T0130004

DIALOGUES *of* Seduction

DIALOGUES
of
Seduction

ROBERTA JAMES

DIALOGUES OF SEDUCTION

Copyright © 2019 James Herndon.

All rights reserved. No part of this book may be used or reproduced by any means, graphic, electronic, or mechanical, including photocopying, recording, taping or by any information storage retrieval system without the written permission of the author except in the case of brief quotations embodied in critical articles and reviews.

This is a work of fiction. All of the characters, names, incidents, organizations, and dialogue in this novel are either the products of the author's imagination or are used fictitiously.

iUniverse books may be ordered through booksellers or by contacting:

iUniverse
1663 Liberty Drive
Bloomington, IN 47403
www.iuniverse.com
1-800-Authors (1-800-288-4677)

Because of the dynamic nature of the Internet, any web addresses or links contained in this book may have changed since publication and may no longer be valid. The views expressed in this work are solely those of the author and do not necessarily reflect the views of the publisher, and the publisher hereby disclaims any responsibility for them.

Any people depicted in stock imagery provided by Getty Images are models, and such images are being used for illustrative purposes only. Certain stock imagery © Getty Images.

ISBN: 978-1-5320-8636-6 (sc)
ISBN: 978-1-5320-8637-3 (e)

Library of Congress Control Number: 2019916961

Print information available on the last page.

iUniverse rev. date: 10/28/2019

1.

∞

The single-engine plane came out of nowhere, swooping down low over the ridge, barely clearing the trees, but gaining a bit more altitude as the terrain dropped down to the valley below. The man who was walking along the ridgeline was a startled witness to the sudden appearance of the plane above the treetops. The plane's engine was making revving noises, signaling a loss of power, and there was no doubt that the pilot was maneuvering for a forced landing. The plane was seeking relatively clear and level ground among the forest-covered hills and was heading for a gently sloping hillside devoid of most vegetation due to a recent rockslide. It was not a good place to attempt a landing–arguably the rocks and boulders afforded a less inviting cushion than the trees of the forest. But there was no time to consider other options.

The man on the ridgeline realized he was not going to see the crash as the rapidly descending plane cleared an intervening ridge and disappeared behind it. He started down the hill towards where the plane had disappeared. After taking a few steps, he heard a far-off, muffled sound that must have been the report of the crash. It was rather anticlimactic after the visual drama he had just witnessed. But he did not doubt the worst for the passengers of the plane. It would take him a while to traverse the rugged terrain to get to the crash site.

He reached the top of the next ridge a half hour later. After a steep descent and an arduous climb, he was exhausted. He had come up too far to the right and would have to climb further up the ridgeline before he expected to get a view of the crash location. He had to stop to rest. He surveyed the surrounding landscape. He knew he was a long way from civilization, and it struck him that any assistance he could bring to injured survivors of a plane crash was limited. He eyed the surrounding terrain a bit longer, a series of unending hills covered by a patchwork of forest and scrub. He continued onward. Another ten minutes of climbing. After pushing through some undergrowth, he caught sight of the plane below. It was about halfway up the next hillside, almost on the boundary of where the rock field met the tree line. It rested nose down with its tail straight up in the air at an almost perfect 90-degree angle to the ground. Nevertheless, the fact that it was basically intact instead of a burning hulk or a mass of debris strewn over the hillside attested to the pilot's skill, or luck.

He saw no human form or movement, but he was not at a good vantage point for that. He could not descend directly to the area since this side of the ridge was too much of a cliff face. He would have to continue along the ridgeline where it descended into a wooded area and, in effect, circle around through the forest to get to the plane.

When he came out of the woods into the hillside clearing, he saw the plane closely for the first time. Again, he marveled at its intact appearance, as if some giant hand had gently set it nose down and propped it up against a boulder. Upon closer observation, he saw that the prop and engine were a mangled mass wedged at the base of a shrub that was growing against the boulder. That was what had absorbed the brunt of the impact. The pilot's door was open. He headed for the cockpit. He took a few steps and stopped. There was a figure sitting on a table-sized boulder a few yards away from the plane. It was a woman. She was sitting bent over, elbows on knees and head buried in her hands. He changed direction to go toward her.

"Excuse me, are you all right?"

She showed no sign of having heard him. She appeared to be unhurt, but probably pretty shaken up or in shock. He continued to approach.

"Excuse me. Are you all right?" She remained still.

Now he did not know what to do. He edged up to her slowly. If he reached out to touch her, he would probably startle her badly. He stopped and looked at her. All he could see was a mass of black hair buried in two hands. She was wearing a plaid flannel shirt like a jacket, unbuttoned and sleeves rolled up to the elbows, and covering a dark green T-shirt. She was also wearing blue jeans and jogging shoes.

He was about to say something else when she suddenly sensed his presence. With a shriek she sat bolt upright. When she saw him, she cringed backward, a look of fear and astonishment on her face, and if he had not taken a step back, she would have begun scrambling backward in panic.

"I'm sorry–I didn't mean to scare you."

She continued to look at him in wide-eyed astonishment and fear, and she gave no indication of having heard his words. He tried to relieve the intensity of her fear with an indirect question that permitted him to avert his eyes from her and glance back at the plane, "Was anyone else in plane?" She did not respond, and a quick glance back at her revealed no change in her expression. He decided to give her some space to compose herself and went over to the plane to look for any other passengers.

No one else was in the plane. He looked around the cockpit. There was a blanket behind the pilot's seat. He took it. He looked in the glove compartment, which was full of papers. Shuffling through the papers he found a granola bar and devoured it on the spot, almost in a single bite. There was nothing else he could find of any use in the cockpit. He exited the plane slipping on a rock, but he caught hold of the wing strut and with an inaudible curse stabilized his balance. Then he stumbled around to the passenger side. No one else appeared to be anywhere.

His weight on the wing strut had slightly shifted the tilt of the plane, and he now became aware of a strong smell of aviation fuel and almost simultaneously noticed smoke coming from the engine. He backed off immediately and returned to the other side of the plane heading back towards the woman. She had been watching his progress around the plane. Although unable to follow his movements in the cockpit, she watched the rest of his fumbling, and it would have been almost comical in less serious circumstances. He was tall and thin, emaciated looking, and he had an advanced start on a beard and an overgrowth of hair that framed a rather intense and worried countenance. When he approached her again, she again evinced an aversion to his close proximity, and he, noticing this, slowed his approach and stopped at a non-threatening distance. She thought he looked like an unkempt scarecrow. When she had first seen him, she had thought in a terrified instance that he was some kind of wild animal that had stalked up to her, and now that he had resolved himself into a human being, she wondered what kind of human being.

"We'd better move further away from the plane," he said. "It looks like a fire in the engine." She followed his gaze over to the plane and saw blue flames now coming from the engine cowling.

"What did you do?" she asked looking at the plane then back at him almost accusingly.

"Nothing," he said, not knowing what else to say.

She returned her gaze to the plane and remained quiet.

"Can you get up?" he prompted. "Are you all right?"

"I hurt my knee," she said and winced as she managed to come to a standing position supporting most of her weight on her left leg. He hesitated, not knowing whether she wanted his assistance, but as she began hobbling in apparent pain, he finally moved forward to take her arm clumsily and tried to support her progress. When they reached a safe distance, she sat down on the ground against a tree while he continued to stand over her for a few seconds. They both looked back at the plane as flames began engulfing it. She buried her face in her hands and again gave herself over to the misery in which she had been indulging when he first approached her. He moved a short distance away from her and continued watching the plane burn.

2.

∞

Arthur O'Neil looked out of his hotel room window at the rapidly diminishing day. It was the time of day that one did not ordinarily think of as dusk, but he knew if he turned on the light of his room, the artificial illumination would dramatically reveal how little light of day was left. The fading light of day appeared to be reflective of his mood and he remained at the window appreciating the natural light that was remaining. He should call Donna. He felt guilty about what had happened earlier in the day. When he told her that their engagement was over, he expected anger, jealously, and threats. But he did not expect her to be hurt. He had expected her to be highly insulted. But he did not expect she would be hurt that much. He should call her–at least to give the matter closure. Of course, he was sure she would not speak to him, and he certainly did not want to talk to any of her family. He was sure that by now her report to her family would make him persona non-grata with her whole clan. That was too bad because he sincerely liked her father Edwin Kittridge who had done much to help his career, as had her brother Lawrence. But as where they wanted to help his career, Donna had felt she had the right to run it. And to run his life in the bargain. She was strong-willed, manipulative, and disdainful. He knew he was fortunate to be disengaged from her, much better now than if they had gotten married. And better now than after launching his political campaign.

There was a knock on the door, and he walked over to answer it. It was Betty. She stood quietly in the doorway waiting for him to speak. God, how he loved a quiet woman. He stood gazing at her for a few moments. He had known Betty for a long time, and only after recent events did he realize how much he loved her. She had been the catalyst that had forced him to seek an end with Donna. She was the "other woman."

They continued to gaze at each other without saying a word. She seemed to know his thoughts and moods. She always let him speak first. That would have been an alien concept to Donna. The contrast between the two women was pronounced. Donna was a brunette with raven black hair, high cheek bones, and probably had something of Native American or Hispanic blood in her. Betty's blonde hair was cut in a page boy style that framed an almost cherubic face. Donna always referred to her as "Doris Day," not that it was ever meant as a compliment. He did not know exactly why. He had always liked Doris Day movies, and this version of Doris Day he liked even better. Betty was the perennial girl next door and always cheerful. Donna was the epitome of the sarcastic aristocrat. If smoking were in vogue, she would probably have one of those long cigarette holders. The only time he saw Donna dress down was when she was flying that dumb airplane of hers, when she would always wear the same type of outfit—that flannel shirt and jeans that was almost a signature costume for her. Donna was a rich, beautiful woman and knew it, and as such she knew she could get away with being a bitch. The fact that he had jilted her must have been a shattering blow to her ego. But he had not expected her to be hurt.

Well, he loved Betty now. He had loved her for a long time without daring to acknowledge it. She would listen to him attentively when he spoke and seemed to take pride when others heard him speak. And best of all, she knew how to communicate without speaking. With a look. With a slight inclination of her head. The way she would take his hand and look into his eyes. He was happy now. The battle was over and won. Like all victors, he was taking a tour around the battlefield lamenting the dead–which in this case were the lingering thoughts about his unhappy relationship with Donna that he needed to exorcize from his mind.

He and Betty continued to gaze at each other a few moments in silence. The waning light served to impart a mood of melancholic longing. She finally came forward and embraced him.

"Hi, Betty," he said.

"My, don't you look nice," she replied, referring to the tuxedo he had donned for the upcoming banquet.

"You look pretty good yourself," he said, holding her apart enough to look down at her dress, and on the way back up stopping to look at her bosom.

Noticing this she smiled and came close to him again, "What are *you* looking at?"

"I was just wondering where your corsage was," he said, picking up on her line in a frisky mood.

"Oh, sure," she said sarcastically. "I know what you were looking at," she added smiling up at him.

He chuckled and held her closer. She became a little alarmed at this. He had a good sense of humor and would normally have had a good comeback line and would not have taken refuge in a hug. He looked a little preoccupied with something.

She looked up at him and said, "We'd better get downstairs. They'll be waiting."

"Oh, yes," he said as if he had temporarily forgotten, and in a quick flurry he went back into the room to pick up his room key card and make sure he had everything he needed. He hurried back toward her with a smile, closing the door behind him. But she noted he took a little longer than normal to look at her again, and now she was sure something was bothering him.

"You're not worried about Donna, are you?"

"Yeah, I guess I am, a little," he said, as he took her arm and walked down the hallway toward the elevator. "You know, she didn't really react at all the way I thought she would."

"What did you expect her to do?"

"I honestly thought she'd make a big scene...slap my face or throw something at me. I never thought she'd just run out of the room crying."

"Well, it was a total surprise to her. It's probably the first time she didn't ever get her own way. She'd probably convinced herself she was in love with you."

He stopped and looked at Betty with surprise. He was surprised that one woman would admit that quality in another woman who was her rival in love.

She looked up at him. "Art, you did what you had to do. Maybe Donna loved you in her own way, but Donna loves people by destroying them. I've known her a long time, and I know what she's like. She has to be in control of everything. You never would have been happy with her. You know that."

"You're right," he said. "I just hope she doesn't do anything irrational."

"Like what?"

"Oh, I don't know..."

"You don't think she'll do anything to hurt your campaign, do you? Do you think her family will withdraw any support?"

No. No, I wasn't thinking about that. And I don't care if they did. I'd rather be dog catcher with you than Governor with her." He said this last sentence in a humorous vein.

"Oh, you say the most romantic things," she said in the same vein.

He laughed and again took her arm and proceeded to the elevator. They were both getting into a frisky mood again, and he grabbed a quick kiss from her while waiting for the elevator to arrive.

When they entered the elevator, he was thankful it was empty. As he pushed the button for the lobby, he queried, "So you don't think she'll throw herself out of a window, or anything like that?" hoping that the exaggeration would impart enough humor to cover up the vestigial concern he still wished to exorcize.

"If she does, she'll land on her feet. Cats are like that."

"Oh ho..." he said, with a mock expression of surprise at the force of her statement, "who's being catty now?"

"Can we please dispense with the subject of Donna for once and for all! She'll be miserable for a couple of weeks, and then she'll find some other poor schnook to make miserable for the rest of his life. So, let's just forget it!"

She was truly miffed, but he had to laugh at her choice of the word "schnook." One of the most endearing charms of her "girl-next-door" image was her use of euphemisms when other people would use stronger language.

She continued to pout over his lingering concern about Donna, but his laughter was infectious, and she finally showed a smile as he snuggled up to her. The elevator stopped at a few intervening floors for other passengers, and they had to contain their playfulness, if not their cheerfulness with each other, an item that was remarked by the other passengers with knowing smiles.

They arrived at the lobby and crossed over to the ballroom where there would be speeches, music, and dancing. He listened to the speeches with only half an ear as he took pleasure, for the first time in a long time, in being somewhere with a woman he loved. And when it was his turn to give his speech, he considered it one of the best he had made. After all, Betty was watching him. And he put the thoughts of Donna out of his mind altogether. Betty was right. Donna always landed on her feet.

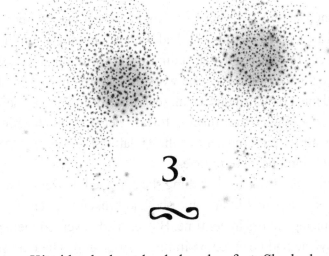

3.

∾

Donna Kittridge had not landed on her feet. She had crashed on a hillside in the middle of nowhere. The fact that she had survived the forced landing and found an apparent would-be rescuer practically waiting on the ground would certainly have been considered "landing on one's feet" by anyone else. But for the moment she was preoccupied with a miserable reliving of the events of the previous hours, and her harrowing crash and present predicament were only nagging worries that came into her thoughts in tandem with the other painful memories that rounded out the totality of her misery. The prospect of imminent death had certainly occupied center stage in her thoughts immediately before and during the crash of her plane. She had spent considerable time afterwards sitting on that rock a few feet from her plane, drinking in the simple miracle of being alive. And for a while that was soothing. But the memory of Arthur's betrayal came flooding back into her mind. Coupled with her current predicament, she knew that things had gone from bad to worse, and she pondered the fact that this must be the lowest ebb in her entire life.

Now she was thinking of Arthur. She had flown to Ellendale to be with Arthur for the entire week, fully expecting to announce their engagement at the banquet tonight and perhaps be married within a couple of months. She had been so supremely confident of herself. Even arrogant, she admitted. Now in retrospect, she felt like a naive idiot. And the worst image was when she had walked into Arthur's hotel room, seeing Betty and him standing together, seeing Arthur turning toward her with a determined look on his face, telling her that their relationship was over. And that Betty and he were in love.

Being jilted was the last thing she expected. Dozens of men had been interested in her, and she had broken the hearts of a few aspiring suitors in her time. But she had never led them on the way she had been led on in this relationship. The man she had made a commitment to—the man with whom she expected to spend the rest of her life—had, out of the blue, turned to another woman. It was more than she could bear. And the woman was one of her friends. That made it more unbearable.

She looked up to see her plane now in the final stages of consumption by fire. Her wonderful plane. It would never be airborne again. Now, tears came to her eyes in earnest. She had loved her airplane and loved to fly. Now, it too was gone, another casualty of a bad day. She had been in a hurry to get away from the fiasco in Ellendale, to get back home, back to something familiar where she could compose herself and make plans. She had not bothered to check out the warning signs her plane engine had been giving her, something that she had never failed to do before religiously.

She had packed her suitcase hurriedly, and in her hurry to achieve the sanctuary of flight, she had left the suitcase and her purse behind in her car at the airfield. Now, she realized she was dangerously stranded and would have to contend with this would-be rescuer. Rescuer? She looked over to the man who had come out of nowhere. More like a serial-killer fugitive from justice. Or at best, some sort of half-crazed hermit who had a tarpaper shack somewhere in these back woods. A chill went through her as she saw him sitting a few yards away against another tree, his head back against the tree and eyes closed–as if he were waiting for something. Why hadn't he gone for help? He opened his eyes and saw her looking at him. He got up, and as he came toward her a pang of dread went through her. She had never felt so helpless. He came down on his knees beside her to be on a level to facilitate talking.

"Are you going to be OK?" he said in a surprisingly soft voice, almost as if he had laryngitis.

She didn't really know the answer to that question and just gave him a confused look.

He continued. "Is anyone going to know where you are? Were you able to radio your position to anyone before the plane crashed?"

Why did everyone she meet always think these small planes had radios? His solicitude gave her a little reassurance, but she continued to give him her confused look. She glanced over to her burnt out plane, and finally shook her head.

"You weren't able to contact anyone about your location?"

It was another version of the same inane question, and she again shook her head and this time said "No" along with it.

"Do you have any idea of how long it'll take before they start looking for you?"

"No."

"Well, how long does it generally take before they start looking for someone overdue?"

"As soon as it's reported, I guess." She was surprised to find she could add a pinch of sarcasm to her answer.

"I mean, when will that be?"

"I don't know," her answers were getting a little snappier.

"Well, won't someone know? Didn't you have to file a flight plan or something?"

What did he think she had been flying? A Boeing 747? Next, he would be asking her for a passenger manifest. She was getting tired of his questions, and her knee was starting to throb. She had been shaking her head while he was asking his last questions. Now she finally spoke up.

"Listen, do you think you could go get some help? I think that might be the best thing to do."

He was a little taken aback by the force of her last sentences. She had been speaking softly with a confused look up until then, perhaps still in a bit of shock. Now she had snapped out of it and appeared to adopt a somewhat reproachful attitude. The force of her tone caused him to glance away, and he directed his gaze over towards the burnt-out plane and said nothing.

She persisted. "I've really hurt my leg," she said hoping this would spur him into action. "I think I'm going to need some medical assistance. Could you call for help?"

She fully expected this scarecrow to have no mobile phone, and when he indicated he did not indeed have such a phone, she continued, "Well, maybe could you get to a telephone or something and call for help..."

He appeared to be contemplating her request, and finally looked back at her.

"I'm afraid we're a long way from the nearest phone," he said.

Both were quiet for a moment, neither knowing quite what to say.

She finally asked, "So, how long would it take you?"

"To get to a phone? I'm not sure."

The look of surprised disbelief on her face caused him to glance away again. They were both quiet for a few seconds. She wondered if he were playing some elaborate game with her, and some of the original dread she had imagined about him came back into her thoughts.

"Can't you go for help?" she asked, almost imploringly.

Now he looked embarrassed.

"It's just that I'm sort of lost, myself," he said trying to soften her disappointment toward him. "I've been walking around in these woods for some time. I don't know exactly where we are or where the nearest help might be."

Now she did not know what to say or think. In the back of her mind she knew this situation must be replete with irony. To crash in the middle of nowhere and find a would-be rescuer practically waiting for her–then to learn that he was lost. She wanted to put her head back in her hands and cry. It was like crashing in an immense ocean next to the life raft of a shipwrecked sailor. She suddenly had the impression that he had come up to her in the hope of being included in any rescue that might be mounted for her.

"Listen," he said, "I don't want to alarm you, but I think this situation is very serious. If you think they might start looking for you, and they have a good chance of finding you, it'd be best to stay put. So, if you can tell what the chances are that they'll be able to find you; you'd know that better than I would."

She had not thought about it before now. She realized it would be some time before anyone missed her. Her family knew she had been planning to spend the entire week with Arthur, and they would not necessarily expect to hear from her during that time. Conversely, she did not think Arthur would call them now. After what had transpired, he would expect that she would be home by now spreading the ill news of their breakup. He would not expect any call he made to the Kittridge family to be well received and probably would not bother. She suddenly realized it could be well over a week before anyone missed her. There was a chance her younger brother, Jeff, would try to call or text her on her cell phone, but this was doubtful. And even if he called and could not get hold of her, he would think nothing serious was wrong.

She finally said, "I still think the best thing would be if you could go for help."

"I could try to get help," he said," but I may not be able to get help anytime soon. You could be here quite a while."

"How long?"

"I'm not sure."

"Then don't you think you'd better get started?"

"OK, but I may not be able to get through or find my way back here. I'm lost and have no idea where I am...so you couldn't put too much hope in my being able to bring any help soon."

She remained quiet trying to digest this latest tidbit of bad news.

He continued. "I think the best thing would be to stay here *if* you think the chances are good that they'll find you within a couple of days."

She remained quiet, again not wanting to admit that chances for a quick outside rescue were practically nil.

"Are the chances good?" he persisted.

After another pause, she said, "I don't think so," finally realizing she did not stand to gain much by not admitting the truth.

He looked as if he finally had some information he could work with. He remained in thought for a while. He got up and walked to the plane that had now been totally consumed by fire and was nothing more than a smoldering hulk. He looked at the wreckage and then around at the surrounding forest. She noted something else about him. The knit T-shirt he was wearing was torn and dirt-stained in a number of places, his bare arms covered in scratches, and the lower part of his left pants leg was stained with what looked like dried blood. He began to appear to her like someone who may have been through the ordeal of being lost. The thought did not inspire any confidence as to his ability to help her, but at least he did not appear to be so threatening now. She suddenly had the conviction that he had gotten lost while on a day hike. Then she wondered if perhaps anyone would be searching for him.

He finally came back and said, "I think the best thing would be for us to try to walk to get help. Can you walk at all?"

"No. I've hurt my knee." She said this as a ploy to get a little more time to think about what he had said. She did not like the idea of either staying here with him or going any place with him.

He again looked around as if he might be searching for some other alternative. "You may have no other choice," he said. "I don't see any other way of getting back to...civilization." She noted that he paused before choosing the word "civilization" to end his sentence. It sounded corny—like a line from some grade B adventure movie.

She remained quiet, and he continued to make his case, "Maybe if I can find something you can use as a crutch, do you think you'd be able to walk?"

She was quiet again. He continued to make his case, this time with a bit of exasperation in his voice, "Please try to understand. We're in the middle of nowhere. I really believe the only choice is to walk out under your own power..." his voice trailed off as he tried to find words to further make his case.

She remained quiet, but he said nothing more and both experienced an embarrassing silence.

"I guess I can try to walk," she finally answered. Then she added, "Where are you from? If you're lost, won't anybody be looking for you?"

"No," he answered ignoring her first question but with no degree of doubt or need to elaborate in answer to her second question. He went back to the hulk of the plane and began working what had been a wing strut loose from the wreckage, evidently to serve her as a crutch. She looked about her, taking a final stock of her situation, and the slow realization came to her that she was in a serious predicament. And this man, who, by rights, should have been able to organize an immediate rescue, was as helpless as she and going to be of no practical use. After everything else she had been through, this was the ultimate injustice.

...

They walked the rest of the day and into the night. They did not cover much distance. The terrain was extremely uneven. They followed the course of the ravines, but they would end up having to climb over ridges when the ravines petered out. The climbing was the most difficult for her. It was dark now, and they were compelled to stop for the night. Walking had been quite painful at first, and her knee was still throbbing as she rested on the ground. But, at least, she had been able to walk with the aid of her makeshift crutch. As she cooled off from the day's exercise, she was surprised at how cold the night was, even though it was summer. He had given her the blanket he had taken from the plane and had sat down against an adjacent tree and now appeared to be sleeping. Sleep was impossible for her. Despite having the blanket, she was cold. Her painful knee made it impossible to achieve a comfortable prone position. But the worst part was the darkness and the sounds of night. She could see absolutely nothing, and the blackness and the strange sounds of the night played havoc with her imagination. She imagined all sorts of wild animals walking around her, and on several occasions, she was sure some flying thing was brushing around her face in the pitch darkness.

She remained in perpetual discomfort until she thought she sensed the dawning light of day. She had not slept and knew she would be exhausted for the next day's hike. She closed her eyes trying to get a little sleep.

"You'd better get up now…we've got a long way to go yet."

She startled herself awake, surprised that sleep had crept up on her so unawares.

He was standing over her to help her to her feet, but she managed to regain her feet by herself with the aid of her crutch. He picked up the blanket and moved a short distance away waiting patiently for her to prepare for the upcoming hike. She was groggy and felt exhausted. The sleep had not done her any good. She looked around the forest where she had spent the night and became immediately depressed. The trees, the underbrush and the rocky and uneven terrain presented a daunting challenge, and she felt totally helpless.

She thought of her family and longed to be with them. She thought of Arthur and Betty and grew angry at the betrayal. She glanced at the man before her and grew angrier at his unhelpfulness.

He turned and began walking ahead of her expecting her to follow.

"Can we get some water?" she called after him.

He turned to face her. "There's none around here. We'll probably come to a stream in a while."

Her pain and tiredness caused her to utter another testy inquiry, "Do you know where you're going?"

"I think so"

"If you're lost, how do you know?"

She was badgering him, but he ignored her tone and responded to her question. "We've got to get out of these woods. And go to a lower elevation. It looks like south is the best way to go."

"Well I flew out of Ellendale from the east, and I'd think that'd be a better way to go."

"OK. We'll go east."

His reply surprised her. If he was so ready to give in and defer to her scarce knowledge of their general location, it indicated that he really did not know where he was. Like the other things he had told her, it did not inspire confidence. "He's hopeless," she thought.

"Do you want to lead the way?" he added.

"No," she said and pointed. "Just go that way."

They walked.

Had she not had her knee injury she could have made better time, and the fact that he seemed to walk tirelessly ahead of her made her simmer.

"You'll have to slow down," she finally called out.

He slowed down. Five minutes later, she said, "It's no use. I've got to stop and rest."

He walked back toward her, plainly concerned about the lack of progress. "We should really keep walking while there's daylight," he said. "We can rest at night."

"I can't go on any further," she said as she found a place to sit on the ground. "Give me the blanket."

He handed her the blanket, and she propped it under her knee. He found a place to sit nearby and glanced at her briefly. Then as he had done previously, he averted his gaze. After adjusting the blanket under her knee, she regarded him critically. There was a furtive timidity in his demeanor. Her other appraisals of him yielded yet more negative regards. For the first time she noticed exactly how haggard he looked. He looked exhausted. There was also something else about his demeanor that disturbed her, but she could not figure out what it was.

"How long have you been in these woods?" she finally asked.

"What?" he said a little startled that she had spoken to him.

In an exasperated tone, she repeated, "How long have you been in these woods?" She enunciated each syllable as if he were hard of hearing.

"A few days, I guess." He ignored the sarcasm.

"How'd you get lost?"

"I ran out of gas on a back road."

"Well, that doesn't make sense. Why didn't you just walk back down the road you were on?"

"I don't know. I just didn't."

"So, you decided to get lost, instead?"

She was badgering him. He got to his feet.

"It's no use talking like this. You should save your energy for walking. We've got a long way to go yet."

"Oh? You've got a knack for getting lost, and now you want me to go with you? No thanks, I think I'll go by myself. Why don't you just go away."

He said nothing, but he was getting mad. She was being intentionally insulting. She seemed to be more upset with him than with her dilemma of being lost. Her refusal to recognize the danger of her situation was galling. Even with his help, there was an even chance that she would not come out of this wilderness alive, and she seemed blissfully unaware of it while indulging her disdain for his company.

He calmed down. He realized that she was in pain and that she was understandably upset over the near fatal crash of her plane. He suspected there was some other issue or issues beyond the crash of her plane that had a bearing on her behavior. At any rate, he was not going to leave her alone. She would die. At some point the danger of perishing in the wilderness would begin to dawn on her. At some point the imminence of death would come upon her in a panic. Then she would be grateful for his help and appreciate his presence. He would ensure her survival. It may not be pretty or comfortable for her, but she would survive. He would see to that. When she was no longer able to walk, she would crawl if she had to. Glancing at her out of the corner of his eye, she suddenly became very real. She was beautiful. She was aristocratic. She was the kind of woman that could easily populate his sexual fantasies. Her survival was very important to him.

She finally took her crutch and struggled to her feet, unable to find any other fault with him for the moment. The first step she took produced an unbearable pain. She shrieked and almost collapsed. He stepped forward to help her, but she exclaimed "Don't!" and waved him off.

With a great degree of concentration, she took about five painful steps and stopped. Then with more painful concentration she began walking in earnest. He picked up the blanket she had left on the ground and fell in behind her.

"Seriously," she said, "you don't have to stay with me…"

"I'm not leaving you alone," he said angrily.

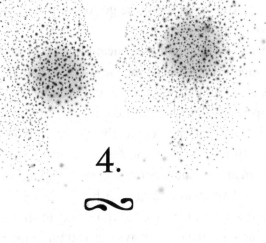

4.

∽

Geoffrey Kittridge wanted to talk to his sister. He thought about calling her on her mobile phone, but he knew she would be busy with her own personal affairs in Ellendale. If he called her, he could well interrupt some important function. But he wanted to talk to her, and on a few occasions, he was close to dialing her number.

He had just returned from his Uncle Dan's ranch, where he normally spent his summers working before returning to grad school. He faced a big decision and wanted Donna's input. For the last ten years, he went to help his uncle and cousins with the work of ranching. At the end of summer, he would come home looking great with muscles and a tan. That was his oft-stated reason for taking on the summer employment. It was a healthy lifestyle, and he enjoyed the hard work. His uncle paid him a token wage as a "ranch hand," but since both families were rich, money was never an issue for the siblings of either family.

More to the point, he enjoyed the company of his cousins. They were a very close-knit and fun-loving family that enjoyed their own company as well as almost adopting Jeff into their family. "Here comes the hired help," they would tease him when he arrived at the ranch in late spring.

"I see you've let the place go to pot since I've been away," he would tease back.

It was one long summer vacation. Not all his cousins lived on the ranch. They also came and went as they pleased. Two of the cousins had gotten married and brought their wives to the ranch as their lifestyles dictated. He would sometimes wonder how his uncle and aunt could always accommodate such a big crowd at times. At one point, Jeff felt a little guilty about taking up a room at the ranch, perhaps crowding out a visiting sibling.

"I got two thousand acres," his uncle told him. "We can always find room for anyone who wants to show up and work. If nothing else, we can always put you up in the cowshed."

Jeff could see where his uncle's kids had gotten their sense of humor and witty personalities.

His uncle was a big bear of a man. Aunt Rosa, his uncle's wife, was a dynamo of a woman with almost no sense of tact who fancied she ran the whole place. She often admitted she would "start talking before I got my mouth connected to my brain." The dynamic between husband and wife would often hold Jeff mesmerized. They would argue in loud, raucous voices but never in anger. Their kids ignored the shouting. He once observed the youngest sibling, Jamie, walk casually between his mother and father en route to the refrigerator while they argued in the kitchen. Maybe "argue" was not the right word. They appeared to enjoy conversing in loud voices. If the noise really became loud and prolonged one or another of their kids would shout in the direction of the argument, "Give it a rest, for God's sake!" After witnessing a few of these shouting matches, Jeff began to suspect his uncle had brought the ranch so that he and his wife could be as loud as they wanted without disturbing any close neighbors.

The ranch was a big place. Jeff joined his cousins in horseback riding, camping, swimming, and any number of ranch activities and other pasttimes. In the evenings everyone often ended up around the fireplace or a campfire, singing, playing games, laughing and just talking. There was also real work to be done: fence mending, cattle herding, stable work, and other ranch chores. His uncle employed a dozen older full-time ranch hands to do most of the work and supervise any of the kids who wanted to lend a hand. No doubt the business of the ranch was profitable enough, but sometimes Jeff wondered if the ranch was really nothing more than a big hobby farm for his uncle and family. He did not think it was the major source of his uncle's wealth, but without doubt the ranch was self-supporting.

His cousins consisted of four males and one female. Leslie was the oldest and the sole female sibling of the clan. Being surrounded by boys, she was the epitome of the tomboy. As such she never seemed to have boyfriends, or even many interests outside the ranch and her family. At any rate she was always happy, friendly, and outgoing. Of all his cousins, he liked her best.

Although Jeff was fairly enchanted with his uncle's family, he nevertheless liked his own family well enough. But there was not the same degree of play and cohesiveness among himself, his parents and his brother and sister. There was some friction. The friction existed mostly between his mother and Donna, his sister. Donna and her mother did not get along because they were almost exactly alike in both looks and temperament. A recipe for disaster. Both women were aristocratic, sparkling, haughty, and forceful. Both women were attractive and vivacious. Lately, his mother had started chiding Donna for not getting married. When Donna turned thirty, her mother stepped up the pressure.

"Sweetheart, when I was thirty, I'd been married to your father five years and had two children. You really must get serious about starting a family. Why do you spend all your time flying around in that airplane? Everyone says you're a beautiful woman, and I know there are many young men who like you and would make good husbands. Let me arrange to introduce you to some. You really need to grow up, dear, and get on with your life."

Donna confided in Jeff. She was not attracted to any of the men her mother tried to introduce to her. She did not want an "arranged marriage," and she did not see any reason to rush into marriage. She wanted to make her own way in the world, and for the time being she did not want to get tied down to a marriage. "Besides," Donna told him, "nowadays people wait longer to get married."

Jeff simplified Donna's stand on the issue—she wanted to enjoy her freedom a while longer. He could understand that. But the constant nagging of her mother had finally compelled Donna to move away from home. Nevertheless, Donna must have continued to feel her mother's admonishments. Jeff was certain that it was her mother's nagging that led Donna to get engaged to Arthur O'Neill. It was a union that her mother approved of highly, and the engagement had gone a long way to mitigate the ongoing conflict between Donna and her mother.

Jeff knew that when he got a little older, his mother would also start reminding him about the need to marry. But for now, like his sister, he wanted to enjoy his youth and freedom for as long as he could.

Pilar Josefina Antunes Marquez de Kittridge was the name of Jeff's mother. She was a descendant of Spanish aristocrats, her own parents having emigrated from Spain to settle in the alpine country of the American West, a place that had reminded them so much of their native Teruel. Jeff's father, Edwin Kittridge, had married Pilar Josefina out of deep love and passion. Edwin Kittridge loved Pilar Josefina so much that he had spent his life giving continuous thanks to the Goddess of love for the happiness of his near-perfect marriage. As such Edwin Kittridge had everything he could possibly want in life and spent his days in quiet contentment and contemplation. Other than being happily married, Edwin Kittridge occupied his time with his business dealings, doubling the family's wealth he had inherited from his parents, who in turn, had doubled the wealth of their own parents. Some time ago a young Edwin Kittridge had been elected a U.S. Senator, an experience he found exceeding unpleasant, whereupon he retired quickly and was content to cast himself in a role of kingmaker for his political party by supporting and grooming ambitious young politicians of note. The Kittridge family's acquaintance with rising politico Arthur O'Neill had sprung from Edwin Kittridge's political activities.

Jeff's older brother, Lawrence, rounded out the Kittridge clan. He was the alpha sibling. He was a practical, hard-headed, no-nonsense type who was his mother's best ally in keeping the younger siblings in line. At age thirty-six, he had already been married fifteen years and had two children. He had already learned the family business and dabbled in politics along with his father.

Being separated in age by ten years, Jeff did not have much in common with his older brother. In fact, the only time they ever came together was at the parties or family reunions at the family estate—about twice a year. The family dynamic had eventually boiled down to two somewhat conflicting factions—the younger faction consisting of Jeff and Donna against the older faction of their mother and older brother. Jeff and Donna's father always remained neutral on the issues that sometimes revolved around the family. When any particular issue produced heated discussion and rising angers, he would sometimes step into the fray with a ruling. Of late, he had been acting as an anchor on the more overbearing actions of their mother in attempting to control Donna's life and marriage potential. Jeff knew that Donna was grateful to her father on these occasions. Pilar Josefina generally had a free hand in guiding and controlling the lives of her children, but she would always yield to her husband's rulings out of marital respect and cooperation. She loved her husband as much as he loved her.

At any rate, Donna's engagement had produced an agreeable climate within the family for the moment. Now, Jeff had a personal problem of his own. Being the younger faction of the family, Donna and Jeff tended to confide in each other before bringing anything up in plenary fashion with the entire family. Unfortunately, Donna was away tending to her engagement with Arthur O'Neill. Jeff knew he really should not bother her now. He hesitated momentarily. Then he picked up his phone and dialed her number.

5.

～

Over the next two days, Donna Kittridge and her acquired companion continued their trek through the wilderness. Conserving their energies for walking, neither spoke much to the other. During the day she found that the more she walked the less painful it became, but her knee was excruciatingly painful when she had to renew the walking at the beginning of the next day.

The more serious problem was water, and they suffered from dehydration. On the third day of their hike, they came out to the rim of a vast valley below them. There was a line of trees running down the center of the valley, and he broke the silence of two days by opining that the trees were growing so lushly there because of the likely presence of water. They had to descend into the valley. It would take them half the day. The downhill hike was extremely difficult for her, but as they reached the floor of the valley the land became more level and prairie like, and walking became easier.

They found a stream where he had indicated it would be, and both fell forward to the edge of the water to drink. She had been truly parched, and despite her champagne tastes, nothing had ever tasted as good and refreshing as the cold water from the mountain stream. She told herself she would never take water for granted again.

"Don't drink too much at once," he suggested.

She settled down at the bank of the stream to relax and imbibe at leisure. She took off her shoes and soaked her feet. She had the feeling that their situation had much improved, being aware of the most basic survival adage that when lost in the wilderness, follow a stream.

"We'd better try to cover some more distance before dark," he said.

Again, as usual, she did not answer, and she settled down for a prolonged rest. After her thirst had abated, she found that she was ravenously hungry.

He stood up and walked along the bank of the creek, and she had the feeling he was finally abandoning her. "Just as well," she thought. "I can follow the stream as well as he can."

He had found a narrow part of the stream and crossed to the other side where he disappeared. She was getting concerned when he returned about five minutes later. He came over to her and handed her something dark and oval she initially thought was a rock.

"Here're a couple of pinecones," he said. "You can open them up and work out the seeds…like this," and after continuing to work open a pinecone with a bit of labor, he popped a seed into his mouth.

He again left her for more foraging, and she began prying open her own pinecone. She finally got a few seeds out, noting the reward was hardly worth the effort.

Returning to her, he indicated he was not able to find anything else edible, but he said the signs were good that they could find some berries or other morsels as they followed the course of the stream. Then he said, "Do you think you can walk some more before dark?"

He had dispensed with his verbal solicitude toward her and spoke in a purely businesslike tone trying to deflect any further disdainful outbursts from her.

She ignored his question and offered her own suggestion, "Listen, why don't you go on ahead and see if you can find help. You'd be able to travel faster without me, and then when you find help, it'll be easy to send it back here upstream."

He hesitated and looked a little perplexed. "No, I can't leave you alone here."

"Why not? I can follow at my own pace."

"You'd want to be alone in this wilderness?"

"Yes, why not?"

"At night?"

"Yes."

He endeavored to explain to her the concept of safety in numbers, that this was bear country, that all kinds of wild creatures would come to the stream to drink at night, and that there was probably a great distance yet to travel, along with other arguments. She finally cut off any other discussion by saying in so many words that he did not inspire any confidence to protect anyone from wild animals. She was kind enough not to say she did not like being with him and would have preferred being on her own.

"I'm not leaving you alone," he finally said trying to terminate the discussion.

"You're being ridiculous," she said.

"Well, we should still try to travel a little more before dark."

"You travel all you want," she said cutting off all discussion and turning away from him to curl up on the ground.

"Come on," he said going to stand over her, "you've got to keep walking. There's a long way to go yet." He bent down to shake her shoulder to get her attention.

"Leave me alone!" she responded angrily, shrugging to throw his hand off her shoulder.

"No, I'm not going to let you stay here. You've got to...."

She whirled to face him and shouted, "God dammit." But she began struggling to come to her feet.

She took a few steps and the pain reinforced her invectives, most of which were directed at him.

"Say what you want. Just keep walking."

"Go to Hell!" She almost screamed.

She eventually calmed down and conserved her energies for walking and fighting the pain in her knee. After another hour of hiking she collapsed on the ground and would not get up again, and this was where they spent the night.

The next morning produced another altercation as he cajoled her to arise and resume the journey. Once they were traveling, no further communication transpired between them. Her fatigue was now permitting her to sleep well on the ground, but the nagging hunger was becoming more acute. After a while they discovered some blackberry bushes growing beside the stream. As with the pine nuts the effort of picking and eating the berries hardly seemed worthwhile. But it was better than nothing.

She awoke early the next day while he still slept. She took advantage of the moment to regard him. She did not have the mental energy to think much about him, but something about him was unsettling. The mystery surrounding him frightened her. She had no idea who he was, and deep down she was afraid of him. Under normal circumstances she would have been more civil, and part of the reason she had been so disdainful to him, apart from her emotional frustrations and physical pain, was to keep him at arm's length. She had thought all along he had been in the wilderness for some suspect purpose. But he seemed to be sincerely trying to get her out of this wilderness, and she should probably show some appreciation. The nagging worry in the back of her mind that he might be taking her to a place of his own choosing did not bear thinking about.

She rested a bit longer then noticed he was awake and looking at her. He looked very tired as he came to his feet.

By way of extending an olive branch, she endeavored to come to a standing position without argument. "Listen," she said, "I'm sorry I...."

In mid-sentence she had put slight weight on her right leg, and the sudden pain shooting through her knee overwhelmed her. All thought of rapprochement with him was driven out of her mind and replaced with the usual invectives. She screamed in pain and tears came to her eyes in earnest. She sank back to the ground, favoring her right leg and lowering herself slowly to rest on her left side. The sight of him standing over her, rather passively, added infuriation to her pain.

As she concentrated on dominating her pain, she waited for him to make the usual inane remark.

After a pause, he said, "We really need to keep moving... come on let me help you get up....?"

"No!" she exploded and broke out crying. Then she implored, "Please let me stay here and go ahead. When you find help just send it back here. Please just let me stay here..."

He appeared to be thinking about her request, but he remained adamant. "No, you can't stay here alone—not by yourself. What if I can't get through? You'll die a slow death."

"If you can't get through, we'll both die anyway," she wailed.

"We've got to try. You can't just give up."

With much coaxing and much reluctance on her part, he finally worried her into making the effort to get up and walk. She was exceedingly slow and whimpered with almost every step. After an hour of walking she half-collapsed and sat on the ground up against a tree. He retraced his steps to come back to her spot. She again noticed how haggard and tired he looked. Now she thought that a possible ploy to get rid of him would be to make him so frustrated with her company, he would finally leave.

"What now?" he said.

She did not answer him. He knew quite well 'what now'.

"Listen," he continued, "I don't have the energy for this… get up!"

"No," she said in a petulant tone. "You don't have to stay here. Go away and leave me alone!"

Out of apparent exhaustion, he sank to his knees to be on a level to face her.

"I've told you…." He could not find his train of thought to complete his sentence.

She sensed she was now getting the upper hand. "I've told *you*," she contradicted, "I'm not taking another step."

"I've told you," he refocused, ignoring her mocking tone, "that you'll die if you don't get up and walk."

It was his same mantra—she was sick of it and it infuriated her. "Then leave me here to die!" she screamed at him.

He slapped her. Hard. Before she could absorb the impact, she found herself flying through the air as he physically picked her up by her shirt lapels and pinned her high up against the tree so that her feet dangled, and her face was on a level to his. He reached around, grabbed her hair, and pulled her head back against the tree, while securing his grip on her shirt front with the other hand. He pinned his body against hers. It happened in a flash and was done with a force that made her gasp in surprised shock. Her eyes were closed from reflex, and when she opened them, she saw his face inches from hers, twisted in anger.

Through gnashed teeth came a menacing, guttural whisper. "Women like you destroy men like me without a second thought… Well, you're with me now, and you'll do exactly as I say…. Do – you – under – stand-me?"

He spoke this last sentence one syllable at a time, emphasizing each one by pulling her head back against the tree in cadence with his words.

She was still in shock, eyes closed again and frozen speechless.

He shook her roughly to get her to focus her attention on him and repeated his last sentence with even more anger in his voice, "*Do – you – under – stand – me?*"

"Y-yes," she stammered, eyes tightly shut. The shock was turning to terror.

He held her subdued against the tree, and when she opened her eyes a few seconds later, she saw his face moving closer— she felt his beard against her face, and his lips touched hers.

"Please, don't," she struggled feebly.

Her struggle enraged him further. He released his hand from her shirt front, reached down and grabbed her crotch with a force that lifted her another couple of inches off the ground and caused her to shriek in pain.

"N-no… please," she uttered.

He held her immobile, and whenever she struggled, he reasserted his grip, keeping her pinned against the tree with his own body. For a second time he brought his lips to hers, and all she could do was shutter with fear.

To further emphasize his control over her, he released her crotch and moved his hand back up to her shirt collar where in a final fit of rage he ripped her tee shirt and her bra from her body, exposing her breasts.

Then it was over. He released her, and she found herself sliding down the trunk of the tree coming to rest on the ground. The fear and shock were absolute, and the only rational thought she could grasp was that she had made a terrible mistake about the motives of this man and had compounded her mistake by antagonizing him.

It took her a few moments to grasp that she was now sitting on the ground at the base of the tree. She looked around in disbelief. She looked up to see him standing over her trembling with rage. He was glaring at her, making an effort to control his anger to the point where he could speak without a quaver in his voice.

"Get up!" he ordered.

She immediately inched herself upwards using the tree for support. When she was in a standing position, putting her weight on her uninjured leg, he came towards her, and the fear on her face was palpable. He went by her to pick up her crutch and thrust it in her hands.

"Walk!" he commanded.

She set out immediately. Her leg still pained her, but it was nothing compared to the fear she now felt. After walking a few minutes, she tried to think rationally again. "God," she thought, "he's going to rape me. He'll probably kill me." A sub-vocal whimper formed in her throat. She was now certain he was taking her to a place as his captive. "That's why he didn't want to go for help," she analyzed. Tears formed in her eyes, but she dared not let him hear any sound of crying, afraid that anything could set him off again.

"Stop," he said.

She immediately came to a standstill, paralyzed with fear.

He had been walking behind her and came around to her front to face her.

"Button up your shirt," he said.

She realized her breasts were still exposed. He had ripped off her tee shirt and bra, but the flannel shirt she had worn over them like an open jacket was intact. She gathered the flannel around her breasts and managed to button up the shirt.

He turned to walk ahead of her, and she followed.

6.

~

Jeff was going stir crazy. He had returned early this year from his uncle's ranch and faced a few weeks of idleness before his post-grad engineering classes began. He could have called up some of his friends for something to do, but he was not in the mood for that. He really wanted to talk to Donna. He got no answer when he dialed her number previously. He had left a message, but she had not called him. He texted her, but still no reply. He was thinking of trying to call her again. If nothing else, he just wanted a brief commiseration with his sister.

He had not enjoyed his summer vacation the way he used to. Maybe he was getting too old to keep going off to his uncle's ranch every summer. Two of his cousins were also absent. After Jeff arrived at the ranch, he asked, "Where's Leslie and Jamie?"

"Leslie went off with her church group to a retreat—they're getting ready to set up a missionary or something in Africa or South America. Jamie's gone off somewhere with his girlfriend."

"Jamie's got a girlfriend?" Jeff reacted with surprise, "And Leslie's a holy roller? When did all this happen?"

"It's been building up for a while. Don't you remember? Jamie brought his girlfriend to the last Christmas party."

Jeff remembered the last family Christmas reunion at his parents' estate. It was an annual event that had been going on for as long as he could remember. Every year, at some time between Thanksgiving and Christmas his parents gave a lavish party, and all the relatives and in-laws had a standing invitation to attend. Sometimes as many as fifty people attended, some coming for the day and some travelling half-way across the country to spend several days at the estate. His uncle's family usually drove down for the day. It was the only time Jeff got together with his cousins outside of his uncle's ranch.

"Come to think of it," Jeff said, "I do think I remember Jamie had a girl in tow. Is it serious?"

"Who knows?"

"And this church thing with Leslie, is it serious?"

"Unknown, cuz."

"I guess that means no more Jesus jokes."

…

Jeff tried to enjoy his ranch visit, but the group dynamic had been changed with the absence of his two cousins. After a couple of weeks, he made an excuse to leave early and headed back home.

Now, that he was home, he was bored. The absence of Leslie and Jamie had a surprisingly negative effect on him. He had wanted his summer retreats to last forever without change, but evidently his cousins wanted to get on with their lives. Jeff thought maybe it was about time he also grew up and started thinking seriously about a career.

When he was not spending his summer vacation at the ranch, Jeff would visit Donna in his spare time, and sometimes she would take him flying. She had been teaching him to fly until she got involved with Arthur. Once at the Wakefield airstrip, where she had taken him for his next lesson, she ran into a fellow flyer. Jeff had immediately forgotten his name, but just as immediately he had also noted Donna's enthusiasm and friendliness toward the man. He was rugged and good looking, and Jeff suspected initially there might something going on between them.

But he knew better. Donna was always hard on her boyfriends. Any man who tried to get close to Donna was put through the wringer. On the few occasions when Jeff saw Donna with a boyfriend in tow, the poor guy would invariably look miserable. And on occasion Jeff would truly feel sorry for Donna's suitors. Donna seemed to have the ability to be friends only with men who had no romantic interest in her. Jeff wondered how her fiancé, Arthur O'Neill, was faring about now. He wondered if Arthur might succeed where others had failed. He was a very forceful person, and Jeff had a suspicion he would not put up with Donna's shrewish behavior. Maybe there was a "Taming of the Shrew" scenario being played out right at this moment.

At any rate, Donna's acquaintance at the airstrip turned out to be a happily married man. Donna talked with him animatedly for a while about flying. He was a competition flyer, and Donna was keen on picking up some flying tips from him.

"I'm hoping he'll teach me some acrobatic maneuvers," she told Jeff, once her fellow pilot had taken his leave. "It's a good way to recover from stalls and spirals and improve your general flying skills."

"Wait a minute. You're not expecting any stalls or spirals on this flight, are you?"

"No, of course not. Come on, get in the plane. I'll let you handle the controls."

If Donna was hard on her boyfriends, she was even harder on her female acquaintances. Jeff was constantly amazed at how much his sister knew about the lives and affairs of other women, and she did not hesitate to display her knowledge of gossip about any of them. Yet she had many friends. Jeff suspected Donna was also the topic of much gossip, so it was probably an accepted form of entertainment among Donna's group of friends. In truth, Donna was a man magnet, and again Jeff suspected that her friends, knowing her reputation with men, congregated about her waiting to catch some prospective ex-boyfriend of Donna's on the rebound.

Donna's ability to perceive the motives of other people revealed itself to Jeff in a very personal way. After the last Christmas party, Jeff came into the kitchen early next morning to find Donna sitting by herself at the table with a cup of tea.

"Bless you, sister dear. You've made a pot of tea." Jeff went to the counter to pour himself a cup of tea and toast a bagel.

When he looked back over to her, she had turned to regard him, sipping the tea with one elbow on the table and the other over the back of the chair. Her eyes were fixed on him. Her pose was remarkably aristocratic, and he became a little uncomfortable.

"Come sit down over here, Jeff," she said, motioning to the table. "Let's have a talk."

"Sure," Jeff said taking his cup of tea to the table. "That was a great party last night, wasn't it? The whole family must have been here."

"You looked like you were having a good time with Uncle Dan's kids."

"Yeah, I was," Jeff responded.

Donna continued to regard him intently. Suddenly, Jeff knew what was coming. "My God," he told himself, "she knows."

And in the next instant, Donna said, "Are you sweet on Leslie?"

...

Jeff was a precocious brat of about twelve when he first met his cousin Leslie. Fortunately, it was a phase of his life he outgrew quickly. But for a year or two he cultivated a "bad boy" image that, in his mind only, others found endearing. It was the first family reunion attended by his Uncle Dan and family. When Jeff first espied Leslie, he immediately lured her into the bathhouse, and before she knew what happened he had unbuttoned her blouse and was working on detaching her bra when, without a word, she turned away from him and made her way back to the plenary festivities of the reunion. Jeff had half expected her to make a full report of his outrage against her to further enhance his "bad boy" stature.

But she made no report, and further into the festivities she showed absolutely no sign of her ordeal nor made any effort to avoid him, short of avoiding any maneuver he made to get her alone again.

In the years that followed he came to appreciate his cousin more and more. He liked visiting with her and her family but was never able to maneuver her into a position of intimacy or even intimate conversation. He often thought about apologizing to her at some point for his indiscretion during their first meeting, but he was thwarted in that effort as well.

Jeff had always assumed that women were ultimately interested in boyfriends and matrimony at some point in their lives. Leslie's apparent disinterest in romantic attachments became a mystery to him. Even if she were not interested in him, he would have expected her to show interest in some other man. During the subsequent summer retreats and holiday parties, he expected to see some evidence of a boyfriend or romantic interest in her life. Yet, he never saw anything of the sort. She appeared to have no burning career interest that might circumvent romantic entanglements. No evidence of a monastic spirit in her. He did not think she was asexual—certainly not lesbian. So, his cousin's sex life remained a mystery. Until the mystery about Leslie could be known, Jeff continued to hold himself out as an unrequited romantic suitor.

He had shared none of these feelings with anyone, not even his sister, his biggest confidant. He had been sure that he had never shown any of these feelings to anyone else. Now his sister had guessed his true feelings. Had his feelings been somehow manifested through his actions when around his cousin? He had been secretive. How many others knew his secret? Had he been obvious?

"What makes you think I'm sweet on Leslie?" he responded to his sister's question.

"I don't know. You seemed to be paying a lot of attention to her at the party."

"I was paying a lot of attention to her whole family. You know I've been spending my summer vacations with them, so, of course, we have a lot in common."

"So, are you sweet on Leslie?"

"Well, I like her a lot—I mean she's very nice and we have a lot of fun together—I mean her whole family and I have a lot of fun together."

"Is that a 'yes?'"

"No. I mean, I've never really thought much about her in that way."

Donna gave him a look that plainly indicated she knew he was lying.

"Well, don't worry," she said, "your secret's safe with me."

"What secret."

"I can't tell you. It's a secret."

In the weeks and months since the last holiday party, Jeff opened up more to his sister about his feelings. Now, after his disappointment over his usual summer retreat, he needed someone to talk to. He reached for his phone again and dialed Donna's number.

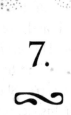

7.

Donna continued to walk the rest of the day. Since the physical attack of the stranger upon her earlier in the day, there was no change in the routine. Walking and more walking. She was doubly exhausted now from the physical exertion as well as from the overwhelming fear that now gripped her. When they stopped for the night, he stood over her as she sat on the ground against a tree. He handed her the blanket as usual, but this time he sat down beside her.

She turned pale with terror. She thought he was cozying up to her as a prelude to sexual assault.

"Don't get excited," he said noting her fear, "I need to share the blanket for warmth."

He sat close beside her, adjusted the blanket to cover them both, and put his arm around her shoulder for a comfortable position. "Here it comes," she whimpered to herself, and wondered if she dared put up a struggle.

He remained still, however, and she noticed he had gone to sleep immediately. Her fear abated a little. She remained stark still, daring to make no move that might awaken him. Unable to think of any other course available to her and hoping he would stay asleep, she yielded to her own exhaustion. She was asleep within a minute of him.

A couple of times during the night, she was awakened by his shifting. The first time, she felt him shivering against her, and he moved closer up against her. It was an indication that he was cold, but she became alarmed as his arm moved further around the back of her neck and over her shoulder, his hand coming to rest on her breast. He was not awake, however. The second time she awakened to find his face buried in her hair and his lips pressed to her temple. She felt his lips move as he mumbled a few sentences in his sleep, none of which made any sense.

She awoke next at first light. He was standing over her, and she was surprised she had not been awakened by the movement of his leaving her side. He gave her a steely stare, and there was no question as to what he expected her to do. She got up immediately and fell into step behind him.

Having not dared to budge during the night, she was sore and cramped more than usual. Her knee pained her as usual, but she dared not voice any complaint. She was desperately hungry. Perhaps, she was getting a little delirious as she considered whether his raping her would be worth it if he first gave her something to eat and let her take a hot bath when they got to his destination.

Shortly after beginning the morning's journey, he veered off to the edge of the stream, peering intently at something in the shallow water. He bent down and cupped his hands in the water. He lifted his cupped hands slowly out of the water.

"There're some minnows here," he said looking back at her. "Do you want to try one? Good source of protein."

He was suggesting she eat a live fish. She shook her head. No matter how hungry she was, she was not going to eat a live fish.

He looked at her a little disappointed. She hoped he was not going to insist. She thought he was going to pop the minnow into his own mouth, but after looking at his cupped hands a few seconds, he let the water and the minnow fall back into the stream.

"Go on downstream," he called to her. "There're some more blackberry bushes there on the right."

She was ravenous. The terror of the previous hours had not diminished her hunger, and for the moment she was looking forward to a blackberry breakfast.

The simple act of walking towards those bushes was about to change her perspectives on things to a considerable degree. She heard rustling among the blackberry bushes and simultaneously spied moving branches as something came through the undergrowth.

Her heart leapt. "Hikers!" she thought. "Or hunters!"

She was saved! She expected to see a couple of hunters bearing rifles and wearing bright flannel hunting jackets emerge out of the bushes.

What she saw, instead, was a huge brown bear that had poked his head out of the bushes and was now looking at her intently as if he were contemplating her as a better meal than the blackberries he had just been feeding on.

What happened next was almost too fast for her to follow. Something from behind her flashed by her screaming and charging toward the bear. The bear was as big as a house, and she never would have expected that something so huge could have moved so fast. The bear took off like a shot, charging through the stream to the other side where it continued its flight through the underbrush. Her companion had chased the bear half-way across the stream and was now standing in the stream looking at the path of the fleeing bear. For a few more seconds, they could hear sounds of the bear crashing through the underbrush as it put as much distance as possible between itself and the humans in the shortest possible time.

He turned and waded out of the stream back towards her. What had just transpired was beginning to register with her. As he approached her, she remained transfixed in wide-eyed shock, looking at him in disbelief, like he was something from another planet.

To relieve the tension, he said, "He got away."

The understated humor and the feigned nonchalance did nothing to alleviate her shock, and he became concerned by the expression on her face. He tried more humor to get her to snap out of her state of shock.

"Man, I was looking forward to some bear steaks tonight."

She now began shivering, and she was close to fainting. He took hold of her arm and said, almost tenderly, "Come on, let's go. Before that bear decides to come back."

How she got through the rest of that day she did not know. The only thing she could think about was his suicidal foolishness in rushing that bear. She knew him to be surprisingly strong; that was proven yesterday when he had picked her up like a feather and thrown her against the tree. But that bear could have snapped him in two with a swipe of its paw. He was evidently insane, in addition to being some kind of sexual predator. Now she had an image of him as an escapee from an insane asylum. He was extremely unpredictable, and she should be doubly terrified of him. But as she sat on the ground at twilight, she felt no fear. She was totally drained. Her strength was ebbing away, and even as he sat down beside her, she could not muster up the apprehension she had felt about him earlier. She could only stare into space with no emotion.

Her passive appearance was an extreme change from her normal aristocratic demeanor. He appreciated her obedience to his commands, but he was saddened by the change from forceful woman to waif-like child, and he was sorry that he had been the cause. She obeyed him now not because of the force of his personality, or because of his use of logic, or because of his ability to make her understand the seriousness of her situation. He had lacked the ability to use any of these devices. Instead he had gotten her obedience like a thug through the use of violence. He remembered the last time he had let his anger get the best of him. The result had been fatal. He had not meant for it to be that way, and he had not meant for it to be that way with this woman. He had wanted her to like and respect him.

"But it doesn't matter," he thought to himself. "The end result is going to be the same, regardless."

As he sat beside her in preparation for sleep, he decided to give her a little encouragement.

"What's your name," he asked her with more of an authoritarian tone than he meant to use.

"Donna Kittridge," she answered with little emotion.

"Mine's Tom Amboy," he said, but she did not seem to note it. Trying to draw her a little more out of herself, he continued, "You know to keep following the stream, don't you….in case anything happens to me?"

She looked at him. "Where are you taking me?" she asked.

"Taking you?" he replied with some surprise. "I'm taking you out of these woods….to safety…"

"Are you going to…?" She could not finish her sentence.

"Am I going to what?"

"Are you going to… to…" Still she could not complete the sentence, afraid of what his reaction might be if she finished the question.

"To what?" he prompted her.

"Never mind," she said.

Then he guessed. "Am I going to hurt you? Is that what you're asking?"

"No, I…"

"No, I'm not going to hurt you," he said growing testy then he added sarcastically, "Why don't I just drop you off at the nearest mall where you can meet your friends at Neiman Marcus. Then I can be on my way."

He went from a sitting to a prone position on the ground and turned away from her.

His statement was significant, but she was too tired to attempt an analysis. As she slipped into sleep, she felt a little reassured by what he said. He wasn't going to hurt her.

8.

Jeff glanced at the caller ID on his cell phone and was surprised. His brother Lawrence was calling. Not having much in common with Lawrence, he had never received a call from his older brother. He answered the call.

"Have you heard anything from Donna?" Lawrence asked him with no preamble or salutation.

"No, not for the last week. Isn't she still in Ellendale?" Jeff responded.

"No, she's not. I just had a call from Arthur O'Neill. He said Donna and him broke up, and she left Ellendale a few days ago."

"What...?"

"They broke up. I've been trying to call her. She's not answering her phone...neither her cell phone or her land phone. I left messages telling her how worried we are, but she hasn't called back."

"Have you called Mom and Dad?"

"Just Dad, he's been trying to call her too...since Mom's still in Europe we don't want to worry her right now."

Despite Lawrence's businesslike command, Jeff noted a growing concern in his brother's voice. Earlier, when Jeff had attempted to contact his sister, he had not considered anything to be amiss when she had not answered.

Jeff's silence prompted Lawrence to continue. "Look, can you try calling her? She might've returned to her apartment and could be in too much of a snit to answer her phone or talk to anybody. She might answer if she knows it's you who's calling."

"Yeah, OK, I'll give her a call..."

"And if there's no answer, can you go over to her place and knock on the door? You don't live too far from her...and, by the way, what's the name of that airport where she keeps her plane..."

"North Wakefield," Jeff responded trying to keep up with the rapid conversation of his brother.

"OK, I'll see if I can get the number and give them a call to see if her plane is there..."

"There probably isn't anyone there," Jeff jumped into the dialog, "it's just a small airstrip and usually pretty unmanned...I'll..."

"Well, there's got to be someone I can call..." Lawrence interrupted.

"Wait," Jeff interrupted back, "I'll go over to her place, and if she's not there, I'll go over to the airstrip and check it out. It's not too far from where she...."

"Good," Lawrence resumed, "and do you know the airport in Ellendale where she went to?"

"No, but..."

"Never mind, I'll call Arthur back and have him check it out on that end...In the meantime let me know what you find out...

Lawrence hung up with the same abruptness with which he had initiated the call. Jeff was left staring at his phone a few seconds. The intensity of his brother's conversation began to infect Jeff with a concern for his sister. He immediately called both of her numbers, getting no answer. He immediately left his apartment and drove to Donna's place.

9.

〜

Donna awoke a little after daybreak. For some reason she had a sense of cozy well-being. The sun was shining, and it was a beautiful day, a little nippier than previous days, and she sensed that a note of fall was in the air. She looked over at her companion. He was sitting up against an adjacent tree, arms folded across his chest. He was awake, but rather than endeavoring to arise to commence the day's hike, his head fell forward on his chest as if he had dropped off to sleep again. Shortly, he lifted his head, let it drop again, and repeated this same action a few times.

"Let's rest a little longer," he finally said.

She was not sleepy and continued watching him. Again, she noted his arms folded across his chest. She had seen him in that position on previous nights as he had sat up against a tree or rock to sleep. It was a natural way to conserve warmth. Why had she not considered that before? She generally had the blanket that covered a warm flannel shirt. She had spent the nights in a relatively warm state. He had always given her the blanket for the night that she used alone, save that night he had insisted on sleeping beside her for warmth.

"Maybe he's been making sacrifices for me all along" she thought. "If I've been wrong about him all this time, I'm going to owe him some big apologies."

Still she was wary of him and frightened of what his true motives might be. The violence he had visited upon her and any possible future treatment he might have in store for her worried her constantly. "Time enough for apologies when and if I get out of this predicament," she reasoned.

Eventually, he arose with an effort. He steadied himself against the tree for a few moments and looked over to her.

"I'm sorry, I think I'm going to need a little help getting up," she said trying to sound agreeable.

He came over, extended his hand, and helped her to a standing position.

"Thanks," she said as she steadied herself against a tree, while he retrieved her crutch. As she took her first step away from the tree, she reeled, and if he had not caught her, she would have fallen.

"I'm sorry," she said. "I'm so dizzy. Wait, I can walk. Just let me hold on to you."

After that, everything was pretty much a blur. Surprisingly, her knee no longer hurt. She was no longer ravenously hungry. Other than the dizziness and an incipient fever, she felt fine.

She lost track of time. She was aware they had stopped again for the night, and maybe another night. She was in a state of semi-consciousness.

"Donna, *Donna!* Come on, Donna..."

His voice came to her out of a haze. She was lying on the ground. His face appeared a few inches above hers.

"No, please...." She wailed in a weak panic, and she struggled to turn away from him.

"Come on, Donna," his arms were around her. "Just let me get you to a standing position."

He was picking her up off the ground. "Stand there just a second, Donna. Now, when I turn around, fall on my back."

She realized he was maneuvering her into a position to carry her piggyback. Even in her feverish condition, she realized he would not be able to carry her like that for any length of time. Yet, that's what he was doing.

Again, everything was a blur and she lost track of time.

Donna! *Donna!* Look, Donna. *A house*!

10.

Jeff Kittridge had never seen his father close to tears.

"My God! Oh, my dear God," his father kept repeating over and over. "My God! She's crashed her plane somewhere. Lawrence, please call Search and Rescue; I'd better call your Mother...."

Lawrence tried to reassure his father, "Take it easy Dad. She may have flown somewhere else. We don't know anything for sure yet. She was pretty upset according to Arthur and maybe just wanted to get away for a while."

"Lawrence!" His father demanded with irritation in his voice, "please call Search and Rescue." His father dropped into a chair and put his head in his hands.

Lawrence had just been on the phone with Arthur O'Neill who had reported Donna's plane missing from the Ellendale airfield, and that the indication was she had flown out of Ellendale almost a week ago.

Jeff had joined his father and brother at the family estate after having called them earlier to report Donna's plane absent from the airstrip where she normally parked it. Her car was there, but not her plane. The clear indication was that she had not flown her plane home.

Arthur O'Neill's report had now confirmed their worst fears. As Lawrence now dialed for Search and Rescue, Jeff and his father struggled to comprehend the enormity of a tragic fate that had likely befallen his sister.

"This is going to be bad," Jeff was thinking. "It'll destroy us," he thought as he conjured up the myriad images of his sister. He realized he was closer to her that he had ever thought. His father was already weeping silently. He felt his own tears. Lawrence tried to maintain his composure as he attempted to contact Search and Rescue. Jeff could feel their universe coming apart.

Jeff nearly jumped out of his skin as the strident ring tone of his cell phone pervaded the solemn atmosphere. Irritated, Jeff quickly answered to prevent a second ring from corrupting the sad silence. A voice said, "Jeffy, this is Donna."

11.

∾

"Bring him, too!" she shouted.

They had given her a light sedative. In her sleep she was reliving the end of her ordeal in the wilderness. Everything was swirling. She could again see the pavement and sidewalk that seemed strange and incongruent after walking so long on natural terrain. But she was not walking on the hard surface, she was floating over it. Then she realized she was being carried piggyback. Then she was resting on porch steps. It was a house. People were gathered around her.

"Please call an ambulance," someone was saying, "she's been lost in the woods. Please call an ambulance. Do you have something she could drink—a coke or something..."

Then another swirl and the sound of an ambulance. Paramedics were examining her.

"She's got a fever and a swollen leg."

"OK, let's get her into the ambulance. You'll be OK, Miss. We'll have you at the hospital in fifteen minutes."

"Are you her husband? Do you want to ride in the ambulance?"

"No, I just found her in the woods, her plane crashed, and...."

"Hey, man, you're not looking too good yourself. You'd better come with us."

"No, I'm OK. Just get her some medical attention…"

More voices, an argument, and another blur. Things cleared up and she was lying on a trolley in the ambulance. She knew that now she was saved. Her relief was boundless. She let herself experience the luxury of passing out altogether. Still, there was something more…something she had forgotten….

"Bring him, too!" She sat bolt upright on the trolley alarming the paramedics with her adamancy.

"Take it easy, everything's going to be OK."

"Bring him, too!"

"Take it easy, Miss Kittridge. You were having a bad dream. Everything's OK."

A nurse had come from the night station upon hearing her cry out in her sleep.

Donna was wide awake now. She looked at the nurse and asked, "Where's the man they brought in with me?"

"He's just down the hall."

"Is he all right?"

"For the moment. Now you need to relax and get some sleep."

"Can I see him?"

"Not right now. He's asleep. And you need to get some sleep too."

"When I can see him, I owe him… I've got to talk to him."

"Tomorrow. Now you get some sleep. Do you want me to bring you something to let you sleep?"

"No, thanks."

Donna was wide awake and had no intention of going back to sleep. She reviewed the events surrounding her rescue to make sure there was not something else she may have forgotten.

She had called her family talking to Jeff and her father just long enough to let them know that she had crashed her plane but that she was OK. The nurse who had placed the call continued talking to her father to confirm that Donna was safe and well, and Donna was grateful to the nurse who had calmed down her father, urging him not to take any dangerous chances in driving the two hundred plus miles to get from the family estate to the hospital in Coulee. (Donna had never heard of the town, attesting to its small size and out-of-the-way location). At any rate, Donna expected her father and Jeff to arrive in the morning. She ached to see her family again. The reunion would be happy and tearful. Donna was going to have much explaining to do. Thank God, her mother was not going to be with them. Eventually, she would have to face the ordeal of explaining things to her mother, but thankfully, that would be later.

She turned her thoughts to the mysterious man who had been with her in the wilderness. She could not settle her mind about him. She had regarded him with dread, disdain, anger, fear, and now gratitude. She remembered vaguely that he had not wanted medical assistance even though he must have been aware that he was half dead. Apparently, it was only at her insistence and the insistence of the paramedics that he had been forced into the ambulance. She had been mostly unconscious en route to the hospital, but she had been aware that the paramedics were working furiously over him. She heard one of them say something about giving him adrenaline.

Had he been close to dying?

The man was a total mystery, and now that she had the luxury of being able to ponder something other than her immediate survival, she knew that the mystery of the stranger would be the topic occupying her mind until it was resolved.

Who was he? And what was he doing in the forest when she encountered him? "God," she thought, "I don't even know his name." Vaguely she remembered that he had told her his name, but she could not remember what it was. "Tom something," she thought.

She slipped out of bed and took up a hospital-supplied crutch. Her knee was almost mended. They had dressed her in one of those unflattering cotton hospital gowns and had taken her clothes. In fact, they had had to slit open the jeans she was wearing to free her swollen leg. A large dose of aspirin had reduced the pain and the swelling. "Of all things," she thought, "aspirin." The doctor who had examined her pronounced her hale and hearty but that they needed to keep her under observation for a couple of days. Then she could be discharged as long as she agreed not to overextend the use of her sore knee for a couple of weeks.

Donna approached the corridor outside her room. She peered cautiously toward the nurses' station to make sure the coast was clear. She stepped out into the corridor and began checking the adjoining rooms. It was late at night, but a few other ambulatory patients and visitors were about, so her own presence in the corridor did not draw undue attention to her.

He was in none of the rooms she checked.

"Just down the hall," the nurse had said.

At the end of the corridor, she encountered a locked double door. This was where the nurse caught her out of bed.

"Hey, you shouldn't be up. You need to keep off your sore leg. Please, Miss Kittridge, let's go back to your room."

"Please, I've got to see him. Where is he?"

The nurse asked, "Is he your husband?"

"No, he's a friend. Can't I please just look in on him?"

"I'm sorry, only close relatives are allowed in the ICU."

"ICU? Intensive Care Unit? He's in Intensive Care?"

"Just as a precaution. They'll bring him out tomorrow. You'll be able to see him then."

Donna was close to tears. Without thinking, she blurted out, "Please, he's my fiancé. I've got to see him."

The nurse relented. She took Donna through the double doors into the ICU.

"You'll have to put on this mask, robe, and gloves," she told Donna. "It's to control any possible contamination from coming into the ICU."

She took Donna into a cubicle and said, "I'll call the doctor on duty to come talk to you."

The sight that presented itself to Donna was shocking. He was in a hospital bed, hooked up to various tubes, IV's, and sensors. She recognized his overgrown hair and beard, but his face was extremely pale. There was a fragile look to him. Now, she felt ashamed for the way she had treated him. Tears rolled down her cheeks as she gazed upon him. He appeared to be totally unconscious, but, surprisingly, he opened his eyes and looked at her.

"Hi," she said moving closer to the bed, "are you OK?"

He said nothing, continuing to look at her. She was not sure he had recognized her, but after a pause, he whispered a barely audible, "Donna?"

"Yes." She moved closer still to the bed and bent down over him to better hear his voice.

"Donna?" he repeated feebly.

"Yes, it's me. Don't worry. You're going to be fine."

He continued to gaze at her. He appeared to be trying to form a sentence. After a few seconds he whispered "Donna, I never would have hurt you."

"I know that."

He closed his eyes and was asleep.

She wanted to break down and cry in earnest. At that point the doctor came into the cubicle to talk to her. He was very young for a doctor, younger than she was. He was also slightly shorter than her. But he exuded the confidence and professionalism of an older man.

"You're Miss Kittridge, his fiancée?

"Yes," she lied.

"He should be out of danger now, but it was touch and go for a while. We'll keep an eye on him overnight, and I think we can release him from Intensive Care some time tomorrow. I think we can put him in your room if you like."

"Thank you."

"So, what happened? I understand you were in a plane crash?"

"Yes, I had a forced landing about an hour after flying out of Ellendale. It was somewhere in the forest in the middle of nowhere, and we had to walk a long time to get out of the forest."

"Was he hurt in the crash?"

"No, he wasn't in..." She checked herself realizing she was about to be caught in a lie. They had all assumed he was in the plane with her when she crashed. Certainly, she would not have met her fiancé on the ground after the crash.

"No, he wasn't," she repeated to cover her near gaff.

The doctor gave her a strange look then looked over to him. She knew what he was thinking. If both had gone through the same ordeal, why was she so much more robust than him?

He asked, "How long were you in the forest?"

She truthfully did not know how many days they had been together in the wilderness. She pondered for a moment and said, "I don't know exactly. What day is today? I flew out of Ellendale on Saturday."

"Today is Saturday."

"You mean it was a week?" she reacted truly surprised.

"It must have been."

She now crafted a further response in anticipation of the next question she knew was on his mind. "I guess I lost track of time. I remember a few days of walking, but I'd hurt my knee and could hardly walk. Then I got sort of delirious, and I know he carried me for a good distance–I don't know how long. I guess it was quite an ordeal for him."

She looked back over to the bed. "He saved my life."

"Well, he's lucky he wasn't out there much longer. His fat reserves were completely depleted, and he'd started to metabolize muscle tissue. There's also a bad gash on his leg, and it looks like it might be infected. We've given him some antibiotics for that. Anyway, we'll have to keep him under observation and monitor his progress for a week or so, but he's relatively young and should recover with time. Just remember, he'll need to take it easy for a few weeks, even after his discharge. Make sure he gets complete rest and limit any physical exertion. His immune system is weakened, so we have to be careful about infections or pneumonia among other things, especially until that gash on his leg is healed."

Donna suspected the gash on his leg must refer to the part of his left leg where she had first seen the dried blood on his pants leg when she first met him.

After a little more conversation, the doctor said, "We need to make a report about what happened–to the police— it's purely routine for accident cases. I'll have the nurse get some information from you, and you'll have to answer some questions about your fiancé. We don't know anything about him at all. By the way, what's his name?"

She remained quiet looking at the stranger and pretending not to have heard the last question in order to get a little time to think. He had told her his name, but she did not remember. She wracked her brain for some clarity of that moment.

"What's his name? The doctor repeated.

"Tom," she said, looking back at the doctor. "Tom Ambrose."

"OK," the doctor said turning to leave. "Just give the information to the nurse. She'll take you back to your room."

"Can I stay here a while longer?"

"Yes, if you want. But I don't think he'll wake up before tomorrow. I'll send the nurse over to you."

The doctor left, and she was not sure he had totally believed her story. Why had she lied about his being her fiancé? It was the only way she was able to see him in the ICU tonight. But why couldn't she have waited until tomorrow?

She continued standing by the bed. She was trying to recall details about their trek in the wilderness that might give her some insight about him. He had claimed to have gotten lost in the forest after his car ran out of gas. It did not make sense. She had initially thought he was a hermit, but if he was, he had been an incredibly long distance from his abode. He had never given her any other information about himself—not that she had been interested at the time. The trek had certainly been an ordeal for him as well as her. He must have been lost as he had claimed. Maybe he had gotten lost fleeing from the law. That might account for his actions. He had also been reluctant to come to the hospital. Yes, that was a definite possibility—he was hiding or running from something. Yet, he had been sincerely trying to rescue her.

As she was attempting to pursue this train of thought, a nurse came into the cubicle carrying some forms clipped to a clipboard. She was not the same nurse who had ushered her into the ICU. This nurse was a slender blonde about the same age as Donna.

"We just need to take down some information about your fiancé," she said. "Do you want to fill out the forms, or I can write down the information if you'll give it to me?"

"Can I get a chair," Donna replied. "I think I need to sit down."

The young nurse gave her an appraising look and said, "Why don't you go back to your bed and get some rest. He'll be asleep until tomorrow, so there's not much for you to do here. I'll go with you, and you'll be more comfortable while I take down the information."

"I guess that would be best," Donna agreed. She wanted to forestall the forthcoming questioning, and in truth, she was beginning to feel fatigued.

The young nurse accompanied her back to her room. Tucked back into her bed, Donna said, "Do you suppose we could wait until tomorrow to fill out the forms? I don't think I can concentrate right now."

The nurse showed a bit of disappointment, but said, "Yes, that'll be fine. The social worker will be on duty then, and I'll have her come see you—but can I just get some quick information about his family, so we can notify them?"

"Well…" Donna paused to dissemble, "I'm not too familiar with his family—I haven't known him that long…"

"Well, that's OK. Let's leave it until tomorrow then. Just relax and get some rest."

The nurse turned to leave the room, bidding Donna good night.

"Wait a minute," Donna called after her.

The young nurse turned to face Donna.

Donna hesitated then confessed, "I'm sorry. I haven't been totally truthful with you. He's not my fiancé. I met him in the forest where my plane crashed, and I don't really know anything about him. I'm sorry I lied. I said he was my fiancé, so I could get in to see him…"

The nurse was puzzled. It showed on her face. Donna suspected she was not making much sense, even though she was telling the truth.

"Well, let's not worry about it tonight," the nurse interrupted, "we'll talk more about it tomorrow."

When she was alone, Donna pondered over how the truth of her situation might sound implausible. She had not thought much about it at the time, but now that she had pondered the whole episode, she had to admit that meeting the stranger the way she did was an almost impossible coincidence. The truth would be hard for people to believe. They would think it much more likely that the man would have been in the plane with her when she crashed. She pondered the odds of meeting a rescuer in a wilderness where no one should be. Then she wondered what would have happened had he not come along. Could she really have saved herself? Pondering this question, she finally fell asleep.

12.

∾

When Edwin and Jeff Kittridge walked into her room, Donna rushed to her father flinging her arms around him with a force that almost made him stagger backwards. Then she hugged Jeff with the same emotional enthusiasm.

"No more flying for you, young lady," her father said trying to sound angry, but his words were laden with nothing but pure relief.

"I'm sorry, Daddy, I didn't mean to worry you." She was already crying as she hugged her father again.

"It's OK, honey, I'm just glad you're safe.

"Oh, Jeffy, I'm so glad to see you." She gave her brother another tearful hug.

"Man, you're really tanned and look like you lost some weight," Jeff said.

After a few more minutes of emotional greetings and displays of relief, her father said, "So, what happened, honey?"

She had rehearsed the story she was going to tell her family, and she intended for it to be mostly the truth, but still she did not quite know where to begin.

"Well, when I got to Ellendale, Arthur decided he didn't want to marry me, and I found him with that tramp Betty Bridger..." she started with an indignant tone in her voice.

"I thought Betty Bridger was your best friend," Jeff interrupted

"Ex-best friend," Donna amended.

"Don't interrupt, Jeff," their father said, "go on, Donna."

"Well, basically, I just turned around and flew out of Ellendale and headed back home. But about an hour after I left, the plane developed some kind of engine trouble, and I had to set down in the middle of nowhere. I hurt my knee during the forced landing, but fortunately I was rescued by someone I met, but we had to walk for days to get back to civilization—and he's here also in the hospital..."

"You gave a ride to someone you met in Ellendale?" her father interrupted.

"No, I met him after I crashed...."

At this moment, a middle-aged woman came into the room, introducing herself as the hospital social worker.

After the introductions, the woman said, "Well, they tell me you'll be able to go home in another day or so."

"We'll take her right now, if you want us to," her father responded happily.

After a few more pleasantries, the woman turned back to Donna and asked, "I don't want to interrupt anything, but we were just wondering if we could get some information about your fiancé. He's still in intensive care and...."

"Arthur's here at the hospital?" Jeff interrupted, as he and his father turned to look at each other with puzzled faces.

"No," Donna said, "it's the man who rescued me who's in intensive care..."

"You mean you got engaged to someone else?" her father interjected. "And he was with you when you crashed?"

"No, I met him on the ground….and he's not my fiancé," she said turning toward the social worker. Donna realized her confession to the nurse last night had not been reported in the proper quarters.

"I'm totally confused," her father admitted.

"I can explain," Donna said with a bit of exasperation in her voice.

However, before she launched into an explanation to clear up the total confusion now reigning in the room, she held up her hand to temporarily ward off more questions from the two men, and she looked again at the social worker who was no less confused than the others.

"I thought he was supposed to be released from intensive care today," she said, "is anything wrong?"

"No, nothing's wrong," the other woman said, "it's just that he doesn't seem to remember anything, and he isn't able to answer any questions. So, they're going to keep him in Intensive Care a while longer until a neurologist can examine him to make sure he hasn't suffered any brain injury. We thought you might be able to give us some information, so we could contact his family"

"I'm sorry," Donna said. "I've only known him for the last week and don't know anything about him other than that. I can only tell you what happened after my plane crashed about a week ago."

"Do you think he might have received a head injury in the crash?"

"No," Donna replied completely exasperated that she could not seem to get across to anyone the simple fact that he had not been in her plane when it crashed.

"Do you want me to talk to him?" Donna added, without trying to clear up the social worker's confusion.

"I'll check with the doctor. He might want you to see him later, but the nurse'll follow up with you on that."

After a bit more conversation, the social worker left, a somewhat confused look still on her face. Donna turned back to face her father and brother who were completely befuddled over Donna's story to this point.

After a lengthy narrative, punctuated with numerous questions from her father and Jeff, Donna managed to recount a fairly complete story of the ordeal of her week in the wilderness. She told them nothing about the shabby way she had treated her rescuer, nor did she say anything about his physical attack upon her person.

"Honey, I don't know," her father said." If you came down in that area north of the Lucinda Valley, I know for a fact that that area is totally unpopulated. I don't know how somebody just happened to be there to save you. I'm glad he did, honey, but it just doesn't sound very plausible."

"I guess it was just a wild coincidence, Daddy."

"Did he ever say anything about what he was doing there?"

"No. We were concentrating on getting back to civilization, and we dedicated our energy to a lot of walking, and we didn't talk much about personal matters. All he said was that he'd run out of gas on a back road and had gotten lost in the forest."

"Well, that sounds suspicious. I'd like to ask him a few questions," her father concluded.

Donna said nothing about her own suspicions that he was running or hiding from something. She simply said, "We can probably see him tomorrow. It looks like he's going to be in the ICU a while longer."

Her father and brother finally took their leave for the day. They would spend the night in a local Marriot on the nearby interstate and pick her up the next day when she could be released. Donna asked Jeff to pick up some new blue jeans and a T shirt for her from any local store they could find. She explained her jeans had been cut off to free her swollen leg. To her relief they did not press her on what had happened to her T-shirt.

…

After the departure of her father and brother, Donna rested a bit then got bored. She expected to be called to assist with the man she saw briefly in the ICU the previous night. After a while, she took action on her on, going to the nurse's station to make inquiries.

"Oh, yes, he's been out of the ICU for a while, but he's being examined by the neurologist now. You can go on in to see him."

Exasperated with the inefficiency of the hospital to inform her about the status of the stranger, she headed to the room the nurse pointed out and introduced herself to the doctor questioning the stranger. The stranger appeared extremely tired. She again felt a pang of remorse at the way she had treated him.

"Mr. Ambrose," the doctor said turning to him, "your fiancée is here. Do you remember her?"

"Oh, can I talk to you a minute," Donna interjected quickly and managed to pull the doctor out of the range of hearing of his patient. "He's not my fiancé," she corrected the doctor in an exasperated but low voice. "I just met him after I crashed in the woods."

"Oh, I'm sorry. They've been saying that you're his fiancée. God, I hope I haven't confused him with some false memory."

Donna was about to try to clarify how the hospital staff might have "assumed" the wrong facts about their relationship, but before she could clarify the facts, the doctor continued, "So you don't know anything about him, other than the time you were in the forest together?

"No."

"But you knew his name. He must have told you his name. But now, he doesn't appear to know his own name or anything else about himself."

"You're saying he doesn't remember anything?"

"Not so far. I've examined him, and he doesn't seem to have any head injury that could have induced amnesia, so there doesn't seem to be any organic reason he can't remember anything. Of course, he's extremely weak, and I'm thinking that maybe the effects of exposure, dehydration, and malnutrition could have caused some trauma leading to loss of memory, but that should only be temporary. I'm trying to point to some memory that I could emphasize as a starting point for him to remember. Maybe if you could talk to him about some shared experience–that might be enough for his own memory to kick in."

"OK, do you want me to talk to him now?"

"Yes, please. Just for a minute."

She went over to the stranger in bed who glanced at her noncommittally as she neared him.

"Tom?" she addressed him. He continued to look at her with no change of expression.

"Do you remember me?"

"Yes."

"And you know who I am?"

He looked from Donna to the doctor, then back to her. "Yes, you're my fiancée."

...

Donna's father and brother talked about her as they drove back to their hotel.

"What do you think about Donna's story, Dad?"

"I guess it sounds plausible to me," Edwin Kittridge answered. "But I still want to talk to this guy to see how he happened to be in that area when she crashed."

"Do you think it was a coincidence?"

"I guess so. I don't think she'd lie about something like that. It was a pretty serious situation."

Edwin again permitted himself to think of the morbid possibility of his daughter perishing in the wilderness. It was unthinkable. He could not begin to fathom the possibility of losing his daughter in that fashion. But she had come so close. When he talked to this guy from the wilderness, he would have to include some profuse gratitude for rescuing Donna.

"Dad?"

"What?"

"Do you believe her story about breaking up with Arthur?"

"She said he broke up with her."

"Do you believe it?"

"Why? Don't you?"

"Yes, I believe every word of it."

"Then, why are you asking all these questions?"

"I guess what I'm saying is do you think Mom will believe it?"

"Ah, yes. Your mother..." Edwin pondered the likely reaction of his wife, Pilar, to these developments, and he knew she was going to be the bump down the road of this happy homecoming.

While Edwin was pondering the possible reaction of his wife to these events, Jeff took advantage of the brief silence to begin again in earnest.

"You know what she's gonna say. She's gonna say that Donna really didn't want to go through with this wedding and that she went back to her old tricks of breaking up with her boyfriends, but I know Donna intended to go through with it. She was…"

"I know," Edwin interrupted his son. "I know what your mother's going to think. But for now, I'm so relieved that I'm not going to worry about that right now."

"Are you gonna call Mom?"

"No, not right away. Everything's turned out OK, so there's no need to alarm your mother right now. Maybe I'll call her in a few days after we get Donna home, and everything will appear normal. We may have to cross a few bridges when we come to them. She'll still be out of the country a few more weeks, so let's just not stir up any sleeping dogs."

"Well, you know, Lawrence is going to call her if he hasn't done so already."

"Let me handle Lawrence. I'll call him tonight. He probably won't call your mother until he gets some word from us, so I'll tell him not to needlessly worry your mother."

At this point they reached the hotel parking lot.

"Let me go up to the room for half an hour, then how about meeting downstairs in the restaurant for some dinner?"

"OK," Jeff responded, the concern in his mind over this whole incident somewhat abated.

13.

He slipped in and out of sleep. He was weak. Even while lying in bed he got dizzy when he turned his head from one side to the other. Answering the simplest questions tired him. Doctors and nurses hovered around him cheerfully determined to make him well. Their presence tired him more. They had unhooked the sensors from him, but he still had the IV through which they were pumping some life enhancing liquids into him—nutrition, medicine, sedatives. He would recover. He would now have to begin things all over again. It would now be doubly difficult. He had come so close. But that woman had spoiled everything. He had been keenly satisfied getting her to safety. It was a small victory in a war of disasters. But why had he lingered? Why was he so determined to see her safely in the ambulance? He had yielded to his attraction to her to be in her presence as long as possible, and it was the worst thing he could have done. They wanted to know who he was. Would an official investigation discover who he was? What if Donna sparked an investigation based on accusations she could have made about his conduct toward her in the forest? He thought about that possibility. He remembered her when they were alone. He was falling asleep thinking of her.

"Tom?"

He opened his eyes to see Donna standing beside his bed. His heart skipped a beat. Two imposing-looking men were with her. She was beautiful, and he was not surprised that she would be surrounded by men.

"I'm being discharged today," she said. "And I wanted to say goodbye and thank you for everything."

"Oh, you're leaving?" He smiled weakly, trying to sound upbeat.

"Yes, but I'll keep in touch to see how you're doing. This is my father and brother who've come to pick me up."

The older man stepped nearer. "Edwin Kittridge," he introduced himself. "I really want to thank you for helping my daughter; if there's anything we can do for you, just let us know."

"Thank you, but I'll be all right."

After a few more pleasantries, Donna bade her father and brother wait outside in order that she could talk in private with him.

When the two were alone, Donna asked, "Do you remember anything about yourself or what happened?"

"No… I'm sorry… Maybe after I recover a little more…"

"The doctor said your memory might kick in if I shared some experiences we had together."

She thought she noted a trace of alarm on his face.

"I guess we could try," he said, "but let me get some of my strength back, so I can concentrate…"

"OK," she said.

After an awkward silence she said, "Well, I guess I'd better get going. I'll call you in a couple of days."

"OK. Good luck."

She remained looking at him, and, true to form, as he had done in the wilderness, he averted his gaze. She continued looking at him, and he became uncomfortable. But he was tired and close to dropping off to sleep again. A last glance at her revealed that she was still regarding him, as if waiting for him to say something more. She gave the appearance of being a little crestfallen. Maybe he should say something encouraging to her.

As he drifted into sleep, he mumbled, "I'm sorry you're not my fiancée."

...

"I'm sorry. I can't leave him like this." Donna balked as her father and brother attempted to shuttle her into the car for the long drive home.

"What's wrong honey?" Her father had noted the crestfallen look on her face as they had exited the hospital.

"I can't just leave him like this. I've got to do something for him."

"Don't worry. He'll get the best of care. He'll be all right. I'll see to that."

"No, Daddy. I need to stay to help him recover his memory. It's the least I can do. He saved my life."

"Look, honey, you've been through a bad ordeal. Let's go home. You'll feel better when you're back home. We can check up on him later after you've had some time to rest and recover."

"Please, Daddy. I'd feel terrible leaving him here if I could help him. Can't we stay here just a couple of days?"

"Look, honey, I've got to get back to some important business. I'm not leaving you here alone after what's happened, so please let's go."

Donna persisted and was on the verge of asserting her independence as an adult or resorting to tears, depending on which course of action she thought would best convince her father of letting her have her way. Finally, her brother Jeff spoke up.

"Why don't we go over to the hotel and discuss all this over some lunch. I think we'll be able to think better about all of this after some food."

That is what they did. In the restaurant, Donna had never tasted any food so good. After a week of berries, pine nuts, and other questionable edibles, even the hospital food had tasted good. But, by comparison, the restaurant food was ambrosia. Of course, she had to restrain her hearty appetite, since she was supposed to be in an emotional state that was not conducive to a hearty appetite. She continued to make her case, knowing she would eventually get her way.

"I'll stay right here in the hotel, Daddy, and I promise I'll call you every day. Jeffy, you can stay here with me for a few days, can't you? Your classes don't start for a couple of weeks, right? We can rent a car. Anyway, it'd be better for me to have something to do by helping Tom; if I go home now, I'll just mope around over Arthur; and I just can't think of facing all my friends right now..."

"Donna, please. You don't know anything about this man. He could be a criminal or some sort of low life, and you could be asking for trouble by getting involved with him."

"I was already involved with him for a week. I was alone with him for a week, and nothing happened. I told you he practically saved my life–and almost at the expense of his own. Seems to me that should be worth a little of our time."

"But you didn't know who he was then or who he is now. OK, so he doesn't remember who he is. That all sounds awfully suspicious for a start. I think we should let the police or the authorities investigate his background and find out who he is."

"Don't you think he could've just been some poor guy lost in the woods? What's wrong with my talking to him–like that doctor wanted me to do so his memory would kick in. Maybe I can actually help someone for a change. It's a small thing to do for someone who saved my life."

After some more discussion, her father finally relented. "OK," he said, "I'll leave you two here till the end of the week. Then you're coming home. Do we agree on that?"

"Yes, Daddy, thank you."

"Just, one more thing. You realize that if this story gets out to the media, they'll have a field day. The longer you stay here, someone's gonna eventually put two and two together and contact the media. This kind of story can end up hurting our family and the campaign we've been working on."

"We'll be careful about that."

"You know the media hates me and would do anything to dig up some dirt on our family…"

"Yes, you've mentioned that before." Donna had heard this broken record many times from her father and now found it convenient to indulge him in his tirade about the vicissitudes of the press.

"That's the nature of the media, and don't forget, honey, I'm a politician, and they're always out to get politicians in this day and age."

The conversation went on about the terms of the agreement. Now that he had lost the main battle, Edwin Kittridge was determined to get as many concessions as possible from his daughter before acquiescing to her plan.

Finally, Edwin Kittridge concluded the family conference. "I'll stay the night and start off early in the morning."

Jeff Kittridge had not said much during this conversation. He finally spoke, "Do you guys want any dessert?"

Donna, who had been engaged in negotiation with her father, had not paid much attention to Jeff. She looked at him now and realized he had been studying her carefully. She knew he was acutely analyzing her arguments. She expected to get some penetrating questions from him, once their father had departed.

...

Later that night, Donna lay on the bed in her hotel room watching TV. She was tired but satisfied with her machinations. Now she was mentally planning her course of action with regard to a certain Tom Ambrose. Her curiosity was in full bloom. She was convinced that Tom Ambrose did not have amnesia and was hiding something. He had certainly recognized her that first night in Intensive Care. The following day his supposed recognition of her as his fiancée was certainly a red herring he had thrown out as a ploy to niftily circumvent answering any real questions on that occasion. She had tried to see him a couple of times since then, but she had found him sleeping (or faking sleeping). Yes, he was hiding something and pretending to have amnesia, so he would not have to answer any questions.

Of course, she could not voice this concern to her father, or tell him the details of her "involvement" with Tom. Had she done so, her father would have thought the worst possible of Tom Ambrose and would have dragged her home kicking and screaming if he had to. Likewise, she could not barge into the hospital proclaiming that their new amnesia patient was faking. The hospital staff would not appreciate her questioning their diagnosis and upsetting a delicate patient.

She would have to be subtle. But that was all right. She was good at that. She looked forward to the challenge of indulging in a few mind games. She knew that Tom liked her. She knew this with the female instinct that had served her so well in the past. Most men liked her. She had always been good at reading the motives of the men around her. True, she had had a few setbacks in that area recently. She had not seen the thing with Arthur and Betty coming. And she had not foreseen Tom's explosive reaction to her shrewish behavior in the forest. But those were unusual circumstances for her. She had been thrown off balance on those occasions. But now she was back. She felt confident again. Before she was finished, she was determined to know everything there was to know about Tom Ambrose.

There was a tap on her door.

"Who's there?"

"Me, Jeff."

"Hi. Come on in." She muted the TV.

"Everything should be all set with the rental car tomorrow. They'll deliver it here in the morning." He sat down in a chair, and they chatted briefly on a few other routine matters.

"Is this arrangement all right with you?" she asked. "I know I sort of railroaded you in to all this."

"I'm fine with it. It'll give me something to do before classes begin." He paused then continued. "Is there anything you want to tell me that you didn't tell Dad?"

"No, not really."

"Nothing you want to confide? You remember, with you and me, it's us against them, right?"

He was invoking their conspiratorial code.

"Yeah, I know."

"So, is there anything you're leaving out about your experience with that guy? Like, what really happened?"

"Pretty much as I told Dad, except that I treated him like dirt, until he finally got so pissed off at me that that he slapped the crap out of me. I thought he was going to kill me."

"What! Kill you? Good God, Donna! That was one hell of a thing to leave out!"

"Don't worry. He didn't hurt me. He could've left me there to die but didn't."

"Good Lord, Donna. Are you sure you know what you're doing? I'm not sure I agree with this. I think maybe Dad is right."

"No, Jeffy. We're in confessional mode now. You can't tell Dad."

"C'mon, Donna. This is serious."

"No, it's all right. Really. It was my fault that he got mad at me. He's really quite nice."

"Oh, yeah. How many times have I heard abused women use that line–'It's my fault he got mad at me' and the next thing they end up dead…No, Donna, I don't care what you say. A normal man would never hit a woman no matter how she acted."

"Then you don't know me very well. I can be pretty god awful when I put my mind to it."

"Oh, really? I don't remember any of your past boyfriends slapping you around, and I know you treated some of them like—well, I know you gave some of them a bad time."

"Not like I gave this man."

"Like what? What the hell did you do to him?"

"Well, I was all upset about breaking up with Arthur, and then my plane crashed on top of that, and I was in a lot of pain from hitting my knee in the crash…so you can imagine the mood I was in… and I ended up taking it all out on him… until he finally got fed up with it… I don't know how he tolerated all of it as long as he did."

Knowing his sister as he did, Jeff had to admit that it all had a ring of truth to it. "Still," he said, "a man should never strike a woman."

"I didn't give him much any other choice. I was pretty much out of control and being a bitch about everything. I'm sure he was trying to get me to cooperate in getting out of the forest alive. So, to be honest, he's more like a hero than anything else."

"A hero? Yeah, a hero. OK, but what's wrong with letting the police or authorities sort out who he is?"

"It's the authorities who want me to talk to him, so they can find out who he is."

Actually, it was only the neurologist who had wanted her to talk to Tom, but that was enough of an authority network for Donna in the present circumstances.

"Well, I still don't like it," Jeff responded, "I'll give you odds he's faking about having amnesia and is hiding something."

"Please, Jeffy. Just see me through this for a few days."

"Listen, I should tell you that before I got your call on my phone, Dad, Lawrence and I thought you were dead. I've never seen Dad so upset, or Lawrence for that matter. The whole bottom dropped out of our world for a few minutes, and it's not something we ever want to go through again. So, please don't take any reckless chances with your life from now on. You mean everything to us…"

Donna was touched by what her brother told her, and tears formed in her eyes. "I'm sorry, Jeffy. Really, I am. I'd never do anything to hurt Dad, or you or anybody else."

"Then, why don't you come on home with us tomorrow? Give us a chance to bask in our relief without having to worry about some unknown man in your life."

"No, Jeffy, I can't. Don't you see? The only reason I *am* alive is because of this unknown man. Our world is still intact because he saved my life. I can't just leave him now."

"Donna, even psychotic killers can do favors for people to get their way."

"Oh, Jeff, now you're being ridiculous. He's not evil."

"How do you know?"

"I just know. Call it female intuition."

"That's a cop out."

They paused realizing their conversation was getting a little heated. Donna softened her speech and continued making her case in a lighter tone.

"Listen, you'll be with me tomorrow. Talk to him and let me know what you think. I think you'll change your mind about him. And if you decide he *is* some sort of monster, it'd be better to check him out now while he's as weak as a kitten, rather than waiting for him to recover his superhuman strength."

Donna and Jeff almost never had a conversation without bringing humor or sarcasm into it at some point. Eventually, Donna got her way with Jeff, as she had with her father. But she had been surprised at the insights he had brought to his arguments, and she knew she would have to be more careful about confiding too much detail in him at this point. She was willing to tell him more than she had told her father, but she was not going to tell him the most intensive details of her experience with Tom Ambrose.

After some more discussion, the conversation eventually wound down to other things.

"OK, sister dear. I guess I'd better be off to bed. I'll see you tomorrow. And believe me, I'm gonna stick to you like glue to make sure nothing goes wrong with that guy."

"His name is Tom."

"OK, that Tom guy, then."

She now changed the subject completely, "By the way, how did things go with you and Leslie at Uncle Dan's place."

"She wasn't there. I came home early."

"Oh, I'm sorry. Wanna talk about it?"

"Maybe tomorrow. It's a little late now, and I guess we'll have plenty of time for conversation between hospital visits."

Jeff headed for the door. On the way out, he turned.

"Just tell me one thing. Is this "Tom" guy going to be the next boyfriend?"

"Of course."

14.

∽

Edwin Kittridge pulled out on the interstate and began the long drive home. Donna had bidden him a sincere, tearful goodbye. He toyed with the idea of cancelling his business appointments for the rest of the week and staying with her and Jeff a few days. It might be a good opportunity to do some long overdue bonding with his younger offspring. But Donna had faithfully promised to call him daily, and since she was with Jeff, he was not worried about leaving her until the end of the week. Before departing he again confirmed her promise to him.

"Remember, I'm expecting to see you both at the end of the week."

He now had a few hours of driving ahead of him, and he was actually looking forward to the solitary journey. In his younger days, he drove all over creation. He figured that he eventually had driven down every road in the state. A couple of times he had driven across country, as well as into Canada and Mexico, and once up to Alaska. He had a convertible and drove with the wind and sun in his face. He would often smoke a cigar, listen to music, and take in the scenery of the landscape and the quaintness of new towns and places. It was a time in his life when he was free and unfettered, and he was taking the opportunity now to relive a bit of that nostalgia.

Unbeknownst to his daughter and son, he had purchased a couple of good quality cigars before leaving Coulee. He peeled the wrapper off one of them and stuck it between his teeth, savoring the taste and bouquet of the tobacco. It had been a long time since he had smoked a cigar. Now, at his age, it would probably make him sick, especially since he had also brought along some soft drinks and junk-food snacks that he thoroughly intended to enjoy in order to make this trip down memory lane as authentic as possible. "Damn the indigestion, full speed ahead," he mused.

Of course, he was not driving a convertible, just the family SUV. Well, he would open all the windows, and that should give him a bit of a wind-blown effect. He would also need to keep the windows open to make sure the tobacco smoke was aired out of the car. He would have a hard time if Pilar noted the odor of tobacco in the family car when she returned home.

He had stoked up the cigarette lighter and was on the point of lighting his cigar.

"Oh, Jeez!" he said remembering something important and laying the cigar aside. He rolled up the windows, reverting the interior compartment to the silent ride often touted by the makers of this model of car. He dialed a number through the car phone console.

"Hi, Lawrence. It's your Dad. Yeah. She's fine, but she's going to stay at the hospital a few more days. No, nothing's wrong. Jeff's gonna stay there with her. No, let's not call your Mom right now, it'll only worry her. Let's just wait till she gets home. OK. No, Donna'll be home by the end of the week, and that'll give us plenty of time to make things look normal for your mother when she arrives. Yeah, let's just downplay this whole affair. She's gonna be upset enough when she learns Donna and Arthur have broken up. Yeah, I'll talk to you more about it later. Look, I'm on my way home now and should be there in a few hours. Can you come over tomorrow? Yes, I want to finish up the business with Malloram–before the weekend. Yeah, bring the documents. I'll see you tomorrow then? Fine. Oh, and Larry, can you do one more thing for me? Use your contacts and see what you can find out about a man named Tom Ambrose. That's Ambrose. A-m-b-r-o-s-e. Yeah, they brought him into the hospital with Donna. He was in the woods with her, and she's saying he found her and rescued her. Well, I want to have him checked out. He's not saying anything about himself, and the doctors are saying he has amnesia. That may be the case, but I'm suspicious. So, see what you can find out. Confine your search to men between thirty and forty. Also, if you can find anyone like that who might have a criminal record, or might be a fugitive, or missing—or anything suspicious. Just see what you can find by tomorrow. I'll tell you more about it then. OK. See you later—everything OK on your end? Good. OK. Bye."

Edwin Kittridge disconnected the phone, rolled down the windows of the car, retrieved and lit his cigar, and continued his journey home.

15.

∾

Tom Ambrose was feeling a little better. Both physically and mentally. They had raised the head of his hospital bed and were encouraging him to eat his first solid food. The nurse said they would see if they could get him to sit up a little later today or tomorrow. He had resigned himself to the fact that he would have to go through with the hospital regimen to regain his health. At least to a certain point. When he had recovered enough strength to walk, he expected it would be easy enough to slip out the front door. No one would expect that a person ostensibly working for a full recovery would steal away from life-giving treatment.

At this point they did not seem overly concerned about his apparent memory loss. They were more interested in his recovering his physical health. The neurologist was now giving him limited visits. So, no one knew who he was, and no one was bugging him about recovering his memory. That was good. He could relax.

He was not sure how much Donna Kittridge had told them about the time they had been in the wilderness. Probably not much. Even if she had told them the details of their most contentious moments, he did not think it would rise to the level of drawing an official investigation. Thinking back on it, he was sure he had not given her significant information about himself. He had told her his name, but from the looks of it, she had gotten that wrong. So, the only thing anybody could investigate him for was as an unknown person. There was not much to worry about. He had no criminal record. So, even if they learned his true identity, they would never find anything to condemn him for. His biggest concern was that someone would figure out the suicidal motives governing his actions over the last few weeks. Then they would consider him a nut case and act accordingly. And it would likely be someone like Donna Kittridge who would be most instrumental in getting the truth out of him.

But she appeared to be out of the picture for now. In the hospital she had been curious about him because she had nothing else to do and because he represented a mystery to her. Plus, the fact that she had finally realized he had been trying to help her and therefore deserving of some of her gratitude. But she had gone home now, and hopefully she would forget about him as she got back to her own life. Funny how he kept thinking about her.

"There's someone else you should be thinking about," he admonished himself.

Still, there was a twinge of regret that he would not see Donna again, even though she had been the cause of his current predicament and had completely derailed his carefully laid plans.

He heard footsteps coming down the hospital passageway. That would be the nurse coming to get him to sit up on the edge of his bed.

He could hardly contain his alarm when Donna and her brother walked into his room.

"Well, hello!" she said, walking up to the bedside with a bright, cheerful smile, "you're looking better today. How are you feeling? Do you remember anything yet?"

"No, not quite–I thought you'd gone home."

"I decided to stay behind a few days to see if I could help you with your memory. Don't worry–I cleared it with the doctor. And I promised not to put too much strain on you or tire you out. You don't mind if we visit you a little while, do you?"

"No, I guess not."

She had achieved total surprise in their first encounter. She knew it, and he knew it. He struggled not to be caught completely off guard.

"But I'm a little surprised," he continued. "Don't you need to get home? Won't your family be worried?"

Jeff spoke up for the first time, "It's all right. We'll be leaving at the end of the week."

She felt like strangling Jeff. He had just given away some tactical information. She had wanted to give the impression that she was prepared to give 24/7 attention to Tom Ambrose for the duration. Now he had a time frame.

"Now he knows he just has to make it to the weekend," she thought to herself.

She pressed on. "Don't you remember anything at all?"

There was concern and expectation in the way she asked her question, and Tom found it difficult to dissemble.

"I think the memories are there, but they're all jumbled up, and I can't seem to sort through them all right now. Maybe when I'm a little stronger, I'll be able to concentrate more."

"Do you remember when we first met?"

Here was a predicament. Even while lying through his teeth, he could not bring himself to say she was forgettable.

"I think...wasn't there something...a plane? A crash, or something...? I hit my head...?"

He was doing it again. Throwing out another red herring, trying to derail the conversation with a false memory he ostensibly picked up from erroneous information floating about among the hospital staff.

She was not going to waste time "correcting" this false memory. She ignored this ploy and pressed on.

"Do you remember the bear?"

"Bear? Uh...no."

He did not like this line of questioning. Did she have any vindictive intentions toward him? How long before she progressively led up to more incriminating questions like, "Do you remember slapping me in the face?" "Do you remember tearing off my clothes?" "Do you remember forcing yourself upon me?"

And how far would she go with her brother present? Had she told him about any of the sordid details? Would any of the males in her life be along to take him to task for his brutish behavior?

After a few more questions which he answered with feeble "no's," he finally rebelled.

"I'm sorry. I think you'll have to excuse me; I'm getting a little tired and don't think I can concentrate right now. Maybe if we postponed this for now..."

Jeff spoke up for the second time, "Donna, let the poor guy get some rest. You're tiring him out."

Donna looked at her brother, then back to Tom. "OK", she said, "I'm sorry. Is it all right if we come back tomorrow?"

"Sure."

"OK. You get some rest. C'mon, Jeffy, let's go."

Her brother led the way out of the room. Before following him, Donna, bent over closer to Tom and gave him a daunting look.

"Don't worry," she said, "tomorrow, I won't ask you any hard questions."

...

The rest of the week yielded disappointing results for Donna regarding her efforts to find out more about Tom Ambrose. The doctors had cautioned her not to tire him out with too many questions. At this point, they were more concerned about his recovering his physical health and stamina, whereupon they judged he would be stronger to battle his amnesia.

"Let's give him another week," the neurologist told her, "then he'll be strong enough to concentrate on regaining his memory."

As a result, someone on the staff would meet her upon her arrival each day to monitor her visits and occasionally accompany her into his room reminding her to limit the length of her visits. As a result, she could hardly discuss more than the weather and time of day. Donna eventually became aware that the staff of the hospital regarded Tom and her as celebrities. The nurses and most of the doctors and staff persisted in thinking that Tom and she were engaged, and that Donna had denied the fact of their engagement to cover up some sort of an illicit love affair between them. "The nurses in the hospital have been reading too many romance novels," Donna told herself.

Jeff also had the opportunity to talk to Tom, and by the end of the week he had taken his measure of Donna's new friend, and he was quite certain that Tom Ambrose was harmless, as Donna had held all along. In fact, he observed that in any predator-prey relationship between the two, his sister was clearly on top of the food chain. Jeff was a little surprised by all this. Tom Ambrose did not strike Jeff as the kind of man his sister would have any romantic interest in. Too passive. Too aloof. Too nerdy? He suspected her interest in him was being sustained by the aura of mystery surrounding him and likely by her need to express some gratitude for what he had done for her.

Since the visits were limited to no more than an hour, Donna and Jeff had plenty of time to kill each day. They would spend the time dining out, and she had Jeff take her shopping for additional clothes.

"Don't take this personally," she told Jeff, "but the clothes you bought for me are not the most fashionable things."

"I expected as much," he retorted. "I noticed you rolled your eyes when I first handed them to you. Well, you know men can't shop."

"That's an understatement."

He faked petulance, "Well, I'm gifted in other ways."

She killed some time talking with her father every evening. A conversation never went by without him interjecting at some point, "Remember, I expect you home on Saturday." She toyed with the idea of telling him that technically Sunday was also the weekend, but she decided not to stretch her father's cooperation to the breaking point.

She had long conversations with her brother and finally got the whole story of his most recent romantic endeavors concerning their cousin Leslie.

"Jeffy, why don't you just come out and tell Leslie how you feel about her?"

"I can't ever get close enough to her to talk about anything in private."

"Then blurt it out over the dinner table some night."

"You've got to be kidding. I'd get beat up by all her brothers."

"Haven't you ever given her any indication about how you feel about her?"

"No. Well, maybe when I first met her. But that was a long time ago"

"Oh, you mean the bathhouse incident?"

"What!?" Jeff exclaimed dumbfounded. "What bathhouse incident?"

"The incident at our bathhouse. About twelve Christmases ago. Remember?"

Jeff was beginning to think his sister had some sort of mind reading capability. The incident was a deep secret that no one but Leslie and he should have known about. He could not conceive of Leslie telling anything like that to Donna or anyone else for that matter.

"How do you know about that?"

"I have my sources," Donna said a little smugly.

"Did Leslie tell you that?"

"Well, no, not the details."

"What *did* she tell you?"

"Nothing, really."

"C'mon, Donna. How did you find out about it?"

"A little bird told me," she teased.

"C'mon, who told you?"

"Tell you what. You fill me in on the details, and I'll tell you who told me."

"Wait a minute," Jeff responded, a clear suspicion growing in his mind. "I have a feeling I'm the one who just told you about the incident. You weren't even at that first party—I think you were off somewhere torturing your second or third boyfriend at the time. Somehow–I don't know how–but somehow you guessed about the bathhouse, and you got me to spill the beans. I don't know how you did it, but somehow you guessed. Well, forget about the details. You're not gonna get anything else out of me. Jeez, you're good. Sneaky and underhanded, but good."

"I didn't guess." Donna was sincerely enjoying the repartee. "Somebody did actually tell me about the bathhouse."

"OK. Who, then?"

"Details first."

"No way, José."

"Well, it's all right. I already know the details."

"Like, Hell, you do."

Donna broke out laughing.

"You're something else," Jeff continued, "I gotta watch you every minute."

Then, he also broke out in laughter then grew semi-serious again.

"So, are you gonna tell me what you know, or not?"

"OK. I'll tell you in exchange for a couple of favors."

"What favors?"

"I'm not sure, but I may need some future help with Tom Ambrose. You may have to run some interference for me between Mom and Dad."

"What kind of interference?"

"I'm not sure, but I just want to make sure I can count on your help if I need it."

"When have you ever *not* been able to count on my help?"

"Is it a deal then?"

"OK. Now tell me what you know."

"All right. I heard Mom and Aunt Rosa talking at the last Christmas party, and they were talking about that first party, and Aunt Rosa was saying she happened to see Leslie come out of the bathhouse, and then saw you come out shortly after that. So, she put two and two together and guessed you had kissed her or something. You know—the "puppy love" thing.

They thought it was so "cute." Anyway, I put two and two together based on what you were saying and came to my own conclusion–like you'd probably ripped her clothes off and had your way with her."

"I didn't rip off her clothes."

"Well, you know, that's probably what I'll think until you put me straight."

"Who cares what you think."

There was a pause in their humorous repartee, until Donna continued in a more serious vein.

"So, since that time you were never able to get close to her again?"

"No, not really."

"Do you think she has any inkling about your interest in her?"

"I don't know. I never have the chance to tell her anything in private. She seems to have such an uncanny way of avoiding me."

"If she's always avoiding you, you can believe it's intentional. Did you ever consider that maybe she's not interested in you, but knows you're interested in her, so she just avoids you to avoid any awkward situations with you?"

"Yeah, I've considered that. And I guess that wouldn't bother me if I knew for sure. I guess the main thing is that I'm just terribly curious about her. I just can't seem to figure her out, and I guess there's something of a mystery about her that I can't get over."

"And there's something else you might consider. Maybe she's just incapable of thinking of you along those lines. You know what I mean? Like if she's religious?"

"What's wrong with her being religious?"

"Well if she's religious, then you know she's got to have a thing about incest. You know–picture yourself going up to Aunt

Rosa and saying 'I want to marry Leslie. You won't be losing a daughter. You'll be gaining a nephew'."

"Yeah, I guess that could also be part of it."

"Why don't you let me see what I can find out, I'll have a talk with Aunt Rosa next time I see her, and..."

"Oh, lord, don't do that whatever you do," Jeff interrupted vociferously. "That's something Mom would do, and I'd die of embarrassment."

"No, no, I don't mean it that way. I'll just find out if she's had any boyfriends or anything like that. I'll be very discrete."

"No, I'd prefer you didn't do that."

"OK, OK. I withdraw the offer," Donna replied, noting to herself that she would certainly have a gossipy little tete-a-tete with Aunt Rosa when she next saw her. She did not like to think of her brother suffering over anything like unrequited love.

...

The end of the week came, and Donna visited Tom Ambrose for the last time.

"Well, you're looking a little better today," she said as she walked into the room, "how are you feeling?"

"OK." He said looking to either side of her. "Where's your brother?"

"Oh, I sent him off to do a few errands. We're getting ready to leave tomorrow. I also told the nurse I wanted to visit with you privately before I left."

He showed no sign of alarm, but he knew his buffers against her coming interrogation were gone. He was apprehensive.

"So, still no memories?" she asked as she sat down in the chair by the bed, crossed her legs and leaned forward to gaze at him intently.

"No. Sorry."

She continued looking at him, trying to give him the impression she could read his thoughts.

He averted his eyes. He could not meet her gaze without the mask of conversation.

She finally said, "You know, you're quite a mystery."

"In what way?"

She ignored his question. He was stalling again.

"Can I ask you a personal question?"

"What?"

"Will you tell me about yourself once you've regained your memory?"

He hesitated. After a pause, he said, "OK," but his answer was weak, and he could not look her in the eye. His body language plainly revealed that he had no intention of telling her any such thing.

She sighed then decided to throw him a curve ball. "Do you remember when we got engaged?"

"We weren't engaged," he responded with surprise and annoyance in his voice. "Why are you saying that?"

For the first time since they were in the hospital, she got something other than a passive response from him.

"Well, what do you remember about it, then?"

"Nothing," he said, letting the annoyance drain out of his voice. He realized he had violated his strategy of remaining passive against her questioning.

"You remember nothing? Then how do you know it's not true?"

"The doctor told me the first day," he replied, unable to look at her, "and you evidently told him."

"Well, how do you think they first got the idea we were engaged?"

"I don't know."

"I told them."

He looked back at her. He was speechless. After a pause, he said, "Why did you do that?"

"You really don't know?"

He really didn't know. He couldn't say anything. She moved closer to him. "Do you remember getting mad at me?"

He did not answer. She was moving too fast for him to verbally fend off her questions.

"Am I making you uncomfortable?"

"Uh…a little."

She changed gears. "I promised my family I'd come home this weekend, but I'll come back next week if you want. Do you mind if I come back? I really want to help you."

She paused to let him formulate some response, but nothing came through the confused look on his countenance.

Again, she asked, "Can I come back next week? I won't if you don't want me to…, but I'd really like to see you again."

He broke through his shock to make a feeble grasp at the escape she just offered.

"Uh, I-I don't think that would be a good idea," he finally stammered trying to sound forceful.

"Please," she said.

"Well… if you really want to."

16.

∽

On Saturday noon, Edwin Kittridge awaited the arrival of his daughter and son. Donna had called him from Coulee to say she and Jeff were starting out and should be home around noon. His other son, Lawrence, was present in order to have the family available to celebrate the happy outcome of Donna's adventure. He would have invited some of Donna's friends, but she said she was not up to that kind of party at present. So, it would be an intimate little family affair. Complete except for his wife, and that was probably a good thing for now.

Edwin and Lawrence killed some time in the morning working together. Four days previously, Lawrence had visited his father to let him know he had learned absolutely nothing about Tom Ambrose. Edwin was surprised by that. His older son was usually pretty good about finding out "information" on practically anyone.

"It just shows that he's not giving his right name," Lawrence said. "I found a lot of Tom Ambroses, but no one who was missing or unaccounted for. Under that name, he'd have to be a complete nobody not to have registered with all my search parameters. So, he's probably using that name as an alias."

"Makes him sound like a criminal."

"Probably is."

"And missing persons or fugitives?"

"Nothing shows up based on the description and picture you provided. It wasn't a very good picture, though."

"I'll see if I can get a better one later." The picture he was referring to was one that he had surreptitiously taken with his cell phone's camera function when he first saw Tom Ambrose in his hospital room.

"Maybe if we could get a good set of his fingerprints, I could search through some of the national fingerprint databases."

"And failing that, what do we have?"

"Nothing, I guess. You have to remember that there are tons of people out there wandering around who are not technically missing but have no fixed addresses or means of support—you know, like the homeless, illegal aliens, society dropouts, some mentally ill people and such. They're on the fringes and don't show up in these kinds of searches, unless they get a criminal record. I mean there *are* still a lot of John Doe's out there turning up all the time."

"Well, he didn't strike me as someone like that. But you never know."

"I guess the main thing is—is Donna going to take up with this guy, not knowing who he is?"

"I don't know. She's never done anything like this before. I'm hoping she'll come home and forget all about it. But she seemed pretty insistent on helping this guy. I don't really ever know what's going through her mind. Maybe, it's all just a reaction from her breaking up with Arthur O'Neil. But I really wish I could find out who this Tom Ambrose is."

"OK. I'll keep working on it."

"Right. And in the meantime, I think I'll give the sheriff's office in Coulee a call. Let's see if I can light a fire under them to get this guy checked out."

17.

∽

Tom Ambrose sat up on the edge of his bed slowly. He remained sitting on the edge of the bed while he slowly fought off the dizziness the effort caused him. After a while, he stood up and managed to walk to the other side of his room fighting new waves of dizziness. They had given him a robe and some hospital slippers. He was able to put on the robe without too much difficulty, but he would have to sit on a chair to don the slippers. Somehow, he managed it and regained his standing position.

He edged out into the corridor. It was about 9:30 pm, late enough for minimal activity but early enough for patients and staff to be around, allowing him to blend in with the crowd as he neared the elevator. So far, so good. There was no way he could descend the stairs. He would have to risk taking the elevator. To his relief the elevator was empty as he pushed the button for the ground floor. He had been on the second floor. He had a brief scare as the elevator stopped at the first floor and a hospital worker pushing a laundry tub entered, touching the basement floor button. They ignored each other, and Tom exited at the ground floor.

He approached the main entrance, but the receptionist and security guard presented an obstacle he did not wish to challenge. He walked the other way down the hall and came out into the emergency room waiting area. A couple of nurses were at the triage desk, and a number of patients were sitting around in the waiting area. Everyone ignored him as he walked through the waiting area and out through the revolving door.

The cool night air hit him. He shivered and was subjected to another wave of dizziness. He leaned up against a post for a few seconds then continued on. He proceeded down the sidewalk and turned a corner where a stronger gust of air hit him causing him to shiver violently and experience a wave of nausea along with the dizziness. He thought he was going to fall. He stood still, slightly bent over, and arms folded across his stomach. He fought to recover his senses. Now he could see that the walk led to the circular driveway at the main entrance. The driveway led down to the street. Just get down the driveway. That was his escape route.

"Mr. Ambrose?"

He whirled around trying not to lose his balance. A figure was approaching him from the other side of the driveway. It was the young blonde nurse. She was wearing a coat. She was just coming on duty.

"Oh, hi," he responded, "I just had to have some fresh air. I get so claustrophobic sometimes..."

She looked at him with concern, but she said nothing as she put her arm through his and walked with him back towards the entrance.

He heard someone call his name. He turned and looked back down toward the street. The nurse continued to tug on his arm.

Again, a high-pitched frantic voice reached his ears. *"Tom!"*

He looked at the nurse. "Did you hear that?"

She had not heard anything.

"Come on," she looked at him with a gentle but concerned smile and led him back toward the entrance, into the warm building, and up to the second floor.

18.

∾

Donna spent two days at her parents' estate. They had a celebration of sorts, and Donna had to admit she was even glad to see her older brother. Her father was overjoyed at having her back safe and sound at home. They had heartfelt conversations, and her father showed an acute interest in anything she had found out about Tom Ambrose. He appeared to be duly disappointed over the scant information she could tell him.

"Maybe it would be better if you told me what you two found out," she asked pointedly.

Her father and older brother disavowed any investigation on their part, but Donna had her suspicions.

After the second day enough of a sense of normalcy had returned to their lives so that she felt secure enough to take her leave of her family and have Jeff drive her to her apartment, about thirty miles away. Again, her father got a promise from her to visit home more often. He admitted it was going to be hard for him to let her out of his sight ever again.

She returned to her apartment and faced the daunting prospect of getting her life back in order. She had left her keys, credit cards, and everything else in her purse in the rental car in her hurry to leave Ellendale. She contacted the management office for a spare key to her apartment. She entered her apartment briefly to pick up a set of spare car keys. Jeff then drove her to the airfield to reclaim her car that she had parked there two weeks ago when she flew out to Ellendale. It seemed like an eternity. She had a twinge of remorse when she saw the airfield minus her plane. She was determined to fly again. "It's like getting thrown off a horse," she told herself, "you've got to get back on immediately." But it would be a while before she could afford a new plane. And she was certain her father would never extend his relief and gratitude to the point of assisting her in getting a new plane. For the time being, she was grounded.

Her car battery was dead, but Jeff gave her a jump-start and then followed her back to her apartment. He did not say anything about her driving without a license. Jeff stayed with her for a long time. Like his father, he was reluctant to let Donna out of his sight.

They had another long brother/sister conversation, until finally Donna said, "Go home, Jeffy. I've got some things to do and I need to check my messages and make some calls. Why don't we get together in a couple of days? I'll have myself back together by then, and then I'll want to have a long talk with you."

"About Tom Ambrose?"

"Yes."

She spent the rest of the day checking her mail and social-media accounts. She had dozens of emails and voicemails. Many emails and calls were from her friends. There were even a couple of messages and calls from Arthur O'Neil.

"Of all the gall," she thought, "he throws me over then expects I'll correspond with him like nothing happened."

She was poised to delete those messages but left them unread without deleting them.

She responded to the messages from close friends. All of them had heard about her ordeal, so she spent some time composing a sanitized, upbeat version of her adventure that she pasted into her replies.

She listened to her telephone voicemails and erased most of them.

Then, she had some incredible luck. One of the voicemails was from the rental car company in Ellendale. When she had originally flown to Ellendale, she had arranged to have the rental car delivered to the airfield for her use. The company was to pick it up from the airfield a week later when she was to fly out. The message informed her they had found her purse and suitcase in the car. Since she had left Ellendale prematurely, the company probably did not retrieve the car for a week. Unable to believe this stroke of good luck, she called the company immediately, and with effusive gratitude she asked the company to overnight her belongings to her. They arrived the next day. Everything was there–keys, driver's license, credit cards, cell phone, even cash.

"Holy moly!" she thought. "Everything should be as hassle-free as renting a car."

She made a mental note to herself that this rental car company would get all her business from then on.

With her life somewhat straightened out, she took a couple of days to relax. For the past two weeks she had been surrounded by people. Donna was a social butterfly, but there were times when she needed solitude. Normally she had gotten her solitude while flying. Now she would have to settle for taking a couple of days off at home.

During those two days she listened to music, watched TV, straightened up her apartment and wardrobe, ordered pizza or Chinese food, and played around on her computer. Her father still called her every day. She expected his calls would taper off as things got back to normal. She called the hospital in Coulee every day. It was not much help. The staff never seemed to know anything new about Tom. The neurologist and other doctors she asked to speak to were never available, and the few times she got hold of Tom, he was more passive over the phone than in person.

So, mostly, she rested. And all during this time, she mentally planned her upcoming road trip to Coulee.

19.

∾

After a four-hour drive, Donna walked into Tom's hospital room and received a series of surprises. The blonde nurse was helping him walk back toward his bed after some clinical outing. Both were chuckling quietly over some bit of conversation they were having. It was déjà vu. It was Arthur and Betty again, standing close together. Arthur turned his eyes toward Donna. He was about to tell her he was breaking off the engagement.

Donna shook off the feeling of déjà vu, and it was replaced with a twinge of daggered jealously as a spark of displeasure flew out of her eye toward the sight of the two of them holding on to each other.

The biggest surprise was that Tom had received a shave and haircut, and for some reason this unexpected sight vexed her most of all. Who had given him the shave and haircut?

For a second or two, she was preoccupied with these poisonous visions and then overcame them. However, the young nurse appeared to have picked up to a degree on Donna's veiled dislike of the scene she had walked in on. As a result, the nurse took refuge in her medical professionalism, as she helped Tom back into bed.

"He's getting stronger all the time," she reported. "Soon he'll be able to get up and around on his own without any help at all. OK, you're all set Tom. Don't forget to take those pills on your tray. I'll leave you two alone to talk."

Donna's gaze followed the nurse out of the room. She had called him "Tom." Since when was she on first name terms with her patients? And now she was giving him pills? What else had she been doing with him the past week?

She turned back to look at Tom. His face had certainly lit up at seeing her, yet he had always shown a degree of apprehension at the third degree he expected from her. Now the consternation radiating from her face exacerbated his apprehension. She had always come into his room with a cheerful smile and bubbly salutation. Now something seemed to be troubling her and he did not know what to make of it.

Donna saw the growing apprehension on Tom's face, and she knew he had not been aware of the internal battle she had just waged against jealousy.

"Typical of men," she thought to herself. "So blissfully ignorant of the motives of women."

She came toward the chair she normally used when visiting him, keeping her eyes firmly upon this new countenance. She did not know what to make of his new look and there were some things stirring in her mind about this new Tom.

"You really look a lot different," she said as she sat down. "Where did you get the shave and haircut?"

"Yes, I got a shave and haircut," he said, so overly anticipating her question that he gave her the answer to the question he had expected.

"Yeah, but who gave you the shave and haircut?"

"Oh, one of the nurses on the staff…I mean she gave me a haircut…I shaved myself…I mean I got a razor from the staff and did it myself…well, I mean, I had to use a trimmer first, then I used the razor…"

"Was it that young nurse who cut your hair?"

"Oh, no. It was another nurse…one who specializes in shaving patients, like, you know, for operations."

She continued to study his face intently. The brown eyes bearing down on him made him uncomfortable.

He finally said, "Is anything wrong?"

She did not answer right away. Then she said, "I can't get over how different you look."

She paused briefly then continued, "I wouldn't have cut it quite so short, but…you know, you're quite handsome."

"Thank you," he said, a little surprised by her generous assessment.

She continued in a lighter tone, "I leave for a few days, come back, and everything's changed."

"I guess that's progress," he said matching her lighter tone.

"Progress?" she asked. "What else has happened? Have you remembered anything?"

"No, I was just saying that things change in general, and that that's progress."

"Oh, I see. Well, has anything else happened since I've been away?"

"Nothing really. Someone from the police came to see me and took my fingerprints."

"Took your fingerprints? Why?"

"I gather it's routine when they're trying to identify someone."

Donna was surprised at his nonchalance. She had assumed all along that he was running or hiding from something and that the last thing he would want was fingerprinting and an attendant investigation by the police. He seemed completely unperturbed by the incident. Could she have been wrong about her assumption that he was some sort of fugitive? For a fleeting instant she thought maybe he really did have amnesia.

No, that was the one thing she was sure about. For a second, she thought about coming right out and accusing him of faking his amnesia.

No that wouldn't work. For the first time in her campaign to discover who Tom Ambrose was she was at a loss as to how to proceed. She was going to have to fall back and regroup.

She spent the rest of the visit in small talk. As she exited Tom's room to return to her hotel, the young blond nurse came up to her while she was waiting for the elevator.

"Miss Kittridge?" The nurse's tone of voice and the look on her face indicated she wanted a confidential word. For some reason Donna experienced another twinge of jealously.

"I thought you should know that he tried to walk out of the hospital on Sunday night," the nurse continued in a low voice.

"What?"

"He tried to sneak out of the hospital on Sunday night."

Donna was dumbfounded. "Why would he do that?" she said.

"I don't know. But if I hadn't happened to be coming on duty and saw him outside, I don't know what might have happened to him. As it was, he nearly suffered a relapse, and now we have a volunteer watching him 24/7."

Donna was still in shock, slightly shaking her head. "Why would he do that?" was the only thing she could say.

"I don't know," the nurse repeated. "I thought you might have some idea."

"No, I don't," Donna answered. "Did he say anything to you?"

"He only said something about being claustrophobic and needing some fresh air."

Donna knew it was exactly the kind of ad hoc answer he would invent to hide the truth. She also remembered that at the end of their wilderness trek, he had not wanted to go to the hospital. He had to be forced into the ambulance, partly at her insistence. What could he be running from that would cause him to jeopardize his health to that extent?

Donna finally responded to the nurse's last statement, "I'm sorry. I really don't know why he did it. I could ask him, but I don't think he'd…"

"Oh, don't tell him I told you," the nurse interrupted her. "He asked me not to tell you; and, actually, I downplayed the whole affair with the medical staff. But I really thought I should give you a heads up about it. I mean, he really seems to like you, and I thought you should know."

"Thank you," Donna replied simply, but deep inside the feelings of jealously she had for this nurse were beginning to reassert themselves. Tom and the nurse were keeping secrets together, the word "affair" used by the nurse conjured up feelings of envy, and now the nurse was being magnanimous toward a possible rival.

"I guess I should tell you," the nurse continued, "that he is getting stronger, and if he tries it again, I don't know if we can stop him. As far as I know there's no legal way we can keep him if he wants to leave. Up to now he's been pretty agreeable about everything and willing to cooperate, but there's no reason he has to stay if he doesn't want to. Of course, I don't know where he'd go."

Donna could see the nurse's concern for Tom. It bordered on romantic attraction. But the nurse had assumed all along that Donna was Tom's fiancée. She was not going to challenge it, since she could see plainly that Tom was in love with Donna and that Donna treated Tom with the familiarity of a lover. She was bowing out graciously.

Donna was still jealous, nevertheless, but she began to respect her rival. After a pause she said, "Will you do something for me?"

"What?" the nurse replied.

"When you see him next just ask him to promise not to leave without telling you. I think he'd keep that promise."

"OK. I'll ask him."

"And can I ask a favor? Will you let me know if anything significant happens with him? Here, I'll give you my number; feel free to call me at any time. And do you have a direct number where I can reach you?"

"Are you going to be away, again?"

"For a little while." Donna had produced a pen and address tablet from her purse.

"OK. What's your name and number?"

"Andrea Barbeau. It's best to reach me at the main number. Just ask for Andrea, and they'll connect you."

"OK, Andrea. And thanks again."

While they were talking the elevator had come and gone twice. Donna took the stairs and left the hospital. There were tears in her eyes as a gust of cold air hit her in the face.

20.

Five days later, Nurse Andrea Barbeau walked into Tom's room. "So, you're leaving us today, Mr. Ambrose."

"Yes, that's what they tell me."

"I guess you'll be glad to get out of here."

"I guess, but it's only a transfer to another hospital. Dr. Murcheson said he wants to put me under the treatment of a specialist."

"I know. It's the Pfister Clinic up north near Davidville. They tell me it's got a good reputation for helping people with memory problems. Anyway, I guess you're strong enough now for a bit of a drive, but you know you still have to take it easy for a few weeks."

"I know."

"No more midnight strolls in the cold weather."

"Yes, ma'am."

Andrea smiled at him. "Anyway, I'm sure they'll be able to help you. Maybe when you recover your memory you can drop us a line. Everybody here is terribly curious about you."

"All right."

"OK, so you just take it easy until your transportation arrives. They'll be here for you shortly."

"OK, and if I don't see you again, I want to thank you for everything. I hope everything works out for you and your family."

"Thanks," she said leaving the room, "and you have a good trip."

During his time in the hospital, Tom had had occasions to talk with Andrea. She was the only staff member with whom he was on a first name basis. She was a down-to-earth woman, and he liked her a lot. She had told him about her family and that she had separated from her husband because of his drinking problems, but that she hoped to get back together with him for the sake of her young daughter. Tom sincerely wished her all the best. He could not believe that someone as pretty and nice as Andrea would have marital problems. In this day and age, no one was happy in their relationships. Everyone seemed to be separating, divorcing or suffering in abusive relationships. He fantasized that if he were Andrea's husband, he would be extremely happy and would cherish her every day. He wanted to pronounce her husband an ogre, but he realized he did not know anything about the dynamics of her marriage and could not really judge anything. His own marriage had been an unmitigated disaster. What had started out with so much joy and happy expectations had had a horrendous ending.

He waited in his room lying on his bed. He was dressed in some new clothes that they had given him, even new shoes, and he was surprised at this expense. The clothes were brand new and appeared to be quite fashionable. He had expected they would have just returned the clothes he had worn when he arrived at the hospital—washed and ironed of course—but his original clothes, nonetheless.

While waiting, he had nothing to do, and was getting a little bored. He did not want to watch TV or read anything, since he expected that such activity would be soon interrupted. He indulged in some reflection on recent past events. He did not want to think about Donna. It had been five days now since she had visited him. During that visit, she seemed somewhat less bubbly and cheerful than previously, and he thought that maybe now her interest in him had tapered off. That was good. The danger of the rich girl/poor guy scenario had been avoided. The last thing he wanted was to be taken under her wing or adopted as some sort of protégé or rehabilitation project so that she could discharge any obligation she might feel toward him. He expected she had returned to embrace her aristocratic lifestyle where she left off. True, he had enjoyed her attentions and concerns for him. But she was beautiful and aristocratic and light years out of his league. He had never been under any illusions as to her true motives toward him. He remained somewhat confused over all that about her declaring him to be her fiancé, but he attributed it all to being part and parcel of her attempts to rehabilitate and reinvigorate him. Now he just needed to put her out of his mind for good.

Tom had given no further thought to "escaping" back into the wilderness. Events had thrown him off course to the extent that his plans were indefinitely in abeyance. Now he began thinking about the possibilities of extricating himself from this second hospital to which they were sending him. Maybe, after a couple of days, he could "regain" his memory to the extent that they could identify him and send him home. Then he could simply begin all over again. The key would be to make sure that Donna did not get wind of any development to that effect.

Why did he keep thinking about Donna?

There was activity out in the hall, and Tom expected they were coming for him.

Donna walked into his room like the sunrise.

"All ready to go?" she asked.

21.

Donna Kittridge had been busy during the five days since she had last seen Tom Ambrose. Now, she and Tom sat in the back seat of the family SUV while her father and brother drove them toward Davidville, where Tom was to receive treatment at the Pfister Clinic for Neuropsychological Disorders. Tom was sleeping, his head resting on her shoulder. He had made a valiant effort to remain awake while her father attempted to converse with him from the front passenger seat. Donna knew her father was trying to form his own opinion about Tom Ambrose through conversation. But the motion of the car had its effect on Tom and after fifteen minutes on the interstate he began to nod off.

"Daddy, he's too tired to talk now. Let him rest."

She pulled Tom over to her, so his head came down on her shoulder. He immediately jerked his head back up cognizant of the appearance it would make to lie against her in the presence of her family.

Donna smiled at this bit of prudishness. "Come on," she told him again pulling him over to her, "put your head on my shoulder. You'll be more comfortable."

She had brought a blanket with her, and she covered the both of them with it. "We can share the blanket for warmth," she told him, trying to evoke the private memory between them when he had slept beside her in the wilderness. She remembered how terrified she had been on that occasion.

But he had not picked up on her reference to that shared episode. He had already been half asleep, and as his head met her shoulder, he was dead to the world.

Without the conversation between Tom and her father, they soon entered a portion of the trip where conversation ceased altogether as her father and brother became absorbed in their own internal thoughts.

Now the motion of the car was having its effect on her also, and she was getting drowsy. She was cozy, warm and contented having her new boyfriend sleeping next to her. It was the acme of all her recent machinations. She chuckled inwardly remembering the completely overwhelmed look on Tom's face when she had walked into his room. When she walked with him out of the hospital, a look of abject defeat also took its place on his overwhelmed countenance. Her father and brother were waiting beside the family car with broad smiles on their faces. The hospital staff had all but broken into applause as they watched the "reunited" couple head toward the car. The hospital staff had never believed that she and Tom were anything else but an engaged couple, despite her earlier protests to the contrary. Donna had used these sentiments to her advantage by letting the hospital staff believe that she was practically part of Tom's family by engagement. Everyone was happy and cheerful about the whole thing.

However, no one had bothered to tell Tom the details of his release and transfer. He wondered if everyone had intentionally conspired to mislead him. He became a little mulish and balked as Donna tried to walk with him arm in arm to his transportation.

He stopped and addressed her father with some agitation in his voice, "I didn't know you were providing the transportation. Nobody told me. I didn't want to put you out."

"Believe me, it's a lot cheaper that paying for an ambulance," her father had replied, clapping him good naturedly on the back to usher him along to the car.

Tom looked back to Donna, even more agitated, "You provided these clothes, too, didn't you?"

It was more a statement than a question.

"And you look very nice," she responded.

He looked over to Jeff who was standing by the driver's door, a broad grin on his face that might have just as well said, "You're in for it, now. Resistance is futile."

With a defeated sigh he entered the car, surrendering his fate to Donna and her family.

...

It had been fairly easy to arrange for the hospital to release Tom into her family's custody. The hospital administration was ecstatic that someone was willing to foot the medical bill for Tom's stay since they had been facing the non-profitable prospect of treating him as a John Doe. Likewise, the doctors who had been treating him at the hospital had done all they could do medically for their amnesia patient and were happy to have him released into the care of the Kittridge family to arrange for his transportation to and treatment with specialists at the Pfister Clinic for Neuropsychological Disorders.

The hard part had been to get her father to agree to the scheme in the first place.

A vociferous "Absolutely not!" had issued forth from his entire being when she first presented her plan to her father.

He had categorically refused the idea of bringing an amnesia patient into his home and among his family, a man no one knew anything about and who could possibly be some sort of dangerous criminal.

"Besides, your mother would kill me, if I did anything like that!"

Donna persisted. Her father resisted. Eventually she played her ace in the hole, "Please, Daddy, I love him."

"How can you love someone you don't know anything about? Are you sure you're not feeling some sense of misguided gratitude, just because you say he saved your life? That's not any reason to fall in love with anybody."

"I know enough about him to know how I feel, Daddy. It's you who doesn't know anything about him. You never objected to anyone I got involved with before, and you didn't know anything about them either. You trusted to my judgment before."

"That's not the same thing."

There was more discussion.

Donna finally played her last trump card. "Daddy if you don't help me in this, I'll just take him home to my place, and he can stay with me."

Eventually they reached a consensus. Her father agreed to help her. In return Donna promised not to do anything "stupid" with Tom until they discovered his identity. Her father reserved the right to investigate him and talk with him extensively for the purposes of identifying him, and most importantly, Donna agreed to have her father and/or brothers present at all times in her dealings with Tom until they were satisfied that he posed no threat. They also discussed how to present these developments to Donna's mother, Pilar.

"I'll try to explain this all to your mother. But you know she's going to have a lot to say about all this, and you know what you're going to be in for, especially when she hears you've gotten involved with an amnesia patient with no memory of his past."

"Can't we just downplay the amnesia angle? That's just temporary. Mother will be more upset with my breaking up with Arthur," Donna conjectured. "If I can present her with another fiancé, maybe that'll help keep her from going ballistic, and maybe she won't ask too many questions."

"Your mother's going to go ballistic and ask a lot of questions regardless. She liked Arthur a lot and was looking forward to seeing you walk down that aisle by his side."

"Just make sure to tell her that *he* broke up with me, so I'm not to blame. Just make sure she knows that."

Her father gave her an appraising look. "I must say, you don't seem to be all that much upset about it. Are you sure you…"

"I was upset at first, but now I could care less."

Her father attempted to read between the lines, and he softened the tone of his questions. "Honey, are you sure you're not taking up with this guy because…"

"His name is Tom," she interrupted a little miffed.

"Are you sure you're not taking up with 'Tom' because you were upset over Arthur—like getting involved with him on the rebound—like to show the world that Arthur wasn't the only man in your life and that you could bounce back…?"

"No, Daddy, no, no, no." Donna answered with frustrated sincerity. "It wasn't like that at all." Donna suddenly found herself in the grip of a strong emotion and suddenly gave her father a tearful hug.

Alarmed at this behavior her father asked, "Honey, what really happened when you were in the forest with that guy—er, I mean Tom? Is there something you're not telling me?"

"No, Daddy, nothing happened. I know what you're thinking, but nothing happened."

"Well, what made you suddenly fall in love with him?"

"I told you before. He saved my life. Even when I was as unpleasant as I could be, and even when I treated him in the worse possible way, he didn't give up on me, and he cared for me and saved me, even almost at the cost of his own life."

"But Donna, that still sounds like gratitude talking. We still don't know the first thing about his past, and a relation built on a short acquaintance—no matter how intense–can't possibly last over the long term. You've got to know more about him to see if you're compatible with each other, and you know...."

"Please, Daddy, I know how I feel and I'm not wrong..."

"But, honey...."

"Wait, Daddy, I know I have to find out about him. I won't do anything until I do. But that's what I'm going to do. I'm going to find out all about him. And when I do, I'm probably going to marry him. So, that should satisfy Mom."

"Honey, are you sure that'll make you happy?"

"Yes, it will."

Her father paused then thought of a different question. "So, does Tom know how you feel? Does he know you're planning to marry him?"

"Not at the moment. I'll fill him in as we go along."

"Then how can you be sure he wants to marry you?

"I'll tell him when the time comes."

"Donna, that's the most presumptuous thing I've ever heard. What makes you so damn sure you can wrap him around your little finger like that?"

"Because he loves me. There's no doubt about that."

...

"Donna."

"Donna!"

The voice came to her out of a mist. She was back in the wilderness, lying on the ground. She could feel his weight on her, and this time she did not try to turn away. She reached out to embrace him. A hand was on her knee.

She awoke out of a deep sleep. He father was shaking her knee. "We thought we'd stop for a bite to eat. Want to join us?"

While asleep, she had shifted down on the seat. Tom was still asleep against her, and she was now a little cramped.

"Oh, OK," she answered her father, and she proceeded to straighten herself up and awaken Tom.

"Tom. Tom, we're stopping for a bite to eat. Do you want something to eat?"

"Huh? Oh..."

He sat up, but he was still plainly half asleep. He looked exhausted.

"Come on," her father said, exiting the vehicle "let's stretch our legs a bit."

They proceeded into the rest area restaurant, and Donna walked arm in arm with Tom to help steady him.

"I don't know why I'm so sleepy," Tom said.

"It's only natural. You'll need some time to get your strength back fully. You'll feel better after something to eat."

"I don't know if I can manage anything to eat right now. Maybe a cup of coffee to help me wake up."

The restaurant hostess showed the four of them to a booth, and they ordered a late lunch. Donna arranged for Tom to sit on the inside of the booth and she secured him to that corner sitting beside him. Tom was so plainly tired that he could not participate in the light conversation around the table. He ordered a sole a cup of coffee, but Donna insisted he share a sandwich with her.

Near the end of the meal, Donna excused herself to go to the restroom. As soon as she was out of sight, Tom addressed her father.

"Do you mind if I wait outside for a few minutes. I think some fresh air will help me wake up. I'll just wait on the bench by the front door."

"OK," her father said, "I'll get the check."

Edwin and Jeff Kittridge watched as Tom exited the restaurant. Edwin turned to his son. "Poor guy. Do you think he might be a little embarrassed that he can't offer to pay his part of the bill?"

"No," Jeff responded, "I think he wants a little fresh air."

When Donna returned to the table, she experienced near panic.

"Where is he?"

"He's waiting outside. He wanted…."

She exited abruptly, hoping her headlong rush to the door, did not come across as a non-decorous stampede.

Outside, she saw an elderly couple sitting on the bench. But no Tom.

With a growing panic, she cast her gaze around.

He was standing in the parking lot, arms folded, leaning back up against the car. He appeared to be gazing calmly at the distant range of mountains that formed the western horizon. Or maybe he had just turned his head toward the western sky to let the warm rays of the setting sun wash over his face.

She heaved a sigh of relief. It was a tranquil enough vision. She was content to watch him for a few moments.

Suddenly there was a change in his whole demeanor. Something on the horizon caught his attention and he stared raptly in that direction. His whole body became rigid. He dropped his arms to his sides and took a couple of slow but intent steps in the direction of his gaze as if he were trying to crystallize in his mind the object in his sight. It reminded Donna of a cat that upon spotting its quarry remains motionless intently regarding its prey, moves stealthily a few paces, and then streaks off in pursuit.

In a wild moment she thought Tom was going to break out into a run through the parking lot and across the highway in pursuit of some unknown quarry on the horizon.

"Tom!" she yelled at the top of her voice, startling a few passers-by outside the restaurant.

As she rushed up to him, he came out of his trance-like gaze and regarded her with the usual passivity.

"What were you looking at?"

"The mountains," he said turning his gaze back toward the horizon. "They're very pretty."

She slipped her arm through his.

"You know," she said, "on the other side of those mountains is the Lucinda valley. That's where you and I were."

"Oh. Really?"

22.

"OK, maybe it won't be so bad," Tom Ambrose thought to himself. "So, they'll just take me to the clinic and drop me off. Maybe, Donna'll still come and visit, but it can't be much different from the other hospital."

They were nearing their destination now. He was lying on Donna's shoulder, still half asleep. She was also asleep. He had felt better after eating, but the coffee had done nothing to help him stay awake. That was probably a good thing because no one was trying to converse with him or ask him questions. He would check into the clinic, get a good night's sleep, and the next day would be...well it would be a new day, and he could think more clearly about the future. It appeared that Donna's interest in him had not waned. In the back of his mind he pondered over whether she might have some sort of romantic interest in him. It might seem that way considering the time she was spending with him, but he rejected that idea. In his younger days, he always misinterpreted the actions of women who paid even the slightest attention to him or showed him the slightest affection, and on more than one occasion he had had terrible romantic disappointments after misdiagnosing the motives of female acquaintances. He did not want to make that kind of mistake with Donna. Even if by some wild confluence of circumstances, she had developed a romantic interest in him, it would be the worst thing that could possibly happen. Yet somewhere in that part of his brain where he indulged the odd sexual fantasy, he allowed himself to cast Donna as the object of his fantasy. Unable to resist, he remembered her in the forest. He had kissed her. He saw her bare breasts. Now he was lying next to her. He buried his face deeper into her shoulder, pursed his lips, pressed them to her neck, and reached across her bosom to embrace her. She stirred beside him, and a barely audible moan came through her lips. She awoke.

An instant later he was fully awake and had retreated with the speed of light to the other side of the seat, a look of wide-eyed unbelief on his face over what he had just done. He wedged himself in the corner between the seat and the door panel. He began shivering.

"Tom? Tom? What's wrong," Donna asked alarmed at his extreme reaction. She tried to reach out to pull him over next to her again, but he resisted.

Another "what's wrong" came from the front seat as her brother turned and checked out the back seat and her father checked out the commotion from the rearview mirror.

"I think he had a bad dream," Donna answered.

"Are you all right, Tom?" she asked.

"Yeah, I'm sorry. I guess it *was* a bad dream."

He still resisted her attempts to pull him closer, so she sidled over to get as close to him as possible.

"How do you feel?" she asked as she repositioned the blanket over him. He pulled the blanket around him like a wall, not because he was cold but because he wanted to erect a barrier between himself and Donna.

She directed a comment to her father and brother in the front seat, "I think the trip was a little too much for him."

The concern on her face and the tone of her voice melted his resolve to resist her. He wanted to put his head back on her shoulder and cry. But he could not do that in front of her family.

"Well, we're here," her father said as he pulled off the road into a long driveway.

"About time, too," Donna said then added for Tom's benefit, "now you can get some proper rest."

They pulled up into a circular drive in front of a building that looked like a mansion. It was nearly dark now, and the building was unlit, but the outside lights had come on as the car pulled up to the entrance. Tom thought it an indication that they were expecting his arrival. Then he thought that the lights might have motion sensors and had probably lit up automatically.

They helped him through the entrance. Someone turned on lights revealing an ample, high-ceilinged lobby. They helped him up the stairs to a room, undressed him, and put him in a comfortable bed.

He heard Donna's voice, "I'll stay with him for a while."

He heard her father's voice, "OK, I gotta get back. I'll call you tomorrow."

There was some additional conversation among Donna and her father and brother, but he was no longer able to follow it. The room became quiet, and he was near to sleep. Someone turned off the room light. He heard Donna whisper softly in his ear, "Good night, Tom," and he was asleep.

…

He awoke the next day to sunlight streaming in through the window of his room. The clock on the bedside table indicated it was almost 9 o'clock. He had slept a long time, and the sleep had done him good. He felt much better and clear headed. He raised himself up on his elbows and took stock of his room. He was surprised at how domestic everything looked. It could have been a normal bedroom, although somewhat larger and more sumptuous than he was used to. There were curtains on the windows, pictures on the walls, comfortable chairs around a table, a love seat and other expensive looking furniture, a modern-looking flat screen TV, even a desk and personal computer. They had gone a long way to impart a homey feel to the place. He thought it was probably one of those sanitarium type places that catered to the long-term care of the wealthy.

The place was very quiet. That was probably by design, but he was a little surprised that no one on the staff had looked in on him by now. He moved to slip out of bed then noticed that he was dressed only in his underwear. He hesitated. There was what appeared to be a closet, next to what was the bathroom. There would probably be a robe or something in there that he could wear. He slipped out of bed and opened the closet. He was surprised at what he saw. There were clothes in the closet, but they were all women's clothes. Finding nothing he could wear, he became concerned that someone might walk in on him while he was half naked, and he thought it prudent to return to the bed. Along the way he took a quick look out the window. He saw ample manicured grounds enclosed by a brick wall. He was looking straight out over a swimming pool with tables and umbrellas. Someone was sitting at one of the tables having a meal and reading a paper. To the left of the grounds he noted the land sloped down to a large, blue lake. To the right the land sloped upwards toward the peaks of several mountains covered in alpine forest. There were other buildings and houses dotted around the lake and on the slopes, and it looked like it might be a ski resort area. While he was taking in the scenery, he thought he heard footsteps coming up the stairs. He returned to the bed and covered himself. A few seconds later the door to his room opened. Donna walked in carrying a tray.

"What are you doing here?" He was totally surprised, but somewhere in the back of his mind he was telling himself he should no longer be surprised whenever Donna showed up unexpectedly.

She looked like she did not understand the question, then looking at the tray in her hands, she said, "I'm bringing you some breakfast."

"But what are you doing here so early?"

"Isn't this the time people normally eat breakfast?

"No, I mean, why are *you* bringing it? Shouldn't someone on the staff be doing that?"

"Staff? We don't have any staff here at this time of year. We have to make do on our own for now."

"Something's not right here," Tom thought to himself. "Is this one of those places that arranges for family members to come and stay with patients to help out with menial chores?" He groaned inwardly.

To Donna he said, "But why are you staying here? I thought you'd go home after dropping me off."

"This *is* my home."

...

Donna spent the next fifteen minutes trying to calm Tom down. He was more agitated than she had expected. For the umpteenth time he protested the fact that Donna and her family had brought him to their vacation estate on Lake Tontino.

"You were supposed to take me to the Pfister Clinic," he persisted in an agitated whine. "No one said anything about me coming to stay in your home."

"We *are* going to take you there, but we'll have to make an appointment for you—probably in a couple of weeks, so…"

"A couple of weeks!?"

"Yes. The idea is for you to continue getting well over the next few days then you'll be ready for your appointment with the clinic."

"But, why am I staying with your family? Can't I just stay at the clinic?"

"No, the Pfister Clinic is an out-patient facility. They don't have any beds there."

"Then why didn't they just keep me in the hospital until I was ready? Why am I staying here? This isn't right."

"Because the clinic is just a few miles from here. So, when you're ready for your appointment you won't have to travel so far. In the meantime, you can concentrate on getting well."

While Tom was casting around for some other objection, Donna continued to make her point.

"Listen, Tom. You've got to take it easy. The hospital released you to our care on the condition that you continue to rest and recover your health. They had done everything they could for you at the hospital, so there was no reason to keep you there when we could look after you here just as well or better. I thought they explained that all to you."

"Nobody explained anything to me."

"Well, I'm sorry. I thought they had. Anyway, my father was paying the hospital bills for your stay—I mean it's not like you had any medical insurance—so we thought we'd save some money by…"

"But I *do* have insurance…uh, I mean, I must have insurance…"

There was a brief pause in their conversation. Donna placed the tray she was holding on the table and pulled the desk chair over to the bedside.

"Tom, I don't see why you don't want us to help you. We just want to show our gratitude for what you did for us."

"What did I do?"

"Well, you practically saved my life."

"I'm not so sure about that. Anyway, you don't owe me anything."

"I think I owe you quite a lot."

"Well, you don't."

There was another pause. Donna continued to regard him trying to gauge his body language. For his part, he seemed content to stare at the foot of the bed. She noted he had been calming down by stages, but his demeanor continued to reflect the perennial worry, fatigue and hopelessness he always exhibited. She had never seen him smile, and she wondered what it would be like to see him smile. She was on the verge of initiating a more intimate conversation with him. But her father's words still rang in her ears–"don't do anything stupid with Tom." But she wanted to say something to mitigate his displeasure.

"I know what's worrying you," she said. "You think that I'm going to bother you with questions every time I see you. Well, don't worry, I won't. And if you want to leave, that'll be fine. I'll take you wherever you want to go. But won't you stay here just for a while? We really want to help you. And I'd like to be your friend."

The last words she spoke had some sort of effect on him. She was not able to determine what it was. He looked at her. She thought he was going to say something, but he seemed to think better of it and turned his gaze back to contemplate the foot of bed.

"So, will you stay?" she repeated. "Just for a while? Please."

He shot her another sideways glance.

"OK," he said, "I guess. If that's what you want."

"Good," she said.

He crossed his arms and maintained his focus directly in front of him without looking at her. She could tell that he was put out by the situation in which he found himself.

She arose to retrieve the breakfast tray.

"Oh, look," she said. "Your tea and toast have gotten cold. Let me run down and heat them up again."

"No, don't do that," he responded. "It'll be all right. Just leave it."

"Well, I was going to ask you what else you wanted for breakfast. Maybe some eggs and bacon?"

"No, just the tea and toast'll be fine."

"Now don't be like that. You know you've got to eat. That's part of your recovery. So, what do you want?"

"Nothing right now. Please. I'll have something else later. I promise."

"All right. I'll come back later. Here let me put the tray on your lap, and you can have breakfast in bed."

"No! Please don't. Just leave it on the table."

"OK, but I expect it to be eaten when I come back."

"OK."

"If you want to eat at the table, let me go and find some pajamas for you to wear. I think Jeff will have a pair that will fit you."

Much to his relief she headed for the door.

On the way out she said, "I've put a toothbrush and some towels for you in the bathroom. Oh, and don't worry about the clothes in the closet, I haven't had a chance to make some space for you. I'll do that later."

"Are those your clothes?" he asked.

"Yes," she replied, "but don't worry. I'll...."

"What are your clothes doing in there?"

"It's where I keep them."

"What?"

"It's where I keep them. It's my closet."

"Your closet?"

"Yes. This is my room."

"What!?"

He jumped out of bed as if he had been sitting on a hot stove. At the last moment he realized he was dressed in his underwear, and he just barely had the presence of mind to catch the bed covers and pull them up around him as he came to a standing position.

Realizing his vulnerability, he checked the flood of protests he had intended to voice. Instead he took stock of himself and heaved a sigh as he sat back down on the bed.

In a calm yet thoroughly frustrated voice he said, "Where are my clothes?"

23.

Edwin Kittridge answered his mobile phone, noting that the incoming call was from Pilar, his wife. She had indicated in an earlier text that she would phone him today to give the details of her upcoming flight back home.

"Hello, sweetheart," he answered.

"Hi, Ed. How is everything?"

"Fine. How was your visit? How's everybody."

"They all missed you and the family. Next time we'll have to take the whole family."

"Why not see if they can come visit us here?"

"Darling, you know Tía Delia is too old to travel now, and there are too many there to be able to drop everything to come visit us all at once."

"Well, I'm not sure we can coordinate everyone here to visit there—you know the children have their own lives to lead and schedules to follow."

"That reminds me. Have Donna and Arthur announced their engagement yet? I'd like to see them as soon as possible to make wedding plans."

"Don't worry about that right now, sweetheart. I have something very important to tell you."

"What is it?"

"I'll tell you when you get here."

"Why can't you tell me now?"

"I don't what to say it over the phone. Just wait until you're home."

"Is it good or bad?"

"Oh, it's very good. I think you'll be pleasantly surprised."

"Pleasantly surprised?" she repeated with a tone of suspicion.

They continued to talk like a long-married husband and wife who had been separated from each other for a couple of months. During the conversation, Edwin got the flight arrival information. She would be arriving late tomorrow, taking a commercial flight to New York, then a charter flight to the local airport. She again asked after the "children," and again he deflected most of the questions with "we'll talk about it when you get home." After a little more chat and a few exchanges of affection, they disconnected.

Edwin heaved a sigh of relief. He had been dreading talking to Pilar and fearing that she might get suspicious over his reluctance to talk about the "children." He thought that he had gotten away with it. She did not seem to be suspicious. If she had the slightest suspicion, she would be dialing Lawrence this minute for the real news. He had cautioned his oldest son to say nothing about recent family events, but if Pilar called him and pressed him on the point, he would definitely spill the beans.

Anyway, the real ordeal was ahead of him, when he would be in the presence of his wife and have to explain to her, face to face, the developments of the last few weeks concerning Donna, her nonexistent engagement, and her new boyfriend.

24.

He was tired and confused. Again. He lay upon the bed trying to clear his mind. The promise of the refreshing, mind-clearing awakening that he had had earlier in the morning had now dissipated under the weight of the surprising revelations that Donna had sprung upon him. Naturally, she had well-reasoned and logical explanations for all the events that resulted in having him brought into her home. Even her explanations for why he was not told in advance about all this sounded perfectly plausible. She was good at convincing him of things he did not want to be convinced about. Nevertheless, he was certain she had orchestrated all this to keep him off balance and under her control. She evidently was not going to let him out of her sight until she knew everything. More than that, she wanted to get a rise out of him. He would have to be careful. At one point he had thought about opening up to her, telling her all his dark secrets. But he knew that each secret he spoke to her would be drawn into those beautiful brown eyes and he would be drawn along with them. He would be captivated along with his secrets. And under such a spell, he would never be able to return to his original mission. He needed to reconstruct the wall of mystery between them. He needed to readopt his air of passivity towards all the stimuli she tossed at him.

He could not help but fantasize that she might actually have some sort of romantic interest in him, given all the attention and apparent care she had been lavishing upon him. But he could not let go of the fact that a beautiful woman like Donna would certainly have a fiancé or serious boyfriend, and he did not want to fall for her only to be subsequently introduced to her lover.

And she had said she wanted to be his "friend." Well, forget about romance. It was a universal axiom that when a beautiful woman told a man she wanted to be "just friends" there was no hope of romance.

She walked briskly into the room carrying another tray. Feeling a little sarcastic, he said, "Hello, friend."

"What?"

"Hello, friend."

She put down the tray and walked over to him. "What do mean, "Hello, friend?"

"You said you wanted to be friends, so I said 'hello, friend.'"

"No, no, no, Tommy. I never said that."

"Yes, you did."

"No, I never said I wanted to be 'just friends.'"

"Well what did you say?"

"I said I loved you like a brother."

"Huh...?"

"Never mind that right now, Tommy. I need you to do something for me. It's very important.

"What...?"

"I have a few friends downstairs that I want you to meet. Can you come downstairs right now? It'll just take a minute."

"I'm not dressed."

"Oh, don't worry about that. Just grab a robe out of the closet." She was practically running out the door. "Hurry," she said.

The urgency in her voice had communicated itself to Tom, and he rushed over to the closet to find a robe. The closet was still packed full of her clothes. He had trouble identifying a garment he could use as a robe. The clothes on hangers were compressed so close together that he could not easily pull them out, and as he pulled one garment out to look at it a few others were pulled off their hangers and fell on the floor.

"Christ!" he muttered and attempted to pick up the garments and re-hang them.

"Tom! We're downstairs. We're waiting."

Out of near panic he grabbed a garment that had a semblance of being a robe and threw it on as he rushed out the door. He hurried down the stairs.

She had said a few friends were downstairs. That was an understatement. A throng of elegantly dressed people were milling around the place. There was some sort of party going on.

But he did not see Donna anywhere. He walked out through a pair of French doors toward the pool patio and saw her standing in the middle of another throng of people talking animatedly to a few friends that were congregated close around her. She was as pretty as a statue of Venus. She had put her raven black hair up in an elegant bun that was in gorgeous contrast to the long flowing white robe that she was wearing. All the women were wearing white as were most of the men. However, a few of the men wore black tuxedos. Most of the people were seated around on the patio furniture so compactly together that there was no way he could navigate through the crowd to get to her.

He became self-conscious. He was almost naked among the crowd. The garment he had donned was not so much a robe as a negligee and barely came down to his thighs. No one paid any attention to him, but he knew some of them must be remarking on his state of undress. Over by the pool, he saw a lone chair by an umbrella table and thought he would be less conspicuous if he sat down. En route, he glanced again at Donna who was now standing between two tuxedo-clad men with her arms around the necks of each. She saw him and raised a hand in a quick wave of recognition as if he had been a late comer to the party.

He sat down on the patio chair and immediately had to busy himself with adjusting the material of the negligee that had ridden up to expose too much of his nether region. To make matters worse the crowd of couples pressed in around him standing over him like a forest. He became claustrophobic. He looked over to the pool. It was empty. To escape the throng, he slipped into the water and shed the negligee to give the casual appearance of a party guest who had decided to take a dip as part of the festivities. He was now a nude swimmer. The water was only waist deep, and he endeavored to move to the deeper end of the pool to cover his private parts more adequately.

Now he saw that all the party guests had congregated around the perimeter of the pool. Again no one seemed to pay any attention to him, but he feared that at any moment their attention would be drawn to him en masse. He felt like a minnow in a jar of water. Why were they all sitting around the edge of the pool? Then the though hit him. "Oh, God," he thought, "this isn't one of those parties where the guests jump into the pool fully clothed?"

He managed to look beyond the humanity ringing the pool and saw Donna again. She was still supporting herself between the two men an arm around each, but now she had turned her head toward one of them and was casually kissing him. Tom turned his head toward the shallow end of the pool and saw Jeff approaching the crowd. Of all the people at the party Jeff was the only person not elegantly dressed. He had been playing fetch with a dog, and the dog jumped playfully in the air attempting to capture the stick that Jeff was holding high in the air. One of the party guests said, "What is this? Mutt and Jeff?" Everyone laughed including Tom.

Jeff laughed also then turned solemn. He took the chair at the table that Tom had previously occupied. Jeff looked directly at Tom and shot him a big smile.

"Resistance is futile," he said and rapped his knuckles on the table.

As if on cue, the entire crowd jumped into the pool, and Tom was surrounded by a splashing mass of swimming humanity.

A woman came up to him. She was as elegantly dressed as all the others, but she wore a veil.

"I know who you are, Tom," she said as she playfully latched onto him, as all the other guests were doing with each other.

"Do I know you?"

"Of course. You know who I am. You can't get away from me."

He recognized the woman and recoiled.

"For God's sake," he said, "you've got to give me a chance."

"I've given you all the chances you're going to get."

He tried to escape.

"Tom!" Another voice called him, and he looked up to see Donna looking down on him from the edge of the pool. There was a scowl on her face.

"Tom, what are you doing here?"

"You said you wanted me to meet a few of your friends."

"I didn't say that."

"I thought you did. I..."

"No, I said the ambulance is here to take you back to the hospital. It's over there in the driveway. And you can take her with you," she said pointing to the veiled woman. She turned on her heel and walked away.

He struggled out of the shallow end of the pool, trying to divest himself of the veiled woman.

"You've got to give me a chance," he said

"No! You're coming with me now."

"No. I can't. I've got to get back to the hospital."

"No, you're coming with me back to the forest."

They rounded the corner of the house to see the ambulance waiting. Two pale, sallow-looking paramedics were standing by the open back doors of the vehicle. Tom looked again. It was not an ambulance. It was a hearse.

With a squeal of glee, the veiled woman ran and dived into the vehicle. Through some kind of mid-air acrobatic turn, she landed in the hearse in a sitting position facing outwards toward Tom. She lifted a solemn arm and pointed at Tom.

"Bring him too," she said.

Tom tried to turn away. He was completely naked. In the distance he saw Donna and her two friends riding ATVs down toward the lake. Jeff was banging on the patio table with his fist like a gavel-wielding judge trying to restore order.

...

"Tom?"

"Huh...?"

"Are you OK?" It was Jeff's voice.

"Oh...uh, yeah."

"I was knocking on your door and didn't get an answer. Hope I didn't disturb you."

"No. It's OK. I must've dozed off."

"Sorry."

"No. It's OK."

"Well, anyway, Donna's making us some lunch and wondered if you felt up to it to having some lunch with us down by the pool."

Tom became fully awake. "Are you having a party down there?"

"No. It'd be just the three of us."

"Oh, right. Well, maybe some other time. I guess I'm not really up to it now. I think I need to sleep a little more."

"OK. I'll let you rest then," Jeff said as he walked to the door. "I'll see you later."

Tom pondered the weird dream. It was disconcerting. It was a disjointed replay of all the nagging worries in his mind, typical of the surreal dreams he occasionally experienced. He was tired. He slept again. This time it was a long dreamless sleep.

...

"So, what did he say?"

"He said he was too tired to come down right now. He's going to sleep some more."

"OK. That's good. I wish I could string a few days together where he'd sleep as much as possible. But he needs to eat. All he's had today is some warm tea and toast."

"Well, I guess he'll wake up sometime and can eat something later."

"Jeffy, would you mind checking on him for the next day or so? He seems to be upset with me for the moment."

"I wonder why?"

It took her a moment to realize he was being sarcastic.

"You think I've been too high-handed with him, don't you?"

"Maybe just a tad."

"Well, what else could I do? I couldn't just leave him in the hospital, could I?"

"Why not?"

"Because I wouldn't've been able to help him there."

"Are you sure he wanted your help?"

"I don't care what he wanted. He needed help. No one else was going to help him."

"You're really getting a thing about him, aren't you?"

"What if I am?" she said.

Before Jeff could respond, Donna was beset by a sudden realization. In a panicky tone she said, "Oh, Jeff, I'm running out of time. What am I going to do?"

"You mean about Mom?"

"Yes. I'm going to have to face her in a few days."

"More like two. She's getting in tomorrow evening, and as soon as Dad tells her what's happened, I'll bet you dollars to doughnuts she'll be over early the next morning demanding a full accounting from everyone concerned."

"Do you think she'll come over here the very next day after she gets home?"

"I don't know, but whenever she sees you, she's gonna have a lot to say."

"Oh, Jeff, why are we so concerned about Mom? We're both adults, and she hasn't got any legal control over us."

"Leave me out of this. I'm not the one concerned. You're the one she'll want to talk to. And if you don't think she's got any control over us, just be sure to tell her that when she gets here. Me, for my money, I think she's gonna have you and Tom Ambrose for lunch."

25.

෴

Edwin Kittridge observed the small white light in the distant afternoon sky that, he knew, was the jet bearing his wife home. The plane would be on the ground in ten minutes, and, again, he mentally rehearsed what he was going to say and do when Pilar arrived. He continued to watch as the small light grew into the recognizable shape of the Lear jet that was approaching for a landing. The Lear jet was a private aircraft that he owned jointly with a partner who used the plane much more often than he. At one point, Edwin had owned the jet outright, but as he had become more settled and had less need for extensive travel, he had sold a half interest in the plane and now had only an occasional need for it. He had never mentioned it to anyone, but the real deciding factor in his getting shed of the plane came about when Donna had started making noises about learning how to fly it.

The plane was housed at the private airstrip that had been built by his partner, and the airstrip was very close to the Kittridge estate. The plane was on the ground now and taxiing toward the spot where he waited by his car. Edwin had a few more minutes to ponder before he could expect to see his wife descend the steps of the plane. He thought about how nice it was never to have to fly commercially anymore, even though on this trip Pilar had flown a commercial jet into New York to make the connection to her private flight. It had been a sixteen-hour trip, and he expected his wife to be tired and suffering from jet lag. He hoped she would rest for a while, thereby giving him a little more of a reprieve before having to explain things to her.

She appeared at the top of the stairs and waved to him almost regally. She was dressed elegantly. She was one of the few people he knew who still dressed up to travel. He went forward to meet her. Unable to contain her joy at seeing him, she forgot her regal stance and hurried down the steps with a beaming smile. A vision of loveliness was coming toward him. He had forgotten how beautiful she was. He had not realized how much he had missed her. Suddenly, every other thought in his mind was secondary, as he rejoiced in having her close to him again. Why had he had such misgivings about her homecoming? They flung their arms about each other in a passionate and joyful embrace, and for the moment that was all he could think about.

He finally led her to the car depositing her in the passenger seat then taking a few minutes to organize the transfer of her baggage into the back of the car. He then took his position in the driver's seat and started out for home. She was eyeing him with those penetrating brown eyes, those eyes of a tyrannical queen or an innocent child. He never tired of the way she looked at him regardless of the reason, whether she regarded him with approbation or criticism. She now leaned across the console of the car and affectionately held his arm, laying her head on his shoulder as well as she could manage over the dividing console. Some thirty years earlier cars had divan seats, and when he first started dating her, she had always snuggled up against him when he drove her places. In more recent times, the all-pervasive bucket seats were not conducive to the snuggling of his day. It was not the first time he pined for things the way they used to be.

She suddenly lifted her head and looked at him. He kept his eyes on the road and could not immediately gauge her look. He thought perhaps she was anticipating additional small talk from him. But she spoke first.

"Have you been smoking?"

"What makes you think I've been smoking?" he said wondering why he ever had thought he could hide that fact from her by simply airing out the car.

"Can't you smell it? What was it? A cigar?"

"All right, I had one cigar. You can't expect me not to have an occasional cigar every once in a blue moon."

"Oh, Ed!" I hope you're not going to take up smoking again. You know how it makes you sick."

"I'm not taking up smoking. A cigar every now and then does not constitute "taking up smoking."

"Well, if you must smoke, please be sure to do it outside from now on."

It was a minor chiding. He still had the ample good will of her homecoming. But he was somewhat discomfited by her acute senses. He knew that her psychic intuition was no less acute, and he wondered if she may have suspected something about the situation with Donna.

"So, what is this pleasant surprise you have for me?"

It was the question he had been dreading. "I'll tell you when we get home."

He could feel her eyes on him. She was studying his face and body language for some clue that would give her an indication of what the surprise was about and whether it was really as pleasant as he had said.

He kept his eyes on the road, and desperately tried to think of something to say to change the topic.

The trip to their estate was not long. He pulled into the driveway and pulled a couple of her larger bags out of the car. She took a couple of the smaller bags and accompanied him through the great foyer of their home and into their ground floor master bedroom. He set the bags by the closet and started out to collect the remaining baggage.

She blocked his way.

"Ed?"

He looked into her eyes and was immediately captivated. It was uncanny how much she resembled Donna.

"It's good to have you home," he told her. "You wouldn't believe how much I missed you."

She smiled quietly. "So, what is the surprise you have for me?"

"Do you want me to show it to you now?"

"Yes, please."

"OK," he said. "Take off your clothes."

26.

∾

"Jeffy, would you go upstairs and see if Tom's awake and if he could manage to eat something now?"

Jeff and Donna had been sitting around watching TV in the late afternoon, and Donna was getting a little restless.

"Why don't you go up and talk to him?" Jeff replied "You haven't been up there since this morning, and he must be wondering where the warden is. Besides, I want to finish watching this program."

"No, I think I'd better give him a little more space. He's probably still miffed at me."

"Oh, go on up, for God's sake."

It did not take much to convince her. She climbed the stairs, tapped lightly on the door and entered Tom's room. He was not asleep. He was lying quietly in the bed and appeared to be deep in thought. Donna suddenly realized that he never seemed interested in watching TV, listening to the radio, or logging onto the computer. In fact, she had never known him even to turn on a light. It was like he never wanted to take the initiative on anything, and she wondered if he felt like an uncomfortable guest who was afraid to use the amenities in his host's home.

"Hi," she said as she walked toward him.

"Hi."

"What're you doing?"

"Nothing."

"Are you feeling OK?"

"Yeah."

"This is some brilliant dialog," Donna thought to herself. She was tempted to begin interrogating him again, but she had promised she would not bother him with questions. She knew he would retreat back into his shell of passivity if she started in on him again.

"Do you think you'd be up to having something for dinner with Jeff and me? We thought we'd order a pizza or something and watch a movie."

"That might be nice."

She helped him don his robe and slippers and accompanied him downstairs. The three of them sat around the living room on large sectional sofas and indulged in small talk. It was getting a little cold and Donna turned on the gas fireplace. The pizza came, and they ate it in front of a large screen TV, where Jeff had called up a movie.

She noted that Tom seemed to be fairly relaxed as she and her brother indulged in light conversation. When smiles or laughter were called for, she could perceive that Tom actually broke into the occasional wry smile as the humor of the moment required. Still, she noted, he could not look at her directly unless they were speaking to each other.

"He's still afraid of me and apprehensive about my motives," she thought to herself. "I'm going to have to be patient with him a while longer."

Nevertheless, she knew that things would come to a head quickly when her mother arrived on the scene. The presence of her mother would certainly circumvent her developing relations with Tom. She gave some thought to the possibility of loading Tom in her car and fleeing with him to her own apartment. But that would not work. She had promised her father. She was going to have to face her mother. Well she had done it before, so she knew she could get through it again. It would be uncomfortable for a while, but it would be just a matter of weathering the storm.

Eventually Tom fell asleep on the sofa, and she lay on the other side of the sectional, continuing to watch TV until she began to doze. Jeff finally arose from the armchair he had been sitting in watching the movie.

"OK. I'm off to bed," he mentioned to Donna in a soft voice so as not to awaken Tom.

"Goodnight," Donna responded, also softly. "I'll think we'll just stay down here and sleep."

On his way out, Jeff extinguished the lights, and Donna continued to watch Tom's sleeping form by the light of the fireplace. It was a peaceful, cozy moment. It was the calm before the storm.

27.

"Well, that was pleasant but hardly surprising."

Pilar Kittridge had rolled over on top of her husband while he was basking in the afterglow of their lovemaking. They tussled playfully for a few moments.

"So, what's this surprise you have for me?" she pressed him.

"I'll have to show you," he answered, and made a playful grab for her.

"Oh, no you don't," she said eluding his grasp. She moved to sit on the side of the bed and he was treated to a profile of her nude body.

"What is it you want to tell me?" She spoke in a serious tone, and she was getting suspicious.

He hesitated. It was a mistake.

She arose from the bed, and he caught one last glimpse of her nude figure as she determinedly put on a bathrobe. She might as well have been donning battle armor.

"Donna's broken up with Arthur, hasn't she?"

"Well, that's not exactly the way…."

"Oh, Ed, how could you?"

The only thing Edwin Kittridge found truly exasperating about his wife was that she tended to hold him accountable for things completely beyond his control as far as their children were concerned.

"Wait, it's not what you think…" he said as he arose from the bed and donned his own bathrobe.

"Why didn't you call me?" she said. She was in the process of building up a full head of steam.

"Wait a minute, honey, calm down. It's not what you think. First of all, she didn't break up with Arthur. He broke up with her."

"If he broke up with her, then you can believe she drove him to it."

"But the main thing is," Edwin continued, "she's found someone else she's in love with and wants to marry. That's the surprise." Edwin was trying to keep a lid on the outburst that Pilar was leading up to, and he had to get his points across in quick succession.

"She says she's in love with all her boyfriends and wants to marry them."

"But it's different this time."

"How so?"

"OK, now, don't get upset, but Donna had a forced landing in the forest north of the Lucinda Valley—she wasn't hurt, and she's perfectly fine…"

Pilar choked back a gasp. "Oh, my poor baby!" she exclaimed

"Don't worry, honey. She's perfectly fine. And I've absolutely forbidden her to fly anymore."

Edwin continued to recount the high points of Donna's adventure in the wilderness. At each successive stage in his narrative about how Donna was stranded in the wilderness, rescued by Tom Ambrose, and became romantically involved with him, Pilar grew calmer and more circumspect.

"So, she's staying with him at the lake house while he's recuperating. Jeff's there with them.

"Why didn't you just bring him here?"

"Because there's a clinic in Davidville they want him to attend, so at the lake house he'll be close to that."

Pilar spent a few moments digesting everything. "OK," she said. "So, who is this Tom Ambrose exactly? Where's he from and who is his family?"

Edwin realized that everything up to now had been a piece of cake. The worst was yet to come, and he realized that he probably should have called Pilar much earlier during this whole episode. At any rate, there was no easy way to say what he had to say next.

"Well, we don't know a lot about him... uh, he's had a temporary loss of memory..."

"What!"

"...as a result of his injuries... that's why they want him to go to the clinic in Davidville..."

There was no way he could contain Pilar's ensuing eruption.

28.

∾

Tom always felt better after a shower. Normally he would dress outside the bathroom, but since Donna had the habit of coming into the room without knocking, he was compelled to put his pajamas back on in the bathroom. He experienced a slight dizziness as he exited the bathroom, but he could tell he was getting stronger. He was not ready to run a marathon, but he was getting stronger none-the-less. Soon he would be able to refocus on his mission and could try to extricate himself from Donna's ministrations. It was not a cheerful thought. Exchanging Donna's cozy attentions for the cold barrenness of an inevitable fate would take an effort. Anyway, it was apparent that Donna was not going to let him go until she had resolved the mystery surrounding him. Maybe he should just go ahead and tell her what she wanted to know. At least enough to satisfy her curiosity. Maybe then he could extricate himself from her and her family.

As he passed the window, he looked out over the forest covered landscape. The late afternoon sun was beginning to cast long shadows. The bright light of the early-autumn day was beginning to give way to an evening that had a touch of chill in the air, and he found himself drawn to it. The leaves would be changing soon at this altitude. He had always liked the autumn, and he had a special regard for it now. Autumn signaled an end. An end to summer. An end to life that was teeming with summer misery. He gazed out into the forest and noticed a mist among the trees. For some reason, the sight quickened his pulse. With a pang of panic, he knew he needed to go there. With a quick calculation, he considered throwing open the window. It would take only a minute to jump to the ground, traverse the grounds, and be among the trees. An unaccustomed dose of adrenaline caused his hands to fly to the sash of the window.

There was a click as the bedroom door opened, and he checked his impulse.

"Hey, what are you doing?" Donna walked into the room.

"Uh, I was in the bathroom," he answered. Then realizing that did not explain his current location, he added, "I thought I'd open the window for a little air."

"You need to stay in bed," she said walking toward him with a suspicious look at the window.

She slipped her arm through his and tried to pull him back toward the bed. But he balked. "No, Donna. I can't."

"What's wrong?" she asked, a little surprised at this sudden rebellion.

"I've been lying down too long. My back is hurting. Just let me sit on the sofa a while."

'A fine time he's picked to get mulish,' Donna thought to herself. She could handle it, but she would have to be quick about it.

"Where does your back hurt?" she asked, standing directly in front of him.

"In the small," he answered, and by way of illustration he brought a fist up to the small of his back and twisted his torso as if trying to massage some kink out of a back muscle.

She came forward and put both of her arms around his torso and kneaded the small of his back.

"There?" she said.

"Uh, yeah….," he uttered completely surprised by her embrace.

She continued kneading his back. It was a full embrace. Her head rested on his shoulder. She gave him an erotic squeeze. He had not quite figured out what to do with his hands; they sort of rested on her shoulders. She looked up into his face. Donna was tall for a woman, but he still towered over her a good six inches. She brought her hands up to caress the sides of his face. She pulled his head down to hers. She kissed him.

29.

Three hours up to the lake. Three hours back. It meant the whole day was wasted. Moreover, they would probably spend the night. Two days wasted.

Lawrence Kittridge was somewhat miffed. He had work to do. His mother had called him last night, and before he could even welcome her back home, she immediately commanded his presence the following morning to accompany her and his father on an expedition up to their lake home to confront the new family "emergency."

"Well, OK," he had said, "but why don't I just go separately and meet you there. It'll give me a little time to..."

But his mother had dismissed his suggestion and insisted he accompany them in the family car so that the three-hour drive could be used as a planning session to discuss the emergency and to lay out a course of action.

Now he sat in the back seat of the car making half-hearted attempts to comment and elaborate on the issues being raised and discussed by his mother and father. And why was it that the dynamics of automotive travel precluded the ability of those in the front seat to hear back seat passengers? After realizing that his father and mother had missed some of his comments, he was compelled to lean far forward practically poking his head between the seats of his mother and father to ensure that he was being heard. It was not the most comfortable position, and at times he would take a break from the discussions and lean back in the seat.

He watched the mountain scenery go by. What started out as a pretty sunny day was beginning to cloud up and show signs of rain. He lamented the waste of time. The shenanigans of his younger siblings were beginning to put a serious crimp in his business affairs. The idle-rich lifestyle of his younger brother had not been anything to worry about up until now, but the potential for future conflict was there as Jeff got older and his mother began regarding Jeff's lack of marital progress with a critical eye. Lately, of course, Donna was the big problem. Larry dearly loved his sister, and his relief that she had survived her wilderness ordeal had been boundless. But now Donna seemed to be making another headlong dash toward disaster by getting involved with a questionable man who was likely some sort of criminal. He always thought Donna's sophistication and wealth would have shielded her from questionable characters. Was she now falling into that typical female death wish scenario that so many other women seemed to be prone to? Destroying herself for some unworthy man?

The Kittridge clan was wealthy and powerful enough to protect its members. Lawrence and his mother were the primary instruments of that protection. They would protect Donna. Regardless. But it would require time. Lawrence again lamented the time that would have to be devoted to this business. At his mother's insistence, he had spent considerable time fixing Donna up with Arthur O'Neil. Arthur O'Neil was practically his best friend. Everyone was ecstatic when Arthur and Donna had announced their engagement. Everything had seemed so logical and appropriate. The whole family breathed a sigh of relief. Then without warning, it all blew up. Lawrence was now back to square one concerning his sister. He would have to deal with it.

Lawrence was the family dynamo. His father depended upon him to help handle the family business and financial matters. His father had certainly been industrious enough, but he had always had a laid-back attitude toward family and business. And as he got older Edwin Kittridge was content to turn over more of the family business to his oldest son. Pilar Kittridge likewise turned to Lawrence as an ally to protect the family's welfare when necessary.

Lawrence returned his attention to the conversation now taking place between his mother and father.

"I still don't know why you're so upset about this," his father was saying.

"I don't understand why you're *not* upset about it," his mother retorted.

"Listen, honey. Donna's a grown woman and you can't keep on treating her like a child."

"Why not? She's acting like a child."

"No, she's not." Edwin Kittridge replied calmly, but he rolled his eyes in exasperation and glanced out his side window. It was raining now, and the day was gray. It was an appropriate reflection of the tenor of the general conversation.

Edwin and Pilar had discussed these issues ad nauseum the evening before and all day today. They were rehashing it all now to put Lawrence into the picture and to confirm their individual stands on the whole affair.

"I'm warning you, honey," Edwin continued, "if you push her too hard on this, she'll simply pack up and go off somewhere with this guy."

"I'm not going to push her too hard. I just want to find out what's going on and try to talk some sense into her before she does anything stupid with a complete stranger."

"Well, I've gotten her promise not to do anything stupid until we can find out more about him, but you're going to have to meet her halfway. Like it or not, she seems to pretty well like this guy, and you're going to have to be patient."

"'This guy,'" Pilar repeated. "Does he even have a name, or has he forgotten that too?"

"His name's Tom Ambrose. Be sure and use that name. She'll get upset if you refer to him as 'this guy.'"

"*Upset!*" Pilar exclaimed. "Who around here has the right to be upset...?"

"Do you know what I think?" Lawrence interrupted, poking his head over the seat from the back. "I think she's gotten involved with this guy on the rebound. If Arthur broke up with her, like she claims, then it wouldn't surprise me if she's gotten involved with the first man who came along just to show everyone that she could have her pick of dozens of men–you know, like Aunt Clarisse did when she got divorced. Right away, she turned around and married some complete asshole alcoholic..."

"Lawrence, please don't use that kind of language," his mother interrupted.

"But you know what I mean..." Lawrence continued his train of thought.

"No, I don't think that's the case," Edwin was the one who interrupted his son this time. "I brought that up with her, and she definitely denied it... Oh, hold on..."

In mid-sentence he had driven into a heavy fog, and everyone contained their conversation to acknowledge the potential driving hazard this represented. They had driven these mountains roads often enough to have experienced fog, and Edwin slowed the vehicle down significantly as a safety precaution. The low visibility lasted only a half-minute. It cleared up then they hit another patch of fog, and Edwin devoted his full attention to his driving. After a few minutes they broke into the clear for good. They were getting close to the lake house, and they continued the trip in silence.

30.

〜

"Tom…? *Tommy?*"

"Huh?"

"Will you do something for me?"

"What?"

"Will you stay in bed until I come back into the room?"

"OK."

Donna was not sure Tom had fully understood her request. He was in shock. He was looking at her in disbelief and the look on his face could not have reflected more surprise than if she had hit him in the forehead with a sledgehammer.

She had embraced him and kissed him. Then with a tenderness that shattered any determination he had to be contrary, she led him to the bed, pushed him down gently and covered him. She sat on the side of the bed poised over him. She had kissed him again. She kissed him with a force and passion determined to break through that passive façade he had always presented to her.

For a few brief seconds, he was not sure of what was happening. Then it all registered. His whole body stiffened as a quantum leap of passion welled up in him. He was on the verge of losing all self-control. He was on the verge of passing out altogether as her passionate kiss overwhelmed him and sucked the oxygen out of him. He was still weak and lacked the robustness for the Olympics of passion.

He managed to get his hands between himself and her body and gently and diplomatically peeled her away to the extent he could catch his breath.

"Wait...Donna...I...!" he stammered unable to form a coherent sentence.

She kissed him again. Again, she overwhelmed him with passion, and again he feared he was about to pass out altogether. Almost in a near panic, he struggled under her and managed to turn his head to the side.

"Wait, Donna, I can't breathe."

"Oh, I'm sorry." She moved her head up a few inches but continued to hover over him holding him penned down on the bed. "Is that better she said?"

"Uh huh."

She continued watching him. When she perceived he had recovered his senses enough, she kissed him again, carefully this time with tenderness more than passion. It was a long kiss. When their lips parted, she remained poised over him, captivating him with her smile and those beautiful brown eyes that were looking into his soul. She caressed his temples. She moved her hands down to his pajama shirt and did something provocative with his collar. She unbuttoned the top buttons. He tried to recover his senses but remained floating on a timeless cloud.

"Donna?" he finally said.

"Mmm?" she answered dreamily.

"Donna, I..."

Suddenly, he had a million questions he wanted to ask her. A million things he wanted to say to her. And he could not think of a single one. She hovered over him. Her nearness. He could smell her perfume. Her weight upon him. Her eyes and smile. Her raven black hair falling down over him. And for now, that was all there was in his universe.

She said something to him that he did not hear at first.

"So, will you stay in bed until I come back?" she repeated.

"Uh, OK."

She sat up on the side of the bed, all business now.

"I've got a few things to do. You stay here and get some rest."

"OK."

"I'll be back later," she said and arose to leave the room.

"Donna?"

"What?"

He hesitated, still not able to form a coherent sentence.

"Yes, what is it?" she prompted.

"Stay with me," he finally said.

The simple elegance of his plea melted her heart. For an instant she was tempted to return to his bedside and smother him with kisses. She went back to the bed and sat down beside him again.

"I'll be back later," she said with maternal tenderness and solicitude. "It's just that my parents will be here any minute now, and I've got to do a few things to get ready. You just stay here and relax. OK?"

"OK," he said.

She watched him a bit longer. He half anticipated she would kiss him again almost hoping she would and fearing she might. She wondered if she should warn him about her mother. She thought better of it and arose quickly to leave the room, finding herself in the grip of a strong emotion and wondering if she had just done something stupid with Tom.

...

After Donna left the room, Tom continued staring at the door through which she had left. He sat up in bed and continued staring at the door. The most beautiful woman in the world had kissed him. It was not a kiss of gratitude or friendship. There was no mistaking the passion in the way she had kissed him. Suddenly, there was a new focus to his life. Up to now Donna had been a beautiful butterfly that teased his senses and that he could not ignore. But she had floated so far beyond his reach that he never thought of getting close enough to possess her. She was a beautiful moth that flittered around the weak flame of his existence. Now she was the flame, and the flame had flared up and engulfed him. He was on fire. He lay back in the pillows of the bed with a sigh of desire. He relived the moments she had been with him. He indulged in a sexual fantasy making passionate love to her. He was back in the forest pinning her up against a tree. He kissed her. He saw her breasts. He relived all the moments they had been together deriving pleasure from her closeness and finding evidence of her love for him from the times she had shown him gentleness and caring. His senses reeled. He was breathing heavily. He put together a thousand scenarios of what he would say and do when she came to him again. He would tell her everything. A thousand thoughts and emotions flashed through his mind until he became mentally drained. He needed to clear his mind and think rationally. But he was tired. He did not want to sleep. A nightmare awaited him in sleep that would counter his carefully constructed scenarios of love. An icy finger came up from the depths of his soul to tap him on the shoulder and remind him of a sealed fate. He ignored the macabre assertion. He looked around the room noticing that it was getting dark. He could have turned on the bedside lamp, but such a mundane action was the farthest thing from his mind. He looked over to the window and saw a cold, grey fog pressing in upon the glass. He turned his gaze from the window and looked back at the door. The ghost in the mist could wait. His plans had just been changed.

31.

⌘

Tom hovered for an indeterminate amount of time between sleep and wakefulness thinking about the way Donna had kissed him. Had it been a dream? He awoke fully finding little change in the ambience of the room since Donna had left. How long had he slept? Now, he could hear voices downstairs. They were loud at times. After a while the voices ceased, and he perceived footsteps coming up the stairs. There was a brief tap on the door and before he could answer, the door opened. Donna came into the room. She had aged thirty years.

During all the projections and scenarios that he had constructed since Donna had last left the room, he never expected anyone else but Donna to be the next person to walk back through that door. He anticipated this so fervently that it took him a few moments to assimilate that the woman now coming toward him was not Donna. It was apparent now that it was Donna's mother. He could not believe the striking similarity. The older woman was followed by a tall, stocky man he had not met before. Donna, the younger, entered the room next followed by her father and Jeff.

Her father and Jeff waited by the door. Donna stood apart from the rest of the group, arms crossed, eyes downcast, and evidently uncomfortable with the unfolding proceedings.

It took Tom a few moments to take in what was happening. He had never known Donna to walk into a room without being the radiant center of attention. Now this older woman and the stocky man were coming toward him like toreadors determined to take this bull by the horns.

"Mr. Ambrose, I'm Pilar Kittridge, Donna's mother. Is there something we can do for you?"

"Uh, I don't know," Tom responded, not immediately understanding what she was getting at. "Your family's done so much for me already."

"I want you to know we're very grateful for what you did for our daughter, but surely don't you think you need to get back to your own family now? Won't they be missing you? Surely, you must remember something about your previous life by now."

"Well, uh, I'm not sure anything comes to mind right now…" He stammered out an almost inaudible trail end to his sentence that neither he nor anyone else in the room could make sense of. But he now understood that unlike the rest of Donna's family her mother was now inviting him to leave. Before his last tryst with Donna, he would have jumped at the chance. Even now he considered telling them enough of what they wanted to know so he could gracefully bow out of their lives. Out of the corner of his eye he glanced briefly at Donna. She remained in the posture she had assumed when she first entered the room, totally put out over the current situation. No, he told himself. If he was going to confess, it would be to her. Alone. She deserved that much. And he desperately wanted to play out the passionate promise of their last meeting, even though now considering the current perspective in the room, he wondered if he had read too much into that episode and was thinking about it all out of proportion by dwelling on it too much.

Pilar Kittridge had paused to let Tom say something more substantial, but when it became evident that he was not going to add anything to his previous feeble sentence, she continued her interrogation.

"What about your family? Do you have a wife? Children? Don't you think that they must be terribly worried about you?"

Donna's mother asked these questions pointedly for Donna's sake, hoping that an appropriate confession from Tom would show Donna the futility of her interest in him. Despite Donna's dislike of this line of questioning, her ears perked up when her mother asked the questions. She held her breath over the answer Tom might give.

"I have no children," Tom said, without hesitation, but he hesitated significantly before saying, "and I have no wife."

Donna was relieved to hear Tom's denial of having a wife. But the look on his face indicated that the question had evoked some painful memory, and Donna wondered if he might be lying about a wife. Or perhaps he had gone through some painful divorce or other marital strife that could have occasioned the sadness that showed through his eyes.

Her mother continued her questions. "OK, Mr. Ambrose, if you know you have no wife or family, it means you must remember something. How far back can you remember from this point?" she asked. "Maybe if you can think back as far as you can, something else will come to you."

Tom responded to these and other questions as passively and noncommittally as he could. He noted the tall stocky man standing slightly behind her and to the side, his eyes boring into Tom, taking his measure of this stranger in their home. He reminded Tom of John Wayne. Not that he looked anything like

John Wayne, but he was definitely there for law enforcement. Tom could almost see him wearing a ten-gallon hat, cowboy boots, a leather vest with a sheriff's star pinned on it and holding a shotgun across his chest. The presence of Donna's entire family within the confines of the room made him feel like some helpless insect under a microscope.

"Surely, Mr. Ambrose, you can understand our concern for our daughter. You must know that this lack of knowledge of anything about you is very worrisome for us. It all has all the appearances that you're hiding something. We'd feel much more comfortable if you could give us even a little more information about yourself and where you're from."

Her questions were so insistent that Tom was hard pressed to continue giving his "sorry-I-can't-quite-seem-to-remember" answers. He finally decided to give her a little information to relieve the pressure she was putting on him.

"I think I came from the East coast area. I remember something like driving for a long time to get to the mountains."

"Good," Pilar Kittridge said with a triumphal tone, "That will give us a starting point." An almost perceptible communication passed between her and the man beside her who slightly nodded his head in recognition of this breakthrough.

"Now, can you narrow it down to the state or city you started out from? Maybe New York? Boston? Philadelphia? Baltimore or Washington?

"I think I can remember driving through Iowa. I remember a lot of corn fields."

"Yes, but where did you start out from? Please try to remember Mr. Ambrose. It's very important."

"I'm sorry, I just can't remember right now..."

"Please, Mr. Ambrose. You must remember something about where you lived."

"Maybe the Washington area."

"OK, that's good. Perhaps we can arrange some transportation for you to return to an area you're familiar with to help you remember. Lawrence, can you see to arranging that....?"

During this questioning Donna's consternation had been growing, and now she finally spoke up.

"Mother, please. Can't you see he's too weak to make a long trip like that? He's just out of the hospital and he's supposed to be recuperating."

Pilar Kittridge shot her daughter a poisonous look. Before coming into the room, she had elicited a promise from Donna not to interrupt her questioning of Tom Ambrose. But Donna could contain herself no longer, and now she was acting like a mother grizzly protecting her cub.

Tom was grateful for the interruption, although he did not like the thought of a woman fighting his battles for him. He also immediately understood why Donna had wanted him to stay in bed. She had been doing a bit of her own staging to present him as a sympathetically helpless figure to her family.

"Donna, please don't interrupt. We're only trying to help."

"No, you're not. You're wearing him out. The doctor said he has to rest completely for a couple of weeks, and you're not letting him."

"Donna, don't take that tone with me. We've got to resolve this situation, and you're being absolutely stubborn about everything."

Donna and her mother continued to have words, and the interrogation of Tom Ambrose had effectively ended. Tom was mesmerized by this mirror image arguing with itself. The heated exchange went up successive notches until the two women were almost screaming at each other.

"¡Mamá! ¡No me fastidies!"

"¡Pórtate bien, hija! ¡Soy tu madre! ¡Ten respeto!"

"¡Es asunto mío! ¡No metas la pata!"

"¡No, hija! ¡Este hombre no es para tí! ¡Fuiste con él por puro antojo!"

"That's enough, you two!" Donna's father stepped forward to put an end to the shouting. He knew that whenever they switched to arguing in Spanish, it was time to put an end to the discussion.

"Everybody out of the room!" he continued. "I'm sorry, Tom."

He ushered everyone toward the door of the room.

"I'll stay with him for a while," Donna said, still flushed with anger.

"No, you get out too. I want to talk to Tom for a bit, in private."

32.

At seventy-five miles per hour, Jeff kept his eyes on the mountain interstate in front of him. He glanced briefly at his brother Lawrence who was sitting in the passenger seat beside him talking to his wife Cora on his mobile phone. The phone call would be good for about ten minutes. After that Jeff would be obliged to indulge in conversation with his brother for the next two and half hours. He did not look forward to that prospect. Hopefully, everyone would stop for lunch somewhere on the road where he could look forward to a little respite by putting the rest of the family between Lawrence and himself when they sat down to a meal.

They had closed up the lake house and formed a three-car caravan that was now en route to the Kittridge family estate about three hours away. Edwin and Pilar led the caravan in the family SUV. Donna followed with Tom in her vintage Corvette, leaving Jeff and Lawrence to bring up the rear. Jeff had fervently hoped Lawrence would travel with his mother and father, but the logic of having two people to each car was too strong to deny.

"We'll be at the estate in about three hours," Lawrence was saying to his wife. "I'm going to have to stay there for a while, so why don't you and the kids come on over this afternoon. Just consider it a welcome home gathering for Mom. What? Yeah, she'll be there too… Yes, him too…"

Jeff knew they were now talking about Donna and Tom. Cora normally did not have a curious bone in her body. She was entirely dedicated to the raising of her two seven-year-old twins almost to the exclusion of any other interests. But the allure of Donna's mysterious situation was an enticement that even the most non-curious could not easily ignore. Cora would come to express her best wishes to Pilar, but in effect she would show up to check out Donna and Tom. Jeff expected that Cora would be the first of numerous curiosity seekers and gossips to darken the door of the Kittridge estate in the near future.

Lawrence continued talking a bit longer to Cora then hung up.

With an inward grimace, Jeff geared himself up for small talk.

"So, how are the little monsters?"

"Monstrous," Lawrence answered.

Lawrence was normally verbose when talking about his children, but his flippant response to Jeff's question indicated that he had other things on this mind, and Jeff knew what those things were and that they were of more intricate stuff than small talk.

Lawrence kept his eyes firmly on Donna's car travelling ahead of them. "Hey, bro, you're lagging behind."

Donna's car was now positioned about a quarter mile ahead of them. "Why does he want me to follow her so close?" Jeff thought to himself. "Probably thinks if she gets out of sight she'll swerve onto an off ramp and make good her escape." Nevertheless, Jeff nudged his car up a few miles per hour to close the gap.

"So, what do you think of this guy?" Lawrence asked.

"You mean Tom Ambrose?" Jeff clarified.

"Of course," Lawrence replied shooting a hard look at Jeff that clearly meant, "Who else would I be talking about."

"He seems nice enough to me." Jeff answered.

Lawrence returned his gaze to the car in front of them, and he was quiet for a few seconds.

"That's right!" he finally said. "He probably *is* a nice guy."

After another pause, Lawrence continued, "So what the hell does she see in *him*?"

"You'll have to ask *her* about that," Jeff responded.

"The guy has no force of personality. He's completely passive, and she'll walk all over him. She can't be serious about wanting to marry him."

"I gather he can be forceful when he has to be," Jeff said in an effort to mount a defense of Donna's interest in Tom.

"When was he ever forceful with her?"

"I gather he had to be forceful when he was helping her get out of the forest."

Lawrence digested this information for a few seconds then shook his head. "No," he refuted, "I still don't buy it. And what's all this about his having amnesia? She would never go for someone like that. No, she's up to something, and I think she's using this guy. And some people are going to get hurt."

"Oh, no, Larry. I don't think she's up to anything mean. Don't forget, he probably *did* save her life, so that's got to be a big deal with her. Why don't we give her a chance and see what happens?"

"Oh, I'll give her a chance, but I've been talking with Mom, and we think maybe Donna went a little crazy when she broke up with Arthur, and maybe got a little suicidal, and maybe took up with the first idiot that came along…"

"Oh, come on, Larry. Give her credit for a little bit of intelligence. And some maturity. She's not a teenager. I think she's knows what she's doing…"

"Well, I don't know. You've got to admit he's not the kind of man she usually gets involved with."

"Well, he's no Arthur O'Neil, that's for sure." Jeff wondered if Lawrence had picked up on the pinch of sarcasm that went with his last retort. Then he continued. "Anyway, sure he's not like her other boyfriends, but maybe that's a good thing considering how she fought like cats and dogs with them until they broke up. Maybe, she needs someone with a different kind of temperament. So, let her give it a try. Maybe that'll be the charm."

"I hope you're right." Lawrence went back to watching the car in front of him. Jeff knew he was forming his own conclusions and mentally drawing up a plan of action on what to do about Donna and Tom. It was a little scary. Jeff hoped Lawrence never found out about his interest in Leslie.

…

Donna and Tom had travelled in silence since they had left the lake house. Donna thought Tom would go to sleep quickly, but he remained awake, watching the road in front of them deep in his own thoughts. He wanted to ask her about last night. He wanted to know the reason she had kissed him so passionately. But in the cold light of day, the episode seemed of much less significance. Try as he might, he could find no way to broach the topic with her, and he remained in a painful and futile analysis of what her motives might be. "I'm thinking too much about this," he told himself.

Some of the consternation in his thoughts must have shown in his face, and Donna finally broke the silence that had characterized their journey up to that point.

"Are you all right?" she asked him.

"Yeah, I'm fine," he responded.

"You look a little worried about something."

"No, I'm fine," he reiterated.

She continued looking at him then back at the road, expecting him to say something more. He felt her gaze and the pressure of her expectations, and he finally said, "I was just wondering about last night."

"Oh, that," she said, "look Tom, I'm sorry about my mother. I should have warned you about her before...."

"No, not that..."

"But don't worry," she continued without hearing his attempted interruption, "she won't bother you like that again. My parents are just insisting we come stay with them, so they won't worry so much. I know you've been jerked around, by all this, but don't worry, everything will be fine. You'll be able to continue your recovery there with no interruptions...

For several minutes Donna continued her commentary which was half tirade against her mother and half justification for the deal she had brokered with her father to bring Tom to the family estate as a house guest. Tom listened perfunctorily as it began to dawn on him that Donna's overwhelming concern last night had been her conflict with her mother rather than any romantic involvement with him. The thought saddened him. He suspected that her displays of affection were yet just another ploy to enlist him as a pawn in an intricate game of chess she was playing with her mother or anyone else she was trying to manipulate.

Donna's near monolog was interrupted by the ringing of her phone. She answered and talked for a few seconds then hung up.

"That's my mother," she told Tom, "they want to stop at the next rest area for some lunch. Is that all right with you?"

"OK," Tom replied.

They continued driving in silence for a few moments when Tom said, "You know you look a lot like your mother." The unspoken implication in his statement was that she also acted a lot like her mother.

"People have been telling me that for as long as I can remember," Donna answered.

"I hope I haven't been the cause of some problem between you and your mother," Tom continued.

"Most things are the cause of problems between me and my mother," Donna admitted.

"I noticed you were speaking in Spanish there at the end."

"Yes. My mother's parents came from Spain. In fact, that's where she just got back from."

"And you speak Spanish too?"

"No, not really. Just enough to argue with my mother."

"I see."

They drove on a while longer in silence. Tom was solely trying to make non-committal small talk, but Donna kept thinking he was leading up to something.

"I guess my mother and I are a little hot blooded at times," she added, "but she drives me crazy when she starts poking her nose into my business."

"I think your mom is just concerned about you. I'm sure she's just trying to do what's best."

"Are you serious? Don't you remember last night? She practically tried to kick you out of the house the first time she talked to you?"

"Yes, but that's because she was just trying to protect you and the rest of her family. I'm a complete stranger to her, and she has a perfect right to be concerned."

"Oh, give me a break, Tom. My mother has been trying to run my personal life forever. She still treats me like a child and wants to decide who I get involved with. I have to keep reminding her to mind her own business."

Donna talked more, and Tom said less. It became apparent that Tom was not going to volunteer any more conversational tidbits, and Donna decided to keep the conversation going hoping for some new insight he might reveal.

"By the way," she said, "what did you and my father talk about last night?"

"Oh, he just wanted to know if it'd be all right with me if I were to come stay at your family home. He sort of said the same thing you said about wanting me as a house guest so that your mother and he wouldn't worry about your being so far away."

"Yeah, that was his plan. I was dead-set against it at first but finally agreed on the condition he keep Mom under control."

Donna thought back on her conversation with her father last night. When he had first come out of Tom's room he went immediately into his bedroom with Pilar, and he must have had a long conversation with her. Donna had thought they had gone to bed for the night. But after a while, he came out of his room and took Donna aside for an equally long conversation, outlining the same deal he had made with his wife to bring Tom into his home as a guest.

"Your mother's agreed not to upset things between you and Tom," her father proclaimed, "as long as you agree to wait until we know more about him, like we agreed to before."

At first Donna had indeed rejected the plan to put Tom anywhere within the purview of her mother. "But Daddy, he needs to stay here to be close to the Pfister Clinic..."

"Oh, Donna, he can easily be brought back here if it's necessary. It'll only be three hours away. Besides," he continued, giving her a knowing look, "he may well recover his memory all together before then."

Now, sitting across from Tom in her car driving en route to her parents' estate, Donna had a growing feeling that Tom had told her father some things he had not told her.

Tom kept his eyes focused in front of himself, taking in the beautiful interstate mountain scenery that was enhanced by the crisp sunshine of an early autumn day. He was not predisposed to continue conversing. Donna noted a highway sign indicating the next rest area to be two miles away.

"What else did you talk about?" she asked.

"Nothing much, really."

"He was in your room for a long time. You must have talked about something else."

"Nothing, really. He just wanted to know if there was any reason he should have any concerns about my coming to stay in your home."

"What did you say?"

"I told him there wasn't."

Donna watched the road ahead of her carefully. She did not want her driving to be distracted, but she was engrossed by Tom's conversation with her. He had said things last night and was saying things now that were clearly at variance with his contention of having total amnesia. He must have known that what he was saying was loaded with memories that gave the lie to what he had told her previously about his inability to remember anything about his past. She was trying to frame a question diplomatically enough to draw more information out of him without appearing to breach her earlier promise of not questioning him too closely about his past.

Before she could ask another question, Tom blurted out forcefully, "Listen Donna, I don't…."

He started to say one thing then changed his mind amending his sentence and stating it with less force, "…it's not fair of me to cause so much conflict in your family. I'm grateful for what you all did for me, but I really think it's time for me to go."

"Where would you go?"

"Home."

"Home?" Donna held her breath. Up ahead her parents took the exit into the rest area. She moved into the exit lane following them, lamenting the unfortunate timing of the lunch break that would put an end to their conversation.

Tom kept his eyes deliberately on the road ahead. "Donna, I don't have amnesia," he said. "I never did."

He paused then looked at her pointedly. "Of course, you knew that."

"Why did you say you did?" she asked as she pulled into a parking space. Her brother's car pulled up beside hers.

"It's complicated," Tom answered. "Give me a few days, and I'll tell you everything you want to know. Is that OK with you?"

"OK."

"But then," he continued, "understand that after that I'll have to leave."

She did not say anything in response to his last statement. They exited the car. Donna walked around to his side of the car and took him by the arm. They joined her parents and brothers in the restaurant.

33.

～∞～

Donna was certain that Tom would not leave her. He loved her, and she loved him. When he finally figured that out, he would stay with her. She had certainly given him hints about her feelings for him, but he was the kind of man who would never believe it until she spelled it out in detail. He would probably want to see something in writing also. Like most men he was naïve enough to think that women played the game of seduction with logic and deductive reasoning. She would confess her love for him in her own appropriately non-logical and feminine way. But only after he revealed the secrets of his past. He was still a big mystery, and she continued to worry that there might be something so awful in his past—something awful he had done—that would preclude a happy ending to the budding romance. She was dying to know all about him. He had said he would reveal all to her in a few days. It had been a few days now, but he gave no indication that he wanted to talk about himself. She was determined not to push him about it. For the moment she wanted to create a tranquil, worry-free environment for him to continue his recovery.

She came out of the shower, and as she dried herself off, she looked out of her second story bedroom window to the outdoor pool patio below. The early autumn day was a little too cool to contemplate swimming, but the patio was surrounded on three sides by buildings of the Kittridge estate, and the area was awash in sunlight making it a perfectly warm and cozy place for sunbathing. Tom was down there in swimming trunks lying on a lounge chair taking in the sun. She continued watching him for a few moments. His eyes were closed, but she did not think he was sleeping. The gash on his left leg seemed to be healed. He was thinner than he should be. He had a "redneck tan." His face and arms that had been bared during their time in the forest still held a dark tan, but the part of his body that had been covered—his torso, legs and feet showed a pallid cast. She hoped a few days in the sun would even out his color. An ample diet should put a little weight on him. And, above all, a quiet week or two would provide the rest that he needed most.

Donna continued to watch him from her window. She smiled remembering the look on his face the day she drove with him through the security gates and up the driveway to the Kittridge estate.

"Are we stopping at a hotel?" he had asked.

"No, silly. This is my parents' home."

As they exited the car, he had looked around almost awestruck, taking in the extensive grounds and buildings of the Kittridge estate.

"Donna, just how rich *is* your family anyway?"

"Filthy."

Other than that initial shock, Tom had adapted without protest to the role of house guest amid the affluence of the Kittridge family. Over the last few days things had been peaceful and quiet enough. Her two brothers had gone home. Donna and Tom took their meals with Pilar and Edwin. Pilar still did not like Donna's involvement with Tom, but she was behaving herself. Tom turned out to be a congenial person for the most part. Although soft spoken, he was polite, cooperative and a good conversationalist. To Edwin's delight, Tom turned out to be a good chess player, and the two of them would have played endless games of chess in the evenings, but the mental strain it caused Tom was apparent, and Donna limited them to one after dinner game in the evening. Pilar also began to warm up to him, but it was evident that she did not like the idea of him as a future son-in-law. However, one evening Donna walked into the family room to find Pilar and Tom chattering away. In Spanish!

"Tom, I didn't know you could speak Spanish."

Her mother looked up at her wearing a keen smile. "He speaks French, too!"

Donna's mother spoke French and Spanish fluently, and Tom seemed to speak those two languages just as fluently. Donna knew that Tom was now "the golden boy" as far as her mother was concerned. Donna was a little miffed that Tom would reveal something as intimate as that to her mother before telling her. For the umpteenth time Donna considered asking Tom to reveal his past to her. But again, she did not want to appear to be the pushy, forward woman she was when she first met him.

"He'll tell me when he's ready," she told herself.

Both her parents now admitted that on the surface Tom was a charming man and worthy of being a possible son-in-law. But both still had the same misgivings about the mystery of Tom's past.

"Honey, please remember, don't make a commitment to Tom until we know about his past," her father told her in a private moment.

"He'll tell me about himself when he's ready," Donna replied.

At another time, her mother gave her similar advice. "Please, sweetheart. Please, please, please make him tell you about himself. Make him tell you before you fall so deeply in love with him that you'll end up suffering badly. We love you sweetheart and couldn't bear to see you hurt."

Her mother had been well aware of Donna's proclivities about shedding past boyfriends, and it was always the boyfriends who suffered most by the breakups. But now she could see that Donna was deeply attached to Tom and that she would be deeply hurt if the romance did not work out.

"It'll be all right, Momma," Donna told her. "He'll tell me when he's ready. It'll be soon, now."

It was a few cautious days. It was an eternity. How many times had she lamented those quiet occasions and conversations in which she was dying to say things intimate to Tom, the things lovers first say to each other to cement their relationships? How many times had she been on the verge of confessing her love to Tom and begging him to tell her about himself?

"He'll tell me when he's ready," she kept saying to herself.

Donna finished toweling herself off and took up her hair dryer and began blowing her hair. She continued watching Tom out the window. If he were to look up to her window, he would see her in the nude. She almost hoped he would. She was being intentionally provocative.

She had developed a salubrious routine for Tom. Between meals and evening gatherings with her parents in the family room, she would deposit Tom by the pool in the late morning or early afternoon to take the sun. She would also show him around her parents' estate or take him on short drives. It was all for the purpose of providing a restful, stress-free environment.

There was one intentional "stress" she put on him. She would usually join him by the pool wearing her most revealing bikini. He sneaked furtive glances at her glorious body. His attempts to contain his gawking at her openly were heroic. If Donna's parents had not been at home, she would have considered letting Tom watch her go skinny dipping in the pool.

Donna left the window and looked at her nude figure in her bedroom mirror. Satisfied with what she saw, she put on a bikini and a pool robe and went downstairs to join Tom by the pool.

34.

∽

Donna had not wanted to get involved with her friends at this point in time. Unfortunately, her mother had arranged a big catered party, and almost every one of Donna's friends had been invited and had shown up bubbling over with curiosity. Her mother organized the party with the dual purpose of celebrating her own homecoming as well as Donna's deliverance from a perilous ordeal. Donna suspected her mother had originally arranged the party, in part, with the objective of illustrating how out of place Tom would appear among her circle of friends. That was before Tom had come up a few notches in her mother's estimation due to his linguistic abilities.

At first Donna intended to keep Tom away from the crowd, but everyone was so insistent on meeting him, she was finally compelled to go to his room to collect him.

Tom was sitting on the sofa reading a book when Donna entered the room. He was awed by the beauty of the vision of Donna who approached him in her party finery. She had donned a shear burgundy dress that enhanced her black hair, her tanned complexion, and the slenderness of her figure. She was truly the closest thing to a goddess he had ever seen.

"Hi, Tom," she said. "We're having a party downstairs, and everyone is dying to meet you. Would you mind coming downstairs for a little bit? If I don't produce you, they'll all be up here pounding on the door."

The expression on his face changed from that of a man hypnotized by beauty to something like a man who had just heard something unbelievable.

"You're having a party downstairs?" he asked plainly apprehensive.

"Yes. You wouldn't have to stay long, or if you don't want to you don't have to… What's wrong, Tom? You look like you've seen a ghost.

"It's nothing. It's just that I had a dream…

"A dream? What kind of dream?"

"A dream about you and a party."

"Oh, really? About me and a party?"

"Yes. It's a little like déjà vu, I guess. Am I dreaming now?"

"No."

"Would you tell me if I was?

"What? No, I mean yes… wait Tom, maybe this isn't a good idea. Maybe you should just stay here…"

"No, it's OK. I'll come down."

"Are you sure you're up to it?"

"Yes."

She took him by the arm and accompanied him out the door toward the grand foyer staircase.

"So, tell me about this dream," she said.

At the top of the stairs, he stopped and turned to face her.

"You were beautiful in that dream."

"Oh, Tom, you're sweet."

"You're more beautiful now."

She positively swooned. She embraced him, and he was suddenly so overcome by desire that he could not resist kissing her.

They had embraced and kissed at the top of the stairs, and some of the party guests in the foyer must have seen them. She was thrilled knowing that the word would spread among her friends at the speed of light. They descended the stairs, a beaming smile radiating from her face. And she was all the more beautiful for it.

Nonetheless, she was concerned about throwing Tom to the wolves—her friends who, spurred on by rabid curiosity, would swarm over them both with the rudest questions and most outrageous party antics.

She escorted Tom among the party guests, introducing him to her friends. There was instantly a throng of people around them asking questions. They wanted to know everything–including all the sordid details. Some of the questions were quite brazen.

"What did you do all that time when you were in the forest alone?"

"Did you have to sleep together to keep warm?"

"That's none of your business!" Donna interrupted continuing to hold on to Tom's arm and preparing to interject her own responses to any questions she felt to be too personal.

She was pleasantly surprised to see that Tom handled the throng of people well, fielding questions and standing his ground. She expected she would have to continue to deflect some of the more invasive questions–especially from some of her more forward women friends, but he answered questions with a degree of aplomb she would never have expected. He was pretending to be circumspect about each question, and before he could deliver more than half a well-measured response to any question, someone else interrupted impatiently with another question.

Everyone was interested enough in learning about Tom, but it was plain to see that her friends were up to their usual party mischief and were probing for weak spots in the armor of the new kid on the block. They were in effect entertaining themselves by trying to embarrass Tom and Donna enough to get some sort of a rise or blush from the new couple. In past gatherings Donna had done the same to some vulnerable guest or couple (good naturedly of course), but this was the first time she was on the receiving end of the mischief. She could stand up to the rigor of such party games, but she was still concerned about how Tom would take to all this.

"Where are you from, Tom?" came one innocuous question from the crowd.

"Washington, D.C."

Donna wondered if Tom was going to reveal some information about himself to a total stranger that he had not revealed to her.

"Oh? What do you do there?" the questioner continued.

"I work for the Government."

"Oh? Really? What part?"

"All of me."

Laughter. It was an old witticism, but Tom had scored a point with the gang.

"No, I mean what part of the Government do you work for?"

"Oh–the NSA."

"The NSA? What's that?"

"The National Secret Agency. I'm a spy."

There was a collective perking up of ears.

"Really? A spy? Who do you spy on?"

"I can't tell you. If I told you, I'd have to kill you."

More laughter. Tom was handling himself well. For a brief instant he looked like a doting uncle entertaining a group of excited children.

Donna began to relax and figured she could cast him loose for a bit on his own. Then she saw a figure approaching the group that made her reassert her grip on Tom's arm.

A woman was approaching the group, a latecomer to the party. She was a mousey brunette who wore glasses and was of average looks and height. Actually, she was even a little plump and one would possibly think she looked a little owlish. But the aura of personality radiating from the woman instantly made her the center of attention and a creature of attraction.

"Oh, no," Donna said for the benefit of all within earshot, "here comes 'Fangs and Claws.' Stay close to me, Tom."

'Fangs and Claws' was Donna's nickname for Fanny Anne Clausen. Donna had hoped that Fanny would not show up at this party. Even though she was Donna's oldest friend, she was also Donna's biggest rival. Ever since that day in junior high school when Donna "stole" Fanny's boyfriend, the two had been rivals–in everything. But especially when it came to men.

Donna did not dislike Fanny. She actually admired her. Fanny had not been endowed with the striking beauty and wealth that Donna and many of her friends had inherited. Fanny's status and position among Donna's clique of friends had been attained through her intelligence and force of personality. She was in fact a desirable woman and had been married and divorced. As such she was the ultimate authority among Donna and her friends on men.

Much of the apparent rivalry between Donna and Fanny was affectation and feigned derision. It was the equivalent to another party game. Normally, Donna had no problem bantering with Fanny. But she was at a tricky point in her involvement with

Tom, and she did not want anyone to upset that balance, and Fanny was exactly the person most likely to do that.

Fanny walked up to the group of people keeping her eyes fixed firmly on Tom in mock fascination. Tom was surprised and a little apprehensive over the behavior coming from this woman.

"Wow, Donna," Fanny said without taking her eyes off Tom, "where did you find *him*?"

"None of your business. And put your eyes back in your head."

Fanny pointedly ignored Donna and continued looking at Tom. "Oh, are you Tom Ambrose? I've heard so much about you."

She insinuated herself on the other side of Tom and took his arm, sandwiching Tom between Donna and herself.

"Why don't we go sit down over there," she said, tugging at Tom's arm. "I want you to tell me all about yourself."

"I don't think so," Donna replied, tugging back.

"Oh, Donna, you've had him all this time. You must be finished with him by now. Let some of the rest of us have a go…I mean, let some of the rest of us talk to him for a while." She gave another tug on his arm.

Donna again tugged back. "Why don't you go talk to some husbands? I hear you're in the market for a new one."

"Why, Donna, you know my liaison with Mr. Burris didn't work out," Fanny adopted a faux accent reminiscent of a coquettish southern-belle. "So, it's only natural that I would cast my eyes about for an unattached young man who might appreciate my charms." She made a dramatic gesture of looking around the room finally letting her eyes come to rest again on Tom. "Why, of course, Tom…"

The party guests around them were all a-twitter over the entertainment afforded by the showdown between the two women. Even Tom, who had initially been anxious about the unfolding dynamic between the two women, had now realized that flippancy and sarcasm were the order of the day, and he was wearing a wry smile. But he was well aware that there was an intense rivalry between the two women with undercurrents of potential behavior that he hoped would never come to the surface.

Fanny reached up to whisper something in Tom's ear.

"Hey, what're you doing?" Donna exclaimed. "Get your grubby hands off him."

The two women continued to exchange sarcastic barbs until one of Donna's friends came over to her saying her mother wanted to see her.

"Good," Donna replied, "come on Tom. Let's go talk to some mature people for a change."

She started to pull him toward another part of the house, but all the surrounding guests objected.

"Oh, let him stay here, Donna. Nobody's gonna run off with him."

She relented, releasing her hold on Tom. "OK," she said, "but everybody keep an eye on her; and Tom, don't let her get you alone."

Having hurled a final jab at her rival, Donna headed off to see her mother.

The Kittridge mansion hosted two large party rooms off the main entrance or foyer. When a party was in progress, the older, more venerable guests generally occupied the room to the right of the foyer, while the younger guests usually gravitated to the room on the left.

As Donna walked across the foyer toward the other party room, she glanced back to see Tom engrossed in conversation with Fanny and the other guests. Despite her concerns over letting Tom out of her sight, she relaxed.

"Donna!"

Donna turned to see another late-arriving guest coming toward her.

"David!" she exclaimed and rushed over to him giving him an enthusiastic kiss. "David, I haven't seen you in ages. Where *have* you been all this time?"

"I was overseas," the newcomer said. "I just got back home."

"Well, fill me in on everything, but first I've got to see my mother. Come with me and I'll introduce you to everyone."

"And I hear you've had some sort of wild adventure, so tell me all about it."

"I will. And later, I want you to meet my new boyfriend."

"And here I was hoping you'd be back in circulation."

They laughed, and she accompanied David toward the adult party room. With an apprehensive afterthought, she cast a glance back toward Tom suddenly realizing he might have gotten the wrong idea if he had observed her enthusiastic greeting for David. Tom's back was toward Donna, and he was conversing with Fanny and a few other people. Fanny kept looking past Tom in Donna's direction and had certainly observed Donna and David. She was wearing an enigmatic smirk, and that bothered Donna. She figured she was going to have to take Tom aside later and perform damage control on any toxic effects of conversations he may have been exposed to during her absence.

Donna and David approached Pilar Kittridge who was surrounded by a number of her friends. Pilar knew David and was evidently pleasantly surprised to see them together.

"Hello, David," she said. "It's so nice to see you again." Then to Donna, she asked, "Where's Tom?"

"He's in the other room with the other guests. I just met David coming in and knew you'd like to see him since he's been away so long."

Pilar's friends had heard of Donna's adventures, and Pilar had summoned her to provide a first-hand account to all interested guests in that group. Between her mother, her mother's friends and David, it took Donna a considerable time to extricate herself and begin working her way back to the other room.

Tom was nowhere to be seen. She spotted Fanny and some of her other friends sitting over in a corner of the room and she approached them.

"Where's Tom?" she asked.

Fanny presented her with the same indecipherable smirk as before. "He excused himself and went upstairs. He looked tired."

"Oh? OK, I'll go check on him."

"Oh, Donna, I don't think he wants to be disturbed. He was going straight to bed and asked us to tell you not to bother him."

"How long ago did he go up?"

"It must be half an hour ago, by now."

Donna turned deliberately on her heel and headed up the stairs.

She opened the door to Tom's room. It was in complete darkness, and Tom appeared to be asleep. She thought about calling out to him softly but changed her mind. She returned downstairs to the party, and before the party wrapped up, her friends had gotten her solemn promise to join them the following day for lunch.

35.

∽

Donna left early the following day to meet her clique of friends at one of their favorite restaurants. She wanted to get it over with as fast as possible then return to Tom. She was lunching with her friends as she had done regularly hundreds of times before. This was the first time she had rejoined the group since returning to civilization. The girls-only clique normally met once a month or so to exchange news, gossip, and mostly to run down husbands, boyfriends, and men in general. This was Donna's inner circle of friends where everyone could let their hair down in earnest without concern for the sensibilities of mixed company. This time, Donna and her recent adventures were the main topic of conversation, and she had to keep up a flippant banter against the barrage of questions now being tossed at her.

The group wanted to know the circumstances and details on the end of her engagement to Arthur. In her younger days Donna had a reputation for being somewhat of a beau snatcher, and her friends believed she had gotten a justifiable albeit long-delayed comeuppance when another woman had "stolen" her fiancé, especially since the other woman was Betty Bridger, a woman who had never seemed to rise above the rank of side kick among Donna's friends. Donna told the assembled company at the table the story she wanted them to hear, saying nothing about how utterly devastated she had been when Arthur broke the engagement with her in favor of Betty. On the surface she gave the appearance of being totally unconcerned about losing her fiancé.

"That man had such a high opinion of himself that I couldn't stand it," she concluded. "I never could have married him."

"Isn't that what he said about you," one of her friends jested, eliciting chuckles from the other girls. It was an open secret that Donna had a reputation for thinking of herself as God's gift to men.

"So, are you going to marry Tom Ambrose instead?" Fanny chimed in. It had become apparent that Donna had no remnant feelings about Arthur that Fanny could use as ammo in her continuing skirmishes with Donna. Now she skillfully guided the topic around to Tom to see if she could push any of Donna's buttons on that score.

"Yes, I'm planning to marry him," Donna replied.

"Has he asked you yet?"

"Not yet. But he will."

"How do you know he will?"

"Oh, Fanny, don't you know anything about men? I thought you were the great expert on the subject. Don't you know that men ask women to marry them when we guide them around to it?"

"Well, when are you going to guide him around to it, then?"

"Soon. I'm just waiting for him to get a little stronger. You know he's just come out of the hospital and is still a little weak."

"So, what are you going to do with him in the meantime? Treat him like you did last night?"

"What do you mean like last night?"

"Well, let's admit it—he didn't look too happy about things. He looked like a fish out of water when you left him and were gone for so long."

"He probably *wasn't* very happy having to talk to you. I can believe that."

Fanny ignored Donna's attempt to turn the tables on her. "Well," she continued, "by the looks of it, I'd say you've probably been jerking him around like all your other boyfriends."

"That's not true!"

"Oh, isn't it? Well, you know, he saw you kissing David Cattermole last night."

"So what? I kiss all my friends. He knows that."

"Oh, does he? Well, when he saw you kissing David, he looked like someone kicked him in the stomach. He didn't even try to hide it, just excused himself and left the room."

Donna was taken aback by that news and could not think of a retort.

Fanny took advantage of Donna's hesitation and continued her crusade.

"So, you keep on treating him like that, and I'm sure he'll ask you to marry him," she crowed sarcastically.

"Oh, I've been treating him well. Don't worry about that."

"Hmmpf," Fanny sniffed. "I bet you haven't even slept with him, yet."

"He's been too weak for…"

"You haven't, have you! You haven't even slept with him!" Fanny exclaimed in triumph. "I knew it!"

"Listen, pickle puss! You know he's just come out of the hospital and isn't strong enough for that!"

"Oh, puh-lease, Donna, give me a break. I think you're the one who doesn't know anything about men. Men'll get up off their death beds to have sex. Especially with their nurses…well, at least, before they're married, anyway." Fanny's last phrase was more of an aside to herself, a private memory of some past marital issue of her own.

"I don't have time for this drivel," Donna said frustrated, "I've got to get home."

She started digging cash out of her purse to pay her portion of the bill.

Fanny loaded up her last barrage.

"Seriously, Donna, can I just ask you one question?"

"What?"

"Can I have him when you're finished with him?"

"In your dreams," Donna retorted in the face of the outright laughter conjured up by Fanny's last question.

Donna left the restaurant abandoning the clique to the skillful ministrations of Fanny who would continue conducting the business of gossip surrounding Donna and anyone else who merited the attention of the group.

...

Donna drove home. She did not much care whether Fanny and her friends would continue gossiping about her in her absence. But she *was* concerned over what Fanny had said about Tom's observing her kissing another man.

"Surely," she told herself, "he wouldn't have taken that the wrong way."

She had not seen Tom since last night. She realized she should have checked with him before leaving in the morning. She would have been able to read anything in his behavior that indicated he was upset. But Tom had not come out of his room in the morning, and she had not wanted to bother him before leaving to meet her friends. She had asked her mother to look after him when he got up in the morning. Her mother had agreed but said that she was leaving a little later in the morning to visit friends. Donna's father was also going out.

En route home, a call to her mother's cell phone verified that her mother was visiting friends and had left home before seeing Tom. Tom had been alone all day.

Donna was beginning to have a bad feeling about this, and she put her foot down a little harder on the accelerator. She should not have left him alone at this time. Suddenly Donna wondered what she had been doing. She was at a delicate point in her relationship with Tom, a man who was in love with her and for whom she had developed sincere feelings. But here she was putting her relationship on hold and falling back into her rich-girl lifestyle enmeshing herself in her old routine of parties, gossip mongering, and one-upmanship with her friends. She should not have left Tom alone at the party, and she should have talked to him this morning before leaving home. She turned into the driveway of the Kittridge estate, wheels squealing, and sped up the long driveway faster than she had ever done before. She jumped out of the car almost before it came to a stop and rushed into the house.

…

He was gone. She went through the house and the grounds calling his name, but he was gone. She was frantic. He had told her he planned to leave, but he had promised to tell her all about himself. She had not thought he would leave before then. Perhaps he wanted to avoid the stress of confessing everything to her about his past and had taken the easy way out. Still, she could not believe it. She had done nothing to drive him away, and she felt betrayed. Even if she had done something that upset him, he would not have left in this manner. Again, she looked through the house calling out for him in vain. She exited the house. In the front driveway she stopped to think. She was near to tears. She wracked her brain on where he might have gone and what course of action she should follow. Maybe call the police? No, that wouldn't work. Without knowing quite what to do next she got in her car and drove down the driveway toward the road. He certainly would not be walking along the road. If anything, he would be headed along an off-road path in search of a forest or wilderness in which to disappear. Maybe he was heading for the distant mountains. But which way to those mountains? He could have gone in any direction. How could she possibly follow him? But she could think of nothing else to do. She reached the end of the driveway planning to turn right on the road that would eventually take her into the higher elevations toward the mountains. It was the only thing she could think of to do. She could only hope that through some impossible circumstance she might cross his path before he got too far away. She paused at the end of the driveway realizing the almost utter futility of heading toward the mountains. In desperation, she played a hunch, and she turned left heading back into town.

She drove down the main street of town hoping against hope that she might spot Tom walking casually along. She had to pull over to the side of the road to spend an agonizing minute punching an address into her GPS unit. Ten minutes later her GPS system delivered her to the gates of the country club. She had been there only a couple of times and was grateful she had use of her GPS to find the place without the trial and error of following her memory. She drove into a crowded parking lot. The country club was busy. Golfers were taking advantage of the waning days of autumn to schedule their last games for the year. Her father and brother often brought clients to the country club for business entertainment purposes. It was unthinkable that her father would bring Tom here without letting her know about it in advance. But she thought maybe her older brother Lawrence could have invited him here to have a "talk" with him in private. That was the hunch she was playing. Tom had won over her mother, but Lawrence had not been disabused of his original opinion about Tom. She should have had her mother talk to Lawrence, but never thought to ask her.

Donna walked around the country club impatiently. She found neither Tom nor Lawrence. She walked over to the restaurant next door. Nothing. She began to lament the waste of time following this hunch. She went back to the country club lobby. The country club was a big place, and she was not familiar with it. More exploration yielded nothing. Could they possibly be in the men's locker room? Finally, she was struck with the futility of her mission. She called Lawrence's cell phone. She got his voice mail. The sinking, empty feeling returned to depress her. She walked benumbed out to the parking lot en route to her car. She had no idea of what to do now.

She almost missed it. She had walked past the car in the parking row before realizing it belonged to Lawrence. He must be here! She rushed back into the building and redoubled her efforts to find him. Even if Lawrence did not have Tom in tow, she would demand his help in finding him.

...

Donna walked into the poolside lounge and immediately spotted two men sitting at a corner table. One man was Lawrence. The other was Tom. Two half-full glasses of beer were on the table in front of them. Her relief was boundless. The tenseness of worry drained out of her leaving her weak-kneed, and she almost had to sit down to recover her composure. But now anger replaced worry and made her all the more intense as she approached the table. She was livid with Lawrence for waylaying Tom and bringing him to this "hideout" without telling her. She was almost as angry at Tom for allowing himself to be dragged off in this manner and for listening to anything Lawrence possibly had to say.

The two men saw her simultaneously, and the furtive looks of each were an acknowledgment of the volcanic anger they saw radiating from her face. Caught off guard, neither man said anything.

"Come with me, Tom," she ordered in a calm voice that belied the barely contained fury churning within her. She turned on her heel and stormed toward the exit.

"I'd better go with her," Tom said softly and arose to follow, both men knowing that any other action or words on their part would have unleashed the full force of Donna's anger upon them causing a tremendous public scene—something that all males avoid religiously when possible.

Donna was halfway across the parking lot before Tom caught up with her.

"So, what was he going to do?" she asked, "drop you off at the bus station?"

"Airport."

"Airport?"

They reached her car. She stood by the driver's side door and looked over the roof of the car to Tom who hesitated by the passenger side door.

"Get in the car, Tom!"

"Listen, Donna, what do you care if..."

"Get in the car!"

They both entered the car, slamming their respective doors. Donna did not make any move to start the car, but rather looked straight ahead through the windshield composing herself enough to begin her accusations in a calmer voice. Tom sat, arms crossed, and likewise staring directly ahead through the windshield.

After a few seconds, Donna sighed and began.

"Listen, Tom, if you want to leave, that's fine. But could you at least have the courtesy of letting me know?"

"I want to leave," Tom responded keeping his gaze in front of him without looking at her.

She looked at him. Something was wrong. He looked more miserable than ever. He was evidently dealing with his own brand of anger. She suspected Lawrence had said some unflattering things about her.

"Tom, what did he say to you?"

"Nothing."

"What did he say to you?" Donna repeated, her anger spiking again.

He hesitated.

"Tom?"

"He was just telling me some things about you I didn't know before."

"Like what?"

Tom hesitated again.

"Tom, what did he say about me?"

"He said you'd had a fight with your fiancé and were using me to get back at him."

"What!?"

"He said you'd had a fight with your fiancé and were using me to get back at him."

Donna listened in stunned disbelief to what Tom was saying. She was absolutely unable to believe that her brother would sabotage her relationship with Tom in that manner. She could only look at Tom in shock, and he must have thought by her hesitation to respond that there was some truth in the accusation.

She continued looking at Tom. He would not look at her. He sat with arms folded looking out the front windshield.

"And you believed that?" she said, still in shock.

For the first time Tom's own anger burst forth. *"Is it true!?"* he snapped at her in anger, looking at her accusingly.

"No, of course not!" she snapped back, "What kind of person do you think I am?"

Tom paused, absorbing the force of her denial.

"And you don't have a fiancé?" he said, still angry.

She had to be careful. She was dealing with a fragile male ego. She knew she could truthfully deny the existence of a fiancé, but her involvement with Tom was so close in time to her breakup with Arthur, that Tom would certainly think she had come to him on the rebound as an unhappy second choice, especially when he learned about her prior engagement to Arthur, as was bound to happen at some point.

"I *had* a fiancé," she began, carefully studying his face, "but that all changed when I met you…"

She paused noting a barely perceptible change in his demeanor as her explanation began to sink in. He turned his head to glance at her.

"…especially after the way you kissed me," she added.

"What?"

"…and tore off my clothes…"

"What!?" he exclaimed.

"I said I *had* a fiancé, but that that all changed when I met you. Especially after the way you kissed me and…."

"Now, wait a minute, Donna!" he said instantly on the defensive, his anger all but evaporated. "You've got to know why I did that."

"Did what?" she asked provocatively.

"What I...did...what you said..." he stammered.

"You mean about kissing me and tearing off my clothes?"

He winced every time she evoked the image of that episode seeing himself as an out-of-control thug in her eyes.

"...uh, ...yes..." he stammered averting his eyes guiltily.

"So, why *did* you kiss me?"

"Well...because we were in a dangerous situation... and you were being...well, difficult. And I had to do something to... uh, to get you to...uh cooperate...so that we could get out of the forest, and I don't think you quite understood how serious the situation was. So, I had to do something to... uh take control..."

He was still stammering. She cut him off.

"You mean I was being a bitch, and you slapped me to get my attention."

"Well, I don't think I'd put it exactly like that..."

"That's the way I'd put it."

"Well, I guess so, but it wasn't anything personal."

"What do you mean 'it wasn't personal'? It was personal to me."

"Oh, well, I'm sorry, I didn't mean..."

"Oh, I deserved it. Don't feel sorry about it."

"Well, then you understand..."

"Oh, I understand all right. I understand why you slapped me."

Tom nodded slightly hoping the matter had now been laid to rest.

"Tom?"

"What?"

"Why did you kiss me?"

"What?"

"Why did you kiss me?"

"Kiss you?"

"Yes."

Tom was taken aback by her continuing line of questioning about that episode. He had assumed the explanations just given covered the entire reach of that angry moment. But now she seemed to want to further dissect the episode into little pieces to dwell upon.

"Well, that was all…it was all part and parcel of my need to…uh get control…" he explained. "I'm sorry, but I was angry and couldn't…"

"You kissed me because you were angry with me?"

"Yes, I…"

Tom looked at her. She was transformed. The look she bestowed upon him was no longer the look of the professional interrogator. She was a vulnerable teenager awash in a sea of emotion searching his face for something. He realized he was on the verge of saying something incredibly stupid.

"…Well, yes, I *was* mad at you," he amended softly, "but I—I guess I kissed you because you were attractive…"

He turned his gaze away from her as if embarrassed over a sordid confession.

"You thought I was attractive?"

"Yes. I'm sorry. I couldn't control myself."

"Oh, Tom!"

She reached over to embrace and kiss him, surprising him with the force of her action and the degree of her passion. The car console presented an obstacle to the successful maneuver of her embrace, but she did a good job. She was all over him.

"Oh, Tommy," she repeated emotionally, "You think I'm attractive?"

"Yes," he answered, "you're beautiful."

"Oh, Tommy, Tommy, Tommy!" She gushed, totally absorbed in the passion of the moment and redoubling her expression of affection. Tom was taken aback by her reaction to his statement of the obvious. She knew she was beautiful. And she knew he knew she was beautiful. He was surprised by her effusiveness.

She finally released him and repositioned herself back in the driver's seat.

"Tom?" she asked composing herself.

"What?" he answered suspecting more questions about that episode in the wilderness.

"I've got to drive. Can we postpone this conversation for now? I should concentrate on my driving."

"OK," he responded.

She started the car. She backed out of the parking space and headed down the drive to the country club exit. She turned and smiled at him. He was looking at the road in front of him but turned and acknowledged her smile with a wry smile of his own. He turned back to watch the road in front of him remaining in deep thought about what had just happened. She had given him a lot to think about. She could practically see the wheels turning in his head. She could almost read his thoughts.

She was happy about the way things had turned out. Her feminine acuity had served her well. She was happy to know that Tom had not tried to steal away from her. He had simply been led astray by her brother. Of course, she suspected Tom would not have put up much resistance if Lawrence had tried to put him on a plane to somewhere far away. Lawrence's stories about her had definitely upset Tom, but she had quickly put him right. She had defused Tom's anger deftly by appealing to his masculine ego, leading him to think that his masterful handling of her rescue had captured her heart and taken her away from another man. He was still trying to absorb all this as he resumed his position back within the ranks of the perpetually perplexed. She looked at him again. He was "deliciously" confused and malleable.

A sudden thought struck her. It came out of the blue. It was a thought that came into her mind with such impact that she had to pull over to the side of the road to confront it.

"What's wrong?" Tom asked turning to look at her.

She continued to look at him saying nothing, experiencing an epiphany. She had told him what was necessary to regain her control over him. She excelled at this sort of manipulation over men, and Tom was no exception. Her rules of manipulation admitted no necessity for truthfulness in getting what she wanted. But she realized that this time she had spoken the absolute truth. She had told him the truth without realizing it. It was his anger at her in the wilderness that had changed her whole perspective about him. It was at that point that she stopped thinking about Arthur and began thinking of him. She had been terrified at the time. Her feminist sensibilities did not want to admit it, but that action was the catalyst that sparked her receptiveness toward him. She spent a few moments absorbing that realization, feeling strange.

"Is anything wrong?" Tom asked her again.

"Nothing's wrong," she answered continuing to regard him in the new light that was shining upon him.

He was perplexed about her strange behavior. But many things about her perplexed him. She put the car in gear and resumed her journey.

"Where are we going?" he asked.

"Home."

"Oh, Donna, I'm not sure I can go back there right now," he said, "I feel a little uneasy..."

"I don't mean my parents' home. I thought you could come stay at my place for a while."

"Your place?"

"Yes. Do you mind? It's not too far from here."

"Oh. Well, I don't know…"

They continued their drive down the highway in the direction of Donna's apartment. She was happy and cheerful, but she realized she had almost lost him. Well, she would take no more chances. No more games or machinations. She would confess her love for him in no uncertain terms, and she envisioned their forthcoming pillow talk when she would confess how she had manipulated things to keep him close to her while at the same time keeping him at arm's length as a promise to her family. She would explain everything to him. She no longer cared about knowing his past. That would come in due course, but it was no longer a condition to her loving him. She realized she would be breaking a vow to her father, but as far as she was concerned, her brother's meddling had abrogated that agreement.

She looked at him again and presented him with a beaming, happy smile. He responded with a nervous smile of his own, realizing she was regarding him as the main course in some upcoming feast.

After about twenty minutes of driving, Donna turned off the road into the parking lot of a big hotel that backed up to a snow-covered mountain. She parked, and they exited the car. Tom looked around confused.

"Donna?"

"What?"

"Is this your place?"

"No, silly. It's the ski lodge. I thought we'd stay here tonight. It's getting late, and it would be another hour of driving to my place, and I don't want to get there in the dark. I think there's a big thunderstorm coming, too."

She took his arm and walked with him happily into the lobby. In addition to the reasons she had enumerated to Tom, she also wanted to stay at the lodge to remain beyond the reach of her family. Knowing Lawrence and her father as she did, they probably would have sent Jeff over to her apartment to check up on her. But for tonight, she wanted to remain incommunicado. To accomplish this in a total way, she turned off the power to her mobile phone.

The ski lodge was gearing up for the coming winter season, but at this point there were still plenty of rooms available. Donna checked in and was able to reserve a suite. She stopped off at the lobby gift shop to buy some toothbrushes and a few other toiletries for the next morning. Then she accompanied Tom toward the elevator.

"Shouldn't we have gotten separate rooms?" Tom asked a little apprehensively knowing she would take him for a prude over the question.

"No," she answered, "why?"

"I was just concerned about your reputation."

"What…?" she started, then realized he was being facetious. She looked at him with a beaming smile and tugged him toward the door of the room. He was actually being humorous.

They entered the room. Tom stood a little way inside the door, wondering what was coming next. It felt strange to be in a hotel room without luggage. Donna walked around checking out the room. There were two sliding-glass doors that led out to a balcony and provided a nice view of the mountain behind the resort. Later, in the winter, the mountain would be plied with ski trails. The living area of the suite contained a sofa, coffee table, and two easy chairs. There were the other usual amenities. A king-size bed was the most imposing feature of the room. Donna sat on the edge of the bed, finding that everything met with her satisfaction. She looked at Tom and patted the bed beside her, an invitation for him to sit next to her. He ignored the visual message she was sending to him and walked gingerly past her into the living area pretending to take his own measure of the room.

"Tom?" she called to him from the bed.

He looked over to her and saw the same visual message she had made before, more pronounced this time. He did not move and could think of no audible response.

She arose from the bed, keeping her eyes upon him. She removed the light jacket she was wearing, and the action could not have been more provocative than if she had disrobed completely. She moved toward him. There was seduction in her eye.

Tom immediately took a step back for every step she took toward him. It was not an activity with any promise of long duration. He backed up against the sofa and was effectively cornered.

"Donna, we've got to talk!"

"Mmmm...?" she replied, looking up at him dreamily and taking in the sound of his voice.

"Donna, please! We've got to talk!"

"Talk?" she replied.

"Yes, we need to talk."

"What about?"

"What we discussed earlier."

"What we discussed earlier?"

"Yes."

"What did we discuss earlier?"

"When we were in the car...and you said...I mean, you indicated some things that...that I think we need to talk about."

"What things?"

"Please, Donna, you know what things—you're driving me crazy!"

"Oh, I'm sorry, Tom."

"Will you please just listen?"

"OK, I'm listening."

"OK," he said and began the speech he had rehearsed mentally in the car, hoping that he was not in some wild way still misinterpreting her intentions.

"Listen, Donna. If you've developed some kind of feelings for me, then it's only because I represent some sort of a mystery to you, and I'm sure that..."

"Tom?" she interrupted.

"What?"

"Can we postpone this talk until later? I'm a little tired..."

"No, Donna, I think we need to get this settled now."

She said nothing but continued looking at him in the same dreamy way as before, and he wondered how much attention she was paying to what he was saying.

After a pause, he continued, "So, listen, Donna. If you've developed some kind of feelings for me, it's only because you're seeing something of a mystery in me that's attracting you, and once you learn about..."

"Tom?"

"Donna let me finish!"

"I'm, sorry, Tom," she said with the wide-eyed look of a chided child.

"Donna, please pay attention. This is important."

"OK, I'm listening."

For the third time he began.

"Donna, you've got to realize that I'm nothing more than a mystery to you, and it's only natural for you to be curious about me. But you've got to know that once the mystery is solved, there'll be nothing left. When you know who I am, you won't find anyone who has anything in common with you. I'm no one special, and you're a beautiful woman who deserves something better. There's nothing I can offer you. You move in different circles than I do, and there's no way I could possibly fit into your life the way you need …"

She listened to him because that's what he wanted. It was the speech he had been rehearsing since she kissed him in the car, when it had finally dawned on him that she loved him. She enjoyed his speaking to her with such avuncular authority. She listened to the tone of his words without paying much attention to the meanings. As near as she could tell he was trying to talk her out of loving him. He was being noble and magnanimous, and he was trying to bow gracefully out of her life–this from the man who had been so jealously angry when the possibility of another lover in her life had been posited. It was some sort of male logic she could not fathom and usually ignored. She wanted him to take her in his arms and kiss her. She wanted him to take her to the bed and make passionate love to her. But for now, he was being logical and pontifical, and she would have to let him run his course. He was talking to her like her father sometimes talked to her. She found it cozy. She put her arms around his waist and lay her head on his shoulder.

As she crowded him with her embrace, he was in danger of toppling backwards on the sofa. He put his hands gently on her shoulders for balance as he stepped to the side to avoid the collapsible position and re-attain the space between them compatible with conversation.

"Donna have you been listening to anything I've said?"

"Yes, I'm listening."

"And you understand what I'm telling you?"

"I understand."

"And what have I been saying?" he asked, testing her attentiveness.

"You said I'm drawn to the mystery and not the man."

"Well, yes..." he said surprised at how succinctly she had summarized his sermon, "I guess that's it in a nutshell. So, then, you understand..."

"Tom?"

"What?"

"Tell me the mystery."

Without realizing it, he had given her an opening big enough to drive a truck through. He did not want to tell her the painful story of his past. Not now. But she was invoking the promise he had made to her, and now, based on the dialog that had just transpired between them, it was natural and correct from her point of view to demand he reveal all.

He turned from her and walked over to the glass doors, looking out at the mountain.

"Tom?" She followed him. He would not answer.

"Tom?" she said again. "Tom, look at me."

He was compelled to turn and face her, but he could not meet her steady eyes. He was transformed from the comfortable, pontifical man she had been trying to seduce to the worried, furtive man she had first met in the wilderness.

"Please, Tom," she continued. "Tell me who you are and what you were doing in the forest. I've got to know, Tom." She was no longer the emotional, love struck girl of a few minutes ago. She had reverted to her assertive, womanly self. Her tone was laden with concern and caring almost maternal in nature.

"Not now," he answered. "It's late, and we're both tired..."

"Please, Tom."

"I'll tell you tomorrow," he countered.

"Tell me now."

In desperation, he looked beyond her to the far wall. She had seen the same look on his face the first day in the forest when she had made an impossible demand from him, and he had cast his eyes toward the far horizon, looking for a metaphorical avenue of escape.

"I need to sit down," he said.

He went to the sofa and sat down. She accompanied him and sat by his side. He leaned back into the sofa. In a nervous gesture, he rubbed his hands up and down his thighs then slid them toward his knees, the action causing him to sit up on the edge of the sofa. It resembled a tense cat-like crouch ready for sudden flight. His eyes reflected a trance-like stare as he continued looking at the wall. He grabbed the sofa arm for support.

He looked at her briefly then turned his gaze again to stare into space in front of him. He sighed. He began.

"I was married, Donna."

He paused. Donna experienced an intense feeling of jealousy.

"My wife is dead. I killed her."

He closed his eyes tightly. He marshaled his inner strength to continue. Donna felt a chill going up her spine. A knot of dread formed in her stomach in anticipation of what he would say next. She prayed that what he said next would not destroy everything.

36.

He stood at the end of the driveway trying to control his rage. She had taken the car. He was not able to stop her. He had tried to reach in through the window to take the key from the ignition as she backed out of the driveway. He was unsuccessful. She backed into the street, running over part of his foot, while the bumper or some part of the vehicle had clipped him on his leg, leaving a cut that was bleeding.

The tires of the car squealed as she sped away in anger. He hurled epithets after her at the top of his voice. It was not like him. In public he had always cultivated the air of a quiet, even-keeled person. It took a lot to upset him to this extent. Even during the seven years of hell that he had been married to that woman, he always maintained a calm, well-measured manner with others. In the privacy of his home, there had been fights and shouting matches in increasing frequency with his wife. And now he was enraged more than he had ever been before, and he hardly cared if any of the neighbors had witnessed the event that had transpired in his driveway. It was the absolute nadir of his marriage.

He had to get his anger under control. He walked back into the house. He had to get to work.

The first order of business was to tend to the cut on his leg. He managed to bandage it up enough to stop the bleeding. He changed his blood covered trousers and socks and ran out the door. Any other day of the year—in fact, any other day of his career, he could have simply called his supervisor to explain that he had had an accident and would be late or not come in at all. But not today. Today happened to be the most important day in his fifteen-year career at the agency. He was scheduled to make his long-anticipated presentation to the Committee. The Committee would have to approve the system of translation procedures that he had formulated as an adjunct to the agency's intelligence operations. If approved, it would increase the efficiency of the agency's intelligence branch to an appreciable degree. It would be a formula that would bear his own name in any future discussions on the effectiveness of agency translation operations. At stake was his own esteem within the agency as well as the esteem of his supervisor and the whole division. But he would have to sell it to the Committee. That was the real hurdle.

He was a dependable employee and punctual. His supervisor considered him his protégé (as much as one government bureaucrat can be the protégé of another government bureaucrat). He was never late for anything, and his supervisor was well aware of it. He was the model employee. Nevertheless, the overbearing importance of the forthcoming meeting had led his supervisor to emphasize a caution.

"Don't be late for that meeting."

Everyone knew that the biggest sin anyone in the agency could commit was to keep congressional members and staff waiting. For anything. It was often emphasized around the office that the only excuse for keeping the Committee waiting was to be dead.

Now as he ran down the street toward the bus stop, he knew he was in danger of committing that unforgiveable sin. Public transportation took twice as long as private vehicle to get to his office. Had he been able to drive his wife's car, he would have been at work about now with an hour to spare. Time enough for a leisurely cup of coffee and to meet with his staff and supervisor to go over any last-minute details. Now he would be lucky to get to work before the starting time of the meeting.

He could not afford the luxury of inwardly railing over his wife's unexpected treachery. Now, he had to dedicate his energies to getting to work on time. Last night, she had agreed he could take her car this morning in view of the fact that his own car was in the shop for repairs. This was something he had done occasionally in the past, and he did not think it would be a bone of contention between them. Now, it was apparent from her premeditated treachery that their mutual animus had reached a new high. She was intentionally tying to damage his career.

But he would have to deal with all that later.

His hastily formed plan was to take the bus to the metro station where he could catch a cab or take the metro downtown where it would be relatively easy to flag down a cab to take him to his office. The real problem would be the time it would take. He waited an agonizing fifteen minutes at the bus stop. In desperation he considered going up to the house of a neighbor to ask for a lift to work or at least to the metro station. He did not know any of his neighbors that well, but he was desperate. While considering this option, the bus arrived. It took another fifteen minutes to get to the metro station. One agonizingly prolonged stop after another. At the metro, there were no cabs cued up waiting for customers. He had to force himself to calm down enough to get the cash out of his billfold to buy a metro ticket.

The ride to Metro Center took twenty-five minutes. He dashed up the escalator to the street and was able to flag down a cab immediately. It began to look like he might make it to work just in time. Nevertheless, he agonized as he watched the blocks go by, praying the cab would not encounter a traffic jam. The cab ride should take about twenty minutes. He should arrive with five minutes to spare. He would still be cutting it close. Too close.

He had taken taxicabs to work before. He usually enjoyed the ride. The urban fleet of cab drivers represented many linguistic nationalities, and he would enjoy striking up a conversation with them, showing off his linguistic skills. The drivers would often be flattered when he was able to speak even a few words in their native languages. Now, the driver ID posted in the cab appeared to be an Ethiopian name. He had no desire to strike up a conversation now. The last thing he wanted was a leisurely conversation with a cab driver. He was trying to use mental telepathy to make the driver go faster. He could only think about getting to his office on time.

Nevertheless, he had a few quiet minutes during the cab ride. He needed to compose himself. He closed his eyes trying to calm down. He could not stop the memory of his wife's treachery from flooding back into his mind. He relived it all again.

He had arrived home last night a little later than usual after putting his car in the shop. Of late, the arguments with his wife had reached a new level of venomous exchange, and, finally, he had given up trying to talk to her at all. Every conversation degenerated into an argument. Every word was an insult. Unfortunately, not talking to her at all seemed to infuriate her more than when they argued. But he did not know what else to do. The anticipation of her presence dragged him down to despair. Her words poisoned him. Normally, upon arriving home, he would immediately go down to the half-finished basement to spend the evening. She hated the basement, refusing to go down there, so he used it as his inner sanctum. Yet he could not avoid communicating with her over the minutiae of daily living, and last evening he approached her about using her car.

"Oh, you're talking to me now?" she had responded sarcastically.

"I don't want to talk to you. I'm just letting you know I need to use your car tomorrow."

"Why can't you use your own car?"

"It broke down. I just put it in the shop."

She gave him the silent treatment trying to mirror the way she judged he had been treating her. She turned away from him.

"Let me know now if I can't take the car," he said. "If not, I'll make other arrangements to get to work. Tomorrow I have an important meeting and can't be late."

Silence.

"Do you hear me!" he continued with a growing edge in his voice.

"I hear you," she responded.

In the morning he arose earlier than usual. He was giving himself plenty of time. He dressed in a casual manner. He came out of the bedroom, took his briefcase, and headed for the kitchen. His wife usually made coffee in the morning, and he had enough time to consider grabbing a quick cup. The only time they were half-way civil to each other was when he bade her goodbye in the morning, when both of them looked forward to the happy absence of the other. He was feeling bad about the arguments, and he wanted to say a few words of encouragement to her. Maybe propose a rapprochement.

But she was not in the kitchen. He looked through the rest of the house, calling her to say goodbye. He got no response from her. Suddenly, he had a sinking feeling in his stomach. He rushed to and threw open the front door. He saw his wife casually backing her car out of the driveway. She had timed it so he would see her defiant action.

He had not been able to stop her. He could only hurl the most vicious threats and insults after her as she sped away.

He came out of his reverie as the cab pulled up to the entrance of the agency building. He leaped out of the cab and took an agonizing ten seconds to get through security. He eschewed the elevator and ran up the stairs to the fifth floor. Coming out of the stairwell he nearly ran headlong into his supervisor. His supervisor had a pale look on his face, and the righteous indignation radiating from his eyes was apparent.

There was no time for explanations. They both ushered themselves immediately into the conference room where the Committee members were just taking their seats. He was hot, sweaty and out of breath from his herculean commute. He began the presentation feeling woefully unprepared. He swallowed a few times and tried to catch his breath. The audience regarded the action as an understandable initial stage fright and indulged him patiently. Thankfully, the projector had been set up the night before and was ready for him to use. But he had to take time to dig his notes out of his brief case. Very unprofessional. He forced himself to focus and concentrate on the topic at hand. Eventually, he warmed up to his subject. By the end of his presentation he knew he had made a good speech and had held the interest of the audience. He fielded several questions during and after the presentation. As normal during the successful conclusions of these functions the Committee members and the agency staff intermingled for a bit of coffee, socializing and shop talk. He had done it! Crisis averted.

After the Committee had left, he heaved a huge sigh of relief. His supervisor came up to him.

"After you get settled, come see me in my office. In about ten minutes."

He knew his supervisor was going to have him on the carpet in about ten minutes for having arrived late. But that would be a walk in the park compared to the ordeal he had just been through. He took a cup of coffee and sought out his office. His cozy cubicle. More and more it seemed the only place on the earth where he felt secure and comfortable. He sat down in his office chair and closed his eyes for a solid two minutes, taking in the tranquility of his space. A couple of colleagues dropped by to congratulate him on his presentation. For a few minutes he looked through some papers in his in-box, initialed a few and sent them on. He checked his voice mails and emails.

By the time he entered his supervisor's office, he felt completely relaxed. He sat down in the chair across from his supervisor's desk.

"I hope you've got a damn good reason for being late this morning."

"I had a bit of an accident on my way out. I cut my leg."

By way of illustration his lifted his trouser leg to show the bandage. He was surprised to see that the bandage was blood soaked.

"Good, lord, Tom. Get down to the nurse's station and have that seen to."

The nurse re-bandaged his leg.

"I've put some antiseptic on the cut, and the bandage should stop the bleeding," she said. "It's not that deep, but it's a long gash, and I'd advise you to call your doctor right away. Don't put it off."

He walked serenely back to his office, thinking he would call his doctor and probably be able to get in to see him on his way home. Then he remembered he had no transportation. He would have to take a cab to the repair shop to pick up his car and from there stop in at the doctor's office.

He sat down at his desk, preparing to make a series of phone calls. He realized that in about six hours he would have to go home. The thought depressed him. He had no idea of what he would say and do when he saw his wife again. He knew that seeing her would reanimate his anger. One thing was sure. His marriage was over. He could take it no longer. Maybe the best thing to do was not to go home at all. He began thinking of the procedures that would be involved in getting a divorce. She would not make it easy and would demand much. It would be messy–the lawyers, the time, the expense, the recriminations, the frustrations, the impact on his career. He would probably have to sell the house. A colleague of his had gone through an awful divorce a couple of years ago. It was not a pretty thought. Still, he simply had no other choice.

He could never really figure out what had gone wrong in his marriage. Perhaps it was a case of two diametrically opposed personalities unwisely united in marriage. He had already been past thirty when he got married. He had always wanted to be married, and at first, he was exceedingly happy to achieve that status. But in retrospect he knew he had rushed too quickly into marriage. This struck home when the arguments started. His wife embarked on a long running litany of complaints accusing him of not meeting her needs.

Over the years, it got progressively worse. He often came home exhausted from a long day's work to find his wife ready for an evening out. It became painfully clear that she was a night-owl partygoer while he was a creature of duty who dedicated much of his energies to earning a living during the day. Things often got crazy at work leaving him drained and exhausted at the end of the day. For a while he tried to meet the "needs" of his wife, but his quiet, circumspect personality was often at odds with her life of the party mentality. His efforts to please her often met with disdain and resulted in more complaining. It finally got to a point where nothing he did could please her.

She ran up huge bills. She stole his credit cards and took large sums of money out of their joint bank account. She was a spendthrift, and he could no longer trust her with the economic well-being of their marriage. He had to cancel his old credit cards and hide his new ones. He opened up a separate bank account in which to deposit his paychecks. He even opened up a private post office box to prevent her from intercepting his mail.

She began staying out all night, and sometimes days at a time. He suspected her of playing around with other men and dreamed of the day she would approach him to tell him she had met someone else and was leaving him. Unfortunately, that was the one "fear" that never materialized. Apparently, other men would party with her, but none of them were foolish enough to get permanently involved with such a woman.

The worst thing she did was embarrass him in front of his friends and family. She disliked his friends and family, and they stopped coming to his home. For a while, the one thing he and his wife continued to do together was attend church–until one day at a function in the church recreation hall, she held court among the female parishioners who listened in shock as she brazenly detailed a litany of his faults that made her life miserable.

It became apparent to all observers that his wife was having psychological problems. He finally confessed this to his priest indicating that his feelings for her were no longer marital but paternal. His wife acted more and more like a petulant child and to the extent that he was somehow the cause of her behavior he felt a responsibility to her as a parent feels toward a child, the difference being that a child knows it is a child and will respond to discipline. His wife refused to acknowledge any behavioral shortcomings, and she categorically refused to seek any sort of counseling. Nevertheless, his priest emphasized the sanctity of marriage and his Christian duty to his wife, even through hard times. He tried to obey the advice. Every Sunday after mass he would return home encouraged to talk to his wife and make his marriage work. Unfortunately, the net result had been more years of misery. In the final analysis his marriage was an abject failure.

Now, reliving this morning's episode reinforced his resolve to seek a divorce. Her treachery had maddened him to the extent that for the first time in his life he would have considered doing physical harm to another person. The vision of her speeding off recklessly down the street was still vivid in his mind. *"I hope you drive under a damn truck!"* he remembered shouting after her. While in the throes of anger, he had wished that outcome on his wife. How convenient such an outcome would be, saving him from a hideous divorce. It was not the first time he wished his wife dead.

But he was spending too much time dwelling on such memories and wishful fantasies. He had to make some phone calls. By coincidence, the phone rang just as he was reaching for the receiver. He answered. It was the police. They informed him with official regrets that his wife had been involved in a traffic accident on the beltway.

37.

"Tom, it was an accident."

Donna sat beside Tom trying to console him after listening to his story. He was inconsolable. At this point, he was sitting forward on the sofa, head buried in his hands. She could not tell if he was crying, but he was in the grip of a strong emotion and could not continue his story. Donna was relieved beyond relief to know that his wife's death had been an accident. Despite his evident belief that he was responsible for her death, he had not killed her. It was an important distinction, and she wanted him to acknowledge it.

"Tom, you didn't kill your wife. You know it was an accident. It wasn't your fault."

"It *was* my fault. I killed her."

"No, you didn't! Don't say that!"

"It's the truth."

"Tom, look at me." She had been sitting close beside him, a comforting arm around his back. She began pulling him closer to her maneuvering for a position to look him in the eye.

He was compelled to face her, but he could not meet her gaze. He put his head forward on her shoulder. They embraced quietly. He held her tightly, and she could feel the tension in his body. She was content to hold him for a while wishing that the tension he communicated to her in his embrace was of a culminating sexual need rather than the static result of mental turmoil. Now she knew what was haunting him. It was guilt and shame. It was the mystery that he had wanted to keep from her and everyone else. It was the reason he pretended to have amnesia.

"Tom, listen to me," she finally said, pushing him gently back to look him in the eye. "The death of your wife was an accident. Even if you did somehow cause the accident, it was still an accident. It was nothing you intended..."

"No, Donna. You don't understand. It wasn't an accident. I willed it to happen. I intentionally wished it would happen. And it did."

"No, no, Tom. You were terribly upset. People can say and wish some terrible things in anger. But you can't make something happen by wishing for it. You didn't do anything wrong or unusual in your circumstances. It was all a coincidence, and you know it."

He slowly shook his head. They faced each other about a foot apart, but he had dropped his head as if in shame, and he would not look at her.

"Tom, please look at me..."

She reasoned with him to the full extent of her powers of persuasion. She had always been good at convincing him of things before. But now nothing she said or did could disabuse him of the notion that he had committed a terrible crime.

"I was so damned concerned about my own career and financial well-being," he said. "I knew she was ill and needed help. I should have been more understanding and compassionate...I should have helped her...she couldn't help the way she was...I should've..."

Listening to his attempt to rehabilitate the image of his wife at the expense of his own psyche was more than she could bear.

"Stop it, Tom! Stop it!"

He looked up at her surprised, realizing he had been in an uncontrollable rant. "I'm sorry, Donna. I got carried away. I'm wallowing here in my own self-pity. I shouldn't be bothering you with all this, I just…"

"No, Tom, I want to hear what you're saying…but you've got to calm down. You've got to change the way you're thinking about all this…"

She pulled him to her again. They held each other. She could feel him shivering against her as he continued to relive the memories that haunted him. His body moved against her, and she felt the force of his anguish. She closed her eyes. She was back in the forest. He was holding her immobile against the tree. His bearded face approached hers. Their lips touched. She shuttered in emotional excitement.

They continued to hold each other for a time. She took a degree of pleasure from his embrace, wishing he could also derive an equal degree of pleasure or solace from her. But he was still living the memories she had forced from him. She put her lips near to his ear and said soothing and tender things.

After a while, he released her and sat back into the sofa staring at the far wall in an exhausted trance. She sat close beside him watching his face intently. He continued to live in that past episode, and now, in hindsight, she was sorry she had insisted he tell her his painful secrets. The telling of it had forced him to dwell upon it, and it reinforced the guilt and shame in which he had been indulging during his entire narrative. More to the point, he could not put the memory behind him. It was a significant trauma, and she did not know how to help him through it.

She wanted to get his mind off the singular image that was overwhelming him. She had to change the focus of his story. She brought her face close to his again interposing herself between him and his view of the far wall.

"Tom," she said, "how did you come to be in the forest when you met me?"

He looked at her with a perplexed look, as if there was really nothing else of significance to tell. But her question had the desired effect. He fought through the inertia of the memory loop in which he was entrapped and forced himself to think about the subsequent history of his odyssey. Donna suspected that the rest of the story would be anticlimactic, serving as a mechanism to pull his thoughts out of the abyss in which they had been imprisoned. Little did she suspect that their subsequent dialog would reveal something even more alarming than anything he had told her up to now.

"I had to get away," he started. "After she died, there were a few days that I don't remember much about. They were sort of a blur. There was some kind of police investigation of sorts. I told them I was responsible for what happened, but after the investigation nothing happened. They said that witnesses saw her driving like a maniac just before her accident, so they determined no one was to blame but her. After that, several people came around to help me, but I couldn't take it. After that I knew I had to get away. I didn't know exactly what to do. I called my work and asked for a leave of absence. Technically, I'm still on that leave of absence. I got in my car and drove. Just drove. For days. I tried to make my mind a blank. I don't remember much about that drive–just that finally I ended up on a mountain road—I guess it was something like a logging road. I reached the end and couldn't go any farther. Then I went into the forest. That's where I was when I saw your plane come down. I guess you pretty much know the rest."

"Why did you go into the forest in the middle of nowhere?"

"I didn't know exactly where I was. I just wanted to get away as far as possible. I wanted to disappear."

"But what did you think you were going to do in the forest. Were you planning to live there like some hermit?"

"I don't think I ever thought it out that far. Besides, that's when I came across you, and I had to get you back to civilization."

"How long were you in the forest before you met me?"

"I don't know exactly. A few days, I guess."

"I thought you were in the forest for some criminal purpose," she said.

"I guess I can understand that. I must have presented a pretty scary appearance by then."

"But you saved my life, you know. I was lucky you came along."

"If you say so."

"I know so."

There was a pause in their dialog. She studied his face.

"Tom," she continued, "I'm sorry I was so mean to you those first few days, after all you had been through."

"You weren't mean to me. You were just upset."

"No, Tom. I *was* mean to you, and I had no right to be. I should have realized that you were trying to help me, but I was so caught up in my own problems."

"I understand."

"No, I should've been more sensitive to what you were going through, and I'm sorry, Tom."

"That's all right. You had your own problems and had every right to be upset."

"You know," she continued, "when you slapped me it's exactly what I deserved."

"No, Donna, I shouldn't have done that…"

"You were so angry at me."

"I'm sorry. It was only temporary."

"When you kissed me, I was terribly frightened."

"I never would have hurt you…"

"I thought you were going to rape me."

She knew she was embarrassing him revisiting that episode. She did not want to embarrass him on top of any other emotional turmoil he was suffering, but she realized she had hit upon a good strategy—to talk about their experience in common to get his mind off that past trauma.

"I'm sorry, Donna. I never would have hurt you. In all honesty I was too tired to even think of anything like that. At that point I was running on pure adrenaline and could hardly even stand up."

"I know. And on top of that you even carried me in the end when I got feverish. How long did you carry me?"

"A couple of days, I guess."

"And you almost killed yourself for me, didn't you?"

"I had to get you some help. That was the most important thing."

There was a pause. She looked at him intently. There were tears in her eyes.

"Tom?" She began again.

"What?"

"Why didn't you want to be rescued at the end?"

"What?"

"You didn't want to get in the ambulance, did you?" Tears were now running down her checks.

"You wanted to disappear back into the forest, didn't you?"

He looked at her saying nothing.

"You wanted to die there, didn't you?"

He cast around for something to say. She had given herself over to her tears.

"Why, Tom? Why?"

"Donna, please don't cry."

"Then tell me why you wanted to die in the forest."

"I hadn't really thought things out that far…"

"So, what did you think was going to happen if you went back into the forest?"

"I didn't really think…"

"I think you knew exactly what you were doing," she interrupted.

"No, Donna, I…"

"You were feeling so much guilt and shame about your wife that you wanted to kill yourself, didn't you?"

"No, Donna…"

"And you kept trying to get away to get back into the forest."

"No, Donna, I…"

"Then why, Tom? Why?"

Her questions were now coming to him with a degree of belligerence and badgering, and he could not calm her.

"Please, Donna, don't get upset…"

"Then tell me why!" she almost shouted, very evidently upset.

"Because, I guess I went a little crazy!" He outshouted her with enough force to quiet her.

She demurred at the anger in his voice. He continued in a forceful but quieter voice.

"Donna, I'm a moral person. I had to identify my wife at the hospital. I had to look at her dead body…"

He paused, the indescribable expression on his face showing that he was again reliving the horrible memory.

"I knew I was guilty of a terrible sin," he continued. "I had to atone for it. And it was then and there that I swore an oath to her and before God that my own life was forfeit. The only thing I held apart and to myself was the manner of my death. Of course, if I'd had any real character, I would've gotten a gun and blown my brains out...."

"No, Tom! Please. Please, Tom, let's not talk any more tonight. We're both tired. Let's go lie down and get some sleep. Things will look better in the morning."

She was thoroughly alarmed now. She had to do something to get his mind off that horrible experience. She had tried to talk to him about their shared experience and that had seemed to soothe him to a degree. But her reckless questioning about his motives in the forest had now caused him to revisit his trauma and fall back into that whirlpool of torment.

She coaxed him to arise from the sofa and walked him to the bed where he lay down on top of the bedspread and turned on his side to face the edge of the bed, leaving no space where she could sit beside him.

"Don't you want to undress and get under the covers?"

"No, I'm fine like this."

"Here, let me at least take off your shoes."

She sat on the bedside at his feet and unlaced his shoes, dropping them on the floor at the end of the bed.

"Tom, it may get a little chilly tonight. Are you sure you don't want to get under the covers?"

"No, I'm OK."

She went to the closet and found an extra blanket. She took her shoes off, turned off the room lights and climbed onto the bed from the other side snuggling up behind him and draping the blanket over them both.

"We can share the blanket for warmth," she said, hoping to evoke the memory of that moment in the forest when he had shared the blanket with her.

"Thanks," he responded, giving no indication that he associated her comment with the memory she wished to evoke. He continued lying quietly on his side at the edge of the bed staring into space.

She knew he was exhausted and would be asleep soon. She wanted to do something to get his mind off his dead wife and back on her as he dozed off.

"Tom," she asked. "Are you comfortable enough?"

"Yes, I'm fine."

"Can I ask you one more question?"

"What?" he answered. She could feel the sigh he heaved as he expected another round of dialog from her.

"I've known you all this time and there's still something I don't know about you."

"What it is?" he asked

"What's your name?"

He turned onto his back and looked up at her in surprised hesitation at the simplicity of her question.

"It's Amboy," he said and rolled back onto his side.

"I got that wrong too, didn't I," she responded contritely.

"Partially."

She snuggled up closer behind him, put her arm around his torso and squeezed. She rested her head over the back of his shoulder and moved her lips close to his ear.

"I'm sorry," she whispered.

"It's all right."

A few minutes later he was sleeping. She was also sleepy, but she stayed awake beside him for a while watching over him and analyzing the issues and revelations of the day. Things had not gone the way she had planned. That was an understatement. Definitively gone were any possibilities of seduction and passion on this night. His traumatic confession had changed him. Reliving the trauma of his wife's death had reinforced a suicidal oath he had sworn, and Donna had no idea of how to deal with it. She was worried now. He had told her a few days ago that he would tell her everything about himself, but that after that he would have to leave. She had not paid much attention to that declaration. Up until tonight she had been supremely confident in her ability to bind him to her because she knew he loved her. Their shared experiences had reinforced his love for her, even though there had been times when she had caused him to be exasperated, angry and even jealous. But those were the emotions that lovers share, and she had manipulated things with consummate skill to keep him close to her and to bring out his love for her.

But now things were different. He was overwhelmed with guilt and shame over the death of his wife. How could she compete with a dead woman? By rights, things should have been simple and straightforward. The convenient demise of a harridan wife should have left him free to come into her arms in search of long delayed love. But in death that woman had a grip on him so strong that he was being dragged down into the grave with her, and Donna did not know how to deal with it. She shuttered at the supernatural image conjured up by the thought of Tom being dragged down into the ground in the grasp of a deathly hand. She did not know what tomorrow would bring. She would do what she could. But would she awake beside the circumspect lover she had gotten to know over the last few weeks, or would she face a stoically morbid stranger who would walk out of her life?

With these thoughts and worries circulating in her mind, she yielded to her own exhaustion and fell asleep beside Tom.

In the small hours of the morning, Tom's tossing and turning disturbed her slumber. She awoke fully and was a little alarmed to find Tom sitting up on the edge of the bed, his face in his hands.

"Tom," she said, sitting up in bed behind him, "are you all right?"

"She gives me no peace," he responded in a low, somber voice more to himself than to Donna.

"Tom, it's all right, I'm here. Come on. Lie back down and let's go to sleep."

She tugged gently on his arm, and he lay back on the bed. He stared vacantly toward the ceiling, and she was not sure he had even been awake.

"It's all right Tom, I'm here," she said propping herself up on her elbow beside him to watch over him.

He turned his gaze to her and focused.

"Donna?" he said in a tone that seemed to indicate surprise at her presence.

"Yes, Tom, I'm here."

"Donna..." He embraced her desperately and pulled her to him.

"Yes, Tom, yes. I'm here..."

He buried his head in her shoulder and wept silently. She soothed him as they embraced. He whispered something inaudible.

"It's OK, Tom...It's OK."

He repeated what he had said. It was almost inaudible, but this time she could make it out.

"Help me, Donna," he whispered, "help me…"

Sleep captured them again as she lay beside him, an arm across his chest. She felt better about what tomorrow would bring. He had asked her for help. Maybe it was subconscious, but it was a plea for help, nevertheless. She would do what she could.

38.

∽

"Larry, have you got a pen?"

"Donna, where the hell have you been? Mom's worried sick..."

"Never mind that now. Take down this information."

"What infor...?"

"His name is 'Amboy' not 'Ambrose.' That's A-M-B-O-Y. He lives in the Washington, D.C. area. He works for the government as a linguist..."

"Wait a minute, wait a minute. I don't have a pen yet..."

Lawrence put down the receiver and returned a few seconds later. Donna gave him the particulars about Tom's work and residence as she had learned from Tom.

"No, I don't know his home address, but you can find that out through his work."

She filled him in perfunctorily on Tom's leave of absence due to the death of his wife, and on other particulars she deemed important for her brother to verify.

"I'll call back tomorrow to see what you've found out... no don't try to call me before then...I'll have my phone off... No, you call Mom for me...everything's all right...goodbye, Larry..."

Donna deliberately cut her brother off and powered down her phone. The abruptness was intended as a rebuff for his interference yesterday. Anyway, he had enough information to get his teeth into his investigation of Tom, and it would keep him out of her hair for the time being. He was probably already making calls, and she would have wagered that he would have everything about Tom checked out before noon.

She spent a few seconds admiring the imposing mountain that was the central feature of the ski resort. She had slipped out onto the balcony of the room to call Lawrence without disturbing Tom who was still sleeping. It had rained last night, but the sun and wind had all but dissipated the clouds and dried up the water, and it would be another bright, sunny day in early autumn. Nevertheless, despite the sunshine, there was a notable chill in the air that heralded the inevitable arrival of the alpine winter.

Shivering slightly, she slipped back into the room where it was warm and still. She looked over to Tom who was asleep. She felt a little guilty about reporting Tom's story to Lawrence. Maybe she was violating a confidence, but Tom had not asked her to treat his confession confidentially. More to the point, she wanted her brother to verify Tom's story to put the matter to rest with her family. She herself had no doubts about the truth of Tom's story, but it could not hurt to have everything verified about who Tom was.

She watched Tom for a while. After last night's confession he was now sleeping the sleep of the exhausted. She felt guilty about stressing him out over the last couple of weeks. The doctors had prescribed a period of rest, and she had not lived up to her responsibility in that regard. But the success of their budding relationship was dependent on her knowing his past, and she had dedicated herself to drawing the story out of him.

It was something that she had to know. But at what cost? Had she succeeded in shoring up their relationship, or had she forced him to relive a past that would destroy him? She would have to see what the new day would bring. They would spend a few restful days together. Beyond that, however, she did not know what would happen. They loved each other, but would that be enough to keep him bound to her? He was still tied to a dead wife, and Donna was not sure that she could be the catalyst to induce him to break that bond. Yet in the still of the night, he had awakened from the nightmare with a plea for help. She would do what she could.

The light of the new day streamed into the room, and it lifted her spirits. She began feeling confident and optimistic. She sat in a bedside chair and continued watching him absorbed in several memories of their time together. From the looks of it, he could well be asleep for some time. She thought briefly about crawling back into bed beside him. They both had slept in their clothes on top of the bedspread. She felt frumpy and wanted to take a shower and change into clean clothes, but, of course, neither one of them had a change of clothes. She would have to go shopping later for them both. She watched Tom a few more minutes then got up quietly and went into the bathroom.

Twenty minutes later, Tom awoke, and as is often the case with people awakening in a strange place and bed, he was momentarily disoriented. A loud click from the bathroom door as it opened, and the noise of the bathroom vent fan had awakened him. Donna exited the bathroom wrapped in a towel from bosom to thigh. She was drying off her hair with another towel. She saw he was awake, and she approached the bed.

"So, you're awake," she said continuing to towel off her hair. "How do you feel?"

"OK, I guess," he responded. The vision of her approaching him wrapped in a towel added a bit of apprehension to the disorientation of awakening, and he immediately sat up against the headboard to be on a level to better confront her approach.

She looked at him pointedly. "You had a bad night last night. Do you want to sleep some more? I'll be quiet."

"No, I'm all right. I'd better get up."

She continued to look at him closely, plainly expecting him to acknowledge something about what had transpired between them last night.

There was an embarrassing silence for a few moments.

"Donna," he finally said, "did I tell you…uh everything last night?"

"Yes, you told me everything," she said sitting down on the bed to be on a level to face him and studying him intently.

He was again embarrassed by her almost nude nearness and her intense scrutiny of him, and he glanced away again.

"So, now you know all about me," he said, still not looking at her.

"Yes, now I know all about you," she answered, moving her head in an attempt to intercept his wayward gaze.

"So, then, you know there's nothing I can…"

"Tom," she interrupted

"What?"

"I love you."

"Wha…?" He was compelled to look directly into those captive brown eyes. He could not look away. He was overwhelmed and dumfounded. Despite all the signals and affection that she had lavished on him over the last few weeks, her simple declaration still left him surprised and speechless.

"I love you," she repeated, moving closer to him and studying his face intently.

"But, Donna, you can't possibly…"

He could not finish his sentence. They remained for a timeless interval looking at each other, their faces inches apart. He again saw the face of an emotional, vulnerable girl. The sparkle in her eyes was tears. She was a fragile thing of crystal, yet a force of passion he could not resist. She kissed him tenderly. He was overwhelmed by her closeness, her still wet hair engulfing him in an aura of desire. It was all he could do to keep from grabbing her and pulling her onto the bed beside him.

Her lips parted from his, and he was again captive to those wonderful brown eyes.

"You do like me, don't you?" she asked.

"Yes, of course…" he replied and paused. He could not look away from those passionate brown eyes. She was so real and so close. Try as he may, he could not resist her. Her eyes searched his face. He took a deep breath and let it out in a sigh.

"I'm madly in love with you," he confessed.

He did not think she could look any more lovely and radiant than she did before, but now, somehow, she did. He bared his soul to her.

"I fell in love with you the first instant I saw you sitting on that boulder with your head buried in your hands. Even before you looked up and I saw your face, I knew you were going to be beautiful. Even when I saw your plane coming down, I think I knew I was going to meet someone special. I think I've been in love with you for a long time. Before I ever met you…"

He spoke about his love for her. But it was a preface for what he had to tell her next. He hoped he could find the words and explanations he needed to tell her that living the love between them was not possible, that he was not the master of his own fate, and that the consummation of their love would end up hurting her badly.

She suddenly kissed him passionately. He could feel her body moving against him through the towel she was wearing. He was overwhelmed. He almost lost control.

"Wait, Donna, this isn't right."

"Oh, yes, yes, Tom! It's right! You do love me!" She exclaimed almost breathless, smothering him with kisses. Her towel became partially dislodged from around her body.

Again, with supreme self-control, he attempted to resist her passion.

"Please, Donna, wait. I've got to tell you this."

She finally focused her gaze back on his face.

"What's wrong, Tom?"

"Donna, please, I've got to make you understand..."

"What?" she asked.

"Donna, please understand. I swear to God that I never thought you were serious about me. I had no idea you thought about me like that. I didn't want you to know about me. I wanted to get away from you. I had no right..."

"Tom, how can you think that? I'm in love with you! Period! Why is it so difficult for you to believe that?"

"Because, Donna, I'm a nobody. There's nothing I can offer you. I can't be the man you want me to be. I'm an emotional basket case. I'm haunted by the ghost of my wife, and I'll never be able..."

"Don't talk to me about your wife!" She stood up suddenly and went back into the bathroom, leaving him looking at the path of her retreat in surprise.

He realized he had upset her just a scant few seconds after she had declared her love for him. He felt ten times worse than ever. He had no idea of what to do now. Again, he was struck by the incredible revelation that the most beautiful woman he had ever seen had just told him she loved him. She was an irresistible force of passion lashing against the immovable object of his past. If he accepted her love, he would have to live with the torture of violating a sacred oath. If he could somehow reject her love, he would end his days with an unhappy honor. It was a dilemma of philosophers.

He arose from the bed and went out onto the balcony looking at the alpine scenery, trying to make his mind a blank. A few minutes later, Donna appeared on the balcony beside him. She had dried her hair and gotten dressed. She snuggled up beside him, and they stood at the railing of the balcony contemplating the view for a few moments.

"I'm sorry I made you mad," he said.

"You didn't make me mad," she replied looking up at him with surprise, "what makes you think I'm mad?"

"Well, the way you reacted when I was talking about my wife..."

"Well sure, I'm mad at your wife, not at you. And you might as well know I'm very jealous of her..."

"Jealous? How can you be jealous? She's dead."

"She's not dead in your mind. And I want you to think about me. Not her."

"Not a second goes by that I'm not thinking of you," he said.

"And how often do you think of her? You seem to be thinking of her all the time."

"It was a bad time—a lot of bad memories–I can't come to terms with..."

"I want you to forget all that and think of me. I want you to love me."

"There's nothing I want more," he replied, "but..."

She snuggled closer to him.

"It's a little cold out here," she said, "why don't we go back into the room."

"But the sun feels good," he replied.

A cold wind whipped around them, and she shivered. She noticed he had walked out onto the balcony in his socks.

"What are you doing out here with no shoes?" she exclaimed. "You'll catch your death! Come on, let's get back inside."

They entered the room. He sat on the edge of the bed to retrieve and don his shoes. She watched him with maternal authority.

"You went out without a sweater yesterday too, didn't you?"

"It wasn't really cold then," he replied.

"I bet you didn't have anything to eat yesterday, either, did you?"

"Well, a glass of beer..."

"I thought so," she said. "Well, don't bother with your shoes now. Go take a shower. You'll feel better after that, and then we'll go downstairs and have some breakfast."

39.

By mid-afternoon, Lawrence Kittridge had investigated and verified the information Donna had given him about Tom, and he called and reported the same to his father and mother.

"She's gonna call me back this evening to see what I found out; otherwise she's not answering any calls or texts and has her phone turned off."

"I know," his father said, "we've been trying to call her too."

"I don't know why she got so upset about my talking to him," Lawrence continued. "I was just trying to help."

"Well, you probably shouldn't have done that," Edwin said. "But we probably should have told you we were OK with him and warned you off. Anyway, based on what you found out I don't see any reason to worry about Donna's interest in him. It's just a little strange that he would take a cross country trip a few days after the death of his wife."

"Well," Lawrence responded, "I spoke to his work supervisor, and I understand he was under a lot of duress and felt he had to get away for a while, hence his leave of absence from work. His supervisor seemed to be most concerned about when he would return to work. He evidently has a pretty important job as a government intelligence analyst."

"Well, I guess we can lay our concerns about this to rest, but I'd really like to talk to him a little more."

"We could send Jeff over to her place to see if she's home."

"Jeff's gone back up to my brother's ranch—he was invited to a surprise birthday they're throwing for Dan."

"Really? That's unusual, isn't it?"

"Well, I guess Jeff's been a fixture up there every summer, so they probably consider him to be part of the family."

"Did they invite you?"

"Lord no, I don't have time to go up there. Besides they'll all be here in a few weeks for the annual party."

"Well, OK. I'll wait for Donna to call and see if I can get her to give you a call."

"Wait a minute Larry. Why don't we do this? You come over here for the evening, and when she calls, I'll answer your phone. That way I'm pretty sure I could get to talk to her and maybe convince her to come back here."

"Well, I'm not sure I can. I've got some stuff to…"

"Oh, come on over," Edwin interrupted his son. "You might as well bring Cora and the kids and have dinner with us."

"OK. We'll be over in a couple of hours."

After disconnecting Edwin turned to his wife who had been standing beside him to hear any news about Donna.

"Well, Lawrence checked him out, and he seems to be a normal enough person," he told her. "So, I guess we don't have anything to worry about if Donna wants to marry him."

"You don't think they'll elope, do you?" Pilar asked apprehensively. Edwin could see that Pilar still fervently wanted to have a wedding ceremony for Donna. Anything else would have saddened her greatly.

"No, they can't elope. Not right now. You need identification to do almost anything nowadays, and he doesn't have any. It'll take time for him to get replacement IDs."

"I wish she'd come back home. I'd just like to talk to her... and him."

"You still don't have any objections about him, do you? Now that we know..."

"No, I don't have any objections. I just don't want them to rush into anything. They should have an engagement period and then have a wedding. I want to be able to talk to them and share in their happiness and help plan her wedding. I just want to be a part of their lives. I don't want to see them go off somewhere on their own and forget about us."

Edwin hugged his wife. "You old softy."

"You do understand that, don't you, Ed? You understand why this is important to me?"

"Of course, honey, I understand. But you've got to expect them to want to spend some time alone together after getting engaged. You remember we did the same thing when we got engaged. We had a long engagement and lived together before getting married."

"I remember," Pilar responded. "In fact, I recall you were quite happy to 'live in sin' all that time, despoiling my innocence without benefit of marriage. You were such a big rebel, fighting against all those traditions and conventions of society. Remember how you found our wedding to be such a big hassle?"

"Well, there were all those people...milling around...most of them I didn't know...and all that choreography...I felt like a gorilla in a tuxedo on circus pony...what with everyone watching and all..."

"But you went through with the ceremony for my sake, and it helped bring both our families together."

"Yeah, both very *big* families."

"I want the same for Donna."

"Honey, Donna's not that much different from you. When the time comes, I'm sure she'll go the whole nine yards with the wedding. I'm sure she'll expect your help and support."

"Do you think so? It seems she's always arguing with me and is at odds with everything I want to do for her."

"That's because you've been trying to rush her into getting married. Just give her a little space and be patient."

"Do you think she's serious about Tom?"

"I think so. She's gone through a lot to be with him. And she's been very possessive about him."

"And do you think he's in love with her?"

"I think so. At least, he didn't look as miserable as all the other boyfriends she's introduced us to. Maybe worried and confused, but not miserable."

"I'm still worried about his past and if that may cause some problem for them."

"Well, I have to admit that it's a little odd for someone to get engaged so soon after the death of his wife. I find his actions somewhat unusual. You'd think he would want a longer mourning period."

"Of course, but that wasn't his decision. Once he met Donna it was all her doing from then on."

"You make it sound like he had no will of his own."

"Well, of course he has a will of his own. But this is Donna we're talking about."

Not for the first time did Edwin Kittridge wonder just how well his male logic actually served him in analyzing the motivations of women.

40.

∽

After a four-hour drive, Jeff Kittridge turned off the secondary road onto the two-mile long dirt road leading up to his uncle's ranch. He had been a little apprehensive about taking the time to visit his uncle's ranch on such short notice given the fact that his graduate classes had just started, and he had planned to spend the weekend getting a start on his studies. But his Aunt Rosa had called him and was adamant. This was a special surprise birthday party for her husband, and she had extended him a special invitation to attend.

"It just wouldn't be a party without you," his aunt insisted, and she convinced him to come to the ranch Saturday morning.

He had spent his summers at the ranch, but there had never been any sort of birthday party. He was not even sure of the birth dates of any of his uncle's family. So why did Aunt Rosa suddenly want him to attend Uncle Dan's fifty-first birthday? It was not a specially numbered birthday. Maybe if it was the fiftieth, or fifty-fifth, or sixtieth, he would understand. But the fifty-first?

He pulled up to the ranch house at almost exactly 11:00 a.m. There were a few cars parked in front of the house, but if this was supposed to be a big party, he would have expected to see more cars and more evidence of the presence of a considerable portion of the clan. He parked and exited his car. A large black Labrador came rushing out of the house barking vociferously until the dog recognized Jeff. The dog continued to rush up to Jeff in a playful mood. It was "Petworth," one of the family pets.

"Hello, boy!" Jeff addressed the dog and played with him a bit. "How's Pets?"

Some years ago, his uncle had gone to the animal shelter to find a dog he deemed to be worthy as a family pet. Hence the name "Petworthy" was given to the new addition to the family. Everyone shortened the name to "Petworth," and eventually to "Pet."

Jeff continued playing with Petworth until the dog trotted back to the porch, having duly discharged his obligation as watch dog and official greeter. He lay down on the porch where the other two family dogs, Tricks and Shucks, were already resting, and all was right with the world. Jeff climbed the porch steps.

"Hey, Tricksy! Hey Shucksy! Didn't you guys want to come out and greet me?"

A chorus of tail wagging and ear perking greeted Jeff. But none of the dogs got up. Jeff knew that Tricks and Shucks were somewhat older than Petworth and neither dog considered the arrival of a guest as anything to waste energy about like a young pup. A stray rabbit, deer or coyote would have been a different matter. Any wild animal coming within the purview of the keen canine senses would cause the dogs to be off like a shot in pursuit.

Jeff entered the house. Everything was quieter and more tranquil than usual.

"Hello. Anybody here?"

Aunt Rosa came out of the kitchen. "Jeffy, dear, how nice to see you. Thanks for coming." She walked up to Jeff and gave him a hug and a kiss.

"Hi, Aunt Rosa. Where is everybody?"

"Dan's gone to town for some stuff. A couple of the kids are around, probably out riding."

"I thought you were having a surprise party for Uncle Dan at noon?"

"That's this evening, dear."

"This evening? I'm sure you said it was at noon."

"I'm sorry, dear. I must've got it wrong. Anyway, you can stay overnight. Why don't you go out and sit on the porch for a while. I'll bring you some ice tea and a sandwich."

Jeff truly loved his Aunt Rosa even though he knew her to be a bit scatterbrained. But she had never gotten anything this wrong before. Anyway, he was stuck with the situation. He went out on the porch and greeted the dogs again. He had had the presence of mind to bring a couple of his textbooks with him, and he went and retrieved one of them from the car, then he ensconced himself in one of the lounge chairs on the porch. He cracked open the book and started to read. He was interrupted by Aunt Rosa who brought a tray out to him. To keep the dogs from begging for food, she went back into the kitchen and out the back door where she rang the dinner bell to attract the dogs. The one thing that got a rise out of the dogs more than the promise of a wild quarry chase was food. When the dogs heard the bell, they slipped, slided, and scampered off the porch in a blur, and rocketed around the corner of the house en route to the back door where they were always fed.

Jeff laughed at the spectacle of the dogs disappearing around the corner. He took a bite of his sandwich, knowing full well that the dogs would wolf down their food and reappear by his side to see if they could inveigle some additional lunch from him. Jeff ate his sandwich and drank his tea. The mountain air always enhanced his appetite. He looked around enjoying the beautiful scenery of his uncle's ranch. The place was idyllic. The peace and quiet was a healthy tonic. No traffic. No noisy people. No drone of machinery.

He again took up his book and started reading. He read and reread the first paragraph of the first page and still could not absorb the meaning. It was no use. The tranquility was soporific. He dozed off.

He slept for a while. At some point he felt a cold, wet nose on the back of his hand. The dogs had returned to the porch hoping for some last morsel of food to be found in his vicinity.

"Too late, guys," he mumbled and went back to sleep.

Later he heard someone clomping up the steps of the porch. He opened his eyes to see his cousin Bobby.

"Hey, Jeffy, shouldn't you be out back chopping wood?" his cousin said facetiously. "D'you think meals around here are free?"

"Yeah, right," Jeff mumbled sarcastically, unable to think of a more pointed rejoinder in his drowsy state.

Bobby went into the house in search of his own lunch. A little later Jeff perceived a slight sound of a TV in the house, indicating that Bobby had decided to take his lunch in front of the TV.

Jeff, lay on the lounge chair somewhat longer drifting in and out of sleep. He was awakened next by the sound of horse hooves coming up to the porch. He opened his eyes to see his cousin Leslie dismounting from her horse.

"Hi, Jeffy," she said pertly, ascending the steps.

"Hi, Lez," he replied coming fully awake. "What're you up to?"

"Oh, I just thought I'd go for a ride."

"Uh-huh. Nice day for it."

He expected Leslie to go into the house, perhaps in search of her own lunch, but surprisingly she sat down on a chair facing him.

"Would you like to come along?" she asked. "I thought we'd go up to Coppy Rock early, so we could get back before dinner."

"I guess it'd give us something to do before dinner."

"Great. You can take the Big Galoot. He's ready to be saddled."

The Big Galoot was the name of the horse he usually rode on their outings. Jeff arose from his lounge chair still a little groggy from his nap and headed for the stable, expecting to see a couple of Leslie's brothers saddling their own horses to form a group for the outing.

No one else was in the stable, and Jeff wondered if part of the group had already headed out. If he had been a little more awake and aware, he would have recalled that Coppy Rock was where the creek widened out into a respectable-sized swimming hole, and that that was where all the boys went to go skinny dipping—minus the girl of course.

The thought finally hit him as he completed saddling his horse. He looked back toward the house where Leslie was still sitting on the steps petting the dogs and waiting for him to join her. Jeff had never seen Leslie at the swimming hole, and the thought of her going there with him now was incongruent. The thought of her riding alone with him for an hour up into the hills was even more incongruent, given the way she had always managed to avoid being alone with him.

"Something's not right here," Jeff told himself.

He mounted the horse and rode out of the stable toward Leslie with a number of questions he wanted to direct to her, but when she saw him she sprang expertly into the saddle with the skill born of the experience of long practice, and she raced out across the meadow toward the high hills. Jeff followed.

All horseback outings from the ranch usually started with a race for a couple of miles, but a more leisurely pace was the norm. This was especially true when ascending to higher elevations. Uncle Dan's law of horseback riding required that everyone use the buddy system, and that no one tear recklessly through the mountain trails on horseback. Jeff knew well of the incident of many years ago when his cousin Tracy suffered a fall while racing his mount down a trail. The horse was hurt and had to be put down. Tracy was in the doghouse for months, but it was not Uncle Dan's ire that devastated him. It was the realization that his irresponsibility had caused the death of a valuable and innocent animal. It served as a cautionary tale, and afterwards everyone took exceptional care when riding.

Leslie reached the foot of the hills and stopped to let Jeff catch up. Jeff's horse was big and strong and had tons of stamina, but in an initial race the horse could not keep up with its smaller, faster stable mates. He pulled up beside her.

Before he could ask any questions, she said, "I thought we'd take the forest trail, if that's OK with you."

"Fine," Jeff replied and watched her trot off ahead of him toward the trail.

The forest trail was generally clear and easy. But it was narrow requiring them to ride in single file. As such he could only watch her back as she led the way, and in second position, he had no chance to strike up a conversation with her. He was still perplexed by the unusual situation in which he found himself. He could not believe Leslie was leading him to Coppy Rock where they would be alone. He started having libidinous thoughts. Then another thought hit him. "Of course," he told himself. "She would never put herself in a situation to be up there alone with me, so it must be that the others are already up there waiting for us. It must be some sort of surprise they want to spring on me."

That was almost certainly the case. They had enlisted Leslie to bring him up there, and he suddenly realized his Aunt Rosa must also be in on the conspiracy by having called him and insisting he visit the ranch this weekend on the pretext of attending a birthday party for Uncle Dan. But what kind of surprise could they have in store for him? He had no idea of what it could possibly be. It was nowhere near his birthday. He had attained no crowning achievement lately; saved no orphans from burning buildings. Perhaps the only claim to fame that would carry any weight with his cousins was his long-standing presence among them every summer. He had always thought his constant vernal presence could have just as well been considered a nuisance in many quarters, and in a humorous aside to himself he thought maybe they were fed up with his recurring invasions of their tranquil home and were luring him up there to do away with the infernal nuisance. But, on the other hand, maybe they wanted to reward him for his "staying" power. He appreciated the unintended pun.

Whatever awaited him at Coppy Rock, he would have to wait and see what it was when they got there.

After twenty minutes the trail ended at the mountain meadow that would take them to Coppy Rock. He was now able to ride up beside her. He had the chance he had been waiting for, but he could not think of anything to say. They rode on in silence for a few minutes. Regardless of the mystery awaiting him at Coppy Rock, he wanted to take advantage of this singular moment to initiate some sort of an intimate conversation with Leslie to investigate the possibility of any romantic inclinations in which he could interest her.

But first a few lead-in questions.

"So, when is your father's surprise party?"

"What?"

"Your father's surprise party. When is it?"

"Oh, that. Uh, I think it'll be this evening during dinner."

Her hesitancy reinforced his suspicion that the surprise party was bogus.

"Will the rest of the family be around this evening? I didn't notice anyone else around today, except Bobby."

"Yeah, I think they all plan to be there."

He asked a few more questions. It gave him the chance to watch her. She was the Leslie he had always known and loved from afar. At first glance she was quite average. Average looks. Average weight and height. She had light brown hair, and half the time she wore glasses that made her look like a librarian, something her brothers often teased her about. But she had the healthy appearance of one who spends much time working and playing outdoors. The thing he liked best about her was her glowing personality. She had a sense of humor and sarcasm that matched his own. She was almost always happy and derived the utmost pleasure in bantering and joking around with her family. She was quickly moved to laughter. She celebrated the interests and accomplishments of her mother, father and brothers with genuine praise and good humor. In short, she was the nicest person he had ever known. Jeff was sometimes jealous that as an outsider, he could not always fit under the umbrella of her glowing munificence. He had always fantasized about doing something great or developing some great skill to impress her as a way to be included within the radius of her approbation and praise.

He continued watching her, trying to make small talk. She was a little less perky and animated than usual, but he attributed that to the nervousness she must be feeling about violating her unspoken rule of not being caught alone with him.

"I missed you when I was up here during the summer," he finally said.

"Yes, I came home after you had left. They said you'd left early."

"Yeah, it just wasn't any fun without the leader of the pack around." He threw out the statement as a reflection of his true feelings for her, but he disguised it in a tone that would allow a facetious interpretation if she so chose.

"Are you serious?" she chuckled shooting him a joyous, playful smile.

"Of course, I'm serious," he responded with enough exaggeration so that she might still interpret his declaration in a facetious manner.

She said nothing and turned her eyes back to the path in front of her, but the contentment he saw radiating from her face was beautiful. He was happy he had been the cause of her response.

He looked ahead. They would be at their destination in another ten minutes, and he wanted to further press his advantage with her.

"So, what's this I hear about your going off on a missionary with your church?"

"Oh, yes. I was hoping to go, but they decided they only wanted married couples to go."

"Oh, really?"

"Yes. My fiancé wanted us to get married so we could go, but…"

"*Fiance?*" The word exploded in Jeff's mind.

The word weighed a ton, and Jeff was crushed by it. His carefully constructed inroad into Leslie's heart was destroyed.

"Damn!" Jeff exclaimed to himself, "why do women take such pleasure in talking to other men about their fiancés and boyfriends."

In a fit of pique, he spurred his horse forward toward the swimming hole leaving Leslie behind him.

"Jeff?" she called after him.

He arrived at the creek bank expecting to see evidence of horses and her brothers. No one was there. He dismounted and walked along the bank to discern if anyone was in hiding.

Leslie rode up behind him.

"Is something wrong, Jeff?"

He looked up at her. "Where is everyone?" he asked her.

"Everyone?" she repeated looking around as a reflex action, then looking back at him. "There's no one else here, Jeff."

"But I thought…"

She was looking at him in alarm, and he knew he needed to regain his cool, or he would reveal himself to be the fool he was.

"I'm sorry, Lez," he began again, "I thought we were going to meet everyone up here."

"But I told you nobody else has arrived yet," she answered. "Except Bobby. The others'll probably be getting in later for the party."

"Oh, I see," Jeff responded. "That's right you did just say they'd be getting in later. I must've misunderstood."

"Do you want to go back?"

"No, no. As long as we're here we might as well stay a bit. But why did you bring me up here?"

"You said you wanted to come."

"Oh, yeah, I did."

"And you know Dad's rule about the buddy system."

"Yeah, I know."

"I asked Bobby if he wanted to come, but he never wants to do anything."

"Yeah, I know about Bobby."

"Besides, I just wanted to visit the place one last time before the weather got too cold."

"I see," Jeff said trying to conclude the discussion. It seemed to him Leslie was explaining more than was necessary, now.

She dismounted and began unsaddling her horse, an indication that she planned to stay for a while. Jeff unsaddled his own mount. They placed their saddles and blankets on the creek bank where they could be used as comfortable supports while they sat on the ground and looked out over the shimmering water of the swimming hole.

"Damn," Jeff thought again, "I can't even go for a swim with her here."

Although he had covered it well, he was still in a funk, not because he had gotten it all wrong about the surprise gathering that he had expected, but rather over the revelation she had sprung on him about her fiancé. His fervent hopes over all these years of getting close to her had been dashed in an instant with her pronouncement of that single word.

Now he would have to face the agony of indulging in small talk with her for the time being, knowing full well that the only cure for him would be to be put distance between him and her as soon as possible and to go back home and try to forget her. He still did not understand why she deigned to be alone with him now at this point, but he didn't care. He suspected that under the aura of a respectable engagement, she probably felt confident enough to face the rogue male and give him his final walking papers.

She sat beside him and took off her riding boots and socks, likely in preparation for a wade in the creek. She said a few things he did not hear. He put his head back on his saddle and pretended he was dozing off, so he would not have to speak to her. In fact, taking a nap in earnest might be the best way to pass the time.

"Jeff!"

"Huh? Oh, I'm sorry Lez. I was dozing off."

"Have you heard anything I've said?"

"Oh, uh, about what?"

She gave him an exasperated look. "I was saying I was…"

She did not complete her sentence. Instead she gave him an appraising look, hesitated, and asked a question instead.

"Jeff, will you answer a question for me honestly?"

"What, is it?"

"Have you been coming up here every summer to see me?"

The question was a bit of a surprise.

"Well, yes," he responded. "I've been coming up here every summer to see you and your fam…" he stopped in mid-sentence, noting the strange look she was giving him. She wanted no flippancy from him. She was demanding an honest answer from him, whereupon, he expected, she would then tell him that she was engaged and that he should not waste his time with any romantic expectations of her. He could see that that was what she was leading up to.

There was nothing to lose now. He looked at her with sadness and restated his answer.

"Yes, I've been coming up here to see you. I mean, your family is hard to ignore, but I've been coming to see you."

She continued looking at him. There was a soft smile on her lips and a sparkle in her eyes.

He waited for her to lower the boom on him, however softly or harshly she wanted to do it.

She suddenly stood up and said, "Come on, let's go for a swim."

To his utter astonishment, she began undressing. The most moral, modest and chaste woman in the world unbuttoned and shed her blouse in front of him. In a crazy instant, Jeff thought she must surely have worn a swimming suit or bikini under her clothes. But the bra around her bosom was not part of a bikini. She unhooked it, letting it fall to the ground. Jeff could only gawk at her bare breasts. She next removed her jeans and panties, turned and walked completely nude into the water. Jeff watched her in stunned open-mouthed silence. When the water was half-way up her thighs she turned to face Jeff.

"Come on in," she called to him. He got a glimpse of her breasts and the dark triangle at the juncture of her legs as she let herself fall backwards into the water and started swimming.

Jeff thought it was a good possibility that he was dreaming. He stood up and walked to the edge of the water.

"What are you *doing*, Leslie?"

"Come on in, Jeff," she called to him again as she reached the deep water at the center of the pool.

Jeff was still stunned and remained on the bank. He knew that something had happened here that he would not have imagined in his wildest dreams. Leslie was behaving in a way that was totally at odds with the innocent girl he had always known, and he wondered what was driving her to behave in this unexpected manner. Nevertheless, fate, or whatever, had dealt him the opportunity to get closer to her (literally), and he fully intended to take advantage of it.

"Jeffy," she called to him again, "come rescue me. I can't swim!"

He almost plunged fully clothed into the water but checked himself. He knew she could swim like a fish.

"Take off your clothes," she teased him. He walked back to his saddle blanket and undressed. He returned to the water's edge, still wearing his briefs—an acknowledgment to a certain male modesty in front of his cousin.

"Take off your underwear, silly."

He complied and dove into the water. He swam out to meet her.

...

Nothing is as conducive to human playfulness as splashing around in a pool of water. Leslie and Jeff were good swimmers, and they played in the water like otters. The clear and comparatively still water of the downstream part of the pool normally had the time to absorb the warmth of the penetrating rays of the sun, while the upstream part of the pool received intrusions of faster-moving cold currents. The effect was exhilarating as the two swimmers moved between warmer and colder areas of the water. All inhibitions were abandoned. With male single mindedness Jeff attempted to latch onto to Leslie's nude body and pull her to him. And with female aloofness Leslie would squeal and break away, and the chase around the pool would continue. Jeff's hands seemed to have the radar-like ability of grabbing onto Leslie's breasts, his fingers probing for her nipples. When he could not latch onto this area of her anatomy, he would just as well as grab her around the waist from front or behind, and somehow his hands would find themselves moving down toward her pubic area or buttocks as she struggled against him. Of course, he had to be careful of the odd knee or foot lodging into the sensitive part of his own anatomy, as she squirmed against him. If he pursued too close behind her, he would find himself the recipient of a significant barrage of water from the expert flipper action of her feet. On these occasions, he would slip under the surface like a submarine where he could observe the glories of her nude figure from the most erotic angles afforded by the buoyancy of the water. This was a particularly pleasing thing to do when he could not catch up to her, and finally after doing this a few times, Leslie caught on to what he was doing, and she responded in kind by diving down to him, embracing him and giving him an underwater kiss.

They surfaced in that embrace. They were spent and out of breath. They slowly made their way toward the creek bank and rested in the shallow water. They continued to hold on to each other giggling but saying nothing while catching their breath.

Jeff was ecstatic and squeezed his cousin as he held onto her. She looked up at him with a beaming, playful smile. Neither one wanted to give up the playfulness just yet. He considered ducking under the water again for another look at her nude body, but he realized he would see her in all her naked glory when they exited the pool. He squeezed her again. She shivered.

"You're cold," he said. "Let's get out of the water."

She held on to him. They moved toward the bank.

"Jeffy, I've got a cramp in my leg. You'll have to carry me." She put her arms around his neck and pulled herself up to a position where he could put one arm around her back and the other under her knees.

She did not have a cramp. He knew that. She just wanted a bit more erotic role playing, and the notion of carrying her nude in his arms gave him an erotic expectation.

The buoyancy of the water made it easy to lift her in his arms, but as he attempted to wade out of the pool, he experienced the full weight of her body without benefit of the buoyant lift of the water. As a result, he lost his balance and they both tumbled into waist-deep water. They surfaced laughing.

"Wait," Jeff said, "I can do this," and he managed to lift her in his arms once more and waded toward shore.

"You're so strong," she said, squirming and kicking her feet in a playful attempt to make him lose his balance again.

"Stop squirming," he said, "you'll fall on the rocks."

He trod diligently over the pebbles and stones of the shore until he reached the blankets that were spread out on the sandier part of the shoreline. He could have easily dropped the arm under her knees to release her into a standing position. But he wanted her prone on the blanket for his purposes, and he carefully sank to his knees lowering her backside to the blanket, but before he could complete the maneuver successfully, he fell forward over her perpendicularly, his arms trapped underneath her, and again they both giggled over his unintended clumsiness. He quickly tried to extricate his arms in order to position himself over her properly, but he had not quite succeeded when she was suddenly seized by a shuttering passion. Her arms were still around his neck, and she pulled his head to her seeking a passionate kiss. He met her lips and kissed her with the same passion.

41.

～

Donna drove into the security parking garage of her condo complex and parked in her designated parking space. She exited her car collecting a number of boxes and bags that represented the day's shopping. She gave a number of the boxes and bags to Tom to carry for her and walked toward the elevator, digging out the security access card from her purse to enter the building. She turned to see Tom still standing by the passenger side of her car, apparently having no intention or desire to follow her.

"Tom?" She called to him. "Come on."

"Donna, I need a little time," he responded, giving every appearance of being a lost orphan holding all his worldly possessions in the bags she had given him to carry.

"What's wrong, Tom?" she asked walking back toward him.

She knew exactly what was wrong. The upcoming evening in her apartment would be the cumulative experience of their day together and, indeed, of all their time together, and he was not ready for it.

"I'm not sure this is a good idea," he answered. "I think maybe we should go back to your parents' place for the time being."

She smiled at him. She shifted everything she was holding over to one arm and slipped her freed arm through his.

"We can go back if you want," she said, "but it's really too late to go over there tonight. We could go over in the morning if you want. Would that be all right with you?"

"Well, uh, I guess…"

"Why don't you come on up to my apartment, for now? We'll, relax and get some rest and start back tomorrow."

"Well, uh, I…"

"Oh, come on, Tom" she said gently tugging on his arm to overcome his hesitation.

"I'm not going to bite you," she added reassuringly.

"At least not right away," she concluded playfully.

He realized her last phrase was a jest, but he was still apprehensive about being alone with her.

"I'm just kidding, Tom." She laughed at the expression on his face.

She led him up to her apartment. As with all the property belonging to the Kittridge family, he was impressed with the size and elegance of her penthouse apartment.

"Just put those things on the bed," she said as she led him into her bedroom.

He complied and quickly left for the living room area of her apartment while she dealt with putting away the new purchases. Then she joined him in her living room. He was standing by the French doors that led out to her penthouse balcony. She noted it was as far away as he could get from her without being outside. She smiled and walked toward him.

"Come sit down and make yourself at home," she said again taking his arm and escorting him over to the big sectional sofa of her living room.

She sat down beside him and snuggled close to him. He looked straight ahead. He was nervous and noncommittal, but he showed no objection to her nearness. She continued to regard him confidently.

"Listen, Tom," she said, "just relax and take it easy. Let's get comfortable and talk for a while. Don't feel that you're under any pressure. OK?"

"OK," he answered.

"Let me get us something to drink. Would you like some wine?"

"OK."

She brought out wine and snacks. She snuggled up against him and they watched television for a while. They engaged in small talk. He began to relax.

"Excuse me a minute," she said at some point, "I need to make a phone call."

She arose, retrieved her cell phone from her purse and walked into the kitchen where she would be out of earshot of Tom. She dialed Lawrence's number.

"Daddy? I thought I dialed Lawrence's number. Oh, I see. Well, what did he find out? So, everything checks out, then? Good. No, we're at my place now, but we'll probably come back to the estate in a few days. No, don't worry about that. OK, I'll leave my phone on, but just tell Mom not to call me every five minutes."

She continued to talk to her father a while, and eventually her father convinced her to talk with her mother. She reassured her mother that she would not run off with Tom and get married.

"Mom, we haven't even talked about marriage yet."

She concluded her call and walked back over to Tom. She stood over him and watched him. She had never doubted the veracity of what Tom had told her about his past. But now, having it "officially" checked out gave her a satisfied feeling, and any questions she may have had about Tom's story were now permanently put to rest. Any objections her family had about him were gone. She had a whole new freedom. As she watched him, he looked at her with a questioning look on his face.

"I love you," she said.

He smiled up at her, but he still seemed to find her declaration surprising. She supposed she could tell him she loved him every day for the rest of her life, and he would find it surprising every time.

"Donna...,"

Before he could continue with his sentence, she lowered herself over him straddling his lap, embracing him and giving him a long kiss.

"I should send you out of the room to make phone calls more often," he said, trying to cut through the intensity of her overture with humor.

She laughed and kissed him again. And again.

They spent a long time on the sofa. They talked about innocuous things. He made no attempt to deflect her advances. He made no attempt to question her motives or explain why their love was impossible. He made no attempt to analyze his own feelings of inadequacy.

Finally, they indulged in a long and passionate kiss. She was left tingling with desire and near to losing all control of her body. She looked at him, and he saw in those beautiful brown eyes all the things she wanted to communicate to him with all the nuances and shades of meaning that could never be described with words. He now burned with a desire that could only be extinguished in one way. He stood up and pulled her up to him and kissed her passionately. Desire overwhelmed her and robbed her body of the energy to do anything but shiver with anticipation. Her legs were weak, and he supported her. He picked her up like a feather and walked with her into the bedroom, placing her on the bed. He was on top of her immediately.

"Tommy, Tommy, wait," she managed to breathe through the passion. *"We need to undress."*

They arose from the bed. He undressed and lay back down on the bed. She stripped down to her panties and bra.

Then she did something extremely strange. She did not come to him in the bed. He watched her as she slowly backed up to the wall of her room. She kept her eyes on him, and the expression on her face was indescribable. She remained with her back to the wall watching him with those infinite brown eyes that looked at him imploringly yet reflecting something of apprehension if not fear. He did not know what to make of her behavior. She had backed away from him. It reminded him of her fearful reaction when he had first come up to her in the wilderness. Had she suddenly changed her mind about making love to him? Had she finally realized she had been entranced with an unworthy man? Had he morphed into a werewolf or something?

"What's wrong?" He asked her truly concerned.

She said nothing and continued looking at him. He arose from the bed and approached her slowly.

"Donna?" He said carefully. "Is anything wrong?"

She remained mute before him. He now feared the reaction she might have as he came closer. He inched forward, now conscious of his nude state and trying to prepare himself for any sudden movement on her part. As he came within arm's reach of her, she held out her arms to him. He came into her embrace, sandwiching her between his body and the wall. She was trembling. She tightened her embrace around him and moved her lips up to his ear.

"Oh, Tommy, Tommy, Tommy!" she whispered in his ear.

"I love you, Donna!"

"Oh, yes, Tommy. Please, please, please Tommy...!"

"Donna, let's go to the bed."

"Wait, Tommy, please, please Tommy. Hold me!"

"What is it, Donna?"

She put her lips again to his ear. She was trembling with uncontrollable passion.

"Tommy," she said, making a supreme effort to control her senses before totally surrendering to passion. "Tommy, please...say to me what you said when you first kissed me..."

"What?" He said not understanding what she wanted.

"...when you were so angry at me," she continued. "In the forest. You remember what you said to me. Say it to me now."

Now he knew what she wanted. She wanted to relive that moment in the wilderness when he had unleashed his out-of-control anger upon her. She had been terrified at the time, but now in retrospect she evidently saw something in that angry moment that excited her sexually. She wanted him to reprise the role of angry, out-of-control thug and to subdue her by making violent love to her. He was taken aback.

But he was on fire. And she was adamant. She trembled in anticipation.

Keeping her subdued against the wall, he somewhat reluctantly took her hair and pulled her head back to the wall. He put his lips close to hers.

"Women like you destroy men like me..." He was not sure he had accurately remembered the words or sequence of that event.

He touched his lips to hers and a shutter went through her whole body as she waited in total submission and anticipation of what was to come.

He pulled her bra away from her breasts. He looked at her beautiful body, nude except for her panties that he would presently strip from her.

As he took in the glories of her body, he wondered what other men had seen her like this and had loved her. She had had a fiancé. He had seen her kiss another man at the party. There must have been other men around her because of her great beauty and wealth. The idea of any other man in her life caused him to be seized with intense jealously. He grabbed her roughly and led her over to the bed. He pushed her with a force that caused her to fall backwards onto the bed. He was on top of her immediately subduing her with his weight. She had wanted a parodied anger. He had just substituted it with a jealous rage. It was more intense than what she had expected. As he roughly pulled off her panties, she looked at him with a degree of apprehension. He again wound his hand around the back of her hair, subduing her roughly. He put his face above hers, inches apart and looked deeply into those brown eyes.

"You're mine, now!" He voiced in a menacing whisper. "You belong to me now! Do you understand? You're mine now and no one else's."

"Oh, yes, Tom! Yes, yes, yes...!"

He kissed her passionately and roughly. He made desperate love to her. She surrendered to him totally. For an endless time, he thrust into her from myriad positions in a campaign to dominate her sexually. She was completely submissive, offering no resistance to him, implicitly inviting him to do whatever he wanted to do to her. As he dominated her, he took in the whole perspective of her naked body, her complete female passivity, and her writhing reactions in response to his tending of her. She was no longer the manipulative aristocrat. No longer the adamant, controlling rich girl. No longer a woman of fashion and vogue. Now she was a naked, submissive creature in his grasp. She was a woman in the throes of lovemaking, with no other goal than to seek out the ultimate level of physical and emotional pleasure, and he was aroused all the more for it. He brought her to a spectacular and sustained climax. He held her tightly and captive in his arms as she shuddered, moaned, and thrashed beneath him. He was completely smitten with her and prayed he was good enough to possess her completely, to drive thoughts of other men out of her memory, and to provide pleasure greater than anything she had known before. It was a campaign he had no intention of ending until he achieved the final subjugation of her by releasing the pent-up energy of his own overwhelming desire upon her.

Neither of them spoke during their lovemaking. They were at the altar of love and words would have been sacrilegious. For an eternity, they made love. After driving her to a final, fulminating climax, he continued driving himself mercilessly in pursuit of his own climax. The effort it required of him began to worry her.

"Tom, take it easy."

He scarcely heard her.

"Tommy, stop. You're killing yourself."

He could not stop. His need was too great for any other course of action. With a final marshaling of energy he dove into her with all the constant force he could muster, and, finally, he ejaculated into her with an explosive shutter that overwhelmed her. A final moan of pleasure escaped up through her lungs as he held her in a breath-crushing embrace while the power of orgasm coursed through his body.

It was over. She reveled motionlessly in his embrace not daring to disturb the aftermath with any word or movement. All was quiet now except for his labored breathing. He still held her in an iron embrace. He slowly lessened his grip, and she felt the tension drain out of his body, and as he settled upon her almost as dead weight, she found the sensation to be almost orgasmic in itself. He finally rolled off her and flopped down on his back breathing heavily. He was exhausted completely.

She wanted to bask a while in afterglow of lovemaking, but she rolled toward him and propped herself beside him. His chest heaved with the effort of taking in air. She was concerned that he had overdone it. He was still in a weakened condition, and the possibility that he could suffer a relapse was a real fear. She should not have let him sustain his unrelenting effort for so long to satisfy her.

"Donna…" he gulped, trying to catch his breath.

"It's OK, Tom," she said. "Rest for a while. We can talk later."

She continued watching him to make sure he was OK. She put her arm over his chest but avoided getting too close to him in order to give him the space he needed for unrestricted breathing.

"Donna…"

"Shhh," she shushed. "Just relax now."

Slowly, his breathing became more regular, and he appeared to be none the worse for wear. He sank into a deep, docile sleep. She continued to watch him. She snuggled up to him, feeling the warmth of his body and the power of his breathing. She was happy, tired, satisfied, and sleepy. She began to drift into sleep. Tomorrow they would awake to the joys of being new lovers.

She laid her head on his chest and began to doze off. There were some things she needed to do to consolidate their love. She was still worried about his health. He was not totally healthy yet. She would also have to talk to him about his past and find a way to pry him apart from the unhappy memory of his dead wife in order to begin his life with her. That would not be easy.

"TOM!"

It was a scream that exploded in her head causing her to jerk her head up with a shriek and look around in fear. She sat up on the edge of the bed and looked around, her ears primed for any further noise. The room was quiet and tranquil and counter punctual to the clarity of the scream. She looked at Tom who was still in a deep sleep. He would not have heard an explosion. She arose from the bed and looked around her apartment. Everything was calm. She finally realized the scream was not a physical noise that reverberated through the peaceful quiet of the night. She must have been dreaming. But the voice had been so real. It was upsetting. She did not have dreams like that. She returned to the bedroom and looked down at Tom as he slept. She suddenly became very possessive as she climbed back into bed and snuggled up to him again. The dream voice still vexed her. She held on to Tom and looked around defiantly.

"He's mine now," she said for the benefit of any ghosts or spirits. "Stay away from him."

42.

∾

Jeff Kittridge awoke early the next morning having spent the night in one of the guest rooms of his uncle's ranch. He was tired and would normally have slept longer, but he wanted to return home as soon as possible. His experience yesterday with Leslie and subsequently with her family left him perplexed and suffering from a number of misgivings.

Leslie and he had spent the entire afternoon at Coppy Rock. She had been happy, affectionate and passionate. They made love. Jeff was ecstatic. The woman he had secretly loved so many years was suddenly receptive to him. Yet, he could not get her to talk to him. She appeared to be unable or too embarrassed to offer any explanations for her feelings. He had wanted to know why she had suddenly changed her mind about him after all these years. When he pressed the point, she had come close to tears. Nor would she talk about the fiancé she had mentioned earlier. Her refusal to explain things was vexing, and he wondered if she had some issue driving her behavior other than feelings for him.

They rode back to the ranch just as it was getting dark. They were both tired–for the obvious reasons. He had tried to caution Leslie about the inadvisability of their riding up openly to any assemblage of her family, since it would not take much insight for anyone to suspect the activity in which the new lovers had been involved as a result of their long absence and late arrival together. And knowing Leslie's brothers as he did, they would be the ones who would voice their suspicions and conclusions with the greatest degree of gusto and humor.

Over the years, Jeff had had ample opportunity to observe the dynamic between Leslie and her brothers. There was no doubt that the whole family was very close-knit and caring of each other. But her brothers were also fun-loving and mischievous. Much of their fun consisted of teasing each other, and it could be intense at times albeit good natured. As the only girl, Leslie had developed a hard shell against any teasing from her brothers, and as the epitome of the tomboy, she always gave as good as she got.

But now things had changed. Jeff suspected she would be experiencing new emotions. She would be more fragile and vulnerable, and he doubted she would be able to stand up to the usual rigors of her brothers' ribbing when it became apparent that she had been away with Jeff all day. This was nothing unusual for her brothers. Each of them had to endure the same kind of ribbing when they first brought a girlfriend or fiancée to visit the family. Leslie would not escape the same treatment.

He suggested they ride up separately to the ranch house or slip into the stable unobserved to unsaddle the horses and subsequently walk separately and nonchalantly up to the porch, or even sneak in the back door of the ranch house or do something else to deflect attention away from their simultaneous appearance. But Leslie held firm to her belief that it was nobody's business as to why they had been in the hills, and she insisted the two of them ride together directly up to the steps of the house as if nothing had happened.

Jeff continued to have misgivings over this course of action. As they neared the ranch house, it was evident that some sort of celebration was in progress. As they rode up to the steps of the porch, he could see three of his cousins engaged in loud, animated conversations, sustained to a degree by the liberal use of a few pre-dinner libations. Jeff had a bad feeling about this gathering, but Leslie continued her approach. When they saw Leslie and Jeff ride up, they immediately set up a chorus of whoops, wolf whistles, and other brash and humorous noises, leaving little doubt of what they suspected Leslie and him had been up to all afternoon.

At first, Jeff thought that Leslie just might stand her ground as they slipped out of their saddles and walked up the porch steps, but suddenly she wimped out over the teasing from her brothers and ran crying in total embarrassment into the house where she clumped up the stairs seeking the sanctuary of her room.

Jeff remained on the porch, watching Leslie disappear up the stairs as framed through the doorway of the house. He would have followed, but Aunt Rosa's imposing figure came into the frame of the doorway.

"Leslie?" she called looking up the stairs "what's wrong."

But Leslie had disappeared up the stairs. Aunt Rosa swung her gaze out the doorway to ascertain the source of Leslie's distress, and seeing Jeff on the other side of the screen she took on a knowing look, and she turned to follow Leslie up the stairs.

Jeff was left out on the porch. He had tried to gesture to Aunt Rosa that Leslie's reaction was not because of his presence but due to the teasing of her brothers. But she did not appear to assimilate that communication as she ascended the stairs. Jeff was left holding the proverbial bag. He was at the mercy of his cousins. And they were merciless.

"You dog, you! You oughta be horsewhipped," came one comment amid gales of laughter.

"Just what are your intentions toward our sister?" Came another comment and more laughter.

"Somebody bring me my shotgun. And call a preacher."

And on it went. Jeff was helpless.

At one point, Jeff finally interjected, "Come on you guys. You're embarrassing Leslie."

"No, we're not. We're embarrassing you."

The laughter and ribbing were endless.

His cousin Bobby appeared from around the corner of the house and came up the steps. Jeff hoped against hope that Bobby's appearance would offer some sort of buffer against the tirades.

"You're not gonna leave those horses unsaddled are you…?" Bobby started, then noting the overwhelming jocularity all around he said, "What's up?"

"Guess who's been up in the hills all day with Leslie," someone said.

Jeff's cousin Bobby was one of the drollest persons Jeff knew. Bobby did not join the laughter, but he looked steadily at Jeff. Jeff was a little worried that Bobby's reaction to the topic of entertainment might not be so jocular.

"It's about time you two got it together," he finally said. He then walked into the house, leaving the others in stitches.

Jeff finally detached himself from the throng with the excuse of having to unsaddle the horses. He hurried down the steps and led the horses into the barn. Gales of laughter and commentary followed after him.

"I bet those horses could tell us a few things."

Jeff was wholly thankful for the relative calm of the stable. The distance of the stable from the porch served to diminish the festive noise but not mute it. He would have to return to face the porch-lounging company, and he knew his cousins where loading up their next barrage of brazen taunts to shower on him when he returned. He was a little miffed that Leslie had left him alone to face the humorous wrath of her brothers, but he could understand how she must feel. He was worried about her and wanted to talk to her. But the antics of her brothers were not helping things.

Things had changed now. Everyone knew that he was here to cut Leslie away from the herd.

Now, there would no longer be those fun-loving summers when Leslie counted herself as one of the boys, and Jeff hovered around the group as the perennial visitor who secretly loved Leslie from afar. Jeff thought back on all those years when he spent the summers with Leslie's family. He remembered those years with fondness. Even though he burned with unrequited love for Leslie, the summer vacations were comfortable and enjoyable. Jeff would regret the loss of those idyllic summers. But he was simply getting too old to continue traipsing up to his uncle's ranch every summer like a kid at camp. He needed to get on with his life, and he wanted to take Leslie with him.

He had nearly finished tending to the horses and was steeling himself to return to the house when he heard Uncle Dan's pickup drive up to the porch.

There was a chorus of birthday greetings for Uncle Dan, and despite the distance from the porch of the ranch house Jeff could clearly make out snatches of Uncle Dan's responses to the well-wishers. Uncle Dan had a lower pitch to his voice than anyone Jeff had ever known. Jeff could often hear and understand Uncle Dan in noisy situations when it was impossible to hear people with normal pitched voices. It was an ability that had served Uncle Dan well in running the ranch, and it was the characteristic that made his "arguments" with Aunt Rosa so voluminous and notable. Jeff had often wished he had been a possessor of the same ability when trying to make himself heard in noisy environments or over long distances outdoors.

Jeff realized it would be a good time to return to the festivities–while the attention of his cousins was in small measure diverted by the arrival of their father. But as soon as Jeff reached the exit of the stable, he noted that his Aunt Rosa had come out onto the porch immediately to talk to her husband, and Jeff knew what that talk was about, especially when he made out a segment of Uncle Dan's response to what Aunt Rosa was talking about.

"So, what about her?" he heard Uncle Dan say clearly to Aunt Rosa as she spirited him into the house.

"Oh, God," Jeff thought to himself, "that makes the evening complete. Now everyone knows, and the topic is open for discussion and commentary."

He knew he would have to suffer through speculation and interrogation for the rest of the evening. He hoped everyone would take it with approbation–along with their humor. His cousins were too fond of their humor to take it any other way, but he wondered if his aunt and uncle might have more serious reactions to what he and Leslie had been doing all afternoon.

Well, he might as well get it over with. He would have to weather the storm. Not for the first time did he envy Leslie who was ensconced in her room. He headed doggedly for the house.

As he neared the porch, his cousins regarded him licking their chops in anticipation of continuing their humorous feast. But before they could build up a head of steam, Aunt Rosa burst through the door, steamrollering the proceedings.

"You boys stop that racket! Now get in here for dinner! And go wash your hands!"

Everyone on the porch contained their carousing and filed contritely into the house under the watchful and admonishing eye of Aunt Rosa. Jeff remained at the bottom of the steps as the assembled company entered the house. He felt like a lonely orphan. After the last of his cousins entered the house, Aunt Rosa looked at Jeff.

"Come on in to dinner, Jeff," she said with considerably less admonishment her in voice than she had expressed to her sons.

As Jeff climbed the porch and entered the house, he thought he perceived his uncle's warning to his sons to tone down their fun. So, there was a relatively quiet hush as Jeff entered the house, but he could feel all eyes on him.

"Jeffy," Aunt Rosa said, "you go sit up at the head of the table by your Uncle Dan."

At the dinner table Uncle Dan said the usual blessing, enforcing a solemnity that would be in stark contrast to the humor that would follow. At first, Aunt Rosa and Uncle Dan made small talk with Jeff, and his cousins observed the enforced silence under the stony stares of their parents. Jeff filled them in on the latest news of his family and the adventures of his sister, Donna.

Near the end of the meal the subject of conversation finally got around to what Jeff and Leslie had been doing all afternoon.

"So, where did you and Leslie go today?" Uncle Dan asked.

It was an innocent enough question, but Jeff's cousins perked up their ears, and Jeff could perceive a few almost audible inward groans from his cousins who were about to bust a collective gut in the effort to stifle themselves. Jeff knew that anything he said from this point on would be replete with double entendres deserving of the most nuanced and witty rejoinders from the cousins.

"We went riding up in the hills," he answered his uncle's question trying to ignore his cousins.

"On horses?" one of his cousins interjected, unable to contain himself.

"Terry!" his uncle admonished. "Listen, no more comments from the peanut gallery. Do you all understand me?"

The cousins nodded their heads collectively, apparently chided but wearing huge grins on their faces with feasting eyes on Jeff.

"Go on, Jeff. So, where did you go today?"

"We went up to Coppy Rock for a while."

"Ah yes. It must be pretty there this time of year. I haven't been up there for ages."

Jeff decided at this point to ask about Leslie, "By the way, Aunt Rosa, is Leslie all right? She hasn't come down for dinner."

"She's fine," Aunt Rosa answered. "She's just being a little emotional right now. I'll take something up to her later. I guess the long ride tired her out a little."

"Yeah, riding will do that." This snide remark came from his cousin Tracy this time who, in turn, wilted under a stony stare from Aunt Rosa.

Uncle Dan was not totally immune to the wit and repartee trying to burst forth at the table, and Jeff noted his lips crinkling up in a slight smile in appreciation of the potential humor in this situation.

"So, Jeffy," Uncle Dan continued, "is there anything you want to tell us?"

At first Jeff was not sure as to what Uncle Dan was referring, but then he understood that the question was meant to cut to the chase. Jeff wanted to say nothing else about the details of his outing with Leslie, but then he decided he had nothing to lose in confessing his love for Leslie and laying his cards on the table.

"Well," he started, "…uh, I guess…it's just that I think Leslie and I have come to…uh, an understanding…and I think we want to get engaged…but we need to talk some more…"

"Are you saying you're in love with Leslie?"

"I guess so."

"You 'guess so?' Don't you know so?"

"Yes, I know so."

"And she's in love with you?"

"I think so."

"And you want to marry her?"

"If she'll have me…"

"Looks like she's already had you!" Not to be outdone by his older brothers Jamie was the one who piped up this time.

"OK! That's it. Everybody out of the room!" Uncle Dan commanded, finally fed up with the antics of his sons.

"You boys go on into the living room," Aunt Rosa added. "We'll have cake and presents in there."

Scolded, but not defeated, Jeff's cousins arose and left the dining room.

"Not you, Jeff," said Uncle Dan. "Stay here and let's talk a little more."

Jeff talked a while longer with his aunt and uncle in the relative privacy of the dining room.

"Jeff," his uncle continued, "are you sure about this? Why now, after all these years, have you suddenly gotten interested in our daughter?

"Well, I always liked Leslie, and when we were out riding today, she said some things that indicated that she liked me too."

"What about the fact that Leslie is your cousin? Do you understand what the implications are for that? And, you know our church frowns upon marriage between cousins, don't you?"

Before Jeff could answer, Aunt Rosa interrupted, "Dan, you know that has nothing to do with it."

While Jeff was wondering why this question had nothing to do with it, Aunt Rosa continued directing her next sentence to him:

"Listen, Jeff, Dan and I have no objection if you and Leslie want to get engaged, but you should know that Leslie just broke up with her fiancé, and she might be a little confused and vulnerable about things right now."

"She said something about a fiancé…" Jeff said. He suddenly had a sinking feeling in the pit of his stomach. "…that means she came to me on the rebound…" he concluded in a pained and barely audible whisper, more to himself than to his aunt and uncle.

The tone of his voice and the look on his face alarmed aunt Rosa.

"Wait a minute, Jeff, it's not what you're thinking. Please promise me you'll have a long talk with Leslie. It's more complicated than what you think. Please talk with her."

"She won't talk to me."

"Yes, she will. Tomorrow. Just be patient with her."

"But what's going on with her? Can't you just…"

"No, Jeff. I can't tell you anything. This is something you and Leslie have to work out between yourselves."

Jeff could think of nothing more to say at the moment, but the perplexed and painful look on his face continued to worry Aunt Rosa.

Uncle Dan took advantage of the pause in conversation to change the subject. "Come on, everybody," he enthused, "how about some cake and presents?" He made a show of rubbing his hands together in joyful anticipation of the goodies coming his way.

They arose from the table and walked into the living room where Jeff's cousins were waiting for them.

"Oh, I left your present in the car," Jeff informed his uncle. "I'll be back in a minute."

Jeff walked through the living room past the gauntlet of his cousins and went out the door.

"And don't come back, you cad!"

En route to his car, Jeff knew that his cousins were not finished with him yet. He knew they must be relishing the prospect of his return to continue being the butt of their wit. But he was not as worried about that as much as he was about the conversation he had had with his uncle and aunt. He entered the car and took up the birthday gift he had brought for Uncle Dan. But instead of going back into the house right away, he sat in the driver's seat of his car and closed the door. He wanted to take a few minutes to think in quiet solitude. He grasped the steering wheel and rested his head on the back of his hands. He was tired and sleepy.

He relived his long afternoon tryst with Leslie. What had been an afternoon of joy had yielded to an evening of questions and concerns over Leslie's unusual behavior. Jeff was beginning to have a bad feeling about everything, and he wondered what ulterior motives Leslie might have had for seducing him. Had it been something other than real affection for him?

Finally, he could neither think nor conjecture any longer. He exited the car and went back to the house, his gift for Uncle Dan in his hand. As he walked into the living room, his cousins again took on a unified look of delightful anticipation.

"We thought you'd lit out for good," was one remark.

"Yeah, we thought maybe you'd gone back up to Copulate Roc–uh, I mean Coppy Rock."

"Oh, God," Jeff thought to himself amid the flood of laughter coming from his cousins. From this time in perpetuity his cousins would refer to that place as "Copulate Rock" in his presence.

Jeff moved closer to the part of the room occupied by Uncle Dan and Aunt Rosa, ostensibly to hand his gift to Uncle Dan, but in truth to remove himself out of the range of his cousins' wit and put himself within the sphere of Uncle Dan's and Aunt Rosa's protection.

Jeff sat down on a nearby chair. Uncle Dan opened the gift.

"Night-vision goggles!" His uncle exclaimed. "Thanks, Jeff. I'll sure be able to use these."

Jeff hardly heard. His fatigue was quickly claiming him. And after a few minutes he asked to be excused and headed up the stairs to the guest room passing within range of his cousins' joyful clutches one last time.

"And be sure to go to your *own* room."

Jeff passed Leslie's room. He was tired, but he wondered if he should try to talk to Leslie. He considered knocking on her door, even at the risk of drawing the attention of his cousins and giving them additional fodder for their brazen fusillades.

He paused to think, but he was too tired. He would not know what to say to her. He went to his room and sat on his bed, taking off his shoes. Fatigue allowed the full measure of pessimism to enter his thoughts. The girl he had made love to earlier in the day was not the Leslie he had known all his life. He had always considered her to be the embodiment of modesty and chastity. He had suspected she was a virgin. Her seductive behavior at Coppy Rock did not fit into that mold. And what was all this about breaking up with her fiancé? An alarming certainty was growing in Jeff's mind. Had she come to him, not with the passion of love, but with the passion of a woman scorned by another man? And what experience had she gleaned from Jeff with which to return and taut her former lover? Jeff lay back into the pillow and was asleep. But the last thought that went through his brain was a picture of himself as the patient lover of a woman who, in one way or another, still carried a torch for another man.

...

Now, early the next morning, Jeff hurried to get himself ready to depart for home before his cousins could arise and plague him anew. He knew that Aunt Rosa was an early riser, and he would have to take his leave of her if no one else. He did not know what to expect from Leslie. But he had resolved to make the attempt to talk to her. He walked over to the door of Leslie's room and tapped on it.

There was no answer.

"Leslie?" He said, tapping a little louder on the door, and hoping he would not draw attention from the whole household.

Still no answer. Jeff opened the door and found an empty room. The bed had been neatly made, or not slept in at all. Had she already left? Had she gone back to her fiancé?

With a sinking feeling he descended the stairs, determined to get on the road as soon as possible, thinking he would never again have the desire or nerve to come to the ranch again.

Aunt Rosa came out of the kitchen to greet him.

"Good morning, Jeff," she said cheerfully. "Come in the kitchen and I'll make you some breakfast."

"No, thanks, Aunt Rosa," he said. "I'm not hungry, and I really need to get on the road."

"On the road? Is something wrong, Jeff?"

"No, it's just that I've got a lot to do before my classes tomorrow."

"Aren't you going to see Leslie?"

"Leslie? Hasn't she already left?"

"No, she's in the stable."

"Oh. OK, I'll go talk to her."

Jeff's tepid statement, and his apparent lack of enthusiasm in going to see Leslie, worried Aunt Rosa, and now she knew that something about her daughter was eating away at Jeff and that he had developed some kind of misgiving about getting involved with her.

"OK, but please come into the kitchen for a few minutes. I need to talk to you about something important."

"Oh, Aunt Rosa, I'm not really up to it."

"Please, Jeff, it'll take just a couple of minutes. And it's very important."

Jeff let Aunt Rosa lead him into the kitchen, and he sat morosely at the table as Aunt Rosa poured him a cup of coffee and sat at the table opposite him. She gave him an appraising look.

"I had a talk with Leslie this morning," she began, "and I need to have the same talk with you."

Aunt Rosa steeled herself to reveal some deep secret. She paused, looked intently at Jeff, and finally spoke.

"It's something about Leslie I've been keeping secret since she was a baby."

"What, Aunt Rosa?" Jeff asked alarmed, thinking maybe Leslie had some rare disease that would preclude the possibility of their union.

"Jeff, what I need to tell you is that your Uncle Dan is not Leslie's biological father."

"What?"

"Your Uncle Dan is not Leslie's father. Leslie was born as a result of my first marriage."

"I never knew you had a previous marriage."

"Yes, it's a long story, and I had a long talk with Leslie about it. I'm just giving you the short version, because I don't want to keep Leslie waiting for you any longer."

Aunt Rosa had become very emotional and had tears in her eyes.

"Anyway," she continued, "Leslie was born when her father was away. His name was Randal. He was killed in the war and never saw his daughter. Your Uncle Dan was Randal's best friend and promised him he would take care of Leslie and me if anything happened to him. That's how your Uncle Dan and I came together. He returned from the war to fulfill that promise, and we were married shortly after. And, I've had four wonderful boys with Dan."

It was a compelling story, and Jeff listened attentively. But he was not sure how all this fit in with the previous discussion.

Aunt Rosa saved him from the necessity of analyzing the implications of her revelation.

"So, do you understand what that means, Jeff? It means Leslie is not a blood relation to you, so there's no biological reason you shouldn't get married."

Jeff listened and absorbed. It began to sink in. Suddenly, he understood that Leslie's long-held concern over an incestuous relationship with him had been erased. The thing that had induced Leslie to avoid him all those years was now a non-issue.

Jeff continued watching his aunt, still absorbing the impact of what she had said. She was in the grip of a strong emotion, and Jeff realized that this was a repeat of the same confession that she had made earlier to Leslie.

"But, Aunt Rosa," he finally spoke, "why didn't you tell Leslie about all this sooner?"

"I would have, if I'd known how she felt about you. But I honestly thought she had no interest in you, and I didn't think it was necessary to tell her."

"Don't you think you should have told her, anyway?"

"I probably should have, but you've got to understand that Leslie is my only daughter. I never wanted her to think that she was anything else than a total member of this family and that Dan was truly her father—I never wanted to take that away from her. I hope you can understand that, Jeff."

"I understand." Jeff responded, seeing the tears and emotion in Aunt Rosa's confession.

She arose from the table and gave Jeff a hug and a kiss.

…

Jeff walked out the front door of the house deep in thought.

He walked into the stable and saw Leslie grooming her horse. She looked at him a little nervously as he approached her.

"Hi, Jeff," she said.

"Hi, Leslie," he responded.

"Thanks for taking care of Billy Girl last night," she added. Billy Girl was the name of her horse.

"You're welcome," Jeff responded moving closer and looking at her intently.

Out of nervousness she had not yet fully met his gaze. She made the pretense of returning to the business of grooming Billy Girl as she spoke to Jeff.

"I'm sorry I didn't come down for dinner last night…"

"Leslie?"

She turned to look at him fully, and idle chit-chat was contained as their eyes met and communicated much more than words ever could.

Suddenly, they threw themselves in each other's arms in a passionate embrace.

43.

After a night of passion, Donna awoke the next morning considering the prospect of true and lasting love. Tom was asleep beside her. She slipped out of bed, donning a negligee, and went to the kitchen to make coffee. She pondered the options of what they would do today. She opted for a quiet day with Tom. Perhaps they could take a drive later. Maybe go to the swimming pool, if it wasn't too chilly outside. Mostly, she just wanted to talk with him.

Donna had a usual morning routine, but as she pondered her normal tasks, she found her attention was not on them. She went back into the bedroom to look at Tom. Giving in to the desire to be by his side, she crawled back into bed beside him, put her arm around him and slept some more.

An hour later she awoke as Tom stirred beside her. She sat up over him so that she would be the first thing he saw this morning. He opened his eyes and looked at her intently.

"Good morning," she said.

"Good morning," he answered.

They continued to look at each other. She smiled at him but said nothing. He directed his gaze downward toward her breasts and seemed a bit surprised that they were covered by a negligee. He looked back up into her eyes. He moved his arms up to embrace her and tried to pull her down onto the bed again.

"Oh, no, Tommy," she said thwarting his embrace, "we've had quite enough of that for now."

He looked at her questioningly.

"I'm fine," he replied. "Please, Donna...I want you...I'm on fire..."

He again made an attempt to embrace her. She almost relented. Instead she managed to coax him out of bed with the erotic promise of a shared shower. She was hoping the water would dampen down his ardor. It had the opposite effect. The two of them soaping each other in slippery embraces served to inflame her as well as him. Leaving the shower, they continued embracing and kissing even before they could dry each other off. His desire could not be ignored. He picked her up and carried her toward the bed.

"No, Tommy. Please, it's too much for you. OK, OK, then... here, let me on top...lie down on your back..."

Being on top, she thought she could control and minimize the amount of energy he expended in lovemaking. But the urgency of her own desire surprised and overwhelmed her, and both of them ended up exhausted and panting for breath. The exquisite result rivaled their lovemaking of the previous night.

Now she lay beside him tingling with contentment and well-being. She had half formulated a plan for the day, but now she considered scrapping that plan and consigning the whole day to be by his side at home. The only problem with that idea was that he would want to have sex with her again, further jeopardizing his fragile condition. She knew she should arise, dress and do something active to defend against any further libidinous overtures from him—without appearing to reject his advances, of course.

She propped herself over him to look him in the eye. He was awake.

"Do you want to sleep some more?" She asked.

"Hmmm, maybe…"

"Are you hungry? Do you want something to eat?"

"Maybe later."

She gave him a tender kiss and parked her face a few inches above his. She caressed his brow and temples. They looked deeply into each other's eyes.

"I love you," she said.

"I love you, too," he answered

"Do you want more sex?" she asked seductively.

"Yes… Later, maybe."

She smiled at him. He was mesmerized by her closeness and those magnificent brown eyes looking straight into his soul.

"Tommy?"

"Hmm?"

"Why were you angry at me last night?"

"What?"

"Why were you angry at me last night?"

Now he tried to avert his eyes.

"I wasn't angry at you…" he answered weakly.

"Yes, Tommy, you were."

"Did I hurt you?" he asked trying to deflect her question with a question of his own.

"No," she answered continuing to peer into his eyes, waiting for him to answer her question.

He offered no further information.

"Tommy, please. If I did something to upset you, I want to know what it was. I know I can be bossy at times, but I don't want to do anything to upset you—if I do, you need to tell me…"

"You didn't do anything to upset me...and you're not all that bossy..."

"Then, why were you angry at me last night?"

"I guess...well...I thought that's what you wanted..."

"Yes, I wanted you to pretend. But you were really mad at me for some reason."

He again hesitated. She prompted him with her eyes.

"I wasn't mad...," he finally admitted, "it's just that...I guess I was just jealous..."

"Jealous? Of what?"

"Nothing really...I guess, maybe other men in your life..."

Now she understood. It never ceased to amaze her–the things men considered important in a relationship. Men always seemed to equate sex with love. Such masculine naiveté.

Still, she was dealing with a male ego, and she needed to be careful.

"Tommy," she said gently, "you're the only man I ever loved..."

He looked at her, trying to correlate this declaration with the fact that he knew other men had been in her life.

"...I spent a long time trying to fall in love," she continued, "but I was never successful until you came into my life."

"But what did I do to...uh...?"

"You kissed me."

"But...how did that cause you to ...uh...I mean...I wasn't the first person to kiss you, was I?"

"It's the first time anyone kissed me like that."

"Like what? I don't understand..."

"If you don't understand, I can't explain it to you," she said smiling at him calmly.

He remained looking at her perplexed.

"Do you love me?" she continued, seeking the assurance that women never get enough of.

"Yes, of course. I'll always love you."

"Oh, Tommy!" she said emotionally, embracing and caressing him.

She was suddenly seized with a frightening premonition and she shivered uncontrollably against him. He was alarmed.

"What's wrong, Donna?"

"Tommy!" she exclaimed in a frightened voice, "Tommy, please don't leave me!"

"I'm not going to leave you."

"Please, Tommy! Stay with me. Don't ever leave me."

"Why would I leave you?"

"Don't go back to that woman," she pleaded.

"What woman?"

"Your wife. Please, Tommy, stay with me."

"My wife? My wife's dead. How could I go back to her?"

He remained alarmed at this strange outburst from her. He shifted to a sitting position in the bed to better attend to her. She had tightened her embrace around him and was shuddering. He tightened his own embrace around her protectively.

"Donna, what's wrong?"

She continued to shiver in his embrace a few more moments and then was still and appeared to be asleep on his shoulder.

"Are you all right, Donna?"

She lifted her head off his shoulder, looking at him with a tired but serene and attentive smile, as if she had just awakened.

"What was that all about?" he asked her.

"What was "what" about?"

"What you were just talking about…about my wife."

"Tom, I know we'll have to talk about these things later, but I don't really want to talk about your wife right now."

"But…but you brought it up…"

"Brought what up?"

"My wife—you asked me not to…"

He stopped in mid-sentence. She was looking at him with a puzzled look on her face.

"Don't you remember?" he asked.

She continued looking at him puzzled, waiting for him to clarify whatever he was talking about. He could not believe she did not remember what she had said a few moments ago. She had been feeling some strong emotions. Maybe the emotional strain caused her to have a temporary lapse.

They continued watching each other, and he ceased his attempt to explain.

Seeing that he was not disposed to say more, she spoke up.

"Tommy," she began with happy anticipation, "lie down beside me and talk to me."

He maneuvered to snuggle up beside her.

"What do you want to talk about?" he asked.

"Tell me how much you love me."

For a while they talked, cuddled, joked and laughed.

At one point he became seriously quiet and looked at her. For a silent eternity they regarded each other basking in the reality of their togetherness. He laid his head on her shoulder and buried his face in the corner of her anatomy where her shoulder curved up to become her neck. He held her in an emotional embrace.

"Donna…" he said and tried to find the words to tell her how he truly felt about her.

"Donna," he repeated. Even the words 'I love you' were inadequate to express his feelings.

"Donna," he repeated for the third time, and he wondered how he could ever be worthy of this fantastic creature in his arms.

She felt the emotion in him through his embrace.

"It's OK," she said to him caressing his face.

"I...I can't find the words..." he said.

"It's OK," she repeated. "I understand."

They slept a little longer in each other's arms.

…

Eventually they bestirred themselves.

"I'm starved," she said, detaching herself from his embrace and springing out of bed. "Let's go get something to eat."

"Sounds good to me," he answered, and made a motion to follow her.

"Oh, whoa….," he uttered as he arose from the bed and sat back down on it.

"Tom! What's wrong?"

"I got a little dizzy there for a second."

She became frantic with alarm. "OK," she exclaimed, "that's it! No more for you. I knew it. You've overdone it, haven't you?!"

"No, I just got a little dizzy, that's all. I stood up too fast. It's nothing to worry about."

"Oh, no! You're going to stay in bed until I get you checked out. I mean it, Tom. You lie down and stay in bed. I'm gonna call and make you a doctor's appointment."

"But Donna, don't you think you're overreacting?"

"No! Come on, now. Lie down."

She pushed him down onto the bed, fussing over him like a mother hen. As she pulled the covers over him her bare breasts came into close proximity with his face, and more out of reflex than anything else, he made a playful grab for her.

She avoided his grasp deftly and walked over to her dresser to pick out clothing and began getting dressed. He watched her nude body, realizing she would soon cover her glorious treasures.

"Donna," he said starting to throw the covers off of himself and moving to get out of bed, "I can't stay in bed all day."

"You stay there!" She said raising her voice at him.

He checked his intent, looking at her in a bit of surprise over her insistence.

"But I can't stay in bed all day," he repeated.

"Yes, you can!"

"But…but I thought we were going to get something to eat."

"I'll bring you something to eat. Now you stay there. I mean it."

She left the room, leaving him somewhat taken aback. She had never been quite this adamant with him before, and he was at a loss as to what to do for the moment. While pondering whether he should disobey her orders, she returned to the room, talking to someone on her phone. She came over to the bedside and sat down beside him, putting a casual hand on his chest as a symbolic way of holding him down on the bed. He could tell that she was making a doctor's appointment for him.

"OK," she said to him as she disconnected, "you have an appointment for tomorrow morning. We'll have to leave early to get there on time."

"How did you get an appointment so fast? I've never been able to get an appointment that fast."

"I told them it was an emergency."

"Oh, come on, Donna, it's hardy an emergency."

She shifted closer to him attaining a position where she could lean over him and look him closely in the eye. It was the position she had assumed to hold him in place that day she first kissed him. Now she gave him an intent look that was equal parts love, concern and playfulness. When she looked at him like that, he was putty in her hands and could not deny her anything or disagree with anything she said.

"OK, sweetheart," she said all business now. "What do you want for breakfast?"

"I don't care..." he answered, "but can I get dressed now?"

"No."

"Why not?"

"I'm not gonna have you lying around in bed all day with your clothes on."

"Well, then, can I put on a pair of pajamas?"

"No."

"Why not?"

"We don't have any. I think we assumed you wouldn't need any, so I didn't buy you any." She gave him a seductively knowing look.

"But Donna, I can't lie around all day with no clothes on."

"Why not? You lay around all night with no clothes on."

"But that's different..."

"Listen, sweetheart," she said ending the discussion, "you stay here. I'll bring you some breakfast in a little bit."

She left the bedroom cheerfully.

"I can't eat anything with no clothes on!" he called after her with a degree of frustration.

In addition to being frustrated, he was a little miffed at her for dismissing his request for clothes so out of hand. Well, she had forgotten to get his promise to stay in bed. He quickly jumped out of bed and headed for the dresser in search of clothes. He would simply present himself to her dressed as a *fait accompli* when she returned. Now, where had she put his clothes? She had put them away when they arrived at her place yesterday, but he could not find them in any of her dresser drawers. He looked in the closet and found nothing he could wear. Even the clothes he had shed and deposited on the floor last night were gone.

"Hey, what are you doing?"

He nearly jumped out of his skin. He turned and saw her coming toward him. He felt naked. He *was* naked.

"I told you to stay in bed, didn't I?"

With an angry look at him, she took him by the arm and led him back toward the bed. Suddenly, an erotic thrill went through him. There was something about a dominant clothed woman in control of a naked submissive man, but she failed to notice the effect of her action upon him as he pushed him down on the bed.

"Now," she said, "are you going to stay in bed or am I going to have to get a rope and tie you down?"

Her threat was figurative with no erotic intention on her part, but it enhanced the thrill he was experiencing.

"You'd better stop it," he said playfully. "You're turning me on."

She suddenly became aware of the erotic trappings of the situation and its effect on him. She laughed.

"You've got a dirty mind," she responded playfully. "I always thought you were such a shy and proper person. Now, I think I've gotten involved with a sex fiend."

"You're the one who mentioned a rope and're keeping me naked in bed."

"Yeah, but not for the reasons *you're* thinking of."

"Will you get in bed with me?" he asked hopefully.

"No."

"Why not?"

"Because you'll want to have sex with me."

He could not argue with that assessment. She remained looking at him in playful anticipation of his next statement. Even in play, he was captivated by her nearness and her beautiful face and smile. He cast around for something else to say.

"Seriously, can't I just get dressed, and I promise I'll sit quietly on the sofa, and..."

"No."

"But I don't see why..."

"No."

"Well..."

"No."

They continued looking at each other. They were both approaching playfulness, and he realized that anything he asked her was destined to get the same flippant response from her until he came to the full realization of the pointlessness of his continued arguments.

"I'm sorry," he said trying a new tact, "but I'm gonna have to insist."

"Oh, you are, are you?" She laughed over his tepid mutiny.

"Yes, I am," he replied with mock defiance.

"Well," she responded, "insist all you want."

"OK, so I'm getting up, right?"

"No."

"Oh yes I am," he contradicted still playfully defiant.

"Oh no you're not."

He gazed at the bright, happy countenance shining upon his soul. He marshaled his thoughts for a response to continue the happy game against her playful adamancy. But he was distracted by the overwhelming force of her presence, he could think of nothing more to say.

She watched him. He looked at her. She shook her head slightly.

"No," she said quietly to his unspoken question.

He looked at her still trying to think of something to say to keep her talking to him.

"So…what are you trying to say, exactly," he ventured frolicsomely.

"No," she emphasized.

"What exactly do you mean by 'no'?"

"When I say 'no' I mean 'no'."

"Well, I…"

"What part of 'no' don't you understand?" she added.

"The 'n' and the 'o,'" he responded.

She laughed and hugged him happily.

The whole episode that had started with serious concern had evolved into a playful banter and now into a happy tenderness.

"OK, Doctor No," he said. "You win."

She giggled in his embrace.

"Donna stay with me," he said tightening his hold on her.

"Oh, Tommy, Tommy…" she whispered in his ear.

He reveled in her presence. Her weight upon him and the movement of her body against him were among the most pleasurable sensations he had ever experienced. He began thinking in terms of a more lascivious activity. Then he sensed her shivering against him, and he heard a series of sobs that wracked her body. He was alarmed.

"What's wrong, honey?" he asked managing to get her to lift her head off his shoulder, so that he could look at her face. He saw a profusion of tears streaming from her eyes.

"Oh, Tommy," she sobbed, "I'm so happy. I love you so much."

He looked at her kindly, still puzzled over her tears.

"But I'm so terribly worried about you," she continued.

"There's nothing to worry about," he answered, "I'm fine."

"I'm so afraid I'll lose you. I'm afraid you might leave me. Please, Tommy, I don't want to lose you."

"Honey, I won't leave you."

"I'm so worried that something will happen to take you from me—I've already almost lost you a couple of times...you were so sad and weak, and I still don't know what's going to happen to you..."

"Honey..." he tried to reassure her.

"Please, Tommy, please. Let me get you checked out. Please be careful with yourself. I know I may be worried about nothing, but I want to be sure. Please, let me do this..."

He acquiesced to her requests. He promised he would never leave her. He promised to stay in bed, and not to overstrain himself. He said other things to put her at ease.

...

Three days later, Tom awoke in bed beside Donna. She continued to sleep peacefully while he took in the pleasing contours of her nude body. For some reason he still could not quite fathom the most beautiful woman in the world loved him. It was beginning to sink in. Her doctor had given him a clean bill of health, with a few provisos, and they had resumed their passionate lovemaking like a honeymooning couple. They had not left her apartment for three days. He supposed that at some point they would have to establish a routine of daily living that would require them to reduce the frequency and length of their bouts of sexual passion. At some point they would have to take trips outside her apartment for shopping and other activity. For the moment, however, there was no indication that they were getting sated with their lovemaking. Even now as he looked at her, there were stirrings within him. When she awoke, she would give him a sleepy smile, snuggle up to him, and present him with a happy, contented face. She might talk to him. He might discern a few tears of happiness in her eyes, and that would tie his loins in knots. She might kiss him tenderly. Or forcefully. Either way he would be carried away on a tidal wave of passion. And he would have no desire or ability to contain it.

But for the moment he needed to think. He needed to think about the future. "What now?" he asked himself.

Things were different now. He had experienced a great awakening. He could not believe that just a few days ago he had pondered a choice between Donna and a return to the insane and suicidal journey that had possessed him when he first met her. He had certainly been insane to think there was ever any choice. He had chosen Donna and rejected the suicidal oath he had made during a time of extreme duress. No man or divinity could hold him to such an oath. He continued to look at Donna and thought about the time they had been together. If he had not encountered her in the wilderness, he would have remained in and perished in that wilderness, and by this time, his cadaver would be deteriorating in some ignominious corner of the forest or would have been devoured by wild animals. She had taken him out of the wilderness—literally and figuratively.

She was his road back to sanity and happiness. And she, in turn, seemed to be contented and happy with him–at least for the time being. But what could he offer her over the long term? She was extremely rich, and there would certainly be no requirement for him to be the provider of her material needs. If he married her, he would not have to work another day in his life. Unlike some men, who might find such an arrangement a blow to their masculine pride, he did not find such a scenario to be unpleasant. He had certain skills, and he would find something useful to do. He could well end up working for her father. He certainly had no intention of going back to his job in Washington. His liaison with Donna and the pristine environment of the mountains left him with no desire to return to that fetid, manic swamp and the memories associated with it. He knew he would have to return there at some point to conclude some unfinished business in his personal and professional life. It would not be a pleasant task, but he had to get his life in order before he could go forward with Donna. He would have to give notice at work, arrange to sell his house, pay some final bills, and clear out his bank accounts. The amount of money from these liquidations would be a pittance compared to Donna's massive fortune, but it was his money, and he felt obliged to manage it. More importantly he needed to apply for replacement identification documents–a driver's license, credit cards, and other IDs to reestablish his existence as a real person. He vaguely remembered that at the beginning of his insane odyssey, he had driven his car as far up an old logging road as possible, and before penetrating the dark forest he pushed the car into a ravine. He had taken his wallet out of his back pocket and hurled it into the ravine after the car in a final gesture to divest himself totally of the trappings of true personhood.

The dark memory possessed him a few moments. He looked over to Donna. There was a bright aura about her, and the dark memory dissipated. Yes, he would have to get his act together if he had any hope of winning Donna.

He sat up on the edge of the bed, carefully so as not to awaken her. He sat a few moments until he was sure he would be able to stand without getting dizzy. That was one of the recommendations from the doctor, and he had promised Donna he would faithfully follow this piece of the doctor's advice. 'If you get tired of what you're doing, stop what you're doing.' That was another suggestion made by Donna's doctor who seemed to have a number of common-sense preventive care recommendations for him. Donna's doctor was a woman, and the two women had greeted each other like old friends. Later, he had suspected that the doctor may have been Donna's personal gynecologist. Donna insisted on being present for the examination and had no apparent inkling of the embarrassment this caused him. It was a full and thorough examination. Donna filled the doctor in on his weakened condition due to his ordeal in the wilderness, and she watched as the doctor poked him, checked his reflexes, looked down his throat, used a stethoscope, and asked him if anything hurt. He feared the examination might require him to undress. His embarrassment grew more pronounced as the two women engaged in a rather clinical discussion about his physical condition, almost excluding him from the conversation. When Donna began asking about whether he was healthy enough to engage in sexual activity, he finally spoke up.

"Donna, you shouldn't be talking about those things," he interjected trying to hide his embarrassment.

The two women realized they had embarrassed him and had excluded him from the discussion. They indulged him apologetically.

"Oh, I'm sorry, Tom," Donna said moving near to him taking him affectionately by the arm.

"He's a little shy," she said to the doctor then looked back to him. "Here we've been talking about you like you weren't even in the room."

Donna's apology and the doctor's return to a professional decorum in his presence served only to heighten his embarrassment.

"I'm sorry, Mr. Amboy," the doctor said looking at Tom then at Donna, "I didn't realize we were embarrassing you. Would you feel more comfortable with a male doctor?"

"No, that's not…"

"Do you want me to wait outside?" Donna interrupted.

"No, it's just that…"

"Well, let me go find my husband," the doctor concluded and left the room in search of her husband who was an internist working in the same office. Donna waited in the exam room with Tom.

"I'm sorry, sweetheart," she said to him diffidently, "I didn't realize you'd be embarrassed by a woman doctor."

"I'm not embarrassed by a woman doctor," he replied, "it's just that I was afraid I might have to get undressed."

"Well, that's not unusual in an examination," she countered.

"Yeah, but not with you in the room."

"But I've seen it all before," she said playfully, embarrassing him again.

He was beginning to fear that the doctor had taken him for a prudish and sexist caveman who required special handling. That was the last thing he wanted her to think, and that, in itself, added to his feelings of embarrassment.

Eventually, the male doctor arrived and completed the examination. Donna waited outside. He tried to explain that he had not had any objection against being examined by a female doctor, but then he suspected that anything more he said would probably be interpreted as a rationalization for an entrenched sexist bias that he possessed, and he thought it best to say nothing more that could further prejudice his standing in the esteem of the professionals attending to him.

At the conclusion of the exam, Donna collected him. She took him by the arm and accompanied him to the receptionist's counter. He felt like a prize bull being led by a ring through his nose. He suffered silently through one final embarrassment as Donna presented her credit card to pay for the exam in full.

There were no requests for insurance information, the filling out of forms, co-pays, or future appointments. It was strange. The super-rich had no need of any kind of insurance.

Upon leaving the doctor's office, she took him to get a couple of prescriptions filled then she took him shopping and to lunch. She took him by the arm or held his hand in a happy display of affection showing off her boyfriend to the world. At times, as they walked along, she would cozy up to him happily laying her head against his arm. He still felt like a bull that she was leading by the ring through his nose, but her exuberance and happiness overwhelmed him, and he was hard pressed to make a big deal over the embarrassment he was feeling. He was uncomfortable because he was totally at her mercy. He had no money or credit cards, and she had to pay for everything. He had no ID or driver's license and had to rely on her for transportation. If the need arose, he could not even prove his identity. He would be totally lost and helpless without her, and he was duly grateful for her attentions and care. Yet, he wanted to explain the embarrassment he was feeling. He finally had a chance to make his point while they were sitting in a restaurant booth for lunch. She sat cozily beside him rather than on the opposite bench of the booth. While she cheerfully examined the menu (with every indication that she was going to order for them both), he endeavored to explain his feelings. She listened to him attentively, almost doe-eyed, and when he saw worry beginning to replace the happiness radiating from her face, he immediately knew he never wanted to be the one to rob her of any sort of happiness. He immediately began backpedaling from the point he had been trying to make.

"I'm sorry, honey," he said. "Don't pay any attention to me. I'm just being masculine. I don't know what I'm saying. I guess I'm just still feeling a little embarrassed by everything."

"Oh, sweetheart," she answered. "I'm sorry." Despite his efforts to sustain her cheerfulness, she was worried about him, and it showed on her face."

"Here," she said suddenly digging into her purse, "let me give you some money and you can pay for lunch…"

"No, honey, don't do that."

She stopped and looked up at him. There were tears in her eyes.

"I'm sorry, honey," he said taking her in his arms. "I love you."

Now, three days later he sat on the side of her bed continuing to watch her as she slept. He continued thinking back on the time he had been with her. He thought about that first day he had met her. Within ten minutes of meeting her, he knew the kind of woman she was. Forceful and demanding. Yet, his subsequent time with her revealed that she was also loving and caring. During the time he was in the hospital and the time he was under her care as a house guest, she had controlled him with consummate and instinctive skill. He had loved her at first sight, and in the final analysis, she easily had her way with him, and he could deny her nothing. On the few occasions when he balked at her authority, she had gotten his cooperation through playful concern, and failing that through caring affection. When all else failed she could resort to tears. She was not being manipulative for the sake of being manipulative. It was an instinctive need she had to relate to him as her lover. Perhaps a less smitten man would not put up with it, but he was totally enthralled with her. As long as she loved him, he would want for nothing else in his existence.

"She's gonna boss you around for the rest of your life," he told himself.

"If you're lucky," he added.

He arose from the bed and walked over to the dresser. He needed to think about the future. What would happen when the fires of passion began to die down? What would they have in common that would bind them together over a lifetime? He looked in the mirror. The face looking back at him was a dark, gloomy visage. Beyond the face in the mirror he saw Donna's bright reflection as she slept on the bed. The contrast between the two images in the mirror came into sharp focus.

At rare times in his life, the fates or the controlling forces of the universe, gave him the ability to see things as they truly were–to glimpse the true nature of things. And now he suddenly saw the two people in the mirror in stark perspective. Donna's bright happy image contrasted sharply with his morose passive façade. The serene happiness in Donna's face, even as she slept, radiated outward in a bright aura. She had the ability to smile and laugh easily and naturally. Laughter and happiness were nowhere to be found in his stony countenance. He tried to force a smile from his lips and form his face into a happy expression. The resulting grimace was a scary thing to behold.

He knew he was the luckiest man in the world, and he should be the happiest. Why couldn't he let it show? Why was he possessed of such an innate streak of pessimism and apprehension? Why did he have such a sense of dread about everything? He looked again at Donna. How could a torpid man like himself aspire to the love of such a magical creature? How could he possibly make her happy? How long would it be before she got tired of him? How long would she continue to lavish her ocean of love upon him only to see her waves of cheerfulness and affection broken and dashed against the immovable rocks of his nature. How long before they began to grow apart?

He continued looking in the mirror. The frame of the mirror took on the appearance of a movie screen, and he could almost hear a surreal projector advancing the images of the film that played out before him. He saw the future between Donna and him. He watched as she awoke beside him no longer happy and affectionate. She became more neutral toward him and found less contentment in his presence. She began finding fault with him, getting bored with his continued morose and passive nature. She began spending less time with him and developed activities that excluded him. She began spending more time among her friends, an action that pointed up a waning community of interest between him and her. Slowly, her happiness was replaced with reserve and coldness in his presence. He saw episodes of argument and fighting between them. She accused him of being incurably negative and not willing to meet her needs. The robust glow began to drain out of her face, and eventually it was replaced by a pale sadness. She no longer had any smiles or laughter for him. He watched as the fire in her eyes was extinguished and her face became bland. Her raven black hair faded and was replaced with an unflattering blondness. He watched the changing image in horror. He suddenly realized that this was a horrific replay of what had transpired between him and his wife. The image in the mirror took on the features of his wife who now spoke to him in a morbid, accusatory voice.

"You know you'll treat her the same way you treated me. And you'll starve her of love and affection like you did to me. And in the end, you'll kill her like you did me."

"No!" he gasped and tore his sight away from the terrible image. He shivered with the horror of what he had seen in the mirror. He fought to compose himself and reject the vicious prediction. He turned his back to the mirror, but he knew the ghost behind him was still attempting to eviscerate him with

its evil intention. He was breathing heavily and continued to shiver almost to the point of nausea.

He looked over at Donna. Without the juxtaposition of the mirror image, he was able to take solace in beholding her alone, letting her brightness fill the entire frame of his existence. As he took in the reality of her presence, the nightmare vision of the mirror was diminished. He wanted to rush over to her, bury his face in her shoulder and cocoon himself in her beautiful aura.

But he could not let her see him in this panicky state.

He knew the kind of man he was and that he could not change his nature. If the evil prediction were a possible vision of their future, he would do everything in his power to prevent it, even if it came to the point where he had to kill himself to prevent any unhappiness in her life. Again, he berated himself for not having had the courage and force of personality to get out of her life before now.

"No!" he suddenly shouted at himself, recoiling from this state of mind. "You've got to stop thinking like this! You can't just give up! You've, at least, got to try."

With supreme effort he dominated his fears and forced himself to calm down.

"You've got to do something to show her that her love is having an effect on you," he said to himself. He wondered what initiative he could take to show her that he was not the passive, morose ninny that she had been coddling all this time.

"Do, something," he thought. "Anything! Anything to show her you have an interest in life and to acknowledge your appreciation of her love."

He walked to the closet, still a bit shaky. He put on a bathrobe and walked back over to the bed where he stood over her and observed her silently for a few moments. She was still sleeping soundly. It was the lazy sleep of a satisfied, contented woman. He again took in the pleasing features of her nude body. He wanted to crawl back into bed and hold her, but he contained his desire. He was on another kind of mission for the moment. He walked toward the bedroom door. He would make some coffee and breakfast to have waiting for her. It would be the small first step in cementing their lives together.

44.

∾

"Donna? *Donna?*"

His voice came to her out of a haze. She was again lying on the forest floor as his face appeared inches above hers. She reached out lazily to embrace him around the neck and pulled him to her.

"Donna, honey," he responded gently trying to unwrap her arms from around his neck. "You've got visitors."

"Mmm?" she said half awake, wondering why he wanted to disengage from her embrace.

"Honey," Tom repeated, "you have visitors. It's your brother Jeff. He's here to see you"

"Jeff?" she queried, awaking fully. "What's he doing here?"

"He wants to see you. He's in the living room."

She sat up on the side of the bed. "Jeff is here?"

"Yes."

She stood abruptly and retrieved her own bathrobe from the closet. "If my mother sent him over here to check up on us, there's gonna be hell to pay."

She walked out of the bedroom fastening her bathrobe securely around her. Jeff was sitting on the living room sectional.

There was a girl with him wearing glasses. It took her a second to realize it was her cousin Leslie.

"Jeff! Leslie! What are you doing here?"

"We had to come in person," Jeff answered. "Someone wasn't answering her phone." Looking at Donna and Tom in their bathrobes, he added impishly, "And I think I know why. Did we interrupt anything?"

Tom looked a bit nonplused, but Donna ignored the insinuation and was more interested in the unexpected presence of Leslie at Jeff's side.

"So, what's with you two?" Donna asked, then glancing at Tom she added, "Oh, Tom this is our cousin Leslie."

Tom and Leslie said 'hi' to each other.

Donna continued to eye Jeff. "So, what's up?"

Jeff hesitated ever so slightly, casting a glance at Leslie. "Well," he answered, "Leslie and I have gotten engaged."

"Engaged! Oh, that's wonderful!" Donna exclaimed almost jumping for joy. "Well, tell me all about it."

The two couples sat comfortably on opposite sides of the sectional. Jeff put his arm around Leslie and recounted the story about how they got engaged. Donna snuggled up to Tom. Donna and Jeff did most of the talking, each trying to ferret out what they wanted to know about the other's love life.

"Would you all like some coffee?" Tom finally spoke up taking an interest in the group dynamic, "I just made some."

Donna looked intently and lovingly at Tom. "You made coffee?"

"Yes, I thought I'd..."

"Oh, honey, that's so sweet." She put her hands up to the sides of his face beaming at him. She brought her lips to his, giving him a tender kiss.

Tom was a little embarrassed by the fact that visitors were witnessing her display of affection. He knew that Donna's affection was genuine, but he knew just as well that her display was a deliberate signal that she was giving to show the assembled company that she and Tom were lovers. Nevertheless, Tom basked in her affection, and there was a momentary pause in the general conversation as the two lovers indulged their attention for each other.

"I was also going to make some breakfast," Tom finally tendered, as if he were carefully yet unabashedly testing and fine tuning the happy formula he had discovered to prolong and enhance Donna's affection toward him. In effect it was a ploy to sustain the humor and good vibes of the situation, and everyone laughed.

Donna laughed heartiest of all, still cuddling his face between her hands, her eyes inches from his, pouring her flood of laughter directly into his soul. And when the laughter was done, her eyes continued to shower him with affection, and he was left tingling from the intensity of it.

"Well, then," she said looking over to Jeff and Leslie, "do you guys want some coffee and breakfast?"

"I don't know," Jeff responded, "are you sure you two don't want to be alone?"

"No... no, we're good," she said repositioning herself to resume the conversation while continuing to snuggle up to Tom. "Let's talk."

"Well, we *had* come over to invite you out to lunch; if you can tear yourselves away...from making coffee, that is."

"That's a great idea!" Donna exclaimed. "Just let us go get dressed."

She arose and headed toward her bedroom. Tom hesitated, wondering whether he should remain behind, ostensibly to entertain the visitors, but, perhaps in actuality, to avoid giving the indecorous appearance of an all too invasive intimacy he had with Donna that would be revealed if he followed closely after her into her private bed chamber. He was debating the course of action to follow when Donna turned after taking a few steps toward her bedroom and ordered, "Come on, Tom."

He arose immediately and followed her into the bedroom.

Jeff and Leslie watched as Donna and Tom disappeared into the bedroom shutting the door behind them. They heard a happy giggle through the door followed by a few muffled sounds, after which all was quiet.

Jeff and Leslie continued watching the door in silence for a few moments.

"Well, that was surprising," Jeff said, feeling a little like some of the wind had been taken out of his sails. He had expected the brilliant news of his engagement to Leslie to occupy center stage in the conversation. But now it appeared that Donna had a rival story of her own to tell.

He looked at Leslie who was sitting beside him, arms crossed, staring intently at the bedroom door, forming her own opinion of what she had just witnessed. Leslie had never had much contact with Donna over the years. She had occasionally interacted with Donna at family reunions during which times she had always regarded Donna as a haughty, opinionated, almost Auntie Mame type figure who would stand atop her aristocratic pedestal handing down her sarcastic and sardonic pronouncements in a way that the men always seemed to appreciate as acerbic wit and the women took as a thinly-veiled cattiness. The last thing she expected to see today was a woman head-over-heels in love.

While she was absorbed in these thoughts Jeff leaned over and kissed her on her temple.

"So, that's the Tom Ambrose you told us about?" she asked.

"Yeah, that's the one," Jeff answered. "I knew she was interested in him, but now it looks like she's really taken with him. I've never seen her like this; I mean, she was positively, uh...positively...uh, what's the word I'm looking for...uh, giddy?"

"Yeah," Leslie responded, "all that just because he made coffee for her–I wonder what she would've done if he'd waxed her floors?"

Jeff laughed and began pulling her toward him to kiss her on the lips.

"Now, don't *you* start," she resisted.

She tried to lean away from him. She almost always resisted his overtures initially, but he knew this was a girlish affectation she had carried over into their relationship. With a bit of persistence, she usually relented willingly to him.

He finally had her positioned where he wanted and proceeded to kiss her, but this time she continued to resist.

"Not now, Jeff," she protested, "we don't have time."

"For a little kiss?"

"They could come back any second, now."

He tried another playful ploy, "Did I tell you that I did the laundry yesterday?"

"So what?"

He feigned disappointment, "Well, I guess the 'domestic chores' line doesn't work with you then, does it?"

They both continued their playful interlude, until Leslie finally said, "What's keeping them?"

"Maybe he *did* wax her floors for her," he conjectured. They both laughed.

Eventually Donna and Tom reappeared, and they all went out to have lunch. It was at the same restaurant where Donna had taken Tom after his doctor's appointment.

It was a long, animated lunch. Donna and Jeff did most of the talking, and near the end of the meal, each had a well-rounded understanding of the other's love story, minus, of course, any explicit descriptions of sex or details best left in the realm of privacy. Tom and Leslie participated in the conversation when appropriate, but for the most part they were content to sit beside their lovers, warming themselves in the camaraderie of the moment yet monitoring the brother/sister conversation in token concern for anything too personal that the exuberance of occasion might reveal.

Not that Donna and Jeff were averse to ferreting out explicit details from each other had either of them been willing to provide that sort of information.

Finally, Jeff and Donna had said all that they were going to say, the meal was complete, and the group contemplated adjournment.

While awaiting the check, Donna regarded Jeff and Leslie as a couple.

"Just think of it," she summarized happily. "My brother and cousin getting married. I can't believe it. I'm so happy for both of you."

She smiled at the happy couple across the table and they responded with satisfied smiles of their own.

"I wish someone would marry *me*," Donna added almost as a perfunctory afterthought.

All eyes from across the table turned to Tom, who, caught off guard by Donna's unexpected sentiment, hastened to remark almost reflexively, "I'll marry you."

"Oh, Tom, this is so sudden!" She turned toward Tom beaming her smile at him, taking his face in her hands and giving him a tender kiss. He realized he had fallen for another playful ploy, as she indulged in an antic similar to the one she had acted out earlier at home in the presence of Leslie and Jeff. As she showered him with calculated yet genuine affection, Tom understood that her performance was for the entertainment of all present.

They continued to gaze into each other's eyes a few moments. As she turned her head aside and proceeded to reposition herself to participate in the next risible moment of the conversation, Tom grabbed her and kissed her forcibly square on the lips.

Caught totally off guard, she resisted momentarily in wide-eyed surprise. A reflexive gasp was stifled in her throat unable to escape through lips that were covered by his. She placed two tentative hands against him in defensive reflex, but her resistance crumbled as he overpowered her. She closed her eyes and melted into the contours of his body. She put her hands up to his shoulders then around his neck in a yielding embrace. She was subdued as he engulfed her in his arms and unleashed his passion upon her. He had proposed to her and was determined to treat the declaration with the force and expression it deserved, overwhelming the initial flippancy with which she had first tried to acknowledge it.

Leslie and Jeff sat in stunned silence as they watched Donna and Tom moving against each other in serious lip lock, oblivious to their surroundings. Customers at nearby tables also observed the amorous display. A momentary silence descended over the place, during which one could have heard a pin drop. A young waitress, who had been en route to the table with the check, slowed her approach and sidled carefully up to the table pretending not to notice the unfolding spectacle.

"I'll just leave this with you," the waitress almost whispered to Jeff.

Jeff took the check, looked up at the waitress, and by way of explanation to her and anyone else within earshot he said, "They just got engaged."

Jeff redirected his gaze back to Donna and Tom, watching the ongoing display of passion for a few more moments.

"For God's sake, you two," he finally blurted out, "get a room!"

Tom responded by loosening his embrace a bit, and Donna was finally able to peel herself tentatively away to the extent where she was able to direct an embarrassed look across the table. She was still enraptured in the raging emotions that Tom's fire and passion had unleashed within her. She struggled to compose herself. She swallowed, took a deep breath, and proceeded to detach herself completely albeit slowly from Tom's embrace. She looked up again into Tom's eyes and saw an unabated fierceness that almost made her swoon again.

"Hold on there, tiger," she managed to say breathlessly, "save a little something for the honeymoon."

She had hoped that the humorous comment would serve to bring her (and Tom) back down to earth. She tried to reposition herself at the table and made a valiant attempt to regain control of her senses to the extent where she could resume her participation in the general festivities. She looked at Jeff then at Leslie. She smiled at them but was not able to think of anything to say. She could not remember what they had all been talking about just a few minutes previously. A couple of times she seemed to be on the verge of uttering something, but she sensed the desire emanating from the man sitting a few inches next to her, and she experienced an overwhelming need to look into those eyes of fire and lose herself in him again.

She dared not look at him. She tried to concentrate on reanimating the group conversation, but the only thing she could think of was the way he had kissed her and held her. It pushed all other thoughts out of her mind. She stared off into space, reliving the whole episode.

"Are you OK?" Jeff asked.

"Yes, fine," she replied, but said nothing more.

She finally became aware that Jeff and Leslie were watching her intently, as were half of the people in the restaurant. She was the focus of an embarrassing silence. She realized that she would not soon regain the poise to continue presiding over the current festivities in the manner that the occasion deserved. She yielded to her discomposure, and simply said, "I think we'd better go."

...

It was getting dark as Jeff drove back towards Donna's place. He kept checking on Donna and Tom in the rearview mirror while Leslie kept turning her head to check on them from the front passenger seat. Donna and Tom sat in the back seat, and it was quite apparent that they were serenely intoxicated with each other and generally oblivious to anything else. They had acted that way since leaving the restaurant.

Jeff pulled into the circular driveway of Donna's building and stopped at the entrance. "We're here," he said again checking the rearview mirror. There was no movement or sound from the back seat to indicate he had been heard. He turned to look at the couple in the back seat and raised his voice a few decibels, "Earth calling Donna, Earth calling Donna!"

Donna came out of her reverie and focused on Jeff.

"We're here," he repeated.

"Oh, thanks, Jeff," she responded dreamily and turned to Tom. "Tommy, sweetheart, we're home." She gave him a gentle push as a signal to exit the car.

Tom exited the car and Donna scooted over intending to exit through Tom's door. She looked at Jeff then Leslie.

"I'd invite you guys in, but I think we want to be alone. Thanks for the lunch."

She looked as if she wanted to say something more, but there was a look of distracted dreaminess about her, and she apparently could not think of what it was she wanted to say. She simply said, "I'll call you tomorrow," and exited the car.

Jeff and Leslie watched as Donna and Tom walked arm in arm toward the entrance of the building. They swayed a bit in their distraction with each other, and, if Jeff had not known better, he would have sworn that they were drunk.

Leslie, likewise, watched the swaying couple with a bit of concern as they entered the building and disappeared from sight.

"Are they going to be all right?" she asked turning to face Jeff.

"They'll be more than all right when they get to her bedroom," Jeff answered.

Jeff pondered a bit more about what happened in the restaurant then added, "That was really incredible. Did you see the way he kissed her?"

"The whole restaurant saw the way he kissed her," Leslie responded in a tone that held an unmistakable trace of disapproving prudery about it. She crossed her arms and repositioned herself in the passenger seat to look straight ahead through the windshield, forming her own evaluation about the spectacle she had witnessed in the restaurant.

Jeff's attention went to Leslie. "Yes, it was all so disgusting," he exaggerated, pretending that he was commiserating with her propriety.

Leslie flashed a glance at him, realizing he was being funny, but said nothing.

"Still," Jeff contradicted, "any man who can leave my sister speechless has got to have some good qualities."

Leslie took in Jeff's comment noncommittally.

"Maybe I could learn a few things from him," Jeff continued.

Now Leslie looked fully at Jeff and saw him looking at her the way Tom had looked at Donna.

"Don't get any ideas," she responded immediately and apprehensively.

"What ideas?" Jeff concluded as he put the car in gear to head home.

45.

"Edwin Perciville (Percy) Kittridge."

He repeated his full name aloud attempting to take in the importance of the sound of it. For the most part he could not hear his utterance. It was drowned out by the noise of the vacuum cleaner.

So, here he was, Edwin Perciville (Percy) Kittridge, one of the richest men in the state. And he was pushing a vacuum cleaner. There was much irony here to appreciate, or perhaps to lament.

Pilar had conscripted him into service. She had assailed his office/study/male bastion/man cave/ inner sanctum, etc. bubbling over with excitement and joy. She told him the "children" were coming to visit for a few days and wanted to discuss future wedding plans.

"Please, honey," she said, "give me a hand to straighten up a little. Could you straighten up the living room? Just run the vacuum over the floor and do something about all those papers and magazines piled up in there. I've got to make some dinner."

"But, honey, the cleaners will be here in a couple of days. They'll do the whole house."

"Yes, but dear, the children will be arriving tonight. Please, it'll only take a little while."

"But, honey, I'm in the middle of something right now."

"What? It looks to me like you were taking a nap."

He realized that his excuse would have carried more weight if she had not walked into the room catching him lying on the sofa.

"I wasn't sleeping," he countered. "I was just lying down to get a few ideas straight in my head."

"No. You were sleeping. I heard you snoring."

"I get some of my best ideas while snoring."

…

Now, as he pushed the vacuum across the living room floor, he began to regret the decision he made a long time ago not to employ live-in domestic staff that could have done these impromptu chores. During his grandfather's day the estate boasted dozens of permanent staff persons to maintain the buildings and grounds and to serve the family's daily needs. But some years after his father had inherited the estate all the old family retainers had died or were pensioned off and were not replaced. His father believed in the nobility of work, and he firmly believed that his children should take on a measure of responsibility for the work of the estate despite being born as sons and daughters of the privileged class.

Percy Cyril Kittridge was the name of Edwin's father. Percy Kittridge had achieved some fame in the state as a politician. He had entered politics knowing full well that his opponents would try to make an issue of his of wealth and privilege. He would have to appeal to a constituency that was brainwashed by the media and by unscrupulous politicians to dislike the wealthy. Thus, another reason he divested his family of domestic staff was to help counter that anti-rich bias.

There was a well-known family anecdote about how Percy Kittridge had won his first election by turning the tables on a political opponent who had been overly eager to make the Kittridge wealth an issue in the campaign. Percy had his operatives plant a story among his opponent's campaign staff to the effect that Percy Kittridge ruled his estate as a mean-spirited Midas who drove his workers and servants with the zeal reminiscent of an antebellum plantation owner. Percy could not believe his luck when his opponent's campaign fell for the made-up story and brought it up as a character issue in the debate. His opponent took smug satisfaction expounding on the Kittridge family wealth, emphasizing that Percy led a life of luxury and ease made possible by an army of hard-pressed servants. He pointed out that Percy was totally ignorant and dismissive about the issues important to normal workaday people and that a man with so many servants in his home could never hope to be a good servant of the people. Whereupon, Percy simply invited reporters to his home who saw no evidence of an army of domestic staff at the estate but rather various members of Percy's family diligently and democratically attending to the work of the estate. Percy won the election by a landslide, especially when it came to light that his opponent had a few servants of his own.

Of course, that was in the days when the media still bothered to do investigative reporting.

As his father's eldest son, Edwin Kittridge remembered that his father had expected much from him and had driven him hard at times. Nevertheless, Edwin had learned much from his father and was the better for his father's discipline. He had followed his father into politics and had already served a couple of terms as a U.S. Senator by the time his father died. As inheritor of the estate, Edwin continued the policy of eschewing permanent domestic staff. His father had called it "maintaining the proper appearances." Edwin called it "political correctness."

Of course, even in his father's time, the great bulk of work needed to maintain the grounds and buildings of the estate could not be accomplished through simple family involvement. His father had instituted the policy of contracting out most of the work needed to maintain the estate, and Edwin had continued that arrangement. Every two weeks a team of cleaners would come into the mansion to do general and special housecleaning as required to keep the place spotless. A crew of contract landscapers and grounds keepers came at scheduled times to maintain and manicure the outdoor areas of the estate. A company specializing in security systems had installed an array of sensors and cameras around the perimeter of the estate and monitored estate security remotely. An acreage of good farmland adjacent to the estate had been rented out to a local farmer. Even the estate's stable facilities were under the management of a horse boarding business that had partnered with the Kittridge family to maintain the family's string of horses and to operate the stables as a business for the local equestrian community. Large parties and reunions held at the estate were catered affairs, although the day to day preparation of meals was undertaken by his wife, Pilar, who loved to cook for the immediate family or for smaller groups of visitors. In her younger days, before she married Edwin, Pilar had received training as a professional chef, and she loved to show off her skills in that regard. Thus, the arrangement of bringing in contractors to do the work of the estate had served him well while he was under public scrutiny as a politician. The watchdogs of political correctness never seemed to mind or even understand that an army of contactors maintained the estate. So long as there was no permanent presence of servants on the estate that could be interpreted in some way as a master/ slave relationship, the powers of political correctness had left him alone on that matter.

Of course, there were a plethora of other issues that had plagued him while he was in office, and, unlike his father, Edwin Kittridge decided not to make a career out of politics. The hypocrisy, double standards, and charlatanism running rampant in political and public life left him sick and depressed. Smear merchants and political opponents constantly probed his life and career for any dirt they could expose or make up about him or his family. The media had developed an animosity toward him that would often lead to their reporting of false accusations and half truths about him in a way that made the allegations appear to be the gospel truth. At best the reporters would conclude their stories with statements such as "Senator Kittridge could not be reached for comment," or "Senator Kittridge's office denies the allegations." It was ten times worse now than in his father's time.

To preserve his sanity, Edwin Kittridge retired from political office while he was still a relatively young man, and now he dedicated himself to managing his businesses and finances, while continuing to serve his party as financier and a "power behind the scenes." As a "retired" politician, Edwin pursued a number of activities for both business and pleasure. He was at a point in his life where he could do exactly as he pleased, except, perhaps for those occasions when he was obliged to serve as helpmate and handyman to Pilar, as he was doing at the moment.

He finished vacuuming and straightening up the family room and headed to the kitchen to report to Pilar. En route, he again pondered the possibility of employing a domestic servant or two to perform these impromptu tasks as needed, especially now that he was no longer in the public eye. Also, since the children had left home, Pilar and he lived in the big rambling mansion alone, and maybe a couple of live-in staff could impart a more occupied feeling to the place. But eventually he rejected the idea. He had gotten used to the status quo. Maybe when he was older and feebler, he would again consider the issue of bringing in domestic staff to help out around the estate.

He entered the large chef's kitchen and approached Pilar who was standing at a counter chopping up some food on a cutting board. He walked up behind her, put his arms around her waist and kissed her on her shoulder.

"I've finished straightening up the living room," he said. "Is there anything else you wanted me to do?"

"Did you put the vacuum cleaner away?"

"Of course."

"And did you put those papers in the recycle bin?"

"Yes, dear."

"OK, then. You'll need to get ready in about an hour. Donna said she and Tom would get here around four."

He gave her a final squeeze and released her.

"Do I have to get dressed up, since it's only family?"

She turned slightly from her culinary chore to appraise his attire but said nothing. However, the look she gave him plainly said, "Change that awful shirt and put on a coat and tie."

"Yes, dear," he responded to her unspoken demand.

He headed off toward the master bedroom to change his clothes, stopping along the way in the family room to put away the vacuum cleaner and transfer the newspapers and magazines that he had stacked up on a chair to the recycle bin.

He then went into the master bedroom, showered and dressed. He returned to the kitchen wearing suit pants and a new dress shirt.

"I thought you were going to put on a coat and tie," Pilar said inspecting his changed garb.

"I laid out a coat and tie on the bed. I didn't think it was necessary to put on the rope and straight jacket until they actually got here."

"You could've worn them for me."

He immediately left the kitchen returning once again to the bedroom to don his dress coat and tie. As he left the bedroom to return again to the kitchen, he met his wife who was en route to the bedroom to get herself ready for the upcoming dinner.

"Oh, Edwin," she said coming up to embrace him, "you look so nice."

She kissed him, and while still in the embrace she looked down to inspect his tie.

"Oh, maybe not that one," she said tugging on the tie knot to loosen it. "Why don't you just leave off the tie and wear the coat over an open collar. Oh, yes, that looks much better."

With his tie in her hand, she looked up into his face again for a final inspection, and when her eyes met his she smiled at him. Of all the women in the world, only Pilar could smile and look at him that way. Edwin comprehended innately that this image of Pilar would be the last memory of this world that he would carry into the afterlife, and if he were to be reincarnated in a future time and place, it would be this image, imprinted on his soul, that would lead him to search for her and love her in an infinite series of lifetimes.

"Oh, honey," she said, detaching herself from the embrace to continue her way into the bedroom, "will you listen for the timer in the kitchen, and if it goes off before I get back, can you turn the heat on the oven down to two hundred and fifty degrees?"

"Is that the middle knob?" he asked, showing apprehension.

"Yes, dear, I've shown you thousands of times. I don't see why you can't remember a little about cooking."

They were about to have the same "discussion" that they had had numerous times before.

"But, honey, you know I can't cook. I'm completely inept in the kitchen."

"That's because you don't try. There's no reason men can't be good cooks. All the best chefs are men. Patty and Mary Jo's husbands know how to cook and help out all the time in the kitchen. And they're not even retired."

"Who're Patty and Mary Jo?" He asked trying to change the subject.

"You know Patty and Mary Jo. They work with me on the Committee. I've introduced you to them dozens of times, and they've been coming to our parties for years…and don't change the subject."

She continued to grill him about his lack of help in the kitchen and he kept casting around for excuses to avoid getting involved in that task.

"Never mind all that for now," she finally concluded. "I've got to get ready. But I want to have a serious talk with you about helping out around the house, and you've got to stop being so stubborn. If you can't figure out the stove, just come and get me when the timer goes off."

"Yes, dear." He watched her disappear into the bedroom.

In her mid-fifties, Pilar was still a beautiful and elegant woman, and he loved her deeply. Of course, after thirty-five years of marriage and three children, the passion of their younger days had cooled off significantly. They were now comfortably ensconced in the minutiae of their daily lives and activities, and often days would go by when they did not see each other except to have meals or to sleep. As he got older, he was no longer possessed of the abiding ache to express his love in a sexual way, and he was often surprised at the lengthening intervals between the times he made love to her. Occasionally, she had to give him a gentle reminder of his responsibilities in that regard.

His love for her no longer required him to be in her constant presence. He was satisfied in knowing that she was in his house, secure in the knowledge that she was in the next room happily involved in the tasks and routines that rounded out her life, while he had a measure of the solitude he craved to indulge in his own interests and activities.

Pilar understood and respected his need for a certain amount of solitude, but she did not need it for herself. She had many friends and was constantly involved in a number of activities outside the home. She served as matron, sponsor or committee member of various community projects and charities. As such she attended a regular round robin of meetings, functions, and other events. Edwin would sometimes accompany her to these events, but generally she left him at home, and during her absences he appreciated an additional measure of solitude for his needs.

He derived the greatest satisfaction when Pilar hosted parties or entertained guests in her home. On these occasions, Edwin would stand at her side as a dutiful husband appreciating the way she related to people around her, and he would bask in her radiant energy while other men could hardly contain the envy they felt for his possession of the most beautiful and elegant of women and the happiness that went with it. Nowadays, he liked nothing more than showing her off to the world.

Edwin chuckled inwardly. It was not always like that. He remembered when he first met Pilar when he was in college. He had not wanted to share her with anyone. He did not want to let her out of his sight. He was so mesmerized by her beauty that he was constantly afraid other men might try to take her away from him. He wanted to elope with her immediately, but she was adamant about having a big wedding, so they had decided to postpone marriage until they finished their studies. He dated her for a year and lived with her another year before introducing her to his family. He had not wanted to put her anywhere near the reach of his younger brothers who, he feared, would have had no qualms about taking her away from him if possible. It was not until they had been married a couple of years and had their first child that he began to relax and feel secure in his permanence with her.

The ringing of the stove timer intruded into his thoughts. He went into the kitchen and deftly turned the heat of the oven down to 250 degrees. He wondered why Pilar was trying to get him to learn how to cook at this late stage of their marriage. She was the professional chef of the family and had perfected her art and science of meal preparation to a degree that he could never hope to emulate. Even if he learned the rudiments of cooking, there was no way he could ever hope to match her mealtime masterpieces, and, more to the point, he did not want to see his comfortable freedoms and routines curtailed by having culinary responsibilities forced upon him. He mentally rehearsed some future excuses to ward off her adamancy in that regard.

"Honey, you know I can't cook. I don't have the cooking gene. I can't cook water."

She might appreciate the witty flippancy of those declarations but would not take them seriously enough to contain her insistence.

"Honey, if you want some help around the kitchen, I'll hire you a cook…"

Good lord no! She would take that as the supreme insult. She might tolerate his fumbling presence in the kitchen as her assistant, but certainly not some stranger who might show a degree of competence in cooking.

"Honey, you know I'd never be able to match your expertise in the kitchen, and even if I did try to make something and failed miserably I'd feel totally inadequate and depressed and would probably not even want to try anymore if I couldn't do something to make you proud of me..."

Hmm. That might work. He would need to develop that line a little further.

"Honey, the reason I married a professional chef was precisely so I wouldn't have to cook."

No, that wouldn't work. And besides it wasn't true. He didn't marry her because she was a good cook. He married her because she was beautiful. In fact, the day he first met her, he lost all appetite for food.

Pilar's uncle had introduced him to her. Her uncle was one of his graduate school professors who had invited Edwin and a select few other students and colleagues to a private dining experience at an exclusive five-star restaurant. Pilar was working as an apprentice sous chef at that restaurant, and she would be in charge of preparing a fine meal for the select group.

Edwin remembered those many years ago when the group had filed into the private dining room, and his professor had brought Pilar out to meet the diners. The first time Edwin saw her, he was totally captivated. Her uncle introduced her to the members of the dining party, and as Edwin stepped forward to be introduced, he was struck speechless. All he could do was stare at her in awe, searching for that slight imperfection that made beautiful women beautiful. He could not detect the slightest imperfection in that face. She was wearing one of those white chef's uniforms that covered her body completely, but she was still the most beautiful woman he had ever seen. He could not take his eyes off her, and as he stared at her openly and unabashedly, a silence filled the room. Pilar became embarrassed while waiting for him to say something–a salutation, an innocuous remark or idle chit chat, or some other appropriate words. But he stood before her spellbound looking at her with desire, and when he finally found his voice he simply said, "You're beautiful."

She said nothing. He had plainly embarrassed her. She blushed and cast her eyes downward, a shy smile on her lips. She withdrew demurely into the kitchen. It was all he could do not to follow her. He returned to the dining table where everyone else had taken their seats. He was so distracted with her vision that he was unaware of the humorous twittering going around the table over his behavior toward Pilar. Waiters served the excellent food, but Edwin had lost all appetite for fine dining and the congenial conversation that went with it. After the meal, the group had taken cognac and smoked cigars on the terrace where Edwin finally approached his professor pleading for a more substantial introduction to Pilar and permission to date her.

Edwin lost himself in the memory of his first two years with Pilar. That time leading up to their wedding had been the happiest and most intensive time of his life. He remembered that nervous second meeting between them arranged by her uncle, when Pilar tried to overcome her initial shyness and he tried to suppress his intensity of feeling for her in order not to frighten her. He remembered when they had first dated and when he met her parents who were old-world and conservative to the point of favoring arranged introductions and chaperoned dating. He had dated her for a year before he was able finally to convince her to move in with him. He remembered the time he first made love to her...

Ah, yes. The first time they made love... Edwin continued to stand by the stove thinking back on the memory of that first intimacy with Pilar. He was spellbound as the details of that moment flashed through his mind, and he shivered from the intensity of that exquisite memory.

Pilar entered the kitchen, dressed regally as usual. His heart skipped a beat, as she walked toward him.

"Good," she said, "you turned the heat down. Now, you see, that wasn't so hard, was it?"

She eyed the stove to inspect his handiwork in turning down the heat of the oven. Then she looked up at him and saw the intensity in his eyes she had not seen for a while. She smiled at him and regarded him with her exquisite dark eyes. He searched her face for that slight imperfection to her beauty, something he still had not been able to discover in thirty-five years of marriage.

"You're beautiful," he said.

They embraced each other. She closed her eyes, and placed her cheek next to his, a brilliant smile on her lips. Her unabashed enjoyment in his strong embrace was apparent. After a long moment, she looked up at him. "So, do you want to help me set the table?"

"OK," he answered.

46.

"What's wrong, Tom? Don't you want to marry me?"

"Of course, I want to marry you."

Donna glanced at Tom in the passenger seat of her car as she drove toward her parents' estate.

"Well, what's wrong then?"

"Nothing's wrong. It's just that everything's moving so fast, and I'm having trouble keeping up."

"Well, you *did* ask me to marry you, right?"

"Yeah, I did…sort of."

"Yes, you did—and don't forget I've got witnesses. So, you can't back out now."

Tom smiled at her. She was trying to brighten up his mood with a bit of cheerful humor and exuberance.

He would gladly spend eternity loving her passionately. And if he was going to love her for all eternity, marriage was certainly a logical thing to consider. Yet the idea of marriage as the next step in their relationship seemed precipitous and incongruent given the whole improbable nature of the events of the past weeks. Her desire to marry him was hard for him to believe because it was still hard for him to believe that she loved him.

"Seriously, Tom, what's the matter?"

He looked at her. "Are you sure you want to marry me?"

"Oh, Tom, you're not going to start that again, are you? I'm gonna get mad in a minute."

"Listen, honey, I know I'm a little dense, but maybe you'd better tell me again what it is you see in me? And don't say it's because I saved your life."

"Well, I'm sorry, Tom, but that had a lot to do with it. You came along and cared enough about me to rescue me."

"But anybody would've done that."

"Not the way you did."

"The way I did? What did I do that was any different from the way someone else would have done it?"

"If you don't understand it, I can't explain it to you."

Tom sighed and looked straight ahead through the windshield. They had had a discussion similar to this previously. Now as then, her "explanation" left him with no better understanding of her thought processes, and she was not disposed to provide him with a scientific analysis of her feelings for him.

"You can't analyze love," he thought to himself.

Still, he would have liked to have some inkling as to why she found him attractive, if for no other reason than to know what he needed to do to maintain and enhance her interest in him. She herself had pinpointed the date she had fallen in love with him, admitting it was that time in the forest when he had slapped her, torn off her clothes, and terrified her into submitting to him. It must have been shortly thereafter that she interpreted those actions as some sort of masculine masterfulness that caused her to fall in love with him. But he was not a masterful person, and he certainly would never again resort to treating her with the angry actions of that day of frustration.

He remained in silent contemplation looking out through the windshield of the car, wondering what he could do to sustain her abiding interest in him.

"Seriously, Tom, what's worrying you?"

He looked at her for a few seconds. He spoke to her very carefully. "Donna, what do you think would have happened to me if I hadn't met you in that forest? Do you think I would have come out of that forest alive if I hadn't come across you?"

She absorbed that. He continued before she could respond.

"I was at the lowest point in my life. I didn't want to live. It was because of you that I came out of that forest, otherwise I would have died.

"O.K." she responded in a mood determined to be upbeat. "So, you saved both our lives. That's even better."

She had not taken his sentiment with the stark realization he had intended. He continued in a tone of serious intensity. "I think you were somehow sent to save me. You were an angel who came down out of the sky to rescue me."

The metaphorical nature of his declaration had its effect on her. "Oh, Tommy, you say the nicest things."

Things were about to get emotional again, and she was afraid her driving was going to be distracted. She pulled over to the side of the road and turned to face him squarely. Her beautiful dark eyes reflected a tearful sparkle as she looked at him intently, saying nothing.

When she looked at him like that it was overwhelming. He glanced away briefly then looked at her again. She smiled and put a gentle hand on the side of his face.

"You lifted me up out of deep despair," he continued, trying not to stammer. "You've given me a new lease on life and put me on top of the world."

"Oh, Tommy! I love you."

"But it's all happening too fast. There's too much I don't understand. I have a feeling that something's going to go wrong...I'm afraid this is all a dream I might wake up from any minute..."

"No, Tommy, everything's going to be all right..."

"And I just can't figure out what you see in me... I looked at myself in a mirror a few days ago; it was a pretty gloomy sight..."

"That's called tall, dark and handsome," she responded, determined to deflect some of his negativity with upbeat humor.

He looked at her and was quiet.

"Listen, Tommy, let's just try to get through this dinner tonight with my parents, OK? Then, I promise we'll have a long talk tonight before we go to bed. Is that OK?"

"All right," he answered.

She put the car in gear and resumed driving. He put his head back on the head rest and closed his eyes for a few moments.

A sudden realization caused him to bring his head erect again and look at her.

"Are we going to sleep in the same room at your parents' house?" He asked with a degree of nervousness.

"Of course."

"But...uh, but do you think that would really be appropriate?"

"Oh, for God's sake, Tom! We're both mature adults. Nobody's gonna care if we sleep together."

"But...uh, but even if we're not married yet?"

"We're engaged."

"Your parents won't mind?"

"They won't mind," Donna asserted then added facetiously, "as long as we're not too noisy."

"Noisy?"

"Yes. You know. During the night."

"Do you think we'd be too noisy?"

"I don't know. But, don't worry, I'll ask them to let us use the soundproof room."

"Soundproof room?"

"Yeah. My parents have a guest room for visiting couples who might be too noisy during the night. If you know what I mean."

"But surely, we don't need a soundproof room," Tom interrupted. "We wouldn't be that noisy, would we?"

"Oh, I don't know. You know how intensive it gets when you're making love to me. I might not be able to control my screaming. You might have to put some tape over my mouth."

"Then maybe we shouldn't..." He stopped in mid-sentence and looked at her. She was beaming at him.

"You're teasing me again, aren't you?" he smiled.

She broke out into laughter.

"I really fell for that one," he said, as she continued to bathe him in the flood of laughter that radiated from her face. He loved it when he was able to cause such heartfelt laughter in her. Unfortunately, most of the time it was unintentional.

"You like to tease me, don't you?" he continued.

"Only when you're behaving like a prude."

"I wasn't behaving like a prude. I was just...concerned..."

"About what?" she prompted.

"About...the rules of decorum."

"That's called being a prude."

"No, it's not."

"Yes, it is."

He smiled and deferred to her exuberance.

"So, I want you to quit worrying and relax. OK?"

"OK," he answered, continuing to watch her, basking in her exuberant personality.

She returned her attention to driving. They were getting close to her parents' estate.

After a few moments of silent driving, he asked, "Have you told your parents we're engaged?"

"Yes."

"Are they OK with it?"

"Of course."

"What about your mother. I thought you were at odds with her over things."

"Not any more. My mother's so happy I'm getting married, she'll be floating on a cloud."

Tom directed his gaze through the front windshield and lost himself in deep thought.

"By the way," Donna continued, "when we get there, I'm gonna have to talk with my mother and probably help her in the kitchen. I'll have to deposit you with my father, and you can talk with him for a while."

"OK," Tom answered. He was still in deep thought, and they drove on in silence.

"Donna," he finally said.

"What?"

"I really do want to marry you."

She smiled at him. "I know," she said.

"But there are a few things we have to consider first."

"What things?" she asked, groaning inwardly to herself. He was going to start throwing up roadblocks again.

"You know that I can't marry you without some sort of identification, don't you? I don't have any."

"Well, let's talk with my father about that. I think he might be able to work something out. If not him, I know Lawrence could do something…"

"No, Donna, it's not just ID. I don't have a driver's license, credit cards, a checkbook or anything. I can't drive a car; there's no way I can access money or anything; I can't even buy you an engagement ring. I'm totally dependent on you for everything."

"But, honey, you'll get straightened out eventually. Don't go around worrying about all that. Everything will be fine."

"But how can I marry you when I can't even identify myself?"

"We'll work something out," she responded, returning her gaze to the road in front of her.

Her face reflected more worry than previously. She was deep in thought. He looked at her carefully. He had again succeeded in robbing her of her cheerful happiness. He never wanted to say anything to her that would cause her any sort of unhappiness, but what he had to say next had to be said.

"Donna, I've got to go back."

She shot a quick look at him then returned her gaze to the road, processing this latest utterance from him.

He took advantage of her introspection to further make his case.

"I've got to go back and straighten out my life. I've got to reclaim my identity. I've got to reconnect with my family and friends. I need to contact my work and face up to all the things I ran away from."

She again glanced at him, assimilating what he was saying, with a quiet intensity. He could not predict what her final reaction was going to be, but her muteness gave him the chance to make his final point.

"And I've got to do this before I can even think about marrying you."

They drove on a few moments in silence. She watched the road ahead and gave the appearance of concentrating on her driving, but she was deep in thought over what Tom had said. Tom kept watching her for an acknowledgment or response from her.

"So, do you understand what I said?" he finally prompted.

"Yes, I understand."

They turned off the main road into the entrance of the Kittridge estate, and Donna's attention was momentarily diverted while she entered a code in her console transponder to open the security gate. They drove up to the front driveway in silence and parked the car.

Before exiting the car, she turned to Tom and asked, "When do you want to do all this?"

"Probably the sooner the better."

"Well, let's talk about it later." She moved to exit the car, but then she changed her mind and asked another question. "How long will it take to get all this done?"

"Probably a few weeks, or maybe a month."

"A month!?"

"Yes, honey. There's a lot to do—I've got to clear out my house and put it on the market, I've gotta give notice at work— at least two weeks' notice; I've gotta apply for a driver's license; I probably need to buy a new car; get replacement credit cards; close my bank accounts; and some other accounts; I need to reconnect with some people—it's gonna take a little time..."

Donna watched him intently. She seemed to be taking it well. She appeared to understand the reasons for his need to return home—at least the more prosaic reasons. He did not want to voice the most compelling reason he had for returning home. He did not want to tell her that he needed to return to clear up all the unresolved issues surrounding the death of his wife. Any mention of his wife would only upset her. But more than anything, he needed to seek closure over his wife's death, exorcise her ghost from his memory and close the book on his previous life for good. Only then would he be able to return to Donna to begin his life anew with her.

She continued to listen to him, processing and accepting what he was saying.

"OK," she finally responded, "a few weeks should still get us back before Thanksgiving; let's talk to my father to arrange to fly us out in a few days, then we can…"

"No, Donna!" he interrupted, "I've got to go by myself!"

The look of introspection on her face was now replaced with one of apprehension. She stared at him in shocked silence, assimilating what he had said. She had assumed all during their conversation that she would accompany him, and he should have realized that from the beginning and spoken accordingly.

"Why can't I go with you?" she said weakly like a fearful child.

"Because this is something I've got to do on my own."

"Why?"

"Because, honey, I've got to prove that I can stand on my own two feet. I've got to go back and face up to all the things I ran away from. I'll never be whole again until I take care of all these issues."

"Fine," she said, "but I don't see why I can't go with you."

"I told you, honey. I've got to be able to stand on my own two feet. You'd be too much of a crutch for me to fall back on, and I've got to do this on my own. What kind of a man would I be if I had to lean on you all the time? You wouldn't want that type of a man, would you? I've got to do this to prove that I'm worthy of you."

"You don't have to prove anything to me. I want you the way you are. We're supposed to support each other. That's all we need."

"I've got to prove it to myself then. It's something I've got to do."

"You know you're being ridiculous, don't you?"

"Please, honey. You've got to let me do this."

A silent tear rolled down her cheek. "You promised you'd never leave me."

"I'm not leaving you. I'm just going away for a while. I'll be back."

"No, you won't."

"Yes, I will. I promise."

"No! I know what you're going to do. You're gonna go find another forest to disappear into, aren't you?"

"No, I won't do that..."

Tears were now streaming from her eyes. She continued to marshal her energies and arguments to assail his resolve. Between her tears, anger, and genuine love for him, there was no way his feeble powers of logic could stand up to her emotional tidal wave. He made a last desperate appeal to her.

"Donna, please, I'm asking you to let me do this."

"No! Absolutely not! End of discussion!" She exited the car abruptly.

He likewise exited the car thinking he should intercept her before she could rush headlong into her parents' house in such an emotional state. But she did not head toward the house. She came around to his side or the car and embraced him, crying profusely on his shoulder."

"I'm afraid, Tom."

"There's nothing to be afraid of."

"Please don't leave me, Tommy. Please don't leave me."

47.

∾

Over the next few days, Tom somehow maintained a gossamer thread of his resolve. Upon entering the Kittridge home, he was obliged to explain to Edwin and Pilar why their daughter was crying and unhappy. She was too upset to explain anything and could only embrace her mother then her father for emotional support. Fortunately, once he outlined the intention of undertaking a solo trip home to put his life in order, they understood and supported his resolve.

Leslie and Jeff showed up a little later that same evening expecting an occasion of enjoyment and lively banter. They were likewise surprised and concerned over Donna's state of dispiritedness, but once they learned of Tom's assertion to return temporarily to his home to put his affairs in order, they too supported his resolve. Tom was relieved that everyone understood his intention. Everyone understood except Donna, of course, who continued clinging to her misgivings with tears and miserere almost to the point of petulance. Feeling that everyone was ganging up on her, she finally lashed out.

"OK," she said addressing Tom, "go if you want! Just don't expect me to be waiting for you when you return!"

She rushed out of the room crying. Her mother followed her and took her aside for a private talk.

"Donna, what's wrong with you? I've never seen you carrying on like this. Why are you making this so difficult for Tom?"

"He wants to leave me," Donna cried miserably through a new set of tears.

"Donna, what are you talking about? He's just going away for a while to straighten out a few things. He'll be back. Why are you making such a big fuss over all of this?"

"He won't come back."

"Of course, he will. Why are you saying that?"

"He doesn't want me to go with him."

Pilar gave her daughter a knowing smile. "Honey, men have been going off for thousands of years to prove themselves, and then return to their wives and girlfriends for approval and praise. It's women's lot to let them do it."

"That absolutely idiotic," Donna replied.

"Of course, it's idiotic. But that's why they're men. This is something that's important to Tom, and that's why you have to let him do it. He needs your support and understanding in this."

"No, mother, it's not just that. It's not that simple."

"Honey," Pilar spoke to her daughter in a firmer voice. "Do love this man?"

"Yes, but…"

"And he's asked you to marry him?"

"Yes, but…"

"Then there's nothing to worry about."

"No, mother, you don't understand."

"What?"

Donna hesitated.

"What?" her mother asked again.

"I think he may be somewhat suicidal."

"*What?*"

"I think he may be suicidal."

Pilar was shocked into silence. Donna had not wanted to reveal this dimension of her relationship with Tom, but she could think of nothing else to do, and at this point she desperately wanted to enlist someone's aid to help her dissuade Tom from going.

Her mother tried to absorb this new revelation about Tom. "What do you mean he may be suicidal," she asked growing truly alarmed.

"When I first met him, he wasn't just lost in the forest. He'd gone into the forest intentionally to disappear. He thinks he's responsible for his wife's death, and that he had to atone for it by sacrificing his own life."

Pilar continued to look at her daughter a few moments then asked pointedly, "I thought she died in a car accident. Why would he feel responsible about that?"

"Because they'd had a big argument before it happened, and he thinks he drove her to it."

Pilar absorbed what Donna said.

"But, even so," she countered, "I can understand why he might feel guilty about it, but it's a long way from guilt to suicide. What makes you think he might have suicidal thoughts?"

"He's as much as admitted it to me. He's been through a horrible ordeal, and I think he's been depressed and confused about things and feeling guilty. I think I've talked him out of it and that he'll be OK, but I really need to keep an eye on him for a while."

Now Pilar looked at Donna a little sternly. "Donna don't tell me you got involved with this man because he's suicidal. That's a terrible reason to …"

"No, mother," Donna interrupted, "I was in love with him before I ever knew anything about his past. He's wonderful and cares about me very much. He told me about his wife's accident just a few days ago."

"Well, honey, if he's in love with you and asked you to marry him, that doesn't sound like someone who's suicidal. Maybe he just needs a little more time. It's understandable for him to want to clear up all the loose ends of his life before thinking about his future. Maybe you need to be patient with him a while longer."

"That's fine. I can wait for as long as it takes. But I don't want him going off on his own. Not now. I need more time with him to make sure he's OK."

Pilar and Donna continued to talk about Tom. They talked calmly, and Donna was able to compose herself and contain her tears. But the talk did nothing to calm her misgivings.

Finally, Pilar said, "There's no way you can keep him from going if he's determined to go. You'll have to trust to the fact that he'll come back to you if he really loves you. In the meantime, you've got to be understanding and accepting of what he feels he has to do. And you'll find you'll have much more influence over him with affection and understanding than with emotional blackmail."

"I'm not trying to blackmail him. I'm just terribly worried about him and want to keep him here until I can be sure he'll be all right. What if I lose him altogether?" Tears welled up in her eyes again.

"Well, honey you're just going to have to chance it this one time." They paused while Donna assimilated this advice from her mother. For a long time, Donna had constantly rebelled against maternal authority and generally rejected her mother's advice out of hand. But now the two women took comfort in sharing their feelings. Pilar felt closer to her daughter now than she had felt in a long time.

"Listen, honey," Pilar encouraged, "you're a beautiful woman, and it looks like Tom is very much in love with you. That means you'll have no trouble controlling him ninety-nine percent of the time. But occasionally you have to give men the freedom to let them do what they want. Even if it's stupid. Your father is no different."

"Daddy? Why? What's he done?" Donna momentarily forgot about Tom as her ears perked up in anticipation of some new revelation about her father.

"I can't tell you," Pilar answered. "He's sworn me to secrecy. But, believe me, it's pretty dumb."

"You can tell me, mother."

"No, I'd better not. He'd be pretty upset if he found out I'd told you."

"He won't find out. Please mother, it won't go any farther than right here."

Pilar resisted telling the secret, but she was so happy to be sharing girl talk with her daughter, that she finally relented.

"OK, I'll tell you, but you can't spread this any further."

"I won't. I promise."

"That means Jeff…"

"I know."

"*And* Tom."

"Yes, yes. So, what is it?"

"Your father's decided he wants to build a doomsday bunker."

"A doomsday bunker? What's that?"

"It's a big underground complex or something. He thinks civilization is going to collapse and that we'll have to seek shelter underground to protect us from roving bands of zombies or something like that."

"Really? Oh, come on, he can't be serious, can he?"

"Well, he's saying it's just a precaution. I wouldn't mind, but I think's he planning to spend a lot of money on it. He wants to stock it with food and water and all sorts of supplies. He even wants me to learn how to shoot a gun."

Both women laughed.

"I thought he'd gotten all of that out of his system when I let him build that basement panic room a few years back. Now, I think he's even planning to link the panic room to the bunker through some sort of tunnel."

The women enjoyed talking more, sharing their feelings and insights about their respective men, until Pilar determined that they should return to the family gathering.

"Come on, sweetheart. Let's get back to the others. They'll be expecting dinner. Why don't you go spend some time with Tom then come help me in the kitchen. And remember to be supporting of Tom's decision. Show him what he's got to come back to."

Donna decided to follow her mother's advice, but she still had misgivings about Tom's course of action. Following her mother back toward the assembled guests in the family room she said, "I just wish he didn't have to leave so soon. I'd like to spend more time with him to make sure he'll be OK."

Pilar said, "Well, maybe if we can't keep him from going, we can at least delay it. Let me talk to your father about it."

48.

Two weeks later, Tom was finally able to take his leave of the Kittridge family. He had not wanted to postpone his departure so long. Donna's father had offered to arrange to fly him home in his business jet, but the jet was currently in use by his business partner for the next few days. Nevertheless, Edwin convinced Tom that it would still be quicker to wait until the jet was freed up for their use rather than attempting to arrange commercial travel for Tom in light of the time it would take due to Tom's lack of identification. It was almost a week later when Edwin informed Tom that his business partner had returned home, but that, unfortunately, the jet now needed its annual routine maintenance before it could be flown again. Edwin apologized for the delay, making a show of chiding himself for not remembering about the scheduled maintenance. Yet, nevertheless, Edwin still held that the maintenance would be done before any commercial flight could be arranged for Tom. The end result was that Tom stayed with Donna and her family two weeks longer than he anticipated.

He had a suspicion that Donna and her family had conspired to delay his departure as long as possible. But otherwise Donna was behaving herself. After her blow up that first evening, she had returned to him with apologies, affection, and understanding. She regained a degree of her usual cheeriness, and she spent the days and nights with him attentively and affectionately almost to the point of clinging to him. She did not speak to him about her misgivings, but he could see the concern in her eyes—eyes that implored him to stay with her forever—eyes that spoke to him with silent tears when they held each other in the night. How many times did her silent pleading eyes tie his heart in knots? How many times during those days and nights did he almost relent and beg her to accompany him on his journey. Yet, he steeled his resolve and came to regard his upcoming sojourn as a grail-like quest that had to be completed before he deemed himself worthy of any possible future with Donna.

The last day came, and Donna and her family accompanied Tom out the front door of their home. Jeff retrieved his car pulling it up to the door to carry Tom the short distance to the airfield. Donna looked at him with soulful, pleading eyes. She had come to the realization that Tom was not going to change his mind, and tears were streaming from her eyes. As Tom embraced her for a final time, he looked into her eyes, and in addition to her silent supplications he saw a hint of defiance, and he knew what she was thinking.

"Promise me you won't follow me," he said to her.

"Promise me you'll come back," she countered.

"I will," he said. "I promise."

Donna turned to embrace her mother, crying profusely but silently on her shoulder.

"Come back to us, Tom," Pilar said.

"Yes, son, come back to us," Edwin echoed.

Tom turned and walked toward the waiting car. It was the hardest thing he had ever done in his life. Every fiber in his being screamed at him to return to those people. He entered the car and Jeff started off slowly down the driveway. Tom dared not look back. As Jeff turned onto the highway, Tom leaned forward and covered his face with his hands.

"Are you OK?" Jeff asked.

Tom posed his own question. "Do you think Donna will be all right?"

"She'll be fine when you get back."

"Would she be all right if I didn't come back?"

"Wait a minute, Tom. What are you saying? You *are* planning to come back, aren't you?

"Yes, I want to. But if something happened to me, and I didn't come back, would she be all right?"

"What's going to happen to you, man? It's not like you're going off to war. I thought this was supposed to be a few weeks to get your stuff in order."

Tom did not respond. He gazed through the windshield at the road in front of him seeing nothing but Donna's image in his thoughts. It wasn't too late. He should turn around and go back to Donna and live with her in her castle in the clouds. Every sensible and rational thought coursing through his brain told him to have Jeff turn the car around.

They continued the trip in silence nearing the airfield. Jeff looked at Tom sternly, waiting for a response to his last sentence. "So why wouldn't you come back? You do love my sister, don't you?"

"I love her more than anything."

"Then why wouldn't you come back to her?"

Tom could not think of a response and remained in silent reflection.

"Tom," Jeff prompted more forcefully, "why wouldn't you come back?"

"I want to. Believe me, I really want to. It's just that... it's just that I'm afraid that...that I'd make her unhappy in the long run."

"What are you talking about, Tom? Where are you getting all these ideas from?"

"I don't know. It's just that...," Tom paused attempting to find an end to his sentence, "...it's just that sometimes I guess I'm not right in the head."

"Well, come on, man! Get your head on straight!" Jeff glared at Tom then added, "Listen, Tom, I'm warning you—if you ever do anything to hurt Donna, I swear, I'll..."

"I don't want to hurt her. Ever. That's why I'm wondering if the best thing I could do for her would be to get out of her life all together."

"Don't be stupid, man! Don't you know that that would hurt her more than anything else?"

"But maybe she'd be able to find someone more suitable than me?"

"You're crazy if you think that. As far as I know you're the only man she's ever found suitable. I've known her a lot longer than you, and she's never found anyone else even remotely suitable as far as I can tell."

Tom was silent a few moments thinking about what Jeff had said. He again thought about having Jeff turn the car around taking him back to Donna. He remained silent as they arrived at the airfield. The jet was waiting on the runway. Jeff parked the car near the runway. Tom remained silent, looking at the airplane that was to bear him away from Donna and her family. A figure appeared in the doorway of the jet waving and beckoning to them.

Jeff regarded Tom sternly. "So, what about it? You're gonna give it a chance, right? You're gonna get yourself straightened out and come back, right?"

"Yes," Tom replied. "I will. Don't worry. I'll come back, and if she still wants me—fine, we'll pick up where we left off. In the meantime, she'll have some time to think things through and put everything in perspective."

"Good man!"

Jeff and Tom exited the car. They shook hands and exchanged a few more words. Tom turned and walked toward the plane. It was his last chance to change his mind. He dared not look back. Again, someone appeared at the entrance of the jet beckoning, and Tom was drawn inexorably into the plane. As the door was closed and secured, Tom's last link with the Kittridge clan was severed. Jeff watched as the plane took off a few minutes later. He had a strange feeling that it was a flight into oblivion. He shivered. He got into his car and headed home. He suddenly had an urgent need to talk to Leslie.

Printed in the United States
by Booksurge

Printed in the United States
By Bookmasters